CHANGE FOR THE MACHINES

Change for the machines. The groups went crazy for it. It was a brand new world out there.

Meet the new world. Same as the old world.

Basically, the job's the same. That's what the Beater said. Hear the music, Gina. Make the pictures.

Except it was better. It wasn't just hearing the music, it was being *in* the music, and the images coming up on the screen of her mind, forming as she looked at them. As soon as she thought it, there it was, and if she thought to change it, it changed, growing from her like a live thing. She suddenly found it hard to remember that she had worked any other way.

It felt so natural, so right. To send a dream out of the inner darkness into raw daylight, where anyone could see it. Once you'd done that, you wanted to keep on doing it, and the more you did it, the easier it became.

For the first time, she had a real understanding of Visual Mark's nature, of what had been happening behind those eyes for so many years. Change for the machines? Nah, the machines had finally changed for him. He was just doing what he'd always done.

SYNNERS

BY PAT CADIGAN

BANTAM BOOKS
NEW YORK · TORONTO · LONDON · SYDNEY · AUCKLAND

SYNNERS
A Bantam Spectra Book / February 1991

ISBN 0-553-28254-9

Published simultaneously in the United States and Canada

Bantam Books are published by Bantam Books, a division of Bantam Doubleday Dell Publishing Group, Inc. Its trademark, consisting of the words ''Bantam Books'' and the portrayal of a rooster, is Registered in U.S. Patent and Trademark Office and in other countries. Marca Registrada. Bantam Books, 666 Fifth Avenue, New York, New York 10103.

PRINTED IN THE UNITED STATES OF AMERICA

RAD   0   9   8   7   6   5   4   3   2

*This one is for Gardner Dozois and Susan Casper,
who got me going on the original idea.
For fifteen years of late nights, wild parties,
talking dirty, and all the other stuff
that makes life worth living
(I've got your dedication right here)*

ACKNOWLEDGMENTS

I could not have gotten through this project without the support of Mike and Rosa Banks. Besides sharing the broad range of his technical knowledge of computers and nets, Mike dropped everything to recover thirty pages of text that a failing disk drive had chomped into garbage, while Rosa dosed me with sanity, wisdom, and several jokes I'd never heard before. You had to be there—I'm grateful they were.

I am also grateful to Ralph Roberts for graciously allowing me an advance look at his book *Computer Viruses* (Compute!) at the very moment I needed it most.

A thank-you to Pat LoBrutto for his patience and care as an editor; to Shawna McCarthy for believing in the first place; and to Betsy Mitchell for getting me home in one piece. Also to Lou Aronica for consideration and good advice.

And many, many thanks to: Ellen Datlow (for Manhattan after dark, among other things), my agent Merrilee Heifetz, Bruce and Nancy Sterling, Lew and Edie Shiner, Barb Loots, Howard "Uncle Chowder" Waldrop, Sherry Gershon Gottlieb, Jim Loehr, Fred Duarte and Karen Meschke, Michael Swanwick and Marianne Porter and Sean, Lisa Tallarico (for the pump), Jeannie Hund (for knowing), Ed Graham, Barry Malzberg (for the fun part), Kathy McAndrew Griffin (for phrasing the coin), Suzanne Heins (for sushi lunches), The Nova Expressions, Robert Haas, Mark Ziesing, Andy "Sahib" Watson, Tom Abellera (for Gödel), Eileen Gunn and John Berry and Angela (for tower accommodations), Patricia "Spike" Parsons, Alan Wexelblat and Jennie Faries, the Delphi Wednesday-Nighters, the Rochester, NY Creative FIST, Malcolm Edwards, James Gunn, Paul Novitski (for food and ferryboats), Gary Knight and Kim Fairchild (for letting me play with their toys), my in-laws George and Marguerite Fenner, my mother Helen S. Kearney, and my husband Arnie Fenner and our son Bobby (for everything).

1

"I'm going to die," said Jones.

The statuesque tattoo artist paused between the lotuses she was applying to the arm of the space case lolling half-conscious in the chair. "What, again?"

"Don't laugh at me, Gator." Jones ran a skeletal hand through his nervous-breakdown hair.

"Who's laughing? Do you see me laughing?" She shifted on her high stool and held her subject's arm closer to the lamp. The lotus job was especially difficult, as it had to merge into a preexisting design, and her eyes were already strained from a full night's work. "I don't laugh at anyone who dies as often as you do. You know, someday your adrenal system is gonna tell you to fuck off, and you won't be back. Maybe someday real soon."

"Just as well." Jones turned from the skull-and-roses design he'd been looking at pinned to the wall of the tent. "Keely's gone."

Gator lifted the needle and dabbed at the decorated flesh, frowning. The cases on the Mimosa generally had terrible skin, but they were docile enough to make a good filing system, considering you could usually find them wherever you left them—they didn't move around much on their own, and unlike other kinds of hardcopy, they seldom got stolen. "What did you expect? Living with someone who keeps dying on you is bound to strain any relationship." She looked at him with large green eyes. "Get help, Jones. You're an addict."

His bitter smile made her look down at the lotuses again quickly. "Jones and his jones? Yah, I know. I don't care. I got no complaints about that, not one. If I'd had to go one more day with that depression, I'd have killed myself anyway. One time, for good."

"I hate to point out the obvious, but you're depressed now."

1

"That's why I'm going to die. And Keely didn't leave me. He's gone."

The tattoo artist paused again, resting the flabby arm on her knee while she reinked the needle. "Is there a difference?"

"He left a note." Jones fished a scrap of paper out of his back pocket, uncrumpled it, and held it out to her.

"Bring it over here and put it under the light for me, I've got my hands full."

He did so, and she studied it for several long moments. "Well?" he demanded.

She pushed his hand aside and bent over her subject's arm again. "Shut up for a minute. I'm thinking."

There was a sudden blast of music from outside as the jammers who had been thrashing all night went at it again. Jones jumped like an electrified chicken. "Shit, how can you think with all that?"

"Can't hear you over the music." Nodding her head to the beat, she finished the lotus and set the needle on the tray. One more flower, and then she could stick the case back under the pier he'd come out from. She straightened up, pushing at the small of her back. "If you're really going to die on me, you could at least rub my neck before you go."

He began kneading her shoulders. The music outside lessened in volume, receding up the boardwalk. Someone was mounting a hit-and-run; have fun, kids, call if you make bail.

A tall man in an ankle-length cape burst through the tent flap, startling Jones again.

"Ow!" Gator slapped Jones's hand off her shoulder. "Jesus, what are you, a Vulcan?"

Even if Jones had understood the old reference, he wasn't paying attention. He was staring at the black patterns writhing on the white material of the cape, strange intricate waves dividing and subdividing almost too fast for the eye to follow, seeming to implode as they swept along the surface.

"Nice," said Gator, wincing as she rubbed the spot Jones had pinched. "Who's your tailor? Mandelbrot?"

The man turned his back and spread the cape wide. "Could you just die for this, or what?"

"Bad choice of words," Gator said darkly. "And if you're here on my account, forget it. I don't do skin animations."

"Actually, I was looking for someone." He swept over to the case slumped in the chair and bent to peer at his face. "Nope. Oh, well." He straightened up, giving the cape another swirl.

It was pulsing with moirés now. "Hit-and-run in Fairfax, if you're interested."

"Fairfax is a hole," Gator said.

"That's why it needs a party." The man grinned expectantly.

"Yes, I do know who you are," she added, as if in answer. "And I'm charmed as all get-out, but as you can see, I'm booked."

He looked from the case to Jones, who was still transfixed by the cape. "You Mimosa people are a strange bunch."

"You should know," she said.

"Last call. You sure?" He leaned in a little. "Kiss me good-bye?"

She smiled. "Dream about it."

"I will. I'll put you in my next video."

"Valjean!" someone yelled from outside. "Are you coming?"

"Just breathing heavily," he called back, and swept out in swirling clusters of slithering paisleys.

"Keep rubbing. Nobody gave you the night off yet."

Obediently Jones went back to massaging her neck and shoulders. The music had faded away, leaving them in relative quiet. Somewhere farther down the strip, someone began improvising something in a high minor key on a synthesizer.

"What I think," she said after a bit, "is you should make your peace with the Supreme Being, however you may conceive of it. Full church confession."

Jones gave a short, harsh laugh. "Oh, sure. Saint Dismas could really help me."

"You never know."

"I'm not of the faith. I don't belong."

"You do now. I'd say you definitely qualify as incurably informed. Let me see Keely's note again."

He gave it back to her, and she read it over as he worked his fingers up her neck to the base of her skull. " 'Dive, dive' could only mean—"

"I know what it means," she said. " 'Divide, the cap and green eggs over easy, to go. Bdee-bdee.' The 'bdee-bdee' is a nice touch, actually."

Jones laughed again. "Yah, sure is. Keely's the one who needs help, not me. That B&E shit. I *told* him someday he'd get caught. I *told* him. And I *begged* him to get help—"

"The same kind of help you got? Implants from some feel-good mill that doesn't give a shit as long as your insurance company comes across?" She shrugged away from him and went to a small laptop on a table in the corner of the tent. The intricate climbing ivy pattern displayed on the screen was rotating through a sequence of views from different angles. She danced her fingers over the keyboard. The ivy pattern grew several more leaves. She pressed another key; the screen partitioned itself into two halves, scooting the ivy over to the right. A menu appeared on the left.

"I'll see what anyone knows," she said, touching a line on the menu with her little finger. "Eat that note."

"I don't like to die with anything in my stomach."

She sighed but didn't answer. On the left half of the screen, the menu had been replaced by the legend, *Dr. Fish's Answering Machine* in large, plain block letters. One-handed, she typed the word *tattoos* on the screen.

U/1 or d/1? came the response.

U/1, she typed, and after waiting a moment she pressed one more key. The partition line in the center of the screen disappeared as the design was uploaded and the two halves merged into one. The rotating ivy froze and then faded away.

The doctor thanks you for your patronage and reminds you to eat right, get plenty of rest, detox regularly, and consult your physician before beginning any exercise program.

She reached for a cigarette as the screen went blank. "Nobody knows a thing," she said. "I'll find the answering machine tomorrow and see if—"

There was a soft thump behind her. Jones had keeled over on the packed sand, dead. She groaned. "You *shit*. You actually *did* it, you piece of useless fucking *trash*. I should just dump you. I *would* dump you, but Keely would care. God knows why."

She turned back to the laptop and called up the stored copy of the skull-and-roses pattern Jones had been looking at earlier. Interesting how he'd been drawn to that one. It supported her theory that everyone had one special tattoo—at least one—applied or not. Of course, the way things were with him, he might simply have been drawn to the skull, but she had other designs that suggested death far more strongly than that one, and he'd barely noticed those.

Partitioning the screen again, she called up the E-mail menu and prepared to upload the skull-and-roses pattern. She added a short form letter:

Here is the latest design in your subscription to the Tattoo-of-the-Month Club. We ask that you pick it up at your earliest

*convenience, and that you consult your physician before skin
integrity is compromised.*

She pressed the upload key and waited. The screen blanked
again except for a small square blinking in the lower right-
hand corner. Minutes passed. She left the buffer open and
went over to the case in the chair. He was passed out or asleep.
She pulled him out of the chair and stretched him out near
the entrance. In a little while the kids would show up looking
for eat-money; she could pay them to drag him back to his
usual spot under one of the piers. Then she hefted Jones into
the chair and bared his left arm.

Maybe she ought to give him the skull-and-roses just to make
him feel better, she thought, and then decided against it. If
he was choosy, let him pay for the privilege. She remembered
him when he'd gone from trying to crack video to just being
a hanger-on, the type who basically helped you get toxed. The
only difference between him and someone like Valjean, was
Valjean had managed to stay detoxed long enough to put together a decent band. Or maybe she was just feeling pissy
because she'd had the inclination to pick a vocation that required her to do it sober.

The laptop beeped discreetly, and she went back to it.

On my way. The words blinked twice and then vanished.
She recalled the ivy pattern, sized it, and set it to print out.
The small cube-shaped printer spat a narrow strip of paper at
her. She took it to Jones and pressed it down on the inside of
his forearm, smoothing it against his flesh with two fingers. A
minute later she peeled the paper away and looked at the ivy
design on the pale skin. Perfect offset. She picked up her
needle.

The tent flap opened, and two kids came in. She knew the
husky fifteen-year-old, but his skinny friend must have been
a recent arrival. Didn't look a day over twelve. Getting old,
she thought.

"Put him back where you got him," she said, pointing at the
case on the ground. "And if you can't, remember where you
end up sticking him so you can tell me exactly."

The big kid nodded.

"And then don't get lost," she went on. "I'll need you to
load this one for a friend." She gestured slightly with Jones's
arm.

The kid took a step forward and squinted at Jones dubiously.
His friend crowded behind him, looking from her to Jones and

back with large, frightened eyes. "Scan *him* flat," said the big kid.

"He *was* dead, he's just comatose now."

"Whack it for a mark." He pointed at the designs.

"You'll do it out of the kindness of your heart," she laughed. "We'll talk tattoos later. *Much* later."

He lifted his chin belligerently. "Hey, I'm packed. Whacked two yesterday."

"Honey, what I've forgotten about finding floating boards it'll take you the rest of your life to learn."

He looked over at the laptop covetously. The ivy design was rotating on the screen again. "Mark me?"

"It's spoken for."

His round face puckered sullenly. "N.g. to leave the cap off," he said. "Someone could crash the party."

"And someone who hacks me could find the doctor is in." She gestured at the case. "Just return my file for me and stick around, and then we'll discuss it. In English, please, I don't talk your squawk. I'm not going to stone you. I never have, have I?"

He pointed at Jones. "That's a stone." He and his friend each grabbed a leg and dragged the case out of the tent.

Kids, she thought, starting on the ivy. She had it mostly done by the time Rosa showed up.

2

The real stone-home bitch about night court was having to stay awake for it.

Sitting at the back of the well-populated courtroom, jammed between some fresh-face named Clarence or Claw and a null-and-void wearing a bail-jumper's Denver Boot, Gina tried to calculate her immediate prospects. Hit-and-run—probably fifty, since she'd only been an attendee, not a conspirator; a hundred if the judge got stoked by the time her turn rolled around. Possession of controlled substances would be another hundred. Public intoxication, disorderly conduct, failure to report a hit-and-run, trespassing, and resisting arrest—call it a hundred and fifty, red-eye special rate, possibly two hundred. The resisting charge was a stone-home joke, as far as she was concerned. She'd only run, she hadn't swung on anybody once she'd been caught. Like it wasn't natural to run like hell when a hyped-up battalion of cops came at you.

Fuck it, what difference did one more charge make, anyway? The fines would clean her out and then some, one more garnishment on her wages, so-fucking-what. All she cared about now was getting back on the street so she could find Mark and take him home. Stupid burnout had let himself get dragged off without a second thought *again*, and here she was paying the price for it. She wouldn't have been at the goddamn hit-and-run in the first place if she hadn't been looking for him.

She'd started out on the Manhattan-Hermosa strip, what the kids called the Mimosa, part of the old postquake land of the lost. She wasn't old enough to remember the Big One, hadn't even been living in the big C-A when it had hit. The kids who shanked it on the Mimosa didn't remember the quake, either. For all they knew, the old Manhattan Pier and Hermosa Pier and Fisherman's Wharf had always stretched out over dry sand, just to shelter the space cases who squatted under them. Some of the cases probably remembered the Big One. Probably not as many as claimed to.

The piers shouldn't have survived the Big One (which everyone was now saying hadn't been the *real* Big One after all, just the Semi-Medium One, but that didn't scan as well). Except for part of the old Fisherman's Wharf, though, they were still standing. Not in prima shape, but standing. Not unlike Mark.

Living through the quake and the postmillennial madness that had followed was one way to end up under a pier talking to your toes; taking some of the stuff available on the Mimosa was another. Mark had always been a candidate for a spot in the sand, even back in the early days before all the hard party-time he'd put in had really begun to take its toll. Sometimes she could almost let the fucking burnout go ahead and flush himself down the rabbit hole in his brain. Like someone had said years ago, some of us can cut the funk, and some of us can't.

But she wasn't ready to let him slip away. Whether he was still salvageable or not, whether he was even worth the trouble, she couldn't bring herself to say fuck it and let him go. So she did another night on the Mimosa, poking into shacks and lean-tos, searching under piers, checking out the jammers and scaring off the Rude Boys, looking to take him home, hose him down, and detox him enough to get him through his corporate debut day after tomorrow.

Several of the regulars had said they'd seen him hanging with a hit-and-run caravan headed for Fairfax. Toxed to the red line, no doubt. The stupe didn't even like hit-and-runs, but someone had probably said party-party-party fast enough to blank out any other thoughts, someone like Valjean and the rest of his no-account band. Like any of them needed to play hit-and-run in the Fairfax wasteland.

She'd ripped over to Fairfax as fast as the toy engine in the little two-passenger commuter rental would allow. The fancy rubble of the old Pan Pacific Auditorium had been hard alive and jumping by the time she made it, bangers and thrashers and the pickle stand in business while the hackers ran fooler loops on their laptops to confound surveillance. All the usual crowd you'd find at an illegal party set up fast in a public place, but Mark had already floated off somewhere else, if he'd ever been there at all. Before she could get a new line on him, the cops had come in and busted things up.

She had almost sulked herself into a doze when most of the crowd that had been waiting ahead of her rose en masse to stand before the judge. To Gina's right a guy with a handcam climbed over two rows of seats for a better angle.

"Another clinic?" the judge said wearily, glancing at the monitor on her bench.

"Three subgroups, Your Honor," said the prosecutor. "Doctors, staff, and patients."

"At this hour?" The judge shrugged. "Oh, but of course. Doctors never keep regular hours. And if you weren't operating round the clock, some of your patients might reconsider. I wish you people would perpetrate insurance fraud in some other jurisdiction. Like Mars. Priors?"

"We'll get to that, Your Honor," said the prosecutor hurriedly as a few hands started to go up.

Gina sat forward, her fatigue momentarily forgotten. Insurance fraud wasn't exactly the kind of thing that called for a raid in the middle of the night. The litany of charges was boring enough: conspiracy to commit fraud, fraud, unnecessary implantation procedures—the usual for a clinic that put in implants under pretense of treating depression, seizures, and other brain dysfunctions. Just another feel-good mill, big fucking deal. She started to drift off.

". . . unlawful congress with a machine."

Her eyes snapped open. A murmur went through the courtroom, and somebody smothered a giggle. The guy with the handcam had climbed over the spectators' rail and was panning the group carefully.

"And what, Mr. Prosecutor, constitutes unlawful congress with a machine?" the judge asked.

"It should come up on your screen in a moment, Your Honor."

The judge waited and court waited. Several long moments later the judge turned away from the monitor in disgust. "Bailiff! Get downstairs right now and inform central we're having technical difficulties. Do *not* call. *Go*, physically, and tell them *in person*."

Next to Gina, Clarence or Claw gave a loud, showy, fake sneeze. The judge banged her gavel. "We can cure the compulsively comedic here, you know. Six months for contempt may be old-fashion aversion therapy, but it works, and we don't have to bill your insurance company, either." The judge's glare fell on the prosecutor. "You have been warned repeatedly about inputting evidence and confiscated material without following proper decontamination procedures."

"The procedures were followed, Your Honor. Apparently they need updating."

"Who was responsible for the storage of this data?" the judge asked, surveying the group sternly. A hand went up timidly from somewhere in the middle.

"Your Honor," said the defense attorney, stepping forward quickly. "Data storage personnel cannot be held responsible for viral contamination and spread. I cite *Vallio vs. MacDougal*, in which it was determined MacDougal had no culpability for an infection that may have already existed."

The judge sighed. "Whose data was it, then?"

"Your Honor," said the defense attorney, even more quickly, "the owner of the data cannot be cited without establishing—"

The judge waved the woman's words away. "I get it, I get it. Viruses form all on their own, input themselves without a human agent, and nobody's ever responsible."

"Your Honor, even leaving aside the issue of self-incrimination, it's very hard these days to prove that any virus in question was not preexisting and inert until triggered by—"

"I'm familiar with the problem, thank you very much, Ms. Pelham. This doesn't alleviate the immediate situation."

"Move for a recess, Your Honor."

"Denied."

"But the virus—"

"Counselor Pelham," the judge said wearily, "it may come as a shock to people of your generation, but courts were not always computerized, and it was not only possible but routine to conduct business without being on-line. We will continue, using hard copy as needed; that is why we maintain court clerks and court reporters. I still want to know what this 'unlawful congress with a machine' charge is supposed to be." She turned her gaze on the prosecutor again.

"Your Honor," said the prosecutor smoothly, "this particular charge also has charges of breaking and entering and industrial espionage attached to it. The complainant wishes to have all proceedings in this matter kept confidential. Permission to clear the courtroom, Your Honor."

"And who is this complainant?" the judge asked.

"Your Honor, the complainant wishes to keep that information confidential, too. For the time being, that is."

"Answer the question, counselor. Who is the complainant?"

Gina glanced around for someone who looked ready to bolt, but the only other people left in court had been pulled in at the hit-and-run with her. And the guy with the handcam, who had been forced back over the rail into the spectators' area by the other bailiff.

"Permission to approach the bench, Your Honor," said the prosecutor.

The judge nodded. "Granted. This had better be good."

They conferred for several moments while the group from the clinic shifted around, nervous but silent. The guy with the handcam was half sitting on the rail, looking sourly at the gag-sticker the bailiff had slapped over his lens.

"Court finds confidentiality will serve the public good," the judge said abruptly. "Before we clear the court, who else is waiting and why?"

The other bailiff herded the clinic group off to one side as Gina straggled up with Clarence or Claw, and the loser clunking his Boot on the floor, and the rest of the hit-and-run people, to stand before the bench. The judge cut off the reading of the charges.

"Is that it? No first-degree murder, no other unlawful-con-gress-with-a-machine perpetrators? Very well. The court is dis-missing the charges against you," she said, her gaze resting momentarily on Gina, "even though I know a few of you have quite a long list of priors. Since we have managed to apprehend none of the conspirators, and since we have more important fish to fry here tonight, the court is letting you off with full knowledge that you will all undoubtedly be back here on some other night. What's one conviction more or less? Except you," she added, pointing at the loser with the Denver Boot. "You can spend the night canned, and we'll pick up the rest of your story in the morning."

Gina had to bite the inside of her cheek to keep from grin-ning. It didn't quite work. The judge shook her head and motioned for the room to be cleared.

"So, you up to do it again?"

Gina looked up at Clarence-or-Claw's smiling face. Didn't this guy ever get tired? Whatever he ran on, it had to be better than most of the stuff you could get from a hit-and-run pickle stand.

"I'm up for getting the fuck outa here," she said, brushing past him. He trotted down the shiny hall after her.

"No, really," he said, in a half whisper. "I know where it's happening right now, hit-and-run, better than the one where they caught us."

"Get the fuck outa my face." She walked faster, pushing through the fatigue that was weighing more heavily on her by the moment.

"Hey, wait—"

She swung around a corner, half turning to slap at him, when something smashed into her, and she went down hard on the polished floor. Sheets of paper rained down and scattered. There were frantic footsteps as someone chased after them.

Pushing herself up to a sitting position, she rubbed the side of her face and then blinked at what seemed to be a solid wall of business suits. She looked up.

"Mount Rushmore," she said. "Little far west of home for this time of year?"

The faces stared down at her impassively, three men and a woman. Attack of the Living Suits. She shrugged and pulled herself up on the nearest one, using his pockets for handholds. He didn't move or change expression, and she was sorry immediately. His face was familiar. At the moment she couldn't remember what it was associated with, but it couldn't have been anything good. The look in his eyes said he knew her, too, and he didn't like her, a lot.

Fuck him. She ran a hand through her dreadlocks and went into a too-toxed-to-live act. "Gotta stop having these crazy-damn dreams," she muttered, and elbowed her way through the middle of the group.

She got down to the first floor without further incident and also without Clarence or Claw or whoever he was. On the way out some instinct made her divert to the doors right of center, so she had a perfect view, without being seen herself, of Hall Galen and Lindel Joslin getting out of the unmarked limo at the curb. The young guy who got out just after them she didn't recognize. But the last guy out was Visual Mark.

The young guy hesitated at the bottom of the steps as the others, including Mark, started up. Gina drew back farther against the wall as Galen paused to turn to him.

"Come on, Keely," he said in that oozy voice that had always reminded Gina of a perverted baby. "You think they come out and fetch state's evidence off the front steps?"

Joslin put one skeletal hand to her mouth and gave a giggle that only dogs should have heard. Gina still couldn't buy the skinny bitch-twitch as an implant surgeon. Anyone lying on a table who saw that coming on with an implant needle had to be stone-home crazy or dead not to jump up and run away screaming.

"You said I'd have a signed hard copy of the deal by now," the young guy said. "I don't see one." He was even younger than Gina had first thought, barely not a kid; an ex-kid.

"S'waiting for you inside with our lawyers."

Gina winced; only a kid would buy Galen doing casual. You could practically see the words stalking around on stilts. *Run, fool,* she thought; *what the fuck, maybe they don't think you've got the nerve so they won't have anyone to chase you.*

"You said I'd have a hard copy *in my hands* before I ever set foot inside," the guy insisted, still holding his ground. But not very well; he was going to let them reel him in any minute. Gina didn't really want to watch, but there was no way to leave without being seen.

"Now, Keely," Galen said, with the lip-smack that had always made Gina want to pop his chocks, "we said we'd pull for you, but there's no way you can speed up a transcription or a hardcopy machine. They can only chug along so fast, you know."

The kid looked down and mumbled something about a hard copy again.

Galen dropped all pretense of congeniality and stumped down the stairs to stand two steps above the kid and just an inch taller. "There's a whole courtroom and an impatient judge waiting. We're going in anyway. You can go in turned over, or you can go in and get turned inside out. It doesn't really make a whole lot of difference to me personally."

Mark yawned noisily, and for a moment he seemed to be looking through the shadows directly at her. Gina tensed; then his gaze wandered past her. She slumped back against the wall. Even if he had seen her, she probably hadn't registered as anything but more of the video playing in his head. Hell, he probably didn't know where *he* was himself. *When I get ahold of you, motherfucker,* Gina thought, *oh, when I get ahold of you, won't be nothing left but shit and blood.*

He didn't look as if there were all that much more to him now—skin and bones, with lank brown Jesus-length hair, a broken nose, dazed, faded green eyes, and a voice permanently buried in gravel. But Mark never had looked like much, even in the early days when they'd first been in the video business together, when it had just been her and Mark and the Beater and a revolving cast of others, hammering simulations into rock-video visions. But that had been back when the Beater had still been the Beater, and Mark had still been a banger instead of a burnout, and Hall Galen the Boy Mogul was still working on hitting the potty with it. And Joslin was torturing hamsters, most likely.

As if Gina's errant thought had activated her, Joslin came to life and went down the few steps to Mark. *Don't touch him, bitch,* Gina said silently, her mouth moving unconsciously with the words as Joslin's dead white hand came to roost on Mark's shoulder. *Get your claw off him, bitch, that meat is mine.*

Joslin's hand stayed there, as if she meant to anchor him against a sudden gust of wind that would blow him away. The way he was going these days, it wouldn't have taken much more than a light breeze. But he still had fire enough to make killer video. Not the only reason she wasn't ready to let him go yet, but it was the one that stood when she couldn't get anything else to stand up with it.

She probably still wouldn't be ready to let him go when he finally went, and he *was* going. They all knew it, her, the Beater, even Mark himself, in some far, as-yet-intact recess of his burning-out head. Galen knew it as well as anyone, and what he wanted in night court with some old wreck teetering with one foot already off his boogie-board, and an ex-kid who obviously didn't want to be state's evidence, and a bitch-twitch whose specialty was brain implants, was one of the better questions of the night.

But the best question was what the *fuck* was Mark doing there all on his own without a word to her. She and Mark were in it together, always had been. They'd been in it together in the beginning, and when Galen had bought most of the video-production company out from under the Beater, and they'd been in it together when Galen had let the monster conglomerate take EyeTraxx over from him, and they were supposed to be in it together the day after tomorrow, when they were due to show up for their first full day working for the monster conglomerate—

The realization came just as the kid gave in and let Galen take him slowly up the steps. That bad-news, familiar face in the courthouse: Somebody Rivera, a minor honcho with the conglomerate, Diversifications, Inc. He'd been around to EyeTraxx a time or three, sniffing at this and that, taking a survey of what his company had bought itself. She'd managed to dodge him every time, but she'd never kidded herself. Rivera had known who she was and what she was, and if he'd really wanted to, he'd have found her no matter where she was. Anyone could. Just follow the trail of court-ordered garnishments on her income.

Surprised that *fucker*, she thought. What little satisfaction she could take in that fact was short-lived. Ace fuckers like Rivera didn't like being surprised. She'd pay for it.

Or Mark would. The sight of him disappearing through the doors at the top of the steps sent a wave of goose bumps along her scalp, around each dreadlock. She had a sudden, wild idea of following him, hiding out till he emerged from the court and then jumping his ass, but there was no telling how long he'd be in there. Besides, Rivera would probably have someone looking out for her now. She'd wait for him at his place.

Something moved above her in the darkness, and for a moment she thought Rivera had already sent a goon for her. Then she saw the outline of the handcam against the darker shadows.

"Pretty interesting scene, huh?" he said. "You seemed to find it pretty interesting, anyway." He came down a couple of steps.

"Got that gag-sticker off okay, then?" she asked.

"Don't happen to know any of those people, do you?"

She blew out a short breath. "You?"

"I asked you first." He laughed a little. "But what the hell. Some of them. Your turn."

"Some of them," she echoed.

"It would be nice to know where we overlap." He moved down to the step just above her. "Can I interest you in a well-dressed cup of coffee?"

Gina wiped her hands over her face. "Right now, you couldn't interest me stark naked in a bathtub of lime Jell-O. Who are you working for?"

He hesitated, and she could practically feel him deciding whether to lie or not. Mark contended that extreme fatigue would do that to you, give you such heightened perception to nonverbal clues as to be all but telepathy. Assuming you could stay awake enough for it to register.

"I gypsy," he said at last. "It's a good living—"

"If you give good tabloid," she said.

He had a sexy laugh, even at this hour. "—if you can find slots for your stuff. I don't think I'd have much trouble finding a slot for this, if I knew a little more about what it was."

Gina yawned. "I don't think you're gonna find a slot for any of that. I think you're gonna find that suddenly nobody gives a fuck about raids on feel-good mills, that it's just another dog-bites-man story and nobody needs it, not even the most desperate tabloid net at the bottom of your market barrel."

"Is that so." No sexy laugh now; no expression in his voice at all.

"And then," she went on, "I think sometime real soon, you're gonna try uploading or downloading, and you'll find a virus has run through your entire file storage and chomped every second bit into garbage before it ran right into your handcam and told it to fuse itself. And maybe you'll have the bad cess to have passed the fucker on to one of your cherished markets, and they'll hand deliver a lawsuit while you're still standing around trying to figure out what happened to the guts in your cam. I think you could even find out that your insistence on scoping out news is classified as a case of obsessive-compulsive disorder, and they recommend you be treated with implant therapy. And the next thing you know, you won't care about what's news anymore. Is that too high up in the stupidsphere for you?"

"You sure about all that?" he asked evenly.

"No." She yawned again. "The only thing I'm sure of is they put a gag-sticker on your lens and the judge cleared the courtroom. Everything you've got is illegal as hell, and you'd go to the can just for attempting to sell it, so they probably wouldn't get to you until your sentence was up."

"You seem to know a lot about this," he said, leaning in a little closer.

"I don't know dick. I'm dead, and I'm going home to lie down decently until it's time to go to work."

"And who do you work for?"

Gina jerked a thumb at the now-empty steps. "Them." She turned and went down the stairs, leaving him to chew on that, if he could.

She was too tired to be able to tell whether she'd really

thrown the fear of God into him or not. With any luck he'd at least bury the stuff if he didn't flush it. And without any luck, it wasn't her worry. She had big problems of her own.

And she was still going to jump Mark's skinny, burned-out ass. She was really going to pop his chocks.

3

LAX went as smoothly and uneventfully as the entire trip. Or trips, actually: K.C. to Salt Lake, Salt Lake to the Bay, and a jumper from the Bay to L.A. Decathlon traveling, but it was the only way to buy three different tickets under three different names—correction, only two; they hadn't asked for a name in San Francisco because it was just a jumper—using anonymous bearer-chips in quantities that wouldn't raise any eyebrows.

Sam hadn't really expected anyone to bother her about the insulin pump hanging on her side. The most attention anyone had given it was to screen it for off-color blips, and the security guard at the Bay jumper hadn't even done that. He'd just grinned at her, displayed his own pump, and said, "Pray for better tissue matching, eh, sister?" Airport security was interested only in weapons and explosives, not unlicensed or bootlegged computer equipment. Besides, it really had been an insulin pump once, before she'd gone to work on it.

She kept her pace to a leisurely stroll through the terminal, letting the crowds flow around her. The pump was out of sight in the pocket of her baggy pants, deactivated for the moment; the tacky sunglasses were hanging on a cord around her neck (tacky but functional; when not turned on, the retinal-projection screen in the left lens was transparent). The chip-player was tucked away in her one small duffel bag. No one had shown much interest in the chip-player, either, but chip-players were far more common than severely brittle diabetics whose bodies rejected all cultured implants. Even if the security guards had been interested enough to pop on the fingertip-sized 'phones and take a listen, all they would have heard was hard-core speed-thrash, in stereo. Speed-thrash was undergoing yet another renaissance as a new generation discovered it was a great way to make everyone over the age of twenty-five give ground in a hurry, hands over ears. Sam was very fond of speed-thrash. She was seventeen.

18

She passed the baggage-claim area, weaving her way through the people waiting to use the closed booths along the wall opposite the carousel. The Cal-Pac modem symbol above the booths buzzed and flickered; not the most confidence-inspiring sight, but nobody gave up a place in line. It never failed to surprise Sam how many people went on trusting Cal-Pac's public modems. Because of their broad compatibility, they were more susceptible to viruses, no matter how many vaccines were pumped into the system. But then, half the vaccines in use were pathetically outdated. Rather than spend money for further research and development, the government and the taxpayers (of which Sam was not one) had opted for stiffer penalties for vandals. As if that would put Humpty Dumpty together again.

She paused briefly next to the end booth. The small graffito was still there, scratched into the plastic in clumsy block letters: *Dr. Fish Makes House Calls.* A new one had been added farther down: *St. Dismas, pray for us.*

At the exit to ground transportation, she ran the usual gauntlet of gawkers and hawkers—a few peddlers, some advocacy groups with handbills to waste, two rival clinics promising that her motivation would come back as if by magic, yes, *magic,* young woman, diagnostic practitioners on the premises, *right there on the premises,* no need to apply for a recommendation from a doctor who probably would refuse anyway since so many doctors these days didn't seem to understand that the healing force of implants was for anyone, *everyone* who felt the *need.*

"Modern life is making you *sick!*" someone called after her.

"And your saying that is making *me* sick!" someone else yelled back.

Sam grinned to herself. My, but the karma was heavy today.

The airport rental lot was as chaotic as ever, impassably jammed with last-minute arrivals trying to turn in vehicles and make the flights they were already late for, and the recently-landed clamoring for service from the bored attendants wandering back and forth seemingly at whim between the *Rentals-In* and *Rentals-Out* blockhouses in the center of the lot. Welcome back to L.A., Sam thought resignedly. After two weeks on the McNabb Nature Reserve in the Ozarks, she wasn't sure her shit-tolerance threshold existed any more.

Against her better judgment she joined the line in front of the blockhouse labeled *Rentals-Out.* No doubt by the time she reached the service window, the attendant would tell her they were all out of everything but the bigger models, sorry, no shortage discount, next please. But she felt too travel-weary to hike over to one of the hotel lots, and getting on one of the privately-run shuttles required producing a scannable ID, something she avoided as often as possible by using bearer-chips. She didn't care to make her movements too traceable.

She dug the chip-player out of her bag and popped on the 'phones. It was some stone-home righteous new speed-thrash Keely had zapped to her, and the translation program she had used on it had left it intact. She hadn't had to remove the encrypted material from the carrier-data to go over it during the flights, looking like any other kid on a boring trip, shades on and plugged into her music. No one had been able to see that, under her shabby satin jacket, the chip-player had been connected to the former insulin pump in her pocket, and the unruly tangle of her hair had hidden how the cord on her sunglasses was plugged into the headphone wire.

She was almost tempted to connect the sunglasses and have another look at Keely's data, but there would be time enough for that later—if she didn't die of old age waiting to rent a commuter unit she probably wouldn't get anyway. She hated the commuter rentals—everybody did—but owning a real car in L.A. was a bureaucratic nightmare, requiring a lily-white record and a king's ransom for the umpty-ump different permits and licenses and taxes that had to be renewed every three months. L.A.'s millennial solution to the car overpopulation problem of the previous century; it was a bad joke. Instead of a mass transit system, there were rental units proliferating like rabbits on fast-forward, little boxes made of masking tape and spit, with shitty little computer navigators built into the dash. For all the good *that* did—GridLid usually ran anywhere from twenty minutes to an hour behind the traffic patterns, so that you were more likely to find yourself in the middle of a clog before the warning about it appeared on the nav screen.

Sam let out a tired breath. Back in L.A. less than an hour, and it was already undoing the smooth that two weeks in the Ozarks had given her. The solitude had been what her father called a tonic. Everything had just gotten so crazy, the whole hacker scene, an information frenzy. Then there'd been the doodah with her parents, speaking of her father, which hadn't helped her feel any less frantic. Old Gabe and Catherine had really done their part to make her crazy, Catherine more than

Gabe, to be fair about it. Why she had expected anything else after all these years—call it temporary brain damage, she thought sourly. Just thinking about them now was giving her that fluttery I-gotta-get-outa-here-or-die-screaming churn in the pit of her stomach.

That had been reason enough to head for the hills, though the stuff she'd hacked out of Diversifications had been hot enough to serve as an excuse for an extended trip out of town. She kept telling herself that was the real reason, the only reason, she'd jumped out. It felt better than admitting that, in spite of everything, the fact that she could not have her mother's love and respect was still a knife in her heart.

She hadn't had to admit anything on the McNabb Nature Reserve; the McNabbs didn't scan IDs, and they didn't ask questions. Few amenities, small cost; each day she had trucked over to the common shower and bathroom area from her tent. If she wanted news, the McNabbs ran a small general store where she could reserve a tailored hardcopy of *The Daily You* printed out from the dataline, if she didn't mind having to reset her defaults each time. Occasionally there was a wait, since the McNabbs had only two printers, and if she didn't want to bother, Lorene McNabb would put hers aside and give it to her the next time she came in.

But as pleasant a change as it had been, she'd known it wasn't her life. She'd already begun thinking about going back to L.A. when Keely had called her.

The one tech thing the McNabbs supplied for each tent was a phone; they did not take messages, and they did not go tramping out to inform people of emergencies. Sam had thought the phone had looked pretty funny sitting on the McNabb-supplied footlocker at the head of the cot. She hadn't expected it to ring; no one had known where she was. But if anyone was capable of tracking her down, it was Keely.

He'd sounded wired as usual—his bizarro relationship with death-crazed Jones was something else that had gotten on her nerves. But for once he hadn't whined about what Jones and his implants were coming to. This time he'd sounded wired and scared, something about some stuff he'd hacked. Keely liked to call it B&E, as if that somehow made it more glamorous than plain old hacking. Sam suspected he'd hit Diversifications. She'd made the mistake of giving him the specs for the modified insulin pump before she'd left.

She'd done all the work on the pump while she'd been out

in the Ozarks, just to see if she had the touch with this kind of hardware. She did, and as it turned out, it was fortunate she had. Keely insisted on zapping something to her over the phone, and she'd left her laptop behind with Rosa.

And then after the zap, he'd just said good-bye and hung up on her. So it had to be Diversifications, she decided, the hackers' Mount Everest and the place most likely to catch you. And when they did, they always prosecuted. Keely had always had this compulsive rivalry with her, needing to match her hit for hit. She'd tried to make him see rivalry was pointless, and the more often you tried Diversifications, the more likely you were to get caught. But Keely had always had more talent than sense.

Perhaps she might have been more convincing, Sam thought, if she'd told him her own little trade secret: she knew her way around their defenses because her father worked there, and she'd picked up a lot about their operation by simple osmosis. Maybe Keely would have seen the wisdom of backing off, or maybe he'd have just taken up hounding her for tips and hints until he drove her mad. And no matter how she tried, she couldn't get around feeling responsible, in an oblique, neurotic way, for whatever had happened to him. Ridiculous, maybe, but there it was. And here *she* was, back in L.A.

". . . new show, free equipment, absolutely no charge!"

The voice that cut through the tumult in her earphones sounded familiar. She clicked off the chip-player and looked around.

The young guy working his way up from the now-distant end of the line she was standing in could have used a few more pounds to fill out his bodysuit and balance off the absurdly full cascade of golden waves spilling down past his bony shoulders. The holo crown bobbing in the air over his head faded in and out with each step, but he didn't bother adjusting the projector on his belt or, for that matter, the bored look on his face. Sam grinned. It had been quite a while, but she'd have known Beauregard in any guise.

"Free tickets!" he called, holding them up between two fingers. "Preview of an exciting new show!" He was about to pass her when she caught his arm.

"Getting many takers?" she asked.

He looked down at her blankly for a moment and then let out a surprised laugh. "Well, fuck me."

"Is that free, too?"

He gave her a ticket. "For this you get an hour's use of a head-mounted monitor and the chance to kill a new series, which you can brag to the folks back in Kansas City about. You wanna get fucked, call my agent. He'll fuck you four times before you even mention my name."

"Thanks, Beau, but I'll give that a miss. I like to know I'm being fucked while it happens." She looked him up and down. "Love the hotbody. You look like an old-time street mime."

"And you look like an old-time vent-hugger. Some things never change. Where the hell have you been?"

She hesitated, looking from side to side. Beauregard thrust two tickets at the man standing behind her. "Here, hold her place in line, will you?" he said. "You can take those down to Hollywood Boulevard and get an easy hundred for them in front of the Chinese Theatre. They're in short supply, everyone in town wants them."

The man frowned dubiously at the tickets in his hand, and Beauregard pressed two more on him. "Okay, this is all I can let you have. That's a guaranteed two hundred you're holding, that'll pay for the best rental you can get here four times over, thanks a lot, pal, you're a prince." Sam laughed helplessly as Beauregard hustled her away from the line.

"Is that true, what you told him?" she asked.

"Fuck, no. They're *free* tickets. He'll probably have to pay someone to take them off his hands."

She stared at him in disbelief. "How do you get away with being you?"

"Same way you do, honey." He tapped her chin with his fist. "Where have you been?"

"The Ozarks. They're real pretty. What are you doing wearing the Para-Versal logo?"

He glanced up at the holo still floating over his head. "I got lucky, for a change. I got a part in *Tunnels in the Void*."

Sam looked at the ticket he'd given her. "This? What is it?"

"A small band of intrepid explorers travel the universe using black holes as a kind of intergalactic subway system, taking you with them as they seek adventure and excitement, sneering in the face of danger and all scientific fact. But hey, it's work. They used me in a bit, on the condition that I hustle passes." He gazed at her evenly as he took the ticket back from her. "Like I said, some things never change."

"I guess not." Sam shook her head. "You know this is prob-

ably all that'll come of it. Intergalactic subway system. Stone
the fucking crows at home. How stupid do they think people
are?"

"You tell me when you see that guy trying to scalp those on
the Boulevard. Diversifications did the finish on it, all the
commercials are from their clients, and gaming rights are being
auctioned right now. Plenty of features have pulled out of a
nosedive on gaming rights alone. Or the wannabee trade."

Sam felt her stomach tighten a little at the mention of Diversifications. "Sorry, Beau, but I don't see why you're wasting
your time."

"Oh, yah. Hacking programs and dodging watchdogs from
a Mimosa squat is *so* much nobler." He shrugged. "I sold my
equipment to Rosa. She's got a use for it."

"You had a use for it, once," she said seriously.

He glanced upward with a labored sigh, making the holo
crown jiggle. "Shit, why can't you be like everyone else and
refuse to have anything to do with me until I, quote, shake it
off, unquote?"

"Beau, if you'd hung in, you could probably be *making* this
stuff yourself. And not garbage like *Tunnels in the Void*, either,
but really good stuff. You know, a lot of people used to think
that you were behind the Dr. Fish virus. 'The one that got
away.' "

"So that makes two of us that got away." His face was stony
now. "You know, it's harder than it ever was now to get a
toehold. All the studios want to go to complete simulation, and
what the fuck is that? Nobody home, you know? No *people*."

"They probably *will* go to complete simulation soon, Beau,"
Sam said, trying to keep the irritation out of her voice. "Maybe
not tomorrow, but soon enough. Too soon for you and your
union and all the other unions. It's gonna be a stone dead end
for you, unless you can make the stuff."

"I don't want to *make* the stuff. I want to *be* the stuff. If that
isn't culturally on-line, then write me off. *I* don't go around
telling people what they're supposed to want."

"Touché, doll." Sam held out her hands. "Peace?"

He curled his fingers around hers briefly, looking momentarily embarrassed. "Well, truce, anyway. I didn't pull you out
of line to fight with you. It's good to see you again, Sam."

"Likewise." She paused. "Haven't seen anyone else lately,
have you?"

"Ha. Like who."

"Oh, Rosa. Gator." She gave a casual shrug. "Keely?"

Beauregard shook his head, making the holo crown wag in sluggish half circles. "I don't see anyone." He ran a wistful finger down the line of her cheek and then looked around. "Listen, I'm on a schedule—"

She nodded. "See you, Beau."

"If I get really lucky, yah, you probably will." He started his pitch again as she went back to her place in the line, smiling apologetically at the man still holding the preview tickets.

"Excuse me," he said as she was putting on her headphones again. "Do you really think I can get anything for these?"

"Oh. Well," she said, "maybe. I mean, sure. I think you might get something."

"You mean something besides taken?" The look on his face was anything but happy.

"Hey, you got them for nothing," she said coldly. "You'll only get taken if you actually go to the preview. Welcome to Hollywood, mister."

Half an hour later she was sitting in a rental that achieved two-passenger status only by virtue of the fact that it had another seat. Sam would not have taxed it with more than her duffel bag, not that it made a whole lot of difference at the moment. True to form GridLid had failed to transmit up-to-date traffic patterns, and she had driven right into the clog on Sepulveda, where, it seemed, she was going to spend most of the morning, kicking herself for not bringing a radio. Some of the smaller free-lance stations operating outside the amorphous mass of the dataline gave traffic reports from phoned-in tips. She glanced at the receiver hanging from the dash. Hell, she could phone one in herself, except it probably wasn't exactly news anymore.

Fez would have told her to accept it as an unexpected opportunity to unwind. *An L.A. clog is just Nature's way of saying it's break time.* But then, Fez had told her that trying to reconcile with her parents was a good idea, too.

She sighed and looked at the nav screen. The map display vanished, to be replaced with a basic, abbreviated dataline menu. Good old GridLid. Gosh, folks, sorry we didn't warn you about the clog, but since you're already sitting in it, you can enjoy some minor diversion, courtesy of the city.

The offerings were limited to the most popular items off several of the networks, text and/or sound only, including, she saw with some amusement, *The Stars, Crystals, and You Show* and *Dear Mrs. Troubles* from FolkNet. If you couldn't pre-guess GridLid with stars and crystals, maybe Mrs. Troubles could help you change your miserable life at two miles an hour.

She pressed the scroll button on the keyboard between the seats, and the categories began a slow roll upward. *Business, Local, Regional, National, International; Sporting Events; Lunar Installation Report; Peccadillo Update*—that was tempting; famous people throw up in public and other gossip to die for—*CrimeTime; The World of Medicine; L.A. Rox, Including !Latest! Video Releases.*

She pressed for the last, feeling slightly mollified. She wouldn't be able to see any videos on the cheap-assed monitor, but at least she'd be able to listen to some new music, maybe find a few good encryption vehicles. Encryption was fun; play this sideways, kiddies, and hear a message from the devil. Keely would certainly have approved.

Keely hated speed-thrash.

Unbidden, the thought came to her and sat in her mind, waiting for her to make something of it. Keely had sent her the information encrypted in speed-thrash, and he hated speed-thrash. *If the Good Lord had really meant speed-thrash to exist, he would have made me deaf.*

Well, so what? He knew she liked speed-thrash; he'd probably figured he'd zap her something she could appreciate.

She made a face. That didn't feel right. Keely had been in a hurry; he'd had plenty of other encryption vehicles to choose from, anything from the Brandenburg Concertos to one of those Edgar Varese things he was so crazy about, and any of those probably far more available to him than a piece of speed-thrash. A *new* piece of speed-thrash.

She pushed for the new speed-thrash listings, tapping the steering wheel impatiently while GridLid's access to the dataline pondered her choice and made a laborious search. *The Age of Fast Information, sure*, she thought sourly.

A full ten seconds later, the screen delivered the page. For once she was lucky; it was the very first item she selected for audio excerpt. *Mechanists Run Loco, by Scattershot.* The credit line for the video made her blink: *created by Aiesi/ EyeTraxx, acq. by Diversifications, Inc.*

EyeTraxx *acquired* by Diversifications? Since when, and how had *that* gotten by her? She topped back to the *L.A. Rox* general menu and selected the news.

There was nothing but the usual collection of gossipy items

on which artists were doing what outrageous or dull things. *General Industry News*, sub-subheading *Rock Videos* gave her nothing but snippets on rights reversions, what artists were signing with what video companies, who had died, and who wasn't doing anything at all.

Rock Video: Acquisitions was just a rerun of who was signing with who, nothing she hadn't been getting in her edition of *The Daily You* back in the Ozarks.

She slid back the sunroof panel and stood up on the seat carefully. There was nothing but an unbroken sea of rentals interspersed with a few private cars in all directions, and no sign of movement. Sam clambered down behind the wheel again and blew out a disgusted breath. "Shit."

"It's awful, isn't it?"

The driver in the car on her left was smiling at her sympathetically. She nodded. "It's worse than that."

"I think we all ought to file a class-action suit against GridLid, force them to clean up their program," he went on. "Or at least provide full dataline access for the rentals. I can't get anything I want."

"Me, neither." Sam looked at him speculatively. "Say, you wouldn't happen to follow rock-video news, would you?"

He managed to look apologetic and bored at the same time. "Sorry. I get *Casting Call* and *Daily Variety*, and the rest of the world can go hang as far as I'm concerned." He looked around at the clog. "Right now I really wish it would. Why aren't all these people home with their families?"

"'Scuse me? Hey, you there?" A woman about her own age was waving at her from another rental directly behind the man. "*I* follow rock video."

Except for the long pink hair, she looked more like a folkie than a thrasher, but Sam wasn't feeling choosy. "I just saw this item on the dataline," she called to the woman, twisting around to lean out the window. "It said EyeTraxx had been acquired by Diversifications, Inc. You know anything about that?"

Now the woman stared at her as if she were crazy. "God, no. That sounds like biz news to me. Snore, snore."

"Oh. Yah," Sam said faintly, pulling her head back in. Business news. Christ, business-fucking-news, what in hell else would it have been. Feeling sheepish, she topped all the way back to the main menu and selected *Business News*. Then she stared at the screen while it asked her which subheading she wanted, Local, Regional, National, or International? There was

nothing more specific. Which figured. Hard-core biz types
didn't register as a target market for GridLid; they wouldn't
be in a clog like this. They'd be in their offices doing everything
by net and email. Like her mother. *Give up*, she told herself.
*At least until you light somewhere with halfway decent ca
pability*.

Fifteen minutes later traffic had moved forward a good fifty
feet only to halt again, but she finally had something, a small
item under *Markets-at-a-Glance/NYSE Most Active*. The listing for Diversifications was footnoted with a comparison box,
giving the trading before and after its acquisition of EyeTraxx.
The date given was roughly two weeks before; nothing about
a topic thread to follow.

Frustrated, Sam sat back, stretching her arms overhead
through the open sunroof. She still didn't know what it meant,
if anything. *If it don't mean a thing, it ain't information*, as
Fez would say.

"Fez, you talk too much," she muttered. She went back to
listening to excerpts from new speed-thrash releases as the sun
climbed higher in the sky.

GridLid finally saw fit to deliver a bulletin about an accident
half a mile from where she was; by then traffic was advancing
regularly in twenty-foot spurts. A few food vendors had materialized to work the clog until the cops appeared and chased
them out. Couldn't redirect traffic fast enough to avoid a clog,
Sam thought sourly, but moved at the speed of light if someone
was out making a profit. Her stomach growled. The cops had
jogged back from the site of the wreck just before one of the
vendors would have reached her.

She had meant to head straight for the Mimosa from the
airport, but she knew if she didn't get something to eat, she
was going to faint. Feeling shaky, she detoured onto Artesia
and cruised until she found a quickie with fewer than five cars
in the drive-thru lane. Quickies were not her cuisine of choice,
but at least she'd had the luck to find one with a decent veg-
etarian offering.

The big menu screen was just out of her reach, and she had
to hang out the window to touch the square next to "Sushi rice
in seaweed cone." Her order appeared in red letters in the
middle section of the screen; a moment later the words *!Good
Choice!* flashed on and off. Cute, she thought. What else would

it say—*!Lousy Choice!* or *!No Good For You!?* Maybe the burger-gobblers got *!Slow Death!*

She selected "Coffee, caffeinated, pot" from the drink menu, and this time the message was unblinking. *The Surgeons General wish you to be aware that caffeine is associated with chromosome breakage, headaches, tension, anxiety, and impaired motor coordination when taken to excess. In pregnant women birth defects can result in those prone to certain inimical chemistries. Abstinence may be advisable; consult your doctor.*

Sam stared. A pretentious quickie; that was new. She slapped her palm against the endit square with a defiant flourish. Too late; she had the guilts over the coffee even as she couldn't wait to drink half of it at one gulp. Modern life was making her sick by trying not to make her sick.

"That's some menu," she said to the guy in the window as she stretched out of the open sunroof to pass him a few crumpled bills.

"Yah, better living through technology," he said, glancing at her without interest. He was tall and good-looking, with icy white hair and luminous green contact lenses, most likely another member of the latest generation of aspiring actors. That may have been the biggest reason simulation hadn't shut down Old Hollywood, Sam thought a little light-headedly. If they stopped taping from live action, who would staff the quickies? "Be a minute," he added as he leaned out to hand her the change. "Just opened a fresh pot of rice."

"Glad to know this place cares so much," she said. "I especially enjoyed the lecture on what caffeine would do to me."

"Oh, *hell.* George!" he roared over his shoulder. "That goddamn virus is back!"

Sam laughed aloud. She should have realized as soon as she'd seen it. A Dr. Fish, no doubt, making a house call with unsolicited health advice. Characteristic of the Dr. Fish strain—almost no destructiveness, just unexpected messages taking up space and slowing things down.

An older man who was definitely not an aspiring actor appeared in the window next to the younger guy. "If it's not asking so terribly much of you, Harmon, could you not screech our troubles to the entire world?"

The young guy gestured at Sam. "She says she got the caffeine message."

"It was just one of those health warnings from the Surgeons

General," she said, shrugging. "I thought it was supposed to be there."

The older man frowned at her as if she were somehow responsible. "Great. We're never going to get rid of that thing. Every time I think it's cleaned out, it pops up somewhere else."

"Just because of the way it reproduces," Sam told him. "Cleaning it out won't take care of any data carrying the infection dormantly. You've got herpes, not cholera."

His expression took on a revolted tinge. "Excuse me?"

Sam glanced at the younger guy, who was grinning behind his hand. "Cholera is a disease you treat by treating the symptoms. Herpes lesions can be treated so they go away, but the infection itself remains in the nerves, waiting to activate again."

"Well, thank you so much, Miz Med School, that was just what I've been waiting all day to hear."

"It's contagious," Sam couldn't help adding. "It can be passed on without being active."

There was a short honk from the rental behind her. "Think it's taking long enough?" called the driver, leaning her head out the window.

"It's coming, lady," the older man called back, and leaned out the window a little more. "You sound like you know a lot about this."

Sam shrugged again. If he was so off-line he didn't know about Dr. Fish, she wasn't going to enlighten him. "Anyone with computer equipment ought to know a lot about it."

"I just manage this place. And hire and fire the help." He gave the younger guy a sidelong glance. "You want a free meal?"

Sam drew back, leaning her elbows on the roof of the rental and folding her hands. "Why?"

"For services rendered. If you know so much, you must know how to take care of it. It'll save me another service call."

"You can do it yourself," she said.

"Me? I don't know dick about computers."

"You know where the off switch is?"

He nodded. "So?"

"So flip it. That'll kill it bang. No matter what your service has been telling you, that's the only way to kill a virus. Cut off the power."

The man rolled his eyes. "Forget about it. The menu's out of a closed-area network so they can monitor our volume; we got nothing here but dumb terminals. I cut us off, they'll be down here with an auditor and a warrant to bust me on suspicion of embezzlement."

Standing behind the man, the young guy was making a familiar up-and-down motion with a fist. Sam bit her lips together to keep from laughing.

"Hey, you don't want a free meal, honey, it's fine by me, but you sure look like you could use one. More than one."

"You only offered one," Sam said evenly, "and for what it would cost you to have someone do the work legally, I should get a free meal here every day for a year."

"Offer's closed." He pulled his head back inside the window and turned to the young guy, who was suddenly scratching the side of his head vigorously. "The virus can stay in there, people can live with a warning about coffee, I don't care. We gotta sell more herbal tea anyway." He marched off.

The young guy grinned at Sam, who shook her head. "Probably wouldn't have worked, at that. The virus is most likely dug in at the node, so as soon as you turned on again, it would be right back here."

"Nobody cares as long as it doesn't actually destroy anything," he said, shrugging a bony shoulder. "It's like graffiti to them, the cheap-asses."

The rental behind Sam honked again. "I said, is it taking long enough?" the driver called, louder.

"Not quite, but we're working on it!" Sam called back. The guy at the window handed her a small bag and a tall covered thermo-cup. She thanked him and pulled up far enough to allow the woman to reach the window before she tore the bag open and attacked her food. The ball of rice sitting on top of the seaweed cone tipped into her lap and shattered on impact, leaving her with a mostly empty seaweed wrapper. "Fuck it," she muttered, and drove back down Artesia toward the Mimosa, scooping rice out of her lap with one hand.

"Where's Gator?" she asked the kid in the tent. He must have been all of fifteen, with a funny-chubby cherub's face and thick, fuzzy dark hair that was tangling itself into dreadlocks.

"At services," he said, hitching up his pants. Hospital surplus; they made him look like an underaged, homeless surgeon.

"Services?"

"Yah. She said to tell you she's off praying for God to forgive you."

Sam blinked. "I'm in hell," she said wonderingly. "The world ended when I wasn't looking, and now I'm in hell." She rubbed her forehead with one hand, trying to think. At least the kid was speaking English. "Gator really told you to tell me that?"

Now the kid looked embarrassed. "Well, actually, that's what she told me I should say to anyone who came by for a tattoo."

Sam laughed and kept laughing as she made her way over to Gator's old barber chair and plumped down in it, alarming the kid.

"Hey, you better not. She said she'd kill me if anyone fucked around in here."

"I'm not fucking, I'm laughing," Sam said wearily. "Can't you tell the difference?" She swiveled around. The printer was in its usual spot in the corner, but Gator had taken the laptop with her. To services. At the St. Dismas Infirmary for the Incurably Informed, of course, wherever that was now.

Abruptly she remembered the ex-pump in her pocket.

"*Hey,*" said the kid, following her over to the corner. "I *know* she wouldn't want you screwing around with that."

"I'm not screwing, I'm hooking," Sam said, unrolling the wires that had been discreetly tucked behind a table leg. "Hooking up, that is." She found the communications jack and plugged it into the ex-pump, then connected it to both the sunglasses and the chip-player. "If Gator comes back, I won't let her kill you more than you deserve."

She settled down on the sand and put on the sunglasses. The screen in the left lens lit up, blurring for a moment before it settled on her focal length. There was a tap on her knee, and she looked over the top of the glasses at the kid.

"Hey, you know you got lice?" he said, pointing at her pants.

"That's not lice, it's rice," she told him. "Now don't bother me, I'm calling Dial-a-Prayer."

"You older women sure are religious," he muttered.

In a few moments she was inside the public net system, flashing through the menus until she reached the listing for the St. Dismas Infirmary for the Incurably Informed. She ignored the public posts and punched for the conference area.

>*You have been misinformed*, said the screen. *No conference area exists on this board. If you wish to pray, please make an offering. If not, please exit.*<

She had to peer under the glasses to watch her fingers work the tiny keyboard on the face of the pump.

>*Are services in progress?*< she asked.

>*Prayer services require an offering.*<

She summoned the basic schematic for the adapted insulin pump system and uploaded it. There was a short pause before the screen said, >*The doctor will see you now.*<

Sam frowned. The doctor? Christ, was St. Diz siccing a virus on anyone they didn't trust? She started to tap the little keyboard again when a new message appeared on the screen.

>*Wonderful to hear from you, Sam! Go to Fez and learn all.*< Abruptly she was disconnected, not just back in the main menu area but off-line.

She took off the sunglasses and rubbed her eyes. Fez. It figured. She probably should have headed straight for his place to begin with. He knew everything, or almost everything. Maybe he knew what had happened to Keely. Or how Diversifications' acquisition of a video-production company corresponded to the schematic drawing of a neuron from a human brain that Keely had zapped to her encrypted in music he couldn't stand. Maybe Fez would know. Somebody had to.

4

The house looked quiet enough, but then the whole street was quiet, and Gabe knew that was all wrong.

On his left Marly nudged him. "It's a lot weirder inside than it is outside," she said in a low voice. "Costa says a guy starved to death in there looking for a way out."

Gabe shook his head. "You believe everything Costa tells you?"

"I'd believe this. Since he's been in, and we haven't." She looked past him to Caritha standing on his right. Caritha held up the handcam projector, her half smile confident. Gabe felt a little more dubious. The projector was the best they could do on short notice, but it was awfully small. Like Caritha herself. The late-afternoon sun seemed to strike sparks in the black hair cropped close to her skull. By contrast, Marly's thick, honey-colored mane hung loose and wild.

As if reading his mind, she suddenly gathered it between her hands and wound it into a knot at the back of her head. Gabe stared, fascinated. He had no idea what was keeping it up there. The force of Marly's will, perhaps. He wouldn't have been surprised. She smiled down at him and threw a muscular arm around his shoulders. "Don't tell me you *want* to live forever."

Gabe winced. Marly was three inches taller than he was and possibly heavier, every pound invested in muscle. "Don't crack my collarbone, I might need it later."

"You want it all, dontcha, hotwire?" Marly gave him an extra squeeze and released him.

"All I really want now is to get in, get your friend, and get out," Gabe said.

"I want that viral program," Caritha said seriously. "I don't like clinics that go screwing up people's brains."

"I don't like clinics, period," said Marly. "Come on. Let's go do a little damage."

* * *

Nobody came to the front door in response to the bell. Caritha tried the doorknob, and Gabe heard a faint sizzling sound.

"Son of a *bitch*," she said, looking at her palm. "It buzzed me."

"I call that blatant hostility," said Marly. She produced a small card from her breast pocket. "I'm glad I thought to get the key from Costa."

Gabe looked the door frame over. "Yah, but where do you put it? I don't see a slot."

"You gotta *look*." Marly reached up to the top of the frame and pushed the card in. It disappeared, and a moment later the door swung open. Caritha went first, holding the projector up and ready. Marly followed, pulling Gabe after her. He glanced behind; just before the door swung shut again, he saw a small figure standing in the middle of the street, a child holding up a hand in a strange gesture of farewell. The sight gave him a brief flash of superstitious dread. He shook it away. It could have just been the clinic playing games with holo, trying to spook them.

They were standing in a murky entrance hall that had been painstakingly antiqued. The highly polished woodwork looked both slippery and cold. Marly tugged his arm, and they followed Caritha down the hall.

Caritha stopped at the first doorway and waved them back. Marly flattened against the wall, throwing one arm across his chest. Somewhere far above he heard muffled footsteps. They stumped the length of the ceiling and then stopped. Gabe waited for the sound of a door opening and closing, but there was nothing. The silence seemed to press on his ears.

"I know you're there," said a woman's voice suddenly. Gabe jumped. Marly patted his rib cage, but he could feel how tense she was.

"You might as well come in and introduce yourselves like citizens," the woman went on. "And if you're burglars, you'll find out you've got a lot more of value to us than we have to steal. Come on, now."

Caritha swung around and stood in the doorway.

"That's right. Now your two friends. Two, I *think*. One of them is awfully big."

Marly joined Caritha in the doorway, and Gabe moved to her side. In the old-fashioned parlor an older woman in a straight black floor-length dress was standing near a round table arrayed with bottles, open pill cases, and several shiny, sterile-looking metal boxes.

Caritha swung the projector up. Half the woman disappeared. "Thought so," she said, and widened the beam to include the table. The bottles vanished. "Cheap holo show. They're buried in the heart of the house, they'd never get so close to an outside wall."

"Wait," Gabe said, looking at the table. The holo of the woman had frozen with a hand to her high collar. A moment later the transmission broke up completely, and the image frayed into nothing. "Not all that stuff on the table is a magic-lantern show." He took a cautious step forward before Marly could yank him back.

"Floor's mined," Caritha said offhandedly.

He kept his eyes on the one metal box that hadn't vanished from the tabletop. "You wanted that program. I'll bet it's locked up in that set of implants."

"*Think*, hotwire," Marly said urgently. "Why would they leave a set of implants out like that?"

"Maybe *they* didn't. Maybe it's a sign from your friend."

A moment later he felt Marly behind him. She hooked one hand in the waistband of his pants. His underwear started to ride up.

"Dammit, Marl," he whispered. "Ease off."

"You'll thank me for this," she whispered back.

He reached the table and put one hand on it carefully, reaching for the metal box with the other. His fingers closed on it, and he dropped through the floor, pulling Marly down after him.

He was sliding down some kind of long chute with a lot of twists and turns in it; his shoulders banged roughly against the sides, and he could feel Marly coming down just above him.

"Push out!" she yelled. "Wedge yourself in!"

It took him a few moments, but he managed to apply his elbows and knees to the sides of the chute, bringing himself to a stop.

"Gabe?" Marly called from somewhere above him.

"Did it," he said a little breathlessly.

"You think you can inch your way back up again?"

He groaned. "Nah, I'll just fly up. Be just as easy."

He heard a slithering sound, and then Marly's hands touched

his shoulders. "How about if you hold onto me and do it?" she said with an effort.

"You can't pull us both up."

"Well, no, but I thought it'd be easier if you were holding onto me."

"Easier for who?"

"Don't waste breath arguing, it's the one thing they're not expecting."

He grunted, pushing himself up against the sides of the chute. "Because it can't be done."

"Dammit, hotwire—" she groaned, and rose a few inches. "Why'd you even come?"

"What was I s'posed to do? Give you the cam and wish you luck?" His elbow slipped. He struggled to regain his purchase on the chute, but the effort was too much, and he was sliding down again with a shout.

"Dammit!" yelled Marly. He heard her coming down after him.

He landed on a pile of musty mattresses and scooted out of the way just before Marly hit.

"See what happens when you don't introduce yourselves properly?"

The woman in the black dress was standing several feet away in front of a white cement-block wall. Gabe got up slowly, brushing himself off, and offered a hand to Marly. She ignored it, keeping her eyes on the woman. "Isn't a trapdoor kind of crude?" she said.

"But effective. Appropriate technology." The woman smiled. "You got what you deserved."

"Hotwire, I don't think this one's any more real than her twin sister," Marly said, and took a step forward.

The woman suddenly compressed to a sharp red point of light.

"*Down!*" Marly yelled.

They flattened just as the point became a red spear that shot out at the spot where Marly had been standing a moment before. It hit the chute with a loud sizzle, and the smell of hot metal filled the air. Marly raised her head slightly to look at him over the mattresses. "They know a few neat tricks with light."

Dumbfounded, Gabe blinked at the spot where the woman's image had been, then at the chute. "I thought the government said the holo-to-laser thing was impossible."

"Impossible for the government," Marly said, looking around warily. "These people hacked the team that worked on it, removed the real specs, and substituted their own." She got up slowly. "Shit, what are we in, a boxcar?"

The room was shaped like a boxcar and not much bigger, all walls and no entrance or exit that Gabe could see except for the end of the chute protruding from the wall. Marly ripped into one of the mattresses, pulling a chunk of ratty yellow foam rubber out of it. She tossed it at the cement-block wall; instead of bouncing off, it vanished.

"That answers *that* question," she said, and got up.

"Wait! What are you doing?" Gabe said as she headed for the wall.

"Ah, it's not like we're not already in sight, hotwire," she said. "If they can see us, I want to see them." She walked through the wall. Gabe hurried after her.

Beyond the white wall was a long room lined with beds, all of them occupied. Gabe braced himself, but no one rushed them. No one in the beds moved or even spoke.

"The ward," Marly said darkly.

"Why aren't there any attendants?" Gabe whispered.

"Don't need them, they're built in." Marly went to the nearest bed and yanked up the man lying there by his shirt-front. He hung bonelessly in her grasp, his eyes wide open but seeing nothing. A thick black cable was driven into the top of his shaven head, held in place by small clamps.

"Jesus," Gabe said.

"The viral program's just a sideline," Marly said grimly, laying the man down again. "You ever wonder where Solomon Labs gets all that fresh, natural-no-synthetics neurotransmitter?"

He stared, unable to speak.

"And if you think this is a deep, dark secret, you're wrong about that, too," Marly added. "They *all* know. Even that outfit you work for, the Dive. You crank out the commercials, and high-level management gets their regular doses of n/t to keep them running at peak brain power. If you could get promoted high enough, you'd get some, too." She looked around at the ward. "If Jimmy's in one of these beds, the best thing we can do is yank his cable and say kaddish before we beat it out of here."

Far down at the other end of the room, the silhouette of a

man appeared. "Hey! You're not supposed to be in here!" The man started to run for it when another red beam speared the length of the ward and impaled him. He fell backwards.

A moment later Caritha materialized at Gabe's elbow, hefting the cam. "Did I mention I made some other modifications to your hardware? Hope you don't mind too much."

"Why did you come down the chute?" he asked incredulously.

"Last thing they'd expect," she said, winking at him. "Find Jimmy? I hope not."

"Haven't looked," Marly said. "Come on." They hurried through the ward, Caritha scanning the beds with the cam. Gabe marveled. It had originally been a simple record/playback holo projector until she'd gone to work on it; now it was the Swiss Army knife of handcams. She had the same easy genius for hardware that Sam did.

He felt himself flushing guiltily at the thought of his daughter, but there was no time to dwell on that; they had reached the end of the ward. He spotted three vacant beds, and then Marly was shoving him after Caritha into what looked like an elevator. Doors snapped shut behind them. Marly was still searching for a control panel when the floor tilted and spilled them out through the back wall.

"Uh-oh," said Caritha in a low voice.

They were looking not into another room but down a long, dark alley strewn with garbage and the shattered remnants of unfathomable machine parts.

"This must be where all the bad machines go to be punished," Marly said. She pulled into a crouch, poised to strike out.

"Can you bust it up, show us where we really are?" Gabe asked Caritha.

"It's worse than you think," Caritha said. She thumbed a switch on the cam, and a bright circle of light appeared on a filthy wall. A moment later the words came up in poison green, precise and annoying:

TIME: 10:30 A.M.
MEETING: 11:15 A.M., NEW MONTHLY
ASSIGNMENTS
!!REMINDER!! LUNCH TOMORROW: 12:30 P.M.
W/MANNY RIVERA, PROBABLY RE QUOTA

ELAPSED TIME: 24 MINUTES, CREDITED TO
GILDING BODYSHIELDS
DISCONNECT: Y/N?

Gabe groaned.

"Rotten break, hotwire," Marly said, and then grinned at him. "Or is it?"

"It is," he said grimly. "I'd rather face the minions of technological evil than another monthly assignment meeting."

Caritha punched his arm. "Just answer *y* or *n* so we can get on with this or not."

"I'll catch up with you later," he promised, pushing himself to his feet.

"*Y* or *n*," insisted Caritha.

"Yes, dammit," he said wearily. "I mean, *y*. But leave it running. Leave it *running!*"

The alley faded to utter black.

The disconnect command automatically opened the clasps on his head-mounted monitor. Gabe eased it off, unplugging the feeds from his hotsuit. The monitor was brand new, lighter than the model he was used to, but it still made him feel as if he had a garbage can over his head.

He stood in the simulation pit, reorienting himself slowly. By afternoon he was going to be aching all over, the way he'd been throwing himself around the room. Like an overgrown, hyperactive eight-year-old playing junior G-man or something. And it was a big room, the biggest Diversifications had; after fifteen years he'd worked his way up to the basketball-court size with the twenty-foot ceilings and full range of equipment—treadmill, stair-climber, scaffolding assembly, modular blocks to stand in for furniture, padded mats.

He had spent a good hour bringing the platform-and-slide arrangement up in the freight elevator and then assembling it for the trapdoor-chute sequence. Looking at it divested of the simulation, he felt embarrassed, even though there was no one to feel embarrassed in front of.

What's the matter, hotwire—too much like kid stuff for you? He could hear Marly's deep, slightly hoarse laughter in his mind.

He looked down at the monitor lying open in his hands like a giant prayerbook, twice the size of his head. Most of the inside front was taken up by the screen, which enclosed the eye area like a diver's mask, surrounded by a multitude of tiny lasers. The beam coverage was particularly effective, better than the previous model's. He could look in any direction, and the laser beams bouncing off his corneas responded instantly, with a screen view-shift so smooth that it was exactly like looking around at a real environment. Which made it more possible than ever to lose himself in the simulation, and he'd been doing a pretty fair job of that before the alarm had gone off.

He took the monitor to the desk and set it down. The desktop screen told him the simulation was running along nicely without him. Not that Marly and Caritha would know the difference if he stopped everything. Hell, they weren't even being imaged anymore; they were just twinklings in the system now.

Now and ever, he thought, feeling suddenly weary beyond what his exertions could account for. Twinklings; fantasies; imaginary playmates.

Well, not totally imaginary. The templates had been assembled from two real, living people who had since vanished into the mass of faces that had failed to raise an appreciable blip in the test-audience ratings. He couldn't fathom that, himself. The Marly and Caritha templates had hit him between the eyes when he'd called them up from Central Filing. Perhaps the original programmer had just had a particularly good day, or maybe he'd been having a particularly bad one. Or maybe he'd just been losing his mind piece by piece all along, and when he had summoned up the Marly and Caritha simulations in tandem, it had been enough to blow out what fragments of sanity he'd still had.

Diversifications had voided their contracts before he got around to requisitioning official usage. His unofficial usage, however, was already extensive; buried in the back of a drawer in his console were chip-copies of the original templates. Every so often, when the running copies got too cluttered up with decision branches, he refocused the programs with the originals—originals once removed, he reminded himself. Or twice removed, if you wanted to count the actual people as the true originals. Normally he didn't; he'd never met the two women in person and didn't know anything about them, except if they'd known that for the last two years someone at Diversifications had been enjoying the benefit of their simulated selves without contract or recompense, they'd be into a sizable financial settlement, and he'd be out of a job.

Jesus, two years? That long? He felt silly. Like some teenager nursing a crush by playing wannabee-format simulations over and over. In the beginning he'd pretended activating their simulations and merging them with some scenario was actually an elaborate warm-up exercise, something to prime the old idea pump, jump start the creative generator. After fifteen years of cranking out commercial spots for body armor and pharmaceuticals, clinic-spas and body-carvers, dataline modules and spray-for-chrissakes-cleanser, you needed the extra stimulation, or you ran completely dry.

Even after he'd gone through half of the stock scenarios and started raiding the wannabee files, he'd kept telling himself it was all for the sake of the old idea pump. His output had been dropping gradually but steadily, and he was spending longer periods of time on the commercials he did complete, or so the automatic log in his system said. He kept spreading the time he spent evenly among his assignments, and the times grew longer and longer, and Manny started making noises about lowered productivity, and still he'd been unable to go a day without spending at least an hour in simulation with Marly and Caritha. An hour? More like four hours; it was so easy to lose track of the time.

He unzipped the hotsuit, peeling it away from himself. Underneath, his skin bore the impression of a baroque pattern of snaky lines punctuated by the sharp geometric variations of the numerous sensors. The coverage was twice as thorough as all but the most expensive 'suits sold to the public. Except for—ahem—genitalia. Only the employees who worked on refining Hollywood feature releases got the complete hotsuits.

Gabe rubbed at the marks, imagining a day when they wouldn't fade after an hour or so—he'd have a permanent tattoo, and when he died (or was fired), Diversifications, Inc., would have him skinned and use his hide as a pattern for new hotsuits.

Great people leave their marks. Everyone else is left with *marks.* He stripped the top part of the suit off and examined himself. There were cases of hysterics who hallucinated being grabbed and managed to produce fingermarks on their flesh like stigmata. Without hotsuits, too.

There was a sudden sensation in his still-gloved left hand, as if someone had taken it gently. Residual flashes of fading energy. It happened sometimes. He took off the rest of the suit in a hurry and changed into his street clothes.

The timer in the bottom right-hand corner of the console flatscreen caught his eye. Somewhere in the computer—in an alternate universe—Marly and Caritha were fighting off a squad of shadowy thugs in a dark alley with a program phantom standing in for himself. He knew how it would come out; the simulation he had merged them with was an old Hollywood B-release—*House of the Headhunters*' a B-title if there ever was one—that had been converted to wannabee format. As a regular feature release, it had done barely modest business, but in wannabee format it had been an over-the-top hit. Apparently it had had more appeal as something to be *in* than to watch. When even that had faded, it had gone into the files as something to be cannibalized for commercial spots.

Gabe had told himself he was accessing it for the sake of the body-armor spot. It would certainly appear more plausible on the quarterly time and productivity audit, which, he didn't need to remind himself, was coming up as quickly as the deadline on the body-armor spot that he hadn't even started on yet. Well, he would replay the whole thing this afternoon and mark the sequences with the best possibilities, assuming Marly and Caritha hadn't wrought more changes in it than was technically legal. They were smart programs, capable of learning and manipulating certain portions of other programs they were merged with. *House of the Headhunters* had a high manipulation quotient; you could die at the end if you wanted to, or even blind-select so you wouldn't know whether you would survive or not.

He toyed with the idea of working that into a finished commercial. *Gilding Bodyshields Can Save Your Life . . . Or Can They?* The Gilding people would shit pears.

Or maybe he should just work up a simulation of his upcoming lunch with Manny Rivera and turn Marly and Caritha loose on that. Then, instead of having to go through it himself, he could just view it later. He knew exactly what Manny would say: *We're facing another quarterly audit of our productivity, Gabe, and you know that for the Upstairs Team, it's all a matter of numbers. How much you're producing and how long it takes. That's all the Upstairs Team understands.* The Upstairs Team was Diversifications-speak for upper management; Gabe imagined it was supposed to make them sound less batch-processed, more like co-workers or something. Sure.

"Ten-forty," said the console clock politely. He used the ladder instead of the small one-person lift to get up to the catwalk, hoping the exertion would keep his muscles from knotting. Just as he reached the top, something in his pocket dug into his thigh. The key to the freight elevator; he'd forgotten to return it to Security. The hell with it. If they wanted it, let them come and get it.

There was a short delay after he pressed his fingers to the printlock; keeping the program active stole a little from the other pit functions.

"Love my work," he muttered.

Likewise, hotwire, said Caritha's voice in his mind.

The lock released, and he went down the hall to the elevators.

5

"You should have come to me first, Sam-I-Am," Fez said congenially.

Sam shrugged. "I guess I took a stupid pill this morning."

In the chair across from Sam, Rosa took a second doughnut from the box on the table between them and then offered the box to the young blond kid sitting on the couch. Fez's grand-nephew Adrian, just in that morning from San Diego, a real bolt from the ether. Fez had never mentioned having any family. The kid was fourteen and looked twelve, and there was something funny about his almond-shaped eyes. They seemed slightly out of focus, as if he'd taken a hard knock on the head moments before. A stunned fourteen-year-old. Sam imagined she must have looked the same way when she'd first been emancipated. The freedom was all you thought about, and when you finally got it, you were scared shitless. Welcome to the world, kid.

"Don't suppose you ate much else," Fez said with some amusement.

"Oh, I managed a little something," Sam told him, finding a stray rice grain on her pants. She rolled it between two fingers and then, for lack of anything else to do, put it in her pocket.

"The usual seaweed and grass clippings?" asked Fez.

"Seaweed and sushi rice."

Fez glanced upward. "Let me have a look in the larder. Maybe I can serve you something real. Besides doughnuts." He went to the kitchenette, a little alcove with a cooktop, zap-box, and midget-fridge built into the cabinets. Sam knew it well. She'd learned to cook there.

"You know how he gets about seaweed," Rosa said, wiping powdered sugar from the corners of her mouth.

"Yah. Fez's four food groups—meat, dairy, vegetables, and doughnuts." Sam sighed and let herself slump farther into the

45

easy chair. "God, I'm tired. Those stupid pills really take it out of you."

"I wouldn't know," Rosa said loftily, and then winked. Sam laughed a little. Rosa probably *didn't* know. She was a canny little woman who had already achieved elder-statesperson status in the electronic underground by the time Sam had bumped into her on the nets three years before.

She'd met Fez right around the same time, along with the rest of them—Keely, Gator, poor lost Beauregard, Kazin, many others, some of them long since vanished, canned or on the move to keep from getting canned. Like Keely, perhaps.

"You know, I thought you'd come for your laptop first thing," Rosa said. "I couldn't believe you'd gone off without it to begin with. Like someone taking a trip around the world stark naked with no luggage."

Adrian giggled and then covered his mouth, embarrassed. Rosa turned her wry, lopsided smile on him. "It's okay, kid. Underneath their clothes everybody's going around naked." The boy giggled again and looked away from her.

"Don't torment Adrian," Fez called from the kitchen. The zap-box hummed and clicked off. "Try to remember that you two were once nervous junior citizens without a shred of savvy."

"If you can prove I was ever that young, I'll pay you a hundred thousand dollars," Rosa said.

"Listen to the old lady of twenty-four," Fez said, coming out of the kitchen with a large mug and a spoon. "Once you'd have paid me a hundred thousand dollars to prove you were ever going to get this old." He presented the mug and spoon to Sam with a slight bow. "Navy-bean soup, in lieu of green eggs and ham."

"Yuck to both." Sam frowned at the lumpy tan mess in the mug. "I told you, I ate."

Fez stabbed the spoon into the soup and curled her hand around the mug. "I find it hard to, um, *swallow* seaweed and rice as a meal. Iodine's fine in its place, but you need something sticking to your ribs, which are still easily countable."

"You peeked," she said, which brought a small flush to his cheeks and sent him bustling over to the couch to sit next to his grandnephew.

Fez was about sixty, as near as she could tell, with a cloud of white hair that reminded her of cotton candy, and bright black eyes, a nose that had been broken once or twice, and a mouth that never quite stopped smiling. The particulars might have suggested Santa Claus, but Fez was neither fat nor bearded. Even if he had been (Sam couldn't imagine it), the angles of his face had a little too much sharpness to them, and in spite of the smile, his face had the wariness of a man perpetually on guard.

She remembered how hard it had been to reconcile this semigrandfatherly presence with the mental image she'd formed from on-line contact, picturing him as a grand old man of perhaps twenty-nine or thirty, with all the looks, charm, and sex appeal that had always been attributed to renegades.

In retrospect she knew she should have figured it out. Fez's knowledge of the past forty years, casually displayed in the course of their many odd-hours on-line conversations, had been too idiosyncratic in detail to be the product of anything but firsthand experience.

Sitting in the old easy chair, trying to choke down enough of the bland/salty soup to appease him, reminded her of the first time she'd come to this one-roomer in East Hollywood. Rosa had brought her, and he'd tried to feed her that day, too, but she'd been too boggled. Rosa herself had been a revelation, Cherokee Rosa as she was known on-line; she really was a Cherokee, and her name really was Rosa, and she had a mass of curly black hair, a knowing look, and a bone-crusher handshake. And, apparently, a mandate to bring her out of the tiny Santa Monica closet she'd been holed up in, making subsistence with gypsy scut work on her homegrown laptop.

We've been watching you, doll. You hack good.

Sam had had mixed feelings about that. *Big Brother, is that it?*

Not Big Brother. More like the relative nobody wants to talk about.

That's me, Sam had said.

Doll, that's all of us.

Sure was. And so Rosa had brought her to be surprised by Fez, and after that she'd kept coming back on her own as often as possible. She found out later that she was one of a very few Fez allowed to visit so frequently or, for that matter, ever (Rosa was another). She might have ended up all but moving in with him if he hadn't always thrown her out eventually. He wasn't looking to host the eastern branch of the Mimosa, he told her firmly, and he was nobody's father figure, he told her even more firmly, both of them well aware that father figure was not how she felt about him.

She settled for the benefit of his extensive knowledge of computer communications, and the privilege of being allowed to use the elaborate computer system sitting on the desk against the far wall. It looked deceptively jerry-rigged with all the mismatched upgrades and add-ons. The configuration had changed again since she'd last visited; there was a second flat easel-type screen now, and a couple of very large housings that had to have quadrupled available memory. She also noticed that the head-mounted monitor sitting off to one side was hooked up to the system, as if it had seen some use recently, which surprised her. Fez had never been especially enamored of Artificial Reality, at least as a place to visit.

The system was on, she realized, even though neither screen was lit. That was unlike Fez, as well, to run anything without screening its progress.

"So, you've been out of town and out of touch," Fez said to her.

"Camping in the *Ozarks*," Rosa said. "I'm still trying to imagine it. That's in Missouri," she added to Fez.

"Yes, I've heard," he said serenely. "Some rather interesting things going on in Missouri, in the realm of nanotechnology —surprise, surprise"—he nodded at Rosa—"but I suppose you were too busy roughing it to check it out. Somehow I always had the idea that you thought camping was an overnight in a Mimosa squat, not hunting and fishing."

"No hunting. And I only tried fishing once. I have problems killing anything." Sam shrugged. "I was hacking around, and suddenly a trip out of town seemed like a good idea."

Rosa laughed. "And you left the hot hardware with me. You're just full of good ideas, aren't you?"

"Oh, the hardware was never hot. Just the software, and I took that with me."

"And what did you do, use it for earrings?"

Sam grinned. "No, but what a great encryption idea."

Rosa looked at her from under her brows. "It's not a real original idea. And I think the word you're looking for is *camouflage*. You've been in a computer too long."

"Whatever." Sam looked at Fez. "Did *you* hear from Keely?"

The lines around Fez's eyes deepened. "Keely is officially

MIA. There's nothing on-line about him, and nobody knows where he is, not even Jones."

"And where's Jones?"

"I've got him," Rosa said. "*Strictly* temporary arrangement. He had the supreme tack-ola to suicide in Gator's tent, and she called me to pick up the body."

Adrian was staring at her openmouthed. "You're keeping a dead guy in your apartment?"

"*Temporarily*. I mean, he's temporarily dead. He's probably not dead anymore, just comatose, but he'll go again in another couple of days."

The kid glanced at Fez a little dubiously. "Jeez, everything's different here. Where I come from, we usually die once, permanently."

"Not if you've got fancy implants," Rosa said sourly. "Our friend Jones—or rather, our friend Keely's friend Jones—was suffering from real bad chronic depression, suicidal, all that. Electroshock didn't work, so he went to this feel-good mill, and they gave him these brain implants that let him kill himself. He flatlines for maybe a minute or two, and then they kick up his adrenal system, and he comes back."

"Oh, she's not making it up," Fez assured his nephew. "It's actually an accepted alternative treatment for certain depressives who don't respond to any other kinds of implants."

"Which probably doesn't describe Jones," Rosa went on, "since he didn't try any others before he let the feel-gooders drill him. So now he's addicted to death, and he'll stay that way until his adrenal system tells him to go to hell. Then he'll go."

"Well, to purgatory, perhaps," Fez said good-naturedly.

Adrian sat back on the couch, hugging himself. "And people think *I'm* weird."

"I'd turn in the goddamn clinic that did him," Rosa said, "but they got canned for feel-gooding this week."

"That leaves Jones really adrift, then," Sam said. "No clinic and no Keely. What's he going to do?"

"Die. Periodically." Rosa turned to Fez. "So, should I take a hike while you look at the zap Sam got from Keely, or what?"

"What," Fez said. "You can keep a secret, can't you?"

Rosa drew a cross over her heart.

"Wait a second," Sam said, and looked significantly at Adrian.

He giggled again. "Don't worry, I'm perfectly safe. I guess Fez hasn't had a chance to tell you, but I can't read."

"Can't read *English*," Fez said pointedly. "Or any other language with an alphabet."

"Makes me safe for anything you wanna screen without a voice-over," Adrian added.

"He has a brain lesion," Fez explained, sounding curt. "He's alexic. For various reasons implants have been unable to mitigate the problem, but we've managed to sneak around it. He learned Mandarin."

Rosa's eyebrows went up. "Really? You can read Mandarin?"

The kid shrugged. "It's not really reading. Not for me. As soon as the world goes to a dual ideogram and alphabet format, I'm really gonna have it made. Or I could just move to China."

"Why not just use Spoken Text?" Rosa asked.

"Same reason you don't," said Fez. "Time. Spoken Text takes at least twice as long as silent reading. If you could stand all that natter-natter-natter. We've been routing the dataline through a homegrown translation program for him. Though I've noticed translation to ideograms does tend to put a slightly different spin on things."

Sam set her untouched mug of soup aside on the floor. "I wonder what it would do with Keely's zap. It's pretty odd stuff. Not that there's a whole lot to read." She looked at Adrian again. "Look, I don't want any innocent bystanders getting hit if they don't have to."

"Adrian's all right," Fez said firmly. "Now, what do you have?"

"I'm pretty sure Keely pulled this out of Diversifications. He wouldn't tell me, but I can't think who else would stampede him. The odd thing was that he encrypted it in some speed-thrash by a group signed with EyeTraxx for videos, and I found out completely by accident that Diversifications just acquired them. Now, my father's worked at the Dive since like the early Jurassic, and they've never, but *never* shown any interest in music videos. Besides hardware, all they do is commercials and Hollywood releases, insty-vacations and tons of that social-expression shit."

"Don't knock the electronic greeting card," Rosa said. "If it weren't for that, some of us wouldn't speak to our mothers even on Mother's Day. —Shit, sorry," she added, looking contritely at Sam. "I caught the news about EyeTraxx kinda by-the-way myself, but I didn't think a thing of it. I mean, lots of companies jump the bandwagons late. Maybe if you hunted around on BizNet, you'd find their profits were down somewhere. If you could actually read anything on BizNet."

"I wouldn't have thought anything of it, either," Sam said, "except there was *nothing* about it in the news. I mean, not even a mention. Now, the Ozarks are picturesque as hell and terribly quaint, but they have datalines there, too, and I didn't see a thing about it anywhere. And EyeTraxx is—*was*—a Hall Galen company, and Hall Galen calls a media conference if he burps."

"Perhaps it was a very small burp by his standards." Fez got up and went to the desk, flipping on one of the screens. "How did you look up the news of the acquisition, dear?"

She told him. "Ah yes, they must have buried that little item in the hard-core biz news. You'd have had to have your defaults set a particular way to get it." Fez beckoned to her and Rosa, and they joined him at the desk. The general dataline menu came up on the screen, and he touched the BizNet listing with his little finger. Immediately the screen filled with BizNet's menu, divided into six dense sections.

Sam could feel her eyes crossing. "Jesus, what a mess."

"Your hard-core biz type can scan this as easily as you can scan a program in your favorite assembly language," Fez said, giving her an amused glance. "BizNet went to great lengths to customize this for their serious subscribers—eye-tracking tests on the layouts, allathat. BizNet is the epitome of narrowcasting. As opposed to old-style broadcasting. Focused information, no waste." He touched an item in the upper left area of the screen; the six sections gave way to a four-part screen, each quadrant containing a new menu.

"Isn't there any faster way than paging through menu after menu?" Rosa asked.

"Like I said, set your retrieval defaults correctly in the first place," Fez replied. "And if we knew what those were, we'd already know what we don't know. Ya know?" He winked at Sam and then flipped through several more menus and pages of small print before he froze the screen. "Here we are." He pointed to a small paragraph.

"Shit," Rosa said, squinting at it. "Can we run this through Adrian's Mandarin translator?"

"That'll be next," Fez said matter-of-factly. "Market-segment translations. In time the language of every subgroup of society will get as specialized as the data it uses, and we'll have a new set of suburbs in the global village. Or rather, the same old suburbs with new names."

"There goes the neighborhood," Rosa said, still gazing at the screen with distaste. "Or here comes the neighborhood. Whatever's right."

Fez shrugged. "People keep looking for ways to chunk themselves. Do you think your average thrash-rockers care if the credit on the latest video firestorm reads 'EyeTraxx' or 'Diversifications' or 'Some Asshole in Detroit'? That's why this didn't make it into the general music news. Anyone who cares about the business end is already tapped into BizNet, not G-Clef. The musicians are all on PerfectPitch, the techies are downloading CircuitBreak—"

"—and the rest of the world can go hang," Sam said thoughtfully.

Fez laughed. "By George, she's got it. Well, anyway, what *this* says, more or less, is that Diversifications investigated the possibility of a takeover of Hall Galen Enterprises as a whole, and Galen cut a deal, divesting himself of the EyeTraxx business unit, and they took that in a settlement."

Rosa put a finger on the screen. "Is that this part here— 'growth opportunities altered in reorganization, closing the aperture around the IBU'? What's an IBU?"

"Independent business unit," Fez said absently. "A term for everything and everything in a term. There's a cross-ref here to MedLine, in Research: Human/Brain/Neurophysiology."

"I can read *that* just fine," Rosa said. "But why in hell would an item like this have a cross-ref in Med-for-god's-sake-Line?"

A small box blossomed in the lower central area of the screen, blinking a notice: *24 min. free access time left.*

"Fucking gougers," Sam said, pointing at the box. The number changed to 23 as she watched. "That makes me so mad. Fucking surcharges."

Rosa shrugged as Fez touched the speed box at the top of the screen and selected the MedLine cross-reference out of the small menu that appeared at the bottom of the screen. "Could be worse. They could have just raised all the rates across the board."

Fez chuckled. "They might yet. 'Truth is cheap, but information costs.' I can't remember who said that."

"Vince What's-His-Name," said Sam. "Died in a terrorist raid or something. I thought you said all information should be free."

"It should. It isn't. Knowledge is power. But power corrupts. Which means the Age of Fast Information is an extremely corrupt age in which to live."

"Aren't they all?" Sam asked him.

He smiled his dreamy little smile at her. "Ah, but I think we're approaching a kind of corruption unlike anything we've ever known before, Sam-I-Am. Sometimes I think we may be on the verge of an original sin."

She didn't get the reference, but she felt a sudden chill run up the back of her neck. "Goose walked over my grave," she said.

"To get to the other side," Rosa murmured. Sam gave her a look.

"Besides being rich," Fez said, "you have to be extra sharp these days to pick up any real information. You have to know what you're looking for, and you have to know how it's filed. Browsers need not apply. Broke ones, anyway. I miss the newspaper."

"Don't you get one?" Sam asked, surprised. "I do. Even while I was out in the Ozarks, I had no trouble at all getting *The Daily You*."

"*Feh*. That's not a newspaper. In my day we called it a clipping service, and it's not even a good one. A bunch of glorified headlines in a watered-down hodgepodge. Ah, at last." Fez froze the screen and began scrolling line by line. "Dr. Lindel Joslin, installed at blah, blah, blah, brain-path research, blah, blah, receptors, receptors, more receptors—" Several more lines marched up the screen. "Here it is. Hm. She's an implant surgeon. Research completed under the auspices of Hall Galen Enterprises and EyeTraxx, any and all subsequent patents now wholly owned by Diversifications, Inc."

"Patents?" Rosa said.

Fez shook his head and read a little farther before straightening up, pushing his hands against the small of his back. "Can't make head or tail of the rest of it. Medspeak."

Rosa laughed. "Crank that translator into overdrive, and let's see what she can do."

Sam was still studying the screen. "It still doesn't explain why some esoteric biz item about a takeover of a rock-video company would have a cross-ref in MedLine."

"Well, obviously because this Dr. Joslin was being funded by EyeTraxx," Rosa said. "Diversifications must have taken over her funding, so they've taken over whatever she was working on. It begs the question of why EyeTraxx was funding her. Tax shelter?" She nudged Fez.

"One possibility." He folded his wiry arms. "Actually, I think I can shed some light on the question of the cross-ref, and Sam, I think you can provide some of the fill-in details."

Sam looked at him, startled. "I can?"

"You only have part of Keely's zap," he said. "I have the other part. You show me what you have, and I'll show you what I have, and between the two of us, maybe we'll have something for real."

She grinned. "You'll show me yours if I show you mine?" She tucked a hand in her right pants pocket where the erstwhile insulin pump was resting against her thigh. "My chips aren't compatible with your system. Mind using mine?"

Fez lifted an eyebrow. "You have a system cleverly concealed about your person?"

She took the pump out of her pocket and showed it to him and Rosa. Fez's surprised expression deepened as he squinted at the palm-sized unit on her outstretched hand. "To my knowledge you're not a diabetic, especially not one whose body keeps rejecting pancreas implants. Very clever." He started to take it from her and spotted the wire snaking under the tail of her shirt. "Oh, God, Sam, not really."

"What?" said Rosa. "What's going on?"

Sam lifted her shirt just high enough to show where the two needles went into the fleshiest part of her abdomen. "You were wrong when you figured I was too busy roughing it to check out the latest in nanotechnology," she told Fez, a little smugly. "The Ozarks turned out to be about the best place I could have gone with my hot hack. I found a lab where I could trade scut work for work space."

"Oh, *God!*" Rosa made a gagging noise. "That's an atrocity! You're *sick!*"

"I'm a potato clock," Sam corrected her.

"You're a potato *head,*" Fez said grimly. "What's wrong with batteries?"

"Not personal enough. No, no, I'm kidding." She laughed at his revolted look. "It's just an alternative power source. You can use batteries, or house current with an adapter, but if the power fails from one or the other, it's crash time. This never crashes. The Dive had this stored in a very out-of-the-way place. I bet my father doesn't even know about it. Probably they meant it for people working in isolated areas under hostile conditions—Antarctica, surface of the moon, places like that."

"Good for espionage, too." Fez winced. "What do you use for a screen?"

She put on the sunglasses. "You'll have to adjust the focal length for your own eye. Projects right onto the retina. How bad's your astigmatism?"

Fez touched the wire. "Hurt much?"

"Stings when I first put it on, but after that I almost forget it's there."

"That's because you're *sick*," Rosa said, refusing to look. "They'd never have put it over, never, never, *never*."

"She's right," said Fez. "Most people will reject anything that requires them to be a pin cushion. The hard-core diabetics and the endocrine cases do it, but ask them if they like it. Someone in Diversifications' research and development lab has a real ghoulish streak." He handed the pump back to Sam. "Give me your software and drive. I've got an adapter."

She fetched the chip-player from her bag and handed it over. He searched through a couple of desk drawers before he came up with a coil of thin cable. Plugging one end into the chip-player, he connected the other end to his system.

A moment later thrash-rock blasted tinnily from a small speaker. Fez looked pained. "You didn't tell me it was still encrypted."

"Of course. You think I was gonna chance getting caught with naked stolen data? You need the potato-head system here to decrypt, unless you want to wait around for one of your own programs to work on it. Might take a few days, though. Keely learned encryption from me."

"Only hours," he said loftily, and then beckoned to her. "Come on. But we'll run it on *my* power, thank you. I've got a first-rate generator in case you're paranoid about the Bigger One hitting just when things are getting good."

"Thanks," Rosa said faintly, still standing with her back to them. "Tell me when it's safe to look."

Fez found the adapter socket on the side of the pump and used another connector to hook it up to his system's power source. When Sam was sure it was running, she slid the needles out of her flesh. "It's safe now, Rosa," she said.

"Now put that away," Fez ordered sternly, "and don't ever let me see you grandstanding like that again."

"Yes, Daddy."

He gave her a look. She punched up the decoding program, and the music cut off immediately. An image appeared on the screen, replacing the dataline. They all stared at it in silence.

"So, what do you think," Sam said finally. "Is that a diagram of some gardener's root system? One little thirteen-year-old dandelion, maybe? Or did things really get weird enough for that to be a synthetic neuron? The only thing that throws me is this here." She pointed at a fairly wide, hollow line extending up from the lumpily triangular blob in the center of the screen. "From what I remember of the brain science I had in biology—"

"You had brain science in biology?" Rosa asked.

"Advanced placement classes, when I thought I was going to college. Anyway, that should be either an axonal fiber to carry outgoing impulses, or a dendrite to receive incoming information. Since this is a cortical neuron, I mean. Still with me, everyone?"

Fez looked at her sidelong. "Go on, Professor Potato Head."

"Okay. Dendrites look like November treetops in New England, and this is too thick proportionally to be an axon." She ran a finger along a line trailing from the base of the blob. "That's a real axon, perfectly in scale. This thing on top reminds me more of a bus than anything—"

"Channel," Rosa said. "Everything's a channel now."

Sam shrugged. "They can put it on the stage and call it Rosebud for all I care. What I really can't figure is why you'd have something like that on a neuron when you already have an axon to do the job. This is wide enough to be a real bus—excuse me, *channel*—and take two lanes of traffic, one going in, one going out." She paused. "I think Keely found out someone at the Dive is making a cortex. Custom-making, I mean. Someone new there. This Dr. What's-Her-Bod, the MedLine cross-ref. That would be the patent, wouldn't it, Fez? And this is going to be their new hardware, and it's going to make every other piece of machinery obsolete. It's kind of weird that Dr. Frankenstein would work on something like this at EyeTraxx. Hall Galen Enterprises is one of those lotta-fingers-lotta-pies things. He could have stuck her in any of his other pies."

"Not if he needed a good tax write-off for EyeTraxx," Rosa said. "Or a good hiding place till they were ready to go public. If the doctor kept volatile records stored on deck, and someone looking for new videos cracked her, they wouldn't know what it was and pass it by. Keep your best whiskey in a bottle marked 'mouthwash.' "

"Yah, but tax write-offs have to be related to the business you put them in," Sam said. "I don't know dick about taxes, but I know that much."

"So he lied. You don't think Hall Galen would lie to the tax man?" Rosa shrugged. "Maybe he called it new video formats or something."

Fez's smile disappeared completely; it was one of the very few times Sam had ever seen that happen. "Rosa, dear, that's exactly what he called it. It's on the part Keely gave me." He turned to Sam, looking troubled. "Keely tried to divide up the data so that if either of us was caught along with him, the other would have enough to raise hell with. When he divided it, he inadvertently saved our asses. But he also destroyed some of the information."

Sam shook her head, confused.

"I found the remains of a sleeping-load flare embedded in what he zapped me. When he spliced the data, he ruined the flare. If he'd just duped it and zapped it whole to both of us, we'd probably be in the can right now. Or somewhere."

"Wherever Keely is," Rosa said soberly. "I'm surprised he didn't spot it."

"It was a very good flare. Good as hacker work. I'd have probably missed it myself if I hadn't found it in the ruins. Anyway, I'll show you what I've got, but I don't know if we're going to be able to make much out of it after all." He took a box from the bottom drawer and selected a chip about half the size of the nail on her littlest finger.

A few moments later the other screen lit up with a 3-D graphic of a human brain seen in three-quarter profile from the left. The legend at the bottom of the screen said, *New-VidFmt*.

"Looks like medporn to me," Rosa said.

"There's an overlay," Fez said, "but it won't make much sense." He pressed a button on the console, and a new graphic superimposed itself on the first. It seemed to be a chart pinpointing several areas of the brain, but the accompanying notations were garbage symbols. "Well, Professor Potato Head? Any ideas?"

"Implants," Sam said promptly. "Stone-home bizarro. I can buy the idea that the Dive is going into music videos faster than the idea that they're gonna open a clinic."

"I thought of implants, too," Fez said, "but from what I know of implantation, there are too many sites here, and they aren't deep enough."

Adrian had been standing behind them looking on silently. Now he leaned forward and touched each pinpointed spot on the brain. "Frontal lobes, temporal lobes, parietal lobes, auditory cortex, visual cortex. My lesion's back here," he added shyly, patting the back of his head.

Fez hit another button on the console, and the image rotated to show the left profile briefly before it was replaced by a diagram of the brain in cross section.

Rosa looked at Adrian. "Name 'em and claim 'em."

He shrugged. "Flank steak, shoulder roast, brisket?"

Another overlay appeared, showing an incomprehensible jumble of lines coming out of the brain stem and radiating throughout the cortex, seemingly at random, as if someone had dropped a wad of tangled yarn on the diagram and photographed the image.

"Can you take the overlay out for a second?" Sam asked, peering closely at the screen.

He obeyed. She studied the image carefully and then shook her head. "You can put it back."

"See something?"

"I see it in that mess, and I thought it was in the underlying graphic, but I was wrong. It's in the overlay. But I can't see it clearly enough with all that spaghetti or whatever it is."

"What does it look like?" Fez asked her.

"Well, it looks a little like it might be the reticular formation—"

Rosa threw up her hands. "You hit my limit for the technical shit. I'm a hacker, not a neurosurgeon. You babble if you want—I quit."

"It's where you dream," Sam said.

Rosa paused in the act of turning away, her eyebrows straining toward her hairline. "Okay, *that's* interesting. If you'll pardon the expression."

"Or is it the part that keeps you from falling into a coma?" Sam frowned. "Dammit, now I can't remember."

"Blah. Just when I thought it was getting good." Rosa plumped down on the couch.

"Never mind. Those scribbles could be just more garbled data." Fez touched the console again, and the screen changed to show a view of the brain from behind, the center portion highlighted. "This is one of the very few readable texts I've found," he said, pointing to a small legend in the bottom left corner of the screen, "and it doesn't tell me a thing. 'Visual Mark.' "

Sam bent to look. "It sure as hell does. It tells you whose brain this is. Which makes this a medical record. Shit, no wonder Keely jumped. They fucking *clobber* you for busting meds." She straightened up and turned to Fez again. "You don't follow any rock video, do you?"

"Not if I can possibly help it."

"Visual Mark is a guy who works—worked—for EyeTraxx. I guess he's at the Dive now. And either he's got implants, or they're going to give him implants."

"So what?" said Rosa from the couch. "Half the world's got implants. Maybe he's some kind of addict, maybe he's burning out. Wouldn't surprise me."

"But what about my neuron?" Sam moved to the other screen again. "Where does that fit in with this? And where's Keely? Did he get away, or did they can him?"

"All good questions," Fez said. "We can do a docket search for Keely, and I'll make some copies of this and turn the doctor loose on them."

Sam stared at him. "You're gonna infect Keely's zap with a *virus*?"

"Not exactly. Let's take a break. You didn't eat your soup." He herded her away from the desk so that she had her back to both screens when the images vanished.

6

Big mistake, Manny thought, putting a few hours sleep between night court and Mexico. He'd boarded the jumper groggy and out of sorts, no better than if he'd decided to tough it out on stimulants, hit Mexico in the middle of the afternoon still groggy, and had to gobble more stimulants anyway.

The stupidities were piling up: the hacker managing to download before the trace-and-freeze kicked in, the goddamn feel-good mill, of all places, and then that obstreperous judge. Then coming face-to-face with the EyeTraxx bitch who'd been dodging him. Four-five visits to the EyeTraxx building, and he'd never seen her in person; one lousy trip into night court, and there she was.

At first he'd thought she might have been in it somehow with the hacker. The whole thing could have blown up then, but her appearance at the courthouse had just been a stupid coincidence. He wasn't completely convinced that she'd been too toxed to recognize him, but he was sure she didn't know anything. And now the hacker was taken care of, and the clinic gang was buried so deep in custody and procedures that by the time they saw daylight again, it wouldn't make any difference.

Sitting in the front passenger seat of the land-cruiser with his eyes half-closed, he managed perfect, if temporary, isolation in which to collect himself. The only time he'd had to move was to shut off the radio when the driver had turned on some gaudy mariachi music. The driver was a blond, pimply-faced kid who had done too much Guadalajara Pink in his short life. He was definitely detoxed today; Manny had done the drug test himself.

Even so, by the time Manny was boarding the jumper back to L.A., the kid would barely remember the drive, or him, or anything else. Pink messed up the transfer from short-term to

60

long-term memory permanently, which was why Manny had okayed him. Fortunately, he'd learned to drive before he'd learned the joy of forgetting.

Manny wouldn't have minded forgetting the previous few hours, or the prize pair sitting in the backseat. Galen and Joslin made a good argument for Pink. Galen was one of those pampered rich boys who liked to play at seeing what his money could do. Joslin was a bonafide twitch-case, thin as a promise, with the hint of a mentality Manny had always associated with the torture of small animals for amusement.

They were probably holding hands back there. They did a lot of that, hand-holding, and whispering and giggling. Reports on their previous stay in Mexico during the installation setup had said they'd spent their downtime holed up in their hotel room, watching videos, chowing down on polyester, and engaging in what they thought of as sex, a routine that never varied.

Picturing that was an exercise in comic thinking. Galen was small, almost boy-sized, flabby without being fat, with a head like a block and an always-grinning face. Joslin was downright spooky looking, pale in a way that suggested she'd never been exposed to natural light. Her hair was the yellow of something gone sour, and her enormous eyes always seemed on the verge of popping out of her head, as if she were perpetually startled. Or revolted. Her thinness implied she found vomiting erotic.

How in God's name could two such people find each other attractive? Manny filed that one under minor mysteries no one really wanted to solve. The EyeTraxx buy-out and subsequent developments would keep them in all the videos and edible polyester they wanted, and out of his sight. Considering their known behavior, they might never come up for air. Hell, when it came time to tell them they were shut out, they might barely notice.

"Here," the driver said abruptly.

Manny roused himself and sat up straight. The low white prefab had appeared on the scrubby landscape like trick holography. With the hurricane fence around it, the place looked more like a warehouse than a hospital.

"After you take us through the gate," Manny said to the driver, "you wait in front till we come out. I'll have a little refreshment brought to you."

The kid giggled.

"Some apple juice," Manny went on, "unless you would prefer milk. Any other refreshment will be handed over back at the hotel."

The kid giggled again and downshifted, working the floor stick with an expertise that belied his mental condition. Manny resisted the urge to shake his head. Implants could have alleviated the kid's condition, at least to a certain extent. Oh, the kid was almost certainly uninsured, which would make his getting help tremendously difficult, but not impossible. As a hardship case, he could have had hot-and-cold-running social workers filing petitions, begging grants, digging up sponsors. But he chose to stay the way he was, illustrating what Manny thought of as General World Rule Number One: some people liked the squirrel cage. Which reminded him—

He twisted around in his seat. Galen and Joslin were fast asleep, his head on her shoulder. Manny reached over and gave each of them a rough shake. "We're here."

Joslin came to with a jump, her big pop-eyes blinking in alarm while Galen floundered clumsily, grabbing at her shirt and inadvertently exposing more of her skin than Manny had ever wanted to see. He had a glimpse of a lattice pattern of thin scars across her chest.

"You *are* prepared to show me the start-up, aren't you?" he said, staring hard at Galen.

"Right, right. Of course." Blinking, he elbowed his twitch and motioned for her to cover herself up. She did so, staring at him as if she didn't know who he was or how she had come to be sitting next to him.

"You told me everything was ready," Manny said.

Joslin turned her head slowly from Galen to look at him. "Everything's ready," she said in her high-pitched monotone. "We've got everything except the heads."

"You'll be getting those soon." Manny turned away from her as they approached the gate. *The heads*, he thought. *Jesus wept.*

"We've got everything except the heads," she said again.

"Manny says we'll be getting those soon," Galen told her soothingly.

"Well, *I* know," she snapped. "*I* heard him."

Manny took a long breath and let it out slowly. The doctors Diversifications had recruited were all experienced in implantation. The assistant chief of surgery, Travis, had assured him there would be no problem learning the technique Joslin had developed; a socket wasn't really so different from the more usual kind of therapeutic implant. Which meant it would be easy for Travis to take over after they squeezed Joslin out, possibly with the help of her own procedure. He would have to ask Travis how it could be engineered.

The guard made the security check into a formal, cautious ritual Manny found more annoying than reassuring. Pulling up to the front door, the kid killed the motor and turned to Manny. "Where are we?"

Manny didn't answer. A minute dragged by in silence; the front door remained closed.

"We gave everyone the day off," Galen said with a vacant giggle.

"Did *not*," said Joslin petulantly. "The staff's in residence."

The door opened then, and a tall red-haired man dressed in antiseptic white stepped out. Manny felt himself relax at the sight of Travis and climbed out to shake hands with him. Travis led him toward the door, started to speak, and then frowned at something over Manny's shoulder. Manny turned to look; Galen and Joslin were still in the cruiser, fiddling with the mysteries of the seat belts. Manny went back to help them.

"You're to wait here," he reminded the kid behind the wheel. Not really necessary; the map on the in-dash screen of the navigational computer had been replaced with the words WAIT HERE TILL FURTHER NOTICE.

"Gotcho, muchacho," the kid said with an idiotic grin. Manny didn't bother giving him a dirty look. But he canceled the kid's refreshment, and later the kid was going to have one of the worst trips of his life on the stuff Manny would give him, without having the slightest idea why.

On the screen two bubbles were moving in a slow dance around a length of complicated braid. Every so often one of the bubbles would hesitate and move to the end of the braid, attaching itself briefly before moving away again, leaving behind a new segment. Manny studied the action for a few minutes and then looked up at Travis. "What's this going to be?"

"The female. The receiver," Travis added.

Manny couldn't help glancing at Joslin, who was wandering around the small room with Galen in tow, pausing occasionally to whisper in his ear. "That's the part that stays in the skull."

"Right." Absently Travis scratched the back of his head.

"When it's finished, it will be a hollow tube only a few molecules wide."

"But alive."

"Living tissue, yes." Travis's gaze remained on the screen. "For the first time implants will consist one hundred percent of living tissue. Therapeutic implants all have some percentage of hardware, so they all qualify as foreign objects, not completely at home in the body, though most recipients accommodate them with no trouble."

Manny made a polite noise.

"This one you see here is for the visual center." Travis tapped the back of his own skull where he had just been scratching. "Injected through the scalp and bone, it makes itself completely at home. So to speak."

"Only a few molecules wide." Manny frowned. "The people who'll be getting the early benefit of this stuff—ah, most of them would be hard put to flip a marble into the Grand Canyon on the first try. How are they going to plug into a socket only a few molecules wide in the backs of their own heads?"

Travis almost smiled. "Each target area will be marked with a small bump the size of a pimple. All they'll have to do is lay the connection against the bump. The connector finds its own way in by tropism. Makes no difference which socket—the software will make the adjustment for the correct input and output, and all the connectors retract automatically at the disconnect command, so there's no danger of damaging the mechanism. It will take a little practice, but your people should be able to receive their implants in the morning and be plugging and unplugging by lunchtime. In theory, that is."

"Clever."

"It's all Dr. Joslin's development."

They looked over at her together. She was standing at a bank of cabinets, gesturing flightily with one pasty hand while she continued to whisper to Galen, who had one arm around her insubstantial waist.

"Amazing." Manny jerked his chin at the cabinets. "What's in there?"

"Very little as yet. Freeze-storage for the completed polymers. They have to be kept frozen so they'll remain in stasis until we're ready to insert them." Travis led him through a door into another room, tiled, white, and bare except for a table with a box about twice the size of a human head at one end.

"Operating room," Travis told him. "Once we start up, we'll keep sterile conditions, of course." He put one hand on the box. "This is a standard combination scanner and insertion device. The scanner pinpoints each area of the brain for insertion. It hardly needed any adapting at all for the new procedure."

"Is it painful?" Manny asked.

"The procedure?" A flicker of amusement crossed Travis's ruddy, oblong face. "Not really. Dr. Joslin's primate subjects indicated some temporary tenderness at the insertion sites, a little itching that we've determined is psychosomatic. Depending on the individual, there may be some slight reactions and discomfort while the sockets become acclimated, but that depends on the individual. Brain tissue itself is incapable of feeling any pain."

"Primates are a long way from knowing for sure about humans," Manny said. "Even running a projection-simulation—"

Travis held up a hand. "Dr. Joslin?" he called loudly. "Could you come in here and help me show Mr. Rivera something, please?"

Joslin appeared in the doorway, still towing Galen. She looked around the room and gave a strange little laugh, as if she'd been caught out at something.

"Dr. Joslin, would you please lie down on the table and put your head in the scanner?" Travis asked.

Joslin disengaged from Galen and hopped up on the table. Travis slid up a panel on the end of the box, and she lay down, moving up until her head disappeared inside the scanner. Travis picked up a small control and danced his fingers over it.

In the wall behind Manny, a mural-sized holo screen lit up with a 3-D display of a human brain in glowing green. Within the brain a network of black lines appeared, all of them coming from separate areas to meet in what looked like an impossible tangle.

"Dr. Joslin supervised the placement of her own sockets," Travis said mildly, facing Manny's frown with an even, noncommittal expression. Manny looked from Travis back to the display. The Upstairs Team wouldn't care much for the idea of Joslin making free with a procedure that was solely the company's property now, even if she had developed it. It made a convenient legal point that could be pressed should she decide to be troublesome later.

"The black lines you see on the screen are the pathways the sockets have generated in her brain. The configuration will vary from person to person, just as brain and mind organization vary."

Manny looked at Travis again. Travis liked this better than standard therapeutic implants for brain dysfunctions, he realized. Travis liked it a lot.

"Eight sockets will serve the purpose," Travis went on, "though we may eventually find that some subjects need more, or even fewer. This procedure, incidentally, makes implants used to treat the dysfunctional obsolete. A totally organic implant can alter brain tissue, replacing dysfunctional cells with healthy ones."

"You included that in the reports to the AMA and the Food, Drug, and Software Administration, didn't you?" Manny said.

Travis nodded. "You're aware that's not necessarily a strong selling point with them."

Manny gave a short laugh. "I know all about them. They'll have representatives in Topanga tomorrow night for a presentation, which will include much stronger selling points."

Travis's face didn't change expression. "The pathways from each socket all end up, without exception, at the limbic system, the seat of our basic emotions—rage, fear, pleasure. When the sockets are engaged, stimuli will induce these things directly, for the duration of the experience. The consumer plugs into the feature presentation—music video, movie release, commercial, standard TV fare—and undergoes a three-dimensional experience." Travis's sudden, brief smile was bizarrely sunny. "Your advertising people will understand how to make good use of this."

Manny nodded, feeling uneasy.

"Now, here"—two areas on either side of the brain stood out in sudden highlight—"sockets feeding into the temporal lobes will enhance whatever data come in. Interactivity again—the consumer can cooperate in the forming of the images. Useful for games of any level of sophistication. It will feel quite extraordinary. Mystical, if you like."

Manny wasn't sure that *liked* was how he'd have put it himself.

"Manipulation of the parietal lobes"—two other areas of the brain stood out—"will give the illusion of movement. Your people will no longer have to move about physically in hotsuits to produce effects like walking, climbing, and so forth. And the consumers will feel it without needing hotsuits of their own."

"Wait a minute," Manny said. "I thought there was no way to stimulate those areas without producing a corresponding movement."

Travis looked impressed, which pleased him. It meant Travis was getting the message: *Don't try to skid one by me, because I know what you're doing.* "There was no reliable way, until now. Dr. Joslin developed a technique to block the physical movement from the sensation. It comes partly from the suppression of movement during REM sleep and partly from the old phenomenon of the ghost limb—where an amputee feels a limb no longer there. It's a kind of combination and reversal of those processes with an extra sideways twist." Travis glanced down at Joslin's gawky form on the table. With her head concealed in the box, she looked too much like a scrawny victim of decapitation. "She's really quite brilliant," Travis said, as if he couldn't believe it either.

"We cover the frontal lobes as well," he went on, "one for each hemisphere. Your people should find they feel more creative. Among other things.

"One socket each goes to the auditory and visual cortices. Technically your video people could use only those two sockets to produce a music video, but it will be a fuller experience using all the sockets. Less like a video, more like a waking dream. More like a real experience." Travis flashed his weird smile again. "What we've done—what Dr. Joslin has done, really—is hardwired an out-of-body experience. The feel of an out-of-body experience, I should say."

Manny had no reply to that. Travis dabbed lightly at the corner of his mouth with his ring finger and shut off the screen. "You can get up now, Dr. Joslin. Thank you."

Joslin squirmed down on the table, and Galen offered her a hand as she hopped off, smiling proudly at Manny. "So," he said, "you want to see mine, too?"

Manny looked at Travis. "Nothing was supposed to be done down here until Diversifications gave the go-ahead."

Travis's chin lifted a little. "Dr. Joslin is the chief of surgery. It was her decision."

"Loosen up, Manuel," Galen said expansively. "When this breaks, even if only a tiny percentage of people jump for it, it's gonna be harder getting a reservation in here than getting political asylum on the moon. And nobody knows what kind of trouble you're gonna have getting it legalized in the States, I don't care how many legislators Diversifications has on their tit. Did you see the look on that judge's face last night?"

"Earlier this morning," Joslin said in a loud stage whisper. She was massaging Galen's shoulders with both hands, making his ill-fitting jumpsuit even more rumpled.

Galen patted her thigh absently. "When I got into that courtroom and found out that goddamn feel-gooder had already modified some twitch's implants, and they were already fooling with direct—"

"That, at least, is taken care of," Manny said, forcing a genteel smile. "I'm sure the Upstairs Team at Diversifications won't have any problems with either of you already having undergone the procedure. But technically you do need permission from us before—"

"Oh, get *off* it, *Manuel*." Galen laughed. "It's *Lindy's* thing."

"Not anymore. When Diversifications took over EyeTraxx, it also took legal possession of all copyrights, trademarks, and patents originating with EyeTraxx. Have your lawyer look it up on the agreement for you."

Galen laughed again. "Big fucking deal. Without us Diversifications wouldn't have shit, so don't go splitting fucking legal hairs with me, *Manuel*. I don't have to be pissed on by some taco flunky whose grandmother went over the border squatting under a load of jalapeño peppers in the back of a pickup truck."

Manny's calm never deserted him. "My full, legal name is Immanuel Castille Rivera. My ancestors were *conquistadores*, and their line had been long established in this hemisphere by the time your forebears were quarantined for smallpox at Ellis Island. Not that such things matter. It has been fortunate for my own advancement that the tradition of the old barrio gangs never took hold in my family, and I grew up without believing that ethnic slurs had to be avenged for the sake of my manhood. I do, however, take a dim view of unprofessional behavior, something I share with the Upstairs Team."

"So? No offense, then." The arrogance was gone from Galen's face. "Hey, I made a few bad investment decisions, and Diversifications was ready to ride in and take over. Like *conquistadores*, eh?" He shrugged. "EyeTraxx had a history of that kind of stuff anyway, but what the fuck. Now I'm gonna be even more fabulously wealthy than I ever was, and after today we don't gotta bother with each other, as long as Diversifications keeps up their payment schedule."

He leaned back against Joslin, who put both arms around

him and rested her chin on his shoulder. Considering the differences in their heights, it was a comically awkward pose. "Frankly, I wouldn't want to be where you are, anyway," Galen went on, regaining a little of his old cockiness. "I still say you're gonna have to go some fucking distance to turn public opinion on what looks like a faster, easier way of mind control and brainwashing, all that shit. There's still plenty of people around who believe that manic-depressives and the schizos and the migrainers and the epileptics and the narcoleptics and *all* those leptics are morally wrong to have little buttons in their heads to keep them even. Hell, there's still plenty that think test-tube babies are a fucking atrocity. And that doesn't even cover the fucking AMA priesthood and the FDSA. They're gonna be screaming rape all over the place. It's gonna be a real mother's mother of a headache, and I don't like headaches."

"And what about you, Dr. Joslin," Manny said. "Do you have any thoughts on the matter?"

Joslin's expression went from vapid to oddly intent. "It's out of control."

Manny gave a politely puzzled laugh. "Pardon?"

"You'll see." She giggled. "Maybe when you lie down on that table, huh? Come on, Hally." She sidled out of the room, pulling Galen after her.

Manny shook his head. "Jesus *wept*."

"For Zion," Travis said, startling him. "In a way she's right. About it being out of control." He cleared his throat and turned the screen on again, recalling the image of Joslin's brain. "We're of a milieu where brain implants are commonplace now, so we won't have to overcome the things many of my instructors in med school talked about. But the full ramifications of this procedure are not apparent yet. Not even to us." He nodded at Joslin's brain on the screen. "We really have little idea of what will come up out of that organ through a direct pipeline. We can make a few educated guesses, and we might even be right about some of it. I understand the, ah, feel-good clinic doctor had already stimulated output through altered implants on one, ah, patient. They were watching pornographic images when the police arrived."

"Indisputable proof of this thing's entertainment value," Manny said dryly. "If rather mundane."

"One wonders about the not-so-mundane. The images were feeding only to a screen, but not from the screen directly to another recipient," said Travis. "We've established that output is far easier than input. But to be frank, we have not clearly established all the effects of input. Except for certain things. For instance—" He indicated the screen again. "The temporal lobes." The highlighted areas shrank, and the color of the area in the left hemisphere changed to orange. "That is the left mesial temporal lobe. If the emotional centers in that particular region do not activate at precisely the right time, a panic attack will ensue. It feels exactly like a heart attack." Pause. "Those prone to the condition can be treated with implants that keep the activation regular. The condition can be induced in a normal brain, however, by an inhibitory neurotransmitter, something that will keep the neurons from firing properly. The inhibitor could be encouraged by input, for example. Just one example."

Several long moments passed in silence as they both gazed at the screen. "I understand what you're telling me," Manny said at last. "I'm just not sure how I should take it."

"You can take it any way you choose," Travis replied. "The world just became that much more subjective. Preparatory to socket implantation a detailed map of the brain is assembled and kept on file." Travis turned the screen off. "The files will be carefully guarded against unauthorized access, of course."

"Of course." Manny felt his energy level sink as the stimulants in his system began to wear off. He glanced at his watch. "Why don't you prepare me a complete report, zap it up to my mailbox. Mark it confidential. I'm due on the evening L.A. jumper. Things are piling up back there. Last night was a real monkey wrench."

Travis's gaze was steady and expressionless. "Would you like those in 3-D or hardcopy flat format?"

"Both. I like to have something I can make notes on in an informal setting. Without hardware."

"And is the Diversifications system secure enough?"

"Now, yes. We have a pet hacker who's already gone to work on it."

He followed Travis out with a thousand different ideas jockeying for position at the forefront of his mind.

7

"Hallelujah," said Melody Cruz with her usual exaggerated good cheer, "it's *another day*! Anybody here care which one?"

"Not me," Gabe muttered groggily as he shuffled into the living room and plumped down on the mile-long couch. Twenty minutes of shower-massage had been either too little or too much; he wanted nothing more than to sink into the sofa and become one with the cushions.

"I just *knew* you'd see it that way. Well, here's the ugly truth of it, big guy: deadline on the Gilding BodyShields spot looms big as life and twice as graphic, you should pardon the expression."

Gabe grunted. "Tell me something I don't know."

"I'm getting to that. But first, this reminder: lunch with Manny Rivera *today*. Another good reason to get the Body-Shields spot wrapped."

"Okay, okay," Gabe said. "Nag." He sat up a little straighter, but his eyes still refused to open all the way.

"And we've got a mailbox close to capacity here. Three more items, and they're gonna hit you with the surcharge. I don't wanna say they're gougers or anything, but if you don't do something soon, they're gonna name the node after you. The Gabriel Ludovic Electronic Postal Node, funded entirely by you. *I* wouldn't want that carved on *my* tombstone."

"Right. What's in it?"

"Only the most comprehensive collection of junk mail in the entire Los Angeles area. Offers so refusable it's amazing they don't implode."

"Anything from Cassandra? Cross-ref Sam?"

There wasn't even a pause. "Not today."

"Delete it all, then."

"You sure about that?"

Gabe yawned. "Real sure. I'm not in the mood. Do we have any grapefruit juice?"

"We should, unless you sneaked into the kitchen in the middle of the night and drank it all without telling anyone."

Gabe grunted again and pushed himself up off the couch. Melody's voice followed him, switching to the ceiling speaker in the kitchen.

"Took another chunk out of your account for your share of the mortgage on this dump, just thought you'd like to know. Wanna know the balance, or would you rather be surprised?"

"Surprise me." Gabe held a glass under the juice tap on the side of the refrigerator and pressed for six ounces, unsweetened. The juice was bitter and icy, hitting his sinuses a moment after it hit his palate. He leaned against the refrigerator, eyes squeezed shut, pinching the bridge of his nose. His sleepiness had dropped away in a rush, leaving him wide-eyed with a lingering undertone of fatigue.

"That's about it as directly concerns your miserable life," Melody went on conversationally. "In the general news Malaysia is still trashed, your tax dollars at work. Another day of food riots throughout the British Isles, while here in town the price of the Gatsby Restaurant's Gourmet Breadloaf goes to twenty dollars per as of this morning. Kinda makes you wonder, don't it?"

"Not really," Gabe said. "I work in advertising, remember?"

"Gilding BodyShields. Deadline: jump it or lump it."

"All right, all right, you said already." He refilled his glass and went back into the living room.

"Hey, you said a trigger-word. Watch the triggers, and you won't cue the nag subroutine when you don't want to."

"Actually, I did want to," Gabe said, settling down on the couch again. "I need to be kept after until I get it done."

The four-screen dataline in the wall across from him was running highlights from *General News* on the two left-hand screens, while a script more formal than Melody Cruz's headline summary ran on the upper right. The lower right screen displayed an abbreviated menu. Gabe picked up the remote and thumbed for the Popular Culture format.

"Pop-Cult comin' atcha," Melody said. "Anything in peculiar or the usual mix?"

"The usual, thanks."

"Don't mention it." Pause. "To anyone. *Ever.* If I'd known I was going to end up like this when I agreed to license myself for dataline modules, I'd have slit my wrists."

"Me, too," Gabe murmured, watching the parade of items

that the summarizer had gleaned from FolkNet, the Public Eye, and the Human Behavior nets, with tidbits from BizNet thrown in. Popular Culture was a bottomless pit of raw material for commercials, and he badly needed some raw material this morning.

A shortened version of his old pharmaceutical spot ran between a segment on new trends in breakfast habits and an item on the sudden jump in popularity of video parlors among people with implants. He'd won a minor award for the pharmaceutical spot, nothing too flashy, just a commendation from the National Pharmaceutical Board for responsible presentation two years ago. Which was as good as a lifetime in the Age of Fast Information.

You know how it is, Gabe: What have you done for us lately, and when are you going to do it again?

Shut up, Manny, he thought. "Melody!"

"You barked?"

"Run down a short list of the contents captured from Pop-Cult for me, will you?" Maybe her voice would drown out the sound of Manny's in his head.

"Okay. Gotta hot report on those breakfast habits, which you saw, and a nonstory about implantees flocking to video parlors, you saw that, too. Also in the queue, we've got—hey, hey!—a big scoop on *pet* implants, is that something? Nobody wants to paper-train Rover anymore. Now you can get an AKC-registered springer spaniel who can walk himself. Hey, get yourself a poodle named Physician and say, 'Physician, heel thyself!' Come on, don't groan—whatcha wanna bet Physician comes up top of the trend for dogs' names inside of a month?"

"A million billion dollars," Gabe said, shaking his head.

"You do and *I'll* own *you*. Won't *that* be embarrassing, in hock to a dataline module. I'll reset all your defaults for food porn."

Gabe slumped farther down on the couch, letting her voice wash over him as she went on listing the items in the recently saved files. He'd bought the Melody Cruz module separately and installed it himself, jamming it permanently in humor mode. At times it could be a bit macabre, and Catherine had accused him of being a throwback to the days of happy-talk news. Catherine couldn't seem to differentiate between *happy* and *funny*.

From where he sat he couldn't see the door to Catherine's office, but he didn't need to. It would be sealed as always, the

white-noise soundproofing engaged so there was no danger of
Melody Cruz's humor offending Catherine's sensibilities or
disturbing her while she punched up real-estate deals on her
console. Hermetically-sealed Catherine Mirijanian. For all he
knew, she ate and slept in there. He was living out of the guest
room himself these days, so he couldn't prove she was making
any use of their bedroom. He couldn't even prove she'd noticed
he wasn't.

Maybe if they'd had more kids, even just one other—he
winced at himself. Considering how things had gone with
the one child they'd had, the idea was absurd. Still, Sam's
babyhood had been the best time between them. If it could
have lasted longer, he and Catherine might have gotten
into the habit of being good to each other, good *for* each
other.

No, still absurd. More children would have meant more
people he could disappoint, while for Catherine it would have
meant more people to disappoint her.

He heard a series of light rattling clicks then; Catherine's
door was unsealing, and she was coming out.

"Melody!"

"What, you again? I mean, huh?"

"Email everything to my office, I'll scan it over there."

"The summary, too?"

"Yah. Go mute. Just leave the dataline on in real time." He
sat up tensely. There was no time to slip back to the guest
room and wait for Catherine to clear. Perhaps she would ignore
the fact that the dataline was on and just go about her business.
It wouldn't have been the first time.

In the next moment he regretted his thoughts, as he always
did when he saw his wife, regretted everything, especially the
way things had gone so awfully wrong with them. She was one
of those women whose looks had improved as she'd gotten
older. Her Middle Eastern ancestry had given her strong, well-
formed features and a head of thick hair most people could
obtain only at cosmetology clinics. Her skin was the shade of
deep honey, a little darker than when he'd last seen her. She
had someone who came in once a month to give her dye jobs,
something he didn't think she really needed. Her own skin-
tone had always looked perfect to him, like her hands; never
given to long, red claws, she kept her hands very plain and
neat. Whenever he looked at her hands, he remembered that
there really were things about her that he loved, things that

were still there, somewhere, if only he could figure out how to reach them.

"I'm showing a house," she said, standing at the far end of the sofa.

He blinked at her without comprehension and then realized she was announcing that she was going out. He turned down the volume on the dataline. "A house? You mean a condo?"

She shook her head, smoothing her long wine-colored vest. "A detached residence. Someone is selling, land and all."

Gabe put on a smile. "And not even on the San Andreas Fault? That's wonderful. Congratulations. I'm happy for you."

"That may be premature," she said, a bit primly. "The deal hasn't gone through yet, but the buyers can afford it." She smoothed her vest again, checked her platinum cuff links, brushed invisible lint from her narrow trousers.

"Well, good luck, then. I hope it comes through."

Her full lips twitched. "If it does come through, luck won't have much to do with it."

Gabe nodded contritely. "Of course. I forgot."

She stood there looking at him steadily, and he found himself suddenly wondering not how she had ever gotten so far away from him, but how he had ever been close to her.

"My commission on this one puts me in house range. I know about another coming up for sale soon." She surveyed the living room slowly before her gaze came to rest on him again.

He frowned, looking around himself. "And?"

She was silent.

"Well, what?" he said. "Are you saying you want to move to a house? Is that it?"

"Yes." She wet her lips. "I want to move to a house."

"Okay. All you had to do was say so—" He broke off, the realization creeping up on him like a hotsuit sensation of rising water. "*You* want to move to a house. Not *me* and you, but *you*. Alone."

Her dignified features took on an expression that might have been regret. "I guess that's what I want to say."

"You guess? That's not like you. You don't trust to luck, and you don't guess."

She lifted her chin defensively. "It's not easy to say."

He blew out a breath and sat back against the couch cushions. "Yah. I know."

"Once it would have been for both of us," she said, sounding suddenly urgent as she leaned forward on the arm of the couch.

"I used to picture it that way. If you think it doesn't hurt even now to let go of that, then it's just as well things have turned out the way they have."

The grapefruit juice seemed to be eating a hole in his stomach. "Really, Catherine? Tell me—does it hurt because it's us, or because it spoils your one hundred percent success rating in the Valley?"

Now she glowered at him. "My success rate with this residence is zero."

"And you'll never forgive us for that, will you?" He shook his head. "Me and Sam, we really put the screws to you."

"Cassandra's a child. What's your excuse?" She came around the front of the couch and sat down on the cushion next to him, well within the borders of her own cushion. Real estate had given her a well-honed sense of territory, he thought, feeling a bit dazed. "We could have had a house together seven years ago, if you'd had any"—she struggled for a moment—"any *anything*. You could have gotten ahead instead of treading water, you could be in a position of power right now. I kept hoping you'd wake up and realize you were wasting yourself. If you had, we'd have that house, and maybe we'd even still have a daughter to live in it with us."

"*I* still have a daughter, even if she's emancipated," Gabe said sharply. "She's not like a goddamn *house*, you know, there's no title, no deed."

"If you'd had the wits to use your job to your own advantage, maybe Cassandra would have wanted to be more than a bum, living in holes with a lot of vermin and outlaws—"

"I think all she ever wanted was to be accepted as she was. And I never wanted the goddamn job to begin with. You wanted me to take it, and then because of all the *things* you insisted we had to have, I had to stay with it, and I got trapped there."

"And what were you going to be instead?" Catherine gave an amazed laugh. "An artist. What the world needs is another artist, especially if his name is Gabriel Ludovic. Was I supposed to support all of us while you answered the call of the muse? You even wasted *that*. You were going to pursue it part-time nights and weekends, remember? I had no problem with that; hobbies are good."

"It wasn't a hobby!" he said.

She laughed again, waving his words away with one hand. "Fool yourself all you want now, but that's all it would have

been. One in two million make it as artists. The rest end up
in little dumps that pretend to be galleries, or doing porn for
next to nothing. *That's* a real prestige career, isn't it. As a
hobby it would have probably done you some good. But—"
She spread her hands and looked around. "I don't see any holo
loops, I don't see any environmental designs, I don't see *anything* that qualifies as even an attempt at fine art, because you
didn't go through with it. You just sat around bitching about
the job until I couldn't stand the sound of your voice. *That's*
why I was always against your quitting your job for art's sake.
Even if you'd been that one in two million, I knew you just
wouldn't produce."

"It was the job," Gabe said, suddenly wanting to make her
understand once and for all, if she was going to leave him.
"The job took too much out of me, I didn't have enough
energy left over for my own work."

"No," she said firmly. "You just didn't want it badly enough.
Otherwise you would have pulled yourself together and just
done it. You'd have done it under any circumstances, in any
condition—Christ, *quadriplegics* used to paint pictures holding brushes in their *teeth*, because they wanted to paint more
than anything in the world—"

"Look, *I* didn't have to live like this, *I* could have lived with
less—"

"But *I wouldn't*." Her dark hair fell forward over her left
shoulder, and she slapped it back. "And we had a daughter to
think about. It wasn't *her* art, it wasn't *my* art, it was *yours*.
It was up to *you*, not *us*, to find a way. It was up to *you* to
work around *our* needs. If you'd wanted to starve under a pier,
you shouldn't have had a family."

"But we didn't have to have my income—"

She sat up straight, looking at him as if from a great height.
"I don't carry *anybody*. And nobody carries me. You knew
that when we got married."

"Poor Sam," he said suddenly.

She looked as if he'd slapped her. "What *about* Cassandra?"

He tried to put it into words, but it wouldn't come. "Never
mind. That slipped out. You're leaving. Case closed. To tell
you the truth, I don't know why you didn't leave me a long
time ago. What's the matter, couldn't you afford a *house* till
now?"

She didn't answer, but her gaze slid away from him. He
burst out laughing.

"My God, I hit it! You've been marking time to put together a down payment on a house!"

"Not a down payment," she said in a low voice. "The whole thing, outright."

He could feel all expression leaving his face. "Damn. You've got *millions*."

"Because I wanted it badly enough!" She had a startlingly desperate look now, as if she were also trying one last time to be understood. "I worked around the clock, no matter how tired I was, no matter how bored, no matter how dead the market seemed. When there were no leads, I made them out of nothing. Instead of sitting around bitching, I kept watch so that when something showed even the slightest hint of promise, I was the first to see it and the first one on it. I kept track of the buyers and the sellers, I charted their spending patterns and their activities so that I knew when they wanted to buy or sell even before they did, and I was right there to make it happen for them."

She rose smoothly, brushing at her trousers and her vest. "I didn't worry about *making friends*. I didn't waste my energy or my work time letting some clown cry on my shoulder and get my expensive clothes all wet. I didn't let myself get marked as a troublemaker, a screwup, or a loser."

"Like me," he said simply.

She glanced upward. "God, you had a very clear grasp of all the politics at Diversifications. You could have played them like a Stradivarius, but instead you chose to bitch about them, show opposition, huddle with the other moaners and whiners. It kept you back. *That's* the pity of it, *that's* the uselessness, *that's* why I'm so mad at you. It wasn't that you *couldn't*. You just said no." She folded her arms and gave a small shudder. "I'd be embarrassed if I were you."

The faint voice-over from the dataline jumped out at him. ". . . don't know how to relax, we have the solution. If you're driven too hard, we have the brakes. The Coves Clinic. We don't do anything to you that you wouldn't do yourself, if you knew how. The only implant clinic with its own on-site spa. Triple-A rating by the Neurological Council, on file with the Food, Drug, and Software Administration."

The beachscape on the screen had been enhanced a little, Gabe knew. LeBlanc had done that spot; she'd thought she was going to get a couple of days on location, but instead Diversifications had jobbed the taping out to some students and called it "intern-work," beating the union fees and LeBlanc's hopes for an incidental vacation.

"You won't be able to keep this place by yourself," Catherine said. "When the time comes, I'll handle the sale for you. You'll do well, even after I take my share and my commission."

He kept staring hard at the dataline as her quiet footsteps went toward the front door. "You gonna find me something else more in my range?" he called suddenly as he heard the lock disengage.

"I don't work in your range."

At least she wasn't a door-slammer. He continued to stare at the dataline, which was babbling a report on consumer spending habits from BizNet, watered down for civilians. Obviously this was supposed to mean something to him, but he couldn't bring himself to care. It was going into the capture buffer anyway, and if he ever did find a reason to care, he could look at it later.

Sam would be happy, he thought after a bit, when his mind began to work again. Well, perhaps not happy. *Relieved* would be more like it. Or maybe it wouldn't matter to her one way or the other—her emancipation had put her beyond having to care about the state of her parents' marriage. If it had come to this three or four years ago, it might have made a difference to her. Even two years ago. She'd only been emancipated for a year then—he might have been able to persuade her to move in with him, go to college, get some legitimate work in programming, or simulations. She had a lot of talent—

Oh, *yah*. Legitimate work with some corporation, perhaps, some company like Diversifications, turn her into another corporate employee. If she'd wanted to have the spirit ground out of her, she could have stayed home and let Catherine do it.

Sure, I'll come back, Dad. As soon as you can give me one goddamn good reason why you didn't leave a long time ago yourself.

What could he have said to that—*Well, Sam, you had to be there*? It would have been just one more way to tell her she didn't understand, and she already knew that. He wouldn't have understood himself, back in the beginning. He hadn't been a whole lot older than Sam was now when he and Catherine had married. There had been no room in him then for the idea of a Plan B, what to do if things didn't turn out the way he wanted. There had been no room for looking ahead to a time when the dreams hadn't come true and there was no love anymore, and instead of the art he had some bootleg simulations he played with on the company clock, the way he passed the days until such time as he dropped dead. Of disinterest, most likely.

"First warning," Melody said suddenly, and he jumped at the sound of her voice.

"What?"

"You can still get to work on time if you leave now. Commuter units are still available at the nearest rental lot. Call ahead and reserve?"

"Yah, sure," he said. *Yah, sure.* Go to work, why not? He had that lunch with Manny, but what the hell—when your wife left you first thing in the morning, how much worse could the day get?

He'd have to remember to feed that line to the Melody Cruz module. Or maybe Marly. Yes, Marly; it was a good line, and it sounded far more like her than it did him.

8

When Gina found out, Mark thought, she was going to kick his ass. She'd done it before, for a lot less.

It wasn't that everything had happened so fast the night before—no, two nights ago. Jesus. It was getting by him, it was all getting by him. There'd been so much happening. It sure hadn't been the night he'd gone out to have.

The Mimosa first, where there was always something going on. Mixed crew down there, the hackers and the bangers, the faces and the cases, roiling around on the sand and the walkways, squatting in vacant buildings, flimsy lean-tos, under piers. Those hacker kids, they really kept it going, the way they could tap a little power with their piggybacks and fooler loops and whatever else they had. They'd have their laptops going, and the bangers'd be jamming, and there'd be some kid, maybe someone's good little girl before she'd gotten her walking papers, coaxing a dream out of her cam with a hacker's laptop running a simulation assembly for her, and someone else'd be jumping an animate around using an exoskeleton and talking about what they could do if they had a hotsuit instead of an exo. While the cases watched like it was all video, which for them it was.

Valjean and his cape. That was it. He'd put the cape in one of Canadaytime's videos, and Valjean refused to live without one in realife. Thing sucked power like Dracula, had to weigh a ton with all the solar collectors in it, and Valjean ran it eighteen, twenty, thirty hours a day, something like that. Valjean and his cape, Ecklestone preening, and Moray jamming with the kids like she used to before Canadaytime hit it on video. That had been pretty fine, he could have listened to Moray and the kids jam all night, but somebody wanted to hit-and-run, and a whole bunch of them had been toxed enough to think it was a good idea. Himself included.

He could remember being crushed into a commuter rental

with some other people. That hadn't been so fine. Once he'd owned a *real* car, but that had been before L.A., L.A. in the big C-A, and he seemed to remember telling someone about that on the way to Fairfax. Or maybe he'd just been talking in his mind. Sometimes with the music going, it was hard to tell. But the program director in his head had orders: play it all the time, and play it loud.

They'd set up in screwy old Gilmore Park, or what was left of it. Someday someone would come up with the cash to finish restoring what the Big One had shaken to shit. Underneath the toss-em chemlights on poles, it looked like the surface of Mars, or how Mars would look after humans got through crapping on it. That had depressed him a little, but the pickle stand was open for business (*Why, officer, this ain't no drug bar, it's a pickle stand*), and he'd wheedled a little cheer out of a young thing in a stone-home lethal flamingo mask with feathers sticking up to heaven.

The hacker kids had their fooler program going—*it's so easy, it's sick, you just bypass the sensors to the surveillance alarm and feed it any simulated data you want, truly stone-home sick, I did this one myself*—he'd tried to look interested for the kid because she'd been so earnest about it, earnest and young. Besides, it was a lot like the story of his life: just bypass the sensors and feed in any data you want. But either the cheer had gone bad in the can, or it hadn't been strong enough in the first place, because he'd gotten a bad feeling he couldn't lose. Nothing he could home in on, but he'd faded before Valjean could pounce on him and talk him out of it.

Well, he'd never really seen what was so high-top about hit-and-runs anyway. See how fast you can have fun before the cops showed. Although one time he'd gone to one set up in the middle of some closed-off lanes on the fucking freeway, and there had been something like stone-home righteous retribution to that one, like he was getting back some of the time he'd lost sitting in the clogs. That one had been worth the arrest and the fines.

So after Fairfax . . . yah, just driving around in the dark thinking he would go home, stick on a header, get toxed, and pass out in videoland, when the phone buzzed urgent. The next thing he knew, they were picking him up. *Don't worry, we'll turn in your rental for you, but it's imperative you come with us.*

Imperative. Im-fucking-perative. That had been Rivera.

Gina had always disappeared when Rivera had come around, maybe because Rivera always came around with Galen, and Gina would just as soon have killed Galen as pissed on him.

He didn't feel any too warm toward the boy himself for what had happened to EyeTraxx, even though Galen had fixed up the deal for him. EyeTraxx had always been the Beater's, as far as he was concerned, even after the Beater had lost most of it to Galen in a bailout. Galen hadn't been there in the beginning, when the Beater had put it together. EyeTraxx Video.

He'd been there. He'd been there the day the Beater had sold off the old tour bus for scrap. Touring was nowhere; video was everywhere. There were billions of little video production companies starting up, it seemed, all over the place, but EyeTraxx was different, because the Beater had still been the Beater, and it wasn't just somebody's money machine. That came later, after Galen took over.

In the beginning they were doing goddamn visions. Video wasn't new even then, but it was getting better all the time, all the stuff you could do, hotsuits and artificial-fucking-reality, shit, you could finally *be* the music. And then that crazy whiz kid—where had he been from? somewhere—the kid had mixed up that simulation of the Great God Elvis burning licks with several later generations of rockabillies too spread apart to have overlapped in realife, though the one he'd really liked was Latin-Satin from 2002 handling Mad-Bad Jim Morrison from 20th C. Damn, but that had been stone-the-fucking-crows-at-home fire.

He'd had big visions for the Beater, bigger fire, and the Beater could have done it, he really could have done it, the Beater's music and his visions, and the Beater had had to go and put it down. Just gave up, covered over his synthesizer and made a desk out of it, full-time bizman. Without anything remotely like a whimper, even.

If it would do any good to kick, old son, I'd kick, but live performance is over. Most of the new ones coming along don't even bother about the clubs. And now I'm over. This is not my synthesizer anymore. You are. You and Gina and the rest of them, you synthesize the sound and the pictures into what they want to see and hear. You're the real synthesizers.

He'd laughed at that one. *I may be a sinner, but I ain't no synthesizer.*

Synner, then. With a y.

And the goddamn name stuck, like a lot of other shit had stuck. And little by little Galen whittled away at them; Guerstein let go, Vlad gone, Kim fired, Jolene packing up and stalking off in a cloud of disgust, until it was the way it had been in the beginning, almost, just him and the Beater and Gina doing the videos. And now look where they all were.

He didn't actually know where they all were, at the moment, particularly himself. Diversifications? Right, some bedroom in the penthouse. They'd told him he could spend the night after, report for work in the morning—which morning?—and then he was free to go home the next night, no problem. He wasn't under arrest or anything. It was that hacker.

None of that was quite straight in his mind, either, the stuff about the hacker, who was occupying another bedroom nearby. Wasn't any hacker he could remember off the Mimosa, he knew that much.

He thought the hacker might have cracked Diversifications and gotten into Galen and Joslin's stuff, the stuff they were going to let him do. Except he couldn't shake the feeling that Rivera already knew the kid, and knew him real well. Galen and Joslin hadn't felt it, but it was a toss-up if Galen and Joslin felt anything. It wasn't like they were paying a whole lot of attention sometimes, anyway, but he'd kept catching these looks between Rivera and the kid, and he was pretty sure it wasn't just his mind playing tricks on him again, the way it did more and more often lately, especially when he was working on a video, which was all the time now. Working on video made him *go away* a lot, as Gina put it. But hell, how else was he supposed to see the pictures and get it right?

He was pretty sure he'd seen at least part of the police raid on the . . . had it been a clinic? Feel-good joint, yah. Jesus, and everybody thought *he* was crazy. *He* didn't have goddamn implants that were supposed to get you toxed without taking any drugs. What the hell was that, anyway—toxed without drugs. That wasn't right, that was *crazy*, that was stone-home *unnatural* was what it was.

Which made the deal Galen had swung for him unnatural, too, he thought uncomfortably. Except he wanted it so much. So what did that make him, another head-geek? It would be different, though, not just brain-buttons to push, but a better way to get the pictures he saw in his head out just the way he saw them, get them out and on video so everyone could see them the same way. Yah, that was different, real different, it wasn't like going to a feel-good joint at all.

He'd wished he could have had it done already while he was sitting in the limo watching the cops march the feel-good people into the van. One of the Beater's old tunes had been stuck in his head with the pictures running, and that had been some stone-home righteous video, running so hot he'd thought for a while that the Beater had been there with him. But he wasn't.

After the raid what had happened? Right, they'd sifted the hacker out from the rest of them, and there'd been a fast visit to somebody important's place. He thought maybe that had been in Bel-Aire because there'd been so many security gates to get through. Or maybe he was just remembering one gate with a stutter because of the way the music had been playing; the program director had been following the pictures and giving the music a house remix that the Beater would have wet his pants over. The old Beater would have, anyway.

He didn't remember much about the Bel-Aire place, except that there'd been hot-and-cold-running phone calls going on the whole time. There must have been about two dozen phone lines and even more terminals and screens—man, the information had been flying so thick and fast, he'd been afraid of getting hit in the head with it. The hacker had looked pretty wired, like he was afraid he was going to take a serious hit from all the shit flying back and forth.

Or maybe from Rivera. By that time he'd been stone-home positive Rivera knew the kid, the way the kid looked at him, like Rivera had a hand grenade with the pin between his teeth, ready to pull it. And meanwhile, they were all talking at the kid, not just talking, machine-gunning him with their voices, ya-ta-ta-ta-ta-tat, bang, bang, *bang*, ya-ta-ta-ta-ta-tat, bang, bang, *bang*. Enough to make you yell, *Dive! Dive!* except Rivera didn't have any sense of humor, that fuck.

The kid took quite a lot of that before he said the secret words: *state's evidence*. But the weirdest part was that Rivera looked even more relieved than the kid, and he flashed on the idea that the kid thought Rivera was going to solve all his problems when really what it was, was he kid had just solved Rivera's and didn't even know it.

So they'd given the kid a bunch of official-looking stuff to thumbprint and made him look into one of those retina-printing scopes. Some more talk, some more phone calls, and then, when he'd thought everything was all over and they could all go home, off they all went to night court. He hadn't really believed they were going there until they'd pulled up at the front steps, and he still hadn't believed it until they all started to climb them.

That was when the kid got balky. Something about copies? He couldn't remember. And then the courtroom—

He'd had a bad moment right then, just before they'd all gone in. He'd started thinking that he was going to run straight into Gina, busted at a hit-and-run or just toxed and disorderly or something. He'd see her, and she'd see him with Galen and Joslin, and boom, nuclear meltdown.

What she'd do when she found out about the deal he'd agreed to—fuck the meltdown, it would be stone-home apocalyptic. *Jesus is coming after all, fucker, but just for you!*

But they'd promised they'd bring her in on it, too, before they opened it up to everyone. She'd go with him, and it would be like it was theirs, together, and that would be good. But she was going to meltdown bad when she found out he'd kept stuff from her, she'd kick his ass just on general principle. In twenty years they hadn't kept any secrets from each other. Then again, he hadn't had any secrets to keep. And then *again*, he'd never been able to imagine having any to keep where Gina was concerned. Until now.

Sorry, Gina.

He wondered if he'd be able to get out even that poor little two-word apology before she nuked him.

Well, like the man had said they would, the times had definitely a-changed, and that made him feel sad beyond the usual morning-after funk.

No, *two* mornings after. Where did the second day go?

Oh, Christ, yes—they'd detoxed him the quick way. Rivera had taken him to a doctor in . . . no, the doctor had come here, to the penthouse, and she'd given him Purge. She hadn't called it Purge, but that was what it had been. He'd had Purge before, and once you'd had it, you didn't forget it. Purge always put a lot of miles on your odometer before it was through with you, and maybe it took a few years off your life and maybe it didn't, but it sure felt like it did. With Diversifications in the person of Rivera picking up the tab. A little trade-off, there— a good life, but a shorter one. *Ars longa, vita* fucking *brevis.*

Fuck it all. He'd just lie here now and watch the pictures. The video show that ran endlessly in his head was coming up to where he could see it better—that, or he was going down to where it was, it didn't matter to him one way or the other. Just as long as he could see it.

The lake, again; the lake with the stony shore. It showed up somewhere in all his videos now, and he didn't know what that meant, but he didn't question it. The pictures ran the way they would, and he was just the medium—

—*synner*—

—all right, synner, now he could believe in that word be-yond its genesis as the Beater's PR device—it could have been worse, the Beater could have dragged out that old chestnut, *cyberwhatsis*, or whatever it was, he couldn't remember, and he didn't have to, because he was standing on the lake with the stony shore, a million-million stones worn smooth as eggs by the lapping of the water, and every stone a secret world to blossom at his touch.

Be careful.

A whisper that came through the music, but whether as part of it or something separate from somewhere else in his mind, he didn't know.

He could feel the stones hard against his bare feet as he made his way unsteadily along the arc of the shore. The sun was high overhead, falling hard on the water like a demand.

Be careful.

He was teetering on one foot, and the sun was demanding that the lake do something, allow something of it. . . .

The stones shifted beneath him, and he felt himself twisting around as he lost his balance. Sky and ground seemed to nod and sway, and he went down, under the glaring demand of the sun.

Water touched his fingertips in a feather-kiss, and his hand closed around a stone.

Be careful. Can you cast this stone?

He brought the stone up close to his face. It was almost bone white, pockmarked and shot through with spidery veins of silver gray. The texture shifted in his sight, and the hard, demanding sun struck a tiny, white-hot spark in it.

On the lake a ripple broke the mirror-smooth surface and sent an echoing spark, briefly blinding him. Or was it still the stone he was looking at, or both stone and lake at once . . . ?

The texture of the stone shifted again; something seemed to part, like water, like veils, and he was looking *into* the stone, his sight traveling toward the heart of the secret—

The surface of the lake rippled again; more flashes of light, brighter, to the point of pain, hot needles driving into his head, needles the size of spears, needles of light and oh God if that was what this stone meant, he wanted to get out, get out get away get away

Be . . . careful. . . .

And then he *was* out, floating away more weightless than weightless, consisting of less than the empty space between his dreams, as if everything that was himself had been distilled down to one pure thought.

It felt right; it felt more than right, something he'd been meant to do all his life.

The bone white was a bed; he was looking down at himself lying in it, and the sight was receding like a tiny image at the wrong end of the telescope.

Stop.

The movement stopped, and he had a sense of waiting.

Rippling on the lake disturbed the air, and he felt how the air pressed up, parted around him; the movement of the kid in the next bedroom turning fitfully in his own bed, tangled in the sheets and in a situation of his own making.

Jones, the kid had said at one point. Aloud? Had to be, he remembered the kid babbling to him when they'd been alone once. *Jones*. Jones was dead. No, Jones *wasn't* dead. No, Jones *was* dead, but only sometimes. Schrödinger's Jones. What was Schrödinger's Jones? Putting cats in boxes with vials of poison gas; strange habit. No stranger than Schrödinger's video, though, the one he kept making over and over because he couldn't seem to get it right, and it wouldn't leave him alone until he did, and the Beater couldn't understand, which was why he was on this deal with Galen and Joslin. That was supposed to fix Schrödinger's video. Maybe it would also do something about Schrödinger's dick, which he also suffered with from time to time. It was a stone-home Schrödinger world, when you came right down to it.

He could feel the stone against his hands, the smooth-rough surface surrounding him as he surrounded it, but his body was still far, far away, sprawled on the bed like a cast-off exo. On the bed, floating on the lake, ripples striking sparks all around,

secret world in the stone, and no mark to point the way
home—

There was a stranger on the stony shore, turning slowly,
turning slowly to him, turning like the seasons, like the moon,
and he was afraid to see what face the stranger would show
him this time, what face, what face, turning from the darkness,
what face face

Gina. Relief shuddered through him. This time, Gina. It
was like seeing her clearly for the first time in a long time, as
if he'd been looking at her through layers and layers of veils
or fog or something. Twenty years would build up a lot of
layers. He had almost forgotten she was beautiful to him.

She had the greatest color of skin, all her own, a gift of
nature, though he'd seen the same shade in various dye-joints
around town, tagged "Wild Forest Hardwood." She'd never
been much of a peacock type, it never seemed that important
to her, she had other stuff to do. Dreadlocks pretty much took
care of themselves, he guessed; they spilled down her forehead, past her ears, onto her shoulders, down her back in
fluid, thickly graceful lines. Strong features, extraordinary
eyes. No one else in the world looked like her, better now
than twenty years ago when she'd first appeared with her laptop
and a homemade simulation, crazy to make videos. Not more
than sixteen or seventeen then, couldn't have been, but he
didn't know. All this time and he'd never gotten around to
saying, *How old are you?*

She knew how old he was. He could see it in her face, still
turning through the light and her gaze sweeping across him,
she knew how old he was, she knew—She knew.

That was in her face as well, and he could see it clearly now,
what he had not seen at the time when he had been standing
on the courthouse steps while Galen and Joslin danced around
the kid (because they *didn't* know), trying to draw him into
the rhythm and the pattern, meaning to strangle him with it,
while he stood there and watched, and the sight that had passed
into him without his noticing and buried itself in his brain
showed itself to him now, the shadow in the deeper shadows,
watching from hiding. Some stray little bit of light had found
her and ignited itself in her eyes. Now he saw the glint he had
not seen then, felt the way her breathing had sent ripples across
the lake.

Gina, I'm sorry.

And she was turning from him, and he saw himself again sprawled on the shifting texture of the bed and knew that it was time to go back. If he was going back.

This was the part of Schrödinger's video that he could never be sure of. Every other time he had gone back, but this might be the time he didn't, this time.

Be careful.

Teetering, about to fall, he could fall either way—

He was lying facedown on the floor, one cheek pressed against the carpet and the afterimages of bright sparks fading in his vision. The fingers of his left hand were curled clawlike around a piece of air the shape of a good-sized stone.

Weird stone fucking shit, he thought, using the bed to help himself up. Have some fucking stone-home crazy dreams and then fall out of bed. With a fucking Purge headache, too. Christ, if they ever did that to him again, he'd take a walk and keep walking, over hill, over dale, over the fucking ocean, he didn't care if they had the stone-home Secret of the Universe in a chocolate candy-fucking-coating, no more fucking Purge, *the*-fucking-*end*.

He found his clothes wadded up in a fat, overstuffed chair and dressed slowly, smoothing away the wrinkles with his hand and wondering if he should be concerned about a change of underwear. Diversifications was a pretty detox/safe-sex kind of outfit. If it hadn't been for Joslin's big-deal project, he was pretty sure Diversifications wouldn't have wanted any part of him, or Gina either.

The memory of Gina was like a physical blow. It caught him off balance with one leg in his pants. He staggered across the room, and for a moment he saw the stony shore in the velour smooth of the carpet before he fell sideways onto the bed.

He lay with the breath knocked out of him, more by surprise than by the fall. She *had* been there, and he'd been too toxed to register the sight of her then, but his brain had saved her for later, for the lake with the stony shore.

Sitting up, he pushed the pants down his leg with his other foot, stamped them into a wad, and tossed them over on the chair again. "Did it wrong," he muttered. He had to be careful about that these days, doing things wrong, because whenever he did, he found himself toppling over onto that shore of egg-smooth stones again, and sometimes it took him a long time to find his way back to where he'd been. And that was different from just going there on his own for Schrödinger's video, because—

But he couldn't say why, really. Except maybe it was just better to jump than to be pushed, the way it was better to burn out than to fade away.

And that was something of the lake with the stony shore, too. One of the multitude of secret worlds there could show him the way out, but the deal with Galen and Joslin was also a way out, and a surer thing. Or so the Beater had convinced him, when the deal was done.

It may be better to burn out than to fade away, Mark, but it's best of all not to do either. And you know you're burning out. Don't you?

Yes, I do, old pal, and how tactful of you to say so. I should have told you when it happened that you had a hand in it as much as anything else, maybe more. You put your ax away too soon, my man; when you closed up your synthesizer for the final time, I heard the lid closing on my coffin as well.

"Woo," he said, and blew out a short breath that might have been a laugh directed at himself. Then he stretched out face-down on the floor and got up again to walk carefully to the chair where his clothes were. And this time it was the right number of steps in the right way according to the music playing in his head. He dressed without any more problems.

The living room was tastefully luxurious, and empty. Over on a desk near the windows, a monitor was flashing his name. But he had to wait for a while, until the program director cued something up with a matching rhythm before he could go to it and press the message-waiting button on the control panel built into the desktop.

Thank you for your help in court, the screen told him. *It was not absolutely vital in terms of legal procedure that you appear before the judge with us, but it did strengthen our case beyond question. Hope you rested comfortably. Press the printout button for a hardcopy map of the building and the areas that directly concern you. The hallway to your left as you face this screen leads to the elevator. Manny Rivera.*

That was it? A Purge detox and not even a fancy French breakfast? What a bunch of cheap-asses.

He was reaching for the map sticking out of the printout slot when he felt the difference in the air.

The kid was standing in the doorway, dressed only in a pair

of colorless jockey shorts that had passed the stage of true wearability. Kindred soul, secret words or not.

"Visual Mark," the kid said.

He shrugged.

"I've seen a lot of your stuff. I always wondered what your real name was."

Mark gave a short laugh. "Who fucking knows? I lost track of that a while ago." Not quite true; some of the stuff he'd toxed out on in the past had had some bizarre lasting effects, but he could remember his real name, if he tried. Mostly, the effort was incompatible with the sound track.

"Yah," the kid said. "Well." He stared distractedly at a spot on the carpet about midway between them.

"Listen, guy—" Mark made a move toward him and stopped. It wasn't like he could help. The kid had said the secret words, and that had locked things up. He shook his head. "Guy, it's a stone-home Schrödinger world." He stuffed the map in his shirt pocket and headed for the elevator.

9

"So, *then*," said Dinshaw, pushing a hand through her frizzy red-gold hair, "after it's all approved and ready to go into the pipe, Manny comes back with 'just one more tiny little fix.'"

Over the civilized din in the Common Room, Dinshaw was holding forth to a less-than-rapt audience gathered more by inertia than choice around the circular table, a scenario more or less duplicated all around the room at the other tables, among the rest of the employees of the Advertising and Entertainment Division.

Gabe tried to give Dinshaw a semblance of attention, since he was sitting right next to her. He'd spent the morning tracking down headhunters in New Orleans with Marly and Caritha, and he was feeling alternately energized and drained. Marly and Caritha had blind-selected a voodoo track, and he had almost been crucified on a cypress tree. The authenticity may have been dubious, but the excitement had been real. Relatively. It seemed more real than Dinshaw's slightly nasal, slightly hoarse complaint, anyway.

Across from him LeBlanc was keeping one eye and ear on the six-screen dataline in the wall behind him, occasionally jabbing the remote in the center of the table, switching between *What's Entertainment?*, *Dear Mrs. Troubles*, and *The Stars, Crystals, and You Show*. Next to her, Shuet was methodically breaking pieces off some unidentifiable snack food and tucking them into his mouth, the designer-sculpted jaws moving in a deliberate way, as if he were counting his chews. On LeBlanc's other side, Silkwood was also watching the dataline, his wide, wholesome face looking alternately anxious and hungry. LeBlanc nudged him. "How's the diet going? Should we switch to food porn?"

"No, thank you," he said primly. "The weight is coming off, I'm fine. I haven't watched food porn since I got my buttons."

"*That's* what you call them?" LeBlanc was amused.

"The buttons that switch off the urge to overeat. Is there something sick about that to you?"

"Hey, they're *your* implants. Excuse me, I mean *buttons*." LeBlanc shared a secret smile with Gabe.

". . . concept's perfect, clothes're perfect, every little detail down to the spear carriers, all perfect," Dinshaw was saying. "*But*, Manny says, the client says I'm not *thinking thin* enough, the viewpoint character just didn't *feel* like a tall, slinky model stalking through the world, she felt like, and I quote, 'just anybody who'd buy off the rack.' Unquote."

Gabe nodded in automatic commiseration as LeBlanc made a sympathetic noise of disgust. "Did you tell Manny to take the test-driver and spin on him? Had to be a him, right?"

"Of course," said Dinshaw. "TexTones employs something like nine hundred women, and they can't spare *one*, not *one*, to test-drive the spot. Instead, we get one of their paunchiest old farts, and we shoehorn him into a hotsuit, stick a header on him, turn on the simulation, and say, 'Okay, now you're this gorgeous woman, roll with it, Zeke.' "

"*Look* at that," LeBlanc said, pointing at the dataline. "Damien Splader's going to do a talk show from prison. They send him up for life, and he gets his own show. Just what we need, another porn show. Prison porn. You know something like sixty-eight percent of all new programming on the dataline is some kind of porn now?"

"Where'd you get a figure like that?" said Shuet. "News porn?"

LeBlanc looked at him evenly. "Hey, a tabloid should know."

"Oh, how could there be prison porn? Who would get hot looking at prison stuff?"

"Who would get hot looking at food?" Silkwood said glumly.

"Are you *sure* those implants of yours are working?" LeBlanc asked him.

"Yes, I'm just thinking of my former bad habits." Silkwood eyed the now-empty wrapper in front of Shuet.

"Manny starts giving me this dissertation," Dinshaw went on, "about how a *really* good simulation can erase barriers and differences and convince a woman she's a father or a man that he's a sexy, high-priced model showing off daywear. And if it can't, it's just not *vivid* and *alive* enough."

"What about the companion spot?" LeBlanc asked. "Or have

they gone budget-slashing cheap-assed, like Kickers, Boots of the Wild? I hope I never see another Kicker in my life."

"Amboy's working on it, from a template lifted off mine. The program'll automatically select it for a male viewer, and it's the default for flatscreen format. That means I can't change mine now."

"Sure you can," Silkwood said distantly. "Just zap a new template over to Amboy."

"Sure I can. And the minute I do, he'll be down in Manny's office, raising hell about how is he supposed to get anything done on time when Big Bad Emily Dinshaw keeps changing everything around on him. Then Manny'll call me in and give me a lecture on how he wasn't asking for a total recompose, just a little more *feeling*."

"Tell him to feel this," LeBlanc suggested.

"Not without a hotsuit. Not even *with* a hotsuit."

"*That's* what we need!" LeBlanc laughed. "*Diversifications* porn! Right? We could tell our horror stories for a cam, let the home audience know what kind of hell we go through to give them those commercials they eat up with two spoons. Sorry," she added to Silkwood. "No offense."

"You did that deliberately, but I don't care." Silkwood gave her a lofty side-glance. "My buttons are working, all's right with the world."

"So did Manny have any helpful advice to offer?" Shuet asked.

"Manny's a veritable *fount* of *helpful advice*—"

Gabe glanced across the room to the drink machines, idly considering another coffee, and then looked again. The skinny figure standing there searching the pockets of his jeans seemed to have congealed out of the empty air, like a special effect suddenly tossed into a particularly realistic simulation. His stringy brown hair trailed over the shoulders of his loose shirt, which had either been yellow once or was going yellow now. The jeans were almost threadbare enough to be translucent, and the shoes seemed about to give up and fall to pieces. As the man turned slightly, Gabe saw the security button attached to his shirt, a twin to his own. The guy was with the company, all right, he wasn't just a lucky wanderer who had managed not to set off any alarms.

"*What* is *that*?" said Shuet in a low voice. "And how the *hell* did it get in here with *us*?" Chatter was dying all over the room as everyone began to notice the stranger.

"Well, I see the new members of our Entertainment department are starting to trickle in." No one turned to look at Clooney, who had come up to the table and was standing behind one of the empty chairs, waiting to be invited to sit down. Gabe could practically feel everyone willing Clooney to go away.

"He goes by the colorful appellation of 'Visual Mark,' " Clooney went on relentlessly, "and he—"

"*That's* Visual Mark?" Dinshaw said, without really acknowledging Clooney's presence. "I'll be damned. He looks like one of his own rock videos."

"Rock videos?" Silkwood raised an eyebrow at her.

"My kids live on them." Dinshaw made a face. "Yah, I know. But this guy actually does some interesting work. Even when he's stealing from himself."

"You *watch* rock video?" LeBlanc put a hand to her throat with an exaggerated flutter. "Emily Dinshaw, a banger? I'm *shocked*."

"Stuff's junk," Silkwood declared. "Worse than all the porn put together. I don't know why we had to go into the music-video business. The company's survived this long without it." The man at the machines was still patting himself down in a way that seemed strangely rhythmic, oblivious to all the attention focused on him.

"It's big money," Clooney said importantly. Dinshaw almost turned her head far enough to give him a dirty look. "*Really big* money, if you've got the means for distribution and promotion that we do. It—"

"It may be *really big* money on the corporate level," Dinshaw said, still not looking at Clooney, "but it doesn't seem to be too rewarding on the individual level. Guy doesn't even have change for coffee."

"I'm going to loan him some," Gabe heard himself say, and got up just as Clooney was pulling out the chair.

"Quick thinking, Ludovic," LeBlanc called after him.

"Video reflexes," he called back, and regretted it immediately. Clooney would probably make something out of that to Manny. It was no secret that Clooney was Manny's self-appointed stooge. The only secret was that Clooney apparently didn't know it wasn't a secret. Nonetheless, he seemed unperturbed that he was openly and actively disliked. Perhaps he figured it as jealousy over his frequent raises, or perhaps he was just thick. *Why are people so weird*, Gabe wondered, and tapped Visual Mark on the shoulder.

He turned slowly, as if he were underwater, his faded green eyes seeming to search Gabe out from a distance. "Can I help you?" He put a slight emphasis on the second and fourth words so that it actually came out, "Can *I* help *you*?" Which, Gabe thought later, was not so unreasonable.

"Ah. I thought you looked like you needed, um, change for the machines." Gabe shrugged self-consciously; he could feel the entire Common Room watching.

The man's smile was unexpectedly broad and sunny. "That's a good way to put it. How did you know?"

Gabe had the sensation of going over a mental speed-bump. "Excuse me?"

"My whole life has been, 'Okay, change for the machines.' Every time they bring in a new machine, more change." He leaned a little closer, and Gabe caught a whiff of several smells, none of them cologne. "They're gonna think I spilled my guts to you, and I don't even know you." He paused, thinking. "Do I?"

Hurriedly Gabe pressed some change into his hand. "Here. Maybe you could use some coffee."

The man's head went up and down in a slow, deliberate movement. "God, the truth is running in the gutters today. Karma so thick you can cut it with a knife." He fed the coins Gabe had given him into the coffee-machine slot. "Gets that way every time there's change for the machines." A few moments later he pulled the cup out of the delivery well and toasted Gabe with it. "And the more change, the more you don't know what the fuck is going on. Right?"

"I don't think I can argue with that," Gabe said, backing up a step.

The man winked at him. "Stone-home right."

Feeling as if he'd had his brains stirred with a swizzle stick, Gabe turned around and started to walk away.

He must have stepped directly into the path of her fist, he thought later, adding his own momentum to hers and making the blow more powerful. At the time all he knew was that his head had exploded with color and sensation that did not register as pain until a full second afterwards, so that the secondary hit of his body against the carpeted floor was too slight for notice.

When his vision returned he was looking up at an uneven ring of faces hovering over him. The growing pain in his cheek suddenly skyrocketed to unbearable. He closed his eyes and waited for it to recede, but it wouldn't. It was like being tortured, like having all the free-floating anxiety and hostility in the room poured into one little area of his face. He drifted away from consciousness while someone demanded that everyone move *back*, move *back*, he needed *air*, goddammit.

Sometime after that he heard Dinshaw's slightly nasal voice saying, very seriously, "You could be fired for this. You could be *arrested* for this."

Marly's face appeared before his inner eye, smiling sarcastically. *Are you gonna take that, hotwire? You can't possibly have done anything that bad already today.*

"Bullshit," said an unfamiliar voice, low and gravelly with irritation. "I just got here. Nobody's gonna fire me *this* week."

That's telling them, Gabe thought. He imagined Caritha leaning over him now, her fingers squeezing his arm gently. *Hotwire, you gonna live?*

"Answer me, Gabe! Are you all right?" The hand on his arm squeezed harder, and he opened his eyes.

LeBlanc was bent over him. "Don't move, the doctor's on her way up. You went down like a stone, I think you even went out for a few moments. Did you lose consciousness, can you remember?"

He blinked into the barrage of words, feeling cheated.

"Now if he lost consciousness, how the fuck is he gonna remember it?" asked the strange voice.

Clooney leaned over LeBlanc from behind. "Gabe, do you know where you are?"

Gabe groaned. "I'm here."

"That oughta be good enough for anyone," the strange voice said, from somewhere to his left. "Get him on his feet, he can go another round."

Gabe struggled to sit up, LeBlanc still gripping his upper arm. He brushed her hand away and looked around. He was sitting on the floor, surrounded by everyone except the crazy man. Visual Mark, who had needed change for the machines. No sign of him at all. Gabe touched the side of his face carefully.

"Maybe that's all right where you come from," Dinshaw said, glaring at someone, "but around here, we don't go trying to break people's faces." She glanced briefly in Clooney's direction. "Usually."

"I wasn't gonna break anybody's face." The edge in the voice hinted at a change of heart. Gabe finally focused on a medium-sized, solid-looking person dressed in what seemed to be odds and ends from the various closets of Rude Boys, mystics, and urban guerrillas. Had she slept in those clothes? It must have been a hell of a night. No wonder he'd gone down, he thought; even the dreadlocks looked mean.

The double doors to the Common Room whispered open. He couldn't remember hearing that before, when this woman had come in to punch his face. What had he done, anyway, and why wasn't anyone asking?

"What happened?" The doctor knelt in front of Gabe and held his chin between her fingers, looking into his eyes.

"That *person* hit him," Dinshaw said, pointing at the woman. "She just swung on him and knocked him down."

The doctor looked over her shoulder at the woman, leaning against the coffee machine with her arms folded. The fateful coffee machine, Gabe thought, feeling a sudden absurd urge to laugh.

"It was an accident," she said. "He stepped into the line of fire."

"Really." The doctor sounded amused. Gabe squinted against the light she was shining in his eyes. "Can you open your mouth?"

He managed to part his lips as she felt his jaw carefully. The strange woman moved a little closer, trying to see over the doctor's shoulder, and Gabe thought he saw her face soften a little with concern. She looked substantial enough to have taken that shot and possibly a bit more without as much trouble.

"No dislocation or break that I can feel," the doctor said, "but we'd better take your picture, in case there's a hairline fracture. And I'll give you some 'killers. That's gonna bother you for a while."

Clooney cleared his throat importantly. "Well, Gabe, do you think you can work on 'killers?"

Gabe wanted to give him a dirty look, but the doctor still had a firm grip on his chin. "Just local stuff, Clooney," she said, "transcutaneous patches. Don't worry your little head, nobody's going to get toxed on the job today."

"*Quel fromage,*" said the stranger.

The doctor looked over her shoulder at her again. "You just said, 'What a cheese.' "

"I let it stand."

The double doors to the Common Room whispered open again, and Manny Rivera came in, looking slightly hurried and rumpled. He paused inside the entrance, forcing the doors to gape around him.

"So *this* is where it's all happening today," he said with false congeniality. Not real emotion but an incredible simulation, Gabe thought, suppressing the urge to laugh again. Manny looked around slowly, as if he were memorizing faces, before his gaze came to rest on him, where he was still sitting on the floor with the doctor holding his chin. The artificial friendliness in Manny's face faded as his eyebrows went up. "Is it physical?" he asked.

"Of *course* it's physical, just *look* at him." The stranger was glaring at Manny as if she wanted a piece of him, too. The crowd around Gabe melted away as everyone else in the room remembered there was someplace else to be. Manny moved away from the doors, releasing them briefly before they flapped open again for the mass emigration. Only the strange woman and the doctor remained where they were.

"It's nice to meet you at last," Manny said to the stranger when the room was empty. "You were always out when I visited EyeTraxx."

"Yah?" The woman tilted her head and frowned at him. "Which one are you, Chang or Rivera?"

The doctor got to her feet. "Downstairs for pictures before you do anything else today," she told Gabe firmly. "Pick up your patches after." She glanced at the woman again and deliberately walked in front of Manny on her way out.

Feeling ridiculous, Gabe pulled himself up on a nearby chair, started to sit, thought better of it, and simply stood, wondering if he could actually get out of the room without further exchange with Manny. But somehow it seemed unfair to leave the woman, whoever she was, to face Manny alone. Even if she had hit him.

Manny turned a mildly bewildered smile-frown on him. "And what happened to you?"

"I hurt my face," Gabe said through his swollen jaw. It came out sounding more like *I hate I fashe*.

"Well." Manny's brow wrinkled with a show of concern. "I presume we're still on for lunch?"

"Shertainly," Gabe said, nodding quickly.

"Good. That's good." Manny gave the woman a sidelong

glance and left, marching through the center of the double doors, which promptly flew open and closed behind him, as if they understood their role in terms of his authority.

Unsure of what else to do, Gabe tried to smile at the woman with the still-functioning half of his mouth, to show her there were no hard feelings, while he waited for her to say something like, *Sorry I hit you*, or *You would have been within your rights to say something*, or even, *Does it hurt much?*

Instead, she turned away to pour coins into the nearest cold-drink machine and hit one of the buttons with the same fist she had used on him. A can rumbled down into the delivery well, and she picked it up, her fingers almost circling it entirely. She had big hands. No long red claws.

She paused and stared at him as if she were surprised he was still there.

"Why the fuck didn't you watch where you were going?"

Without waiting for an answer, she strode out of the Common Room, swinging around the left-hand door and giving it a shove as if it hadn't opened widely enough.

10

He knew trying to phone out was as futile as trying to walk out, but he'd had to make the attempt anyway. It was logged on the record of activity now, and Rivera would have something to say about it. But then, Rivera had probably been expecting it. The last surprise he'd given Rivera was the double cross; there wasn't going to be another one.

Keely shifted on the couch, putting a cushion under his knees and an extra pillow under his head. The corporate-issue mattress had been a little softer than what he was used to. So were the amenities; even the fresh-air-scented clothes they'd left for him were as soft as a baby blanket. *Cush* was the word, except for the extra-hard stuff on the phone line.

With a little concentrated effort, he should have been able to get around that, but the key word there was *concentrated*, or to be more precise, *concentration*. He just didn't have any. His mind was fogged over, in a very funny way. He felt alert enough, but his ambition was gone.

This was not exactly mysterious. Rivera had seen to it personally that he was fed and watered in this fancy stable, after he'd beefed up the watchdog program. The effects of whatever had been in the food or water or both would wear off eventually, certainly in time for the full overhaul of the security system Rivera had said he wanted. Along with a number of other things. Rivera was expecting plenty out of him. The only thing that really surprised him was that Rivera hadn't already had an in-house pet hacker to call his own.

But then, if he'd had, he wouldn't have needed to pay someone to crack EyeTraxx.

Keely looked over at the nine-screen dataline. The programs popping on and off barely registered with him. Occasionally he used the remote to turn up the sound on something that looked interesting, but everything took too much effort to follow. He wondered idly what Rivera had given him—mild

Blank? Or just a garden-variety Thorazine derivative? Whatever it was, it was clever. He could think all he wanted, even dream up whole programs, but when he tried to do anything more complicated than press a button, the system failed. Not enough RAM, he thought with bitter amusement. Or too much RAM allotted to pure processing.

Jones was probably dead about it, dead several times over. Trying to *deal with it*. Because, as all therapy victims knew, it was not what happened, it was how you *dealt with it*. Thanks, brother, you're a big fucking help.

Not that he was going to win the Einstein Award for Smart Thinking himself. He wasn't sure which was more stupid—trying an end run around Rivera, or throwing in with him in the first place.

He'd sworn he wouldn't get involved with industrial espionage; in the past he'd turned down plenty of other offers from middle-management sharks looking for a way to turbo out of the corporate pack. But Rivera had interested him. Maybe because he'd been getting bored, or maybe because he'd felt the need to show Jones that B&E could be useful beyond personal gratification. Yah, play the big man for a dead man. The need to posture had gotten him more than he'd bargained for. Shit.

The fresh-air aroma from his shirt came up strong as he rolled over onto his side. Somehow he'd put disaster porn on the top-middle screen, and they were running the *Twenty-Five Worst Air Crashes* series. Pretty disgusting. He would change it as soon as he could muddle through a decision as to what to put on instead. Today was not his day for decisions. He hadn't been doing too well in that area lately anyway; his decision to hack Hall Galen Enterprises for Rivera had been the start of a sequence of bad career moves. So to speak.

Maybe if he'd known that Rivera had been Diversifications, he would have given him a hot dose of the Fish instead of service with a smile. But Rivera had been well shielded, communicating through an anonymous email-drop. They used the same one later to catch the data hacked out of HG.

Not an easy hack, but a pretty safe one, routed through a tangle of different nodes; in case HG detected anything, the cutoff would kick in on all the nodes simultaneously, frustrating even the swiftest trace-and-freeze. Of course, that had meant he couldn't access the data during the transfer, and Rivera was the only one with entry to the email-drop. Or so Rivera had thought. He had honored Rivera's request in letter but not in spirit, piggybacking a small catch-and-copy on the channel into the drop. If Rivera was stupid enough to think he would leave himself totally ignorant of what they were hacking, then Rivera deserved to get hacked himself, which was what he'd had in mind all along.

What the hell. The guy was a fucking thief, a pampered corporate thief who couldn't even do his own dirty work, and his mistake was trusting another thief. While his own mistake, Keely reflected ruefully, was believing that Rivera couldn't do *any* dirty work. And believing that everything Rivera said *wasn't* a fucking lie. *Yah, I'm after financial records; I want to know if this company's teetering and what it would take to buy them out.* That was a good one, just because it was so typical. Or maybe it hadn't been a lie, maybe that had been all Rivera had thought he was going to get.

The socket stuff must have been the first shit to hit the Rivera fan, so to speak, which had probably made it that much easier for Rivera to be so openhanded. Bearer-chips waiting in this or that electronic teller. He'd spent the chips happily enough and bided his time until Rivera closed the E-mail drop, which would trigger the catch-and-copy to zap its contents directly and untraceably to him.

Rivera's final message containing the promised bonus had come just before the C&C. The bonus had turned out to be the specs for Sam's system.

When he'd decrypted the data and seen that wild little nanothing you could make from an old insulin or endocrine pump, he'd had a mental blowout. He hated Diversifications from the bottom of his heart, them and their overpriced crap ripped from hacker designs, repackaged and foisted off on a gullible public as hot, new product. Like the Dodge-M program, a little facade the busy career person could stick on the electronic mailbox; made it look like you hadn't picked up your email when you already had—that was nothing more than a fooler loop, dumbed down enough so that it responded only to the E-mail system and called *dedicated* so the public would think of it as reliable instead of an idiot release of a smart program.

And then the C&C had come in and his blowout had become a meltdown. Sockets, *fucking brain sockets*, and he'd given it to Rivera on a silver platter in exchange for a set of specs Sam had given him for free. Rivera had had the benefit of that for fucking *weeks*, while he'd been sitting with his thumb up his ass figuring he was dealing with some CPA whose idea of porn was a stolen spreadsheet.

He'd begun to wonder then if Diversifications hadn't cooked up the nano-system just for hackers, as a decoy. Maybe there was a sleeping load in the specs, and as soon as you ran them on your system, the alarm went out. Which meant Sam could be in danger.

A fast Dr. Fish search routine had traced her to the Ozarks. He still didn't know how the Fish had done it, and there hadn't been time to find out. Apparently she was safe, though. Safer than he'd been.

The sleeping load in the copied files hadn't awakened until he'd zapped the stuff to the clinic, after he'd divided another copy between Sam and Fez. The clinic had been his final stupid brainstorm. Later he thought he must have gone over the edge, thinking how it would be a great case of giving Diversifications a taste of their own medicine, see how they'd like finding out some cheap feel-good clinic had beat them out just by modifying some already existing implants and making them over into sockets.

Sockets from a feel-good joint, not some antiseptic, respectable corp like Diversifications—the government would have had a ban on them before you could say, well, *feel-good*. Not a whole lot of profit opportunity there for Diversifications. Wow, Rivera, what a bad bounce.

He couldn't say what had made him decide to split another copy between Sam and Fez any more than he could have said what they would do with it once they got together and figured out what they had, but it had seemed like a good idea at the time. Backup in case something went wrong.

And he'd still been sitting at his laptop feeling like he'd bitten the biter when the cops had popped his lock and taken him straight to Rivera for a deal. A new deal.

You go state's evidence against the clinic, and nobody'll charge you for hacking Diversifications and violating confidential medical records in the process. How does that sound? Rivera hadn't had to explain how it could fall that way—there was no record of the email-drop, and since Diversifications had finessed EyeTraxx out of Hall Galen Enterprises weeks before, he was the only one holding a bag, and the bag was labeled *Felony Hack*. If they prosecuted the clinic with him as state's evidence, it would muzzle them and keep the sockets under wraps until Diversifications was ready to go public with their hot new development. And under the current state's-evidence law, he was bound over to the victim—i.e., Diversifications —for reparation service, in exchange for the felony charge being dropped. Reparation service didn't usually amount to house arrest in a corporate penthouse, but he imagined Diversifications' lawyers had been very persuasive with the judge. The meds had clinched it; if Visual Mark's medical records hadn't been in the data, he'd have been able to get a public defender to knock it down to a misdemeanor. But once you busted someone's meds, you might as well just bend over and kiss your ass good-bye. Even other hackers had no sympathy for you. Too many people had suffered from having their meds used against them some years back, during the Age of the Retrovirus.

The only satisfaction he'd gotten out of the whole thing was seeing the discomfiture on Manny Rivera's face when he realized the project that had taken the construction of a fancy installation in Mexico had been up and running in a lousy little feel-good mill with no amenities, no big salaries, and no Manny Rivera to boss it. Might take a while for the corporate brass to figure that out, but sooner or later someone was going to take note of the fact. And when they did—well, it was already too late for himself, but he could enjoy knowing that he'd shot Rivera with a sleeping load of a different but no less volatile kind.

He glanced over at the phone again. It might have been imagination, but he thought he felt a little more competent. Rest a bit longer and maybe he'd be ready to try canoodling around the outcall block again.

Or maybe a miracle would happen and Visual Mark, Diversifications Guinea Pig Number One, would come back and agree to get a message out for him. He'd been too dumbed down to ask before. Not that Visual Mark had seemed a whole lot better himself, but at least he was free. For the time being, anyway. Damn but he had to admire Diversifications' strategy on this. Pushing the implants by way of the artificial reality of rock videos—the ground swell of prelegal demand alone would probably kick things over in the States. Fuck the bribes to the AMA and the FDSA and the politicians—the vidiots would kill for it.

Truth to tell, he'd have killed for it himself. He wanted it as bad as everybody else was going to when the news broke, he couldn't deny that. He just didn't like the idea that Diversifications was in the driver's seat. All he'd wanted to do was steal the wheel and toss it out for grabs.

Nice try. He would remember it for as long as he could, because he had a feeling that by the time he saw anything besides the inside of this penthouse again, he might have forgotten all about it.

He looked at the phone again. Just a few more minutes and he was sure he'd be up for another try. Another wave of fresh-air aroma from his corporate-issue shirt hit him, and he dozed.

11

She could see why they called it a pit. It was cush; even the walls were carpeted. Down at the other end was enough junk for a personal gym—treadmill, stair-climber, a rack of pulleys with assorted handles, scaffold and platform assemblies, stacks of modular units that would probably make better furniture than what she had in her apartment. Hanging from the ceiling was a flying harness complete with joystick, in case she needed to levitate. They seemed to have thought of everything here, just like the Beater had said, and if you didn't see it, all you had to do was get your ass down to Central Stores.

The system was equally elaborate. It had a flatscreen as well as a headmount for the state-of-the-art hotsuit, a full sound system, and a keyboard about as wide as the farthest reach she could make stretching out both arms without locking her elbows. Plenty of capacity—two dozen programs in volatile storage wouldn't have taxed it. The phone was built in along with the controls for the room, including the printlock on the door, which she had left open. She could close it now just by touching a small lighted panel, but she didn't. The idea of being shut in completely had zero appeal.

She looked up at the open door, as though Mark might pop his head in at any moment and say, *Wanna jam?* And then, like the old days, they'd play a few rounds of Dueling Videos. *Run this one, lover. Can you top it?*

Not today. He'd about left a hole in the air after she'd popped the corporate stud—damfool just stepped between them at the wrong moment, and she hadn't been able to pull her punch. Christ knew where *that* clown's mind had been. There'd been a certain small amount of sour satisfaction in knocking him down—in knocking anyone down at that point—but it had dissipated right after. Guy looked even more lost than Mark, if that was possible.

Figured, though; go to get a few hard answers out of Mark,

and he slipped out from under. It was the story of their life. Not the same as the story of their lives. They had their lives, and then they had this overlapping life, two circles intersecting each other, with the eye-shaped common ground between them. Sometimes she thought she knew that territory better than her own mind; other times she was sure it was a frontier only Mark knew. And then there were times like today, when neither one of them seemed to have any idea which end was up or which way was out.

Mark had always been a flake. By the time she'd managed to crack the video business, she'd practically memorized most of his work. He'd already been Visual Mark by then; it should have been Visualizing Mark. It was as if he had a pipeline to some primal dream spot, where music and image created each other, the pictures suggesting the music, the music generating the pictures, in a synesthetic frenzy.

Synner. Yah. The Beater's cutie-pie-tech term. If a synner was someone who continually hallucinated, then Mark was the original. Sometimes it seemed that when he looked at her, just looked, he had to search her out of some kind of wilder, larger, more baroque vision his brain had laid over the world. She'd wondered how long that could go on with him, how long it would be until some kind of critical threshold was reached inside that picture-filled brain, and what would happen then.

Twenty-umpt years ago that hadn't been a big worry. It had been a vague, not terribly real future they hadn't bothered to think about. Mark hadn't been burning out then, and she hadn't had crazy debts the size of Canada from the goddamn father who'd booted her ass into the Boston streets at fucking fourteen and years later took such a long fucking expensive uninsured time dying that the hospital had hunted her down with a court order to pay it off.

The Beater's old career had started to drag, but that hadn't been so real then, either. The Beater had still been young enough to feel immortal, at least on his better days. It was all, *Wow, if we don't slow down, we're gonna die before we get old*, except somehow it hadn't happened that way. So they'd all assumed it never would, not dying, not getting old—hell, not even growing up.

She looked around the pit. Definitely a place for grown-ups. Either they'd all gotten old, or they'd died and gone to video hell. Maybe both, and not necessarily in that order.

Someone was standing in the open doorway. The Beater.

The guy in the drab suit had only a vestige of the gong-banging wild animal she'd known when she'd first gotten into video. The straight chin-length hair had been slicked back, and she could see there was more gray among the brown. For that confidence-inspiring corporate look, no doubt. Most of the people he'd be moving among now wouldn't remember him from his performance days—his *real* performance days, when there had still been plenty of concerts, and video had been the come-on for the studio releases and the live events, not an end in itself.

If anyone had remembered him, Gina doubted that all the corporate grey in the world would have put him over. *Hey, kids, this guy used to wear more paint than the Sistine Chapel and still holds the world distance record for projectile vomiting from a tour-bus window.*

Just seeing him now, you could tell the party was definitely over, had been for some time. Everything's business, let's work again like we worked last century.

Did he know about the night-court follies starring Mark? Gina doubted it. But he had to know something; he had to know why Mark would have been with Galen and his twitch and Rivera. Maybe. The way the Beater told it, his new position at Diversifications was supposed to be something roughly equal to Rivera's. *Yah, I'll still be your boss, you just gotta show up washed.*

Yah. Twenty-umpt years and that was the first time the word *boss* had come up in polite or even impolite conversation, even back when there'd been half a dozen of them cranking video, before Galen had taken over and pushed the others out. And if you couldn't tell who was the real boss, you were probably flatline.

"Pretty posh, huh?" he said. "May I come in?"

She folded her arms. "Sure. Fly on down."

He started toward the little platform lift.

"I said, *fly*."

He stopped and looked at her.

"Go on, jump. Or I'll drag your ass back up there and push it off."

He leaned on the rail. "Tell you what—I'll just get down any old way I can, and you can take a swing at me. I won't even duck."

She grinned flatly. "Heard about that already, did you."

"You've made your usual good impression, yes." He stepped

onto the lift and pressed the down button. "Manny Rivera told me that a chemical leash would be available if you got completely out of control."

"Chicken-fucking-shit. He didn't say dick at the time."

"I'm your supervisor, I'm supposed to take care of your misbehavior." The lift thumped to a stop, and the Beater stepped off. All fifty-plus years were showing hard on him today, mostly in the slumping posture of his softening body and in the hint of jowls on his oblong face. She had an urge to rumple his hair, but there was so much lacquer on it, it would probably break off in her hand.

"Supervisor. It's come to that already." She sat down and put her feet up on the console. "What have they got here, a demerit system? Five black marks and I don't get my fucking Christmas bonus?"

"Stop it," he said quietly, resting one haunch on the desk a careful distance from her. "I didn't want this any more than you did."

"Hey, you had no control, right?" She spread her hands. "They musta given you a fat little package for your share of EyeTraxx, so if you don't like what you see, you can walk away. Not like some of us."

"Where would I go?" The Beater's face was expressionless. "I don't have enough to start up a new production company, not with what it takes today, and I couldn't deliver the artists if I did have it. Our groups are contractually bound to Diversifications now. And I can just see me strolling the Mimosa or hunting the clubs looking for talent. Sign with me, boys and girls, I'm real old, and I know what I'm doing." He sighed. "It worked out shitty. Go with the money you'll get. Maybe you'll pay off your father before you get to be my age."

"Except for Mark, I'd walk," she said. "They could put me in fucking debtors' prison, and I'd walk anyway. Except for Mark." She gestured at the pit. "How long do you think he's gonna make it in a place like this?"

There was a funny change in the Beater's face then, as if a wall had gone up somewhere inside him. "Maybe a lot longer than you think."

"Yah." She offered him a leg. "Pull this one, it's got bells on it."

"Shit, how long do you think he'd last anyway?" the Beater said, disgusted. "You've seen what he's been doing lately—the same goddamn thing over and over, stealing from himself.

We had to redo most of the last video he made behind his fucking back, or don't you remember?" He leaned forward. "*He* doesn't remember. He doesn't even know. Half the time he doesn't know where the fuck he is or how he got there. He needs to be taken care of."

"And Diversifications is gonna look after him like a *mother*."

"They've got ways to help him."

Gina's mouth dropped open. "Shit, what did you do, put him in for implants? You gonna turn him into that corporate vegetable I popped in the goddamn company cafeteria, make him deliver *good product*? You're his friend, shit, he *lived* for you, he saw fucking *visions* for you, and you quit on the music and you quit on him, too." She stood up and grabbed the front of his crisp white shirt. "I oughta give you the beating I was saving for him."

He pried her hand off him and held it. "Badass Gina Aiesi, always looking for a head to punch. I can see why you'd want to punch mine, but not Mark's."

She gazed at him for a moment and then laughed without humor. "I thought so. You *don't* know."

"What." His expression didn't change, but the grip on her hand tightened a bit.

"Mark made an appearance in court night before last. With Boy-Wonder Galen, Frankenstein Joslin, and Manny Fucking Rivera. Do the words *state's evidence* do anything for you?"

The Beater was mystified. "Mark was state's evidence?"

"No, that part was played by an unknown," she said sarcastically, slipping her hand out of his. "But Mark was in on it. I thought you were, too. Guess not. Maybe you want to talk to Rivera about your *career path*. Isn't that what all you hot executives talk about when you lunch it up?"

Now he looked troubled. "Mark in court . . . with Galen, Joslin, and Rivera . . ."

"It was some big deal. Instant gag order. Unlawful congress with a machine."

The Beater snapped to attention. She shrugged at his alarmed expression.

"Maybe Joslin was fucking an earth-mover, and they caught her at it. You figure it out, son." She paused. "*Can* you figure it out?"

"Some of it," he said slowly. "I think."

She grabbed his shirt again, closer to the collar this time. "Then you better fucking tell me what's going on."

He shook his head, pulling her hand off. "Not till I find something out for sure. I'll talk to Rivera." He started to get up, and she seized the waistband of his pants, yanking hard.

"*Fuck* Rivera and his mother, too, my man, you oughta be talking to *me*!"

The Beater pulled away from her, shoving her back into her chair. "Goddammit, Gina, will you grow the fuck up? What do you think this is, a hit-and-run? We lost EyeTraxx, it's over! The corporations took over the world, that's not my fault! Mark spent the last twenty-five years toxed, and now he's paying the price for it. Nothing stays the same, Gina, nothing works forever. If I don't like it, that's too bad. If *you* don't like it, that's *still* too bad."

She stared up at him darkly. "All I wanna know is just what it is I don't like. And how bad is 'too bad.' "

The Beater pressed his lips together. "Just do the videos. Just do the videos and hope for the best."

He stood on the lift with his back to her.

She sat for a while, thinking nothing, the pit so much empty space around her. In the old days at EyeTraxx, they'd have killed to get something like this. Or the Beater might have. Operating out of a converted warehouse hadn't made much difference to the videos. Sometimes they'd all been practically on top of each other, especially when the groups came in. Valjean and that cape, the crazy skiffle-revival group, the Little Cares; Vlad had done most of their videos, usually bouncing one of his seven kids on his knee while they all watched a rough cut on flatscreen. Galen had laid Vlad off early, and when Vlad had gone, he'd taken the Little Cares with him in a show of solidarity that had lasted through one more video, a gypsy production, and when it had failed, they'd all dropped out of sight.

Kim had gone next, Galen insisting they were losing money like crazy, and Jolene had stomped out after her. Kim had taken off for parts unknown, but Jolene was still around, picking up the work wherever she could. Guerstein had been Galen's final cut, Guerstein who did news like other people did dope, and that left just the three of them, the way it had been in the beginning, except that someone else owned them now, and Galen partitioned the warehouse and rented out three-fourths of it for storage. And that had lasted something over a year before the real end came.

It was strange, but sometimes she couldn't remember what it had been like; it was almost as if those years had never happened. Except for Mark; that was where the mileage really showed.

Just do the videos and hope for the best.

Sure. Do the videos. Do it *their* way. She looked around the pit. This was a place to make commercials, and fool with feature releases, and maybe play a few nifty games, but it wasn't rock'n'roll. Rock'n'fuckin'roll. Jesus. Yah, what the hell, we'll just put *that* in a nice clean box and keep it business, keep it all business, and maybe she'd go out of her mind in the nice clean box.

Grow the fuck up. She might give the Beater that one, but she wouldn't give him the rest of it, at least not until she knew what it was. If you had to surrender, you at least ought to get to know what you were surrendering to. They owed her that much, Mark most of all.

Just do the videos. Hope for the best. Wanna jam? Can you top it, lover? Not today.

She had just stepped out into the hall when the door directly across from her own opened, and she was face-to-face with the guy she'd punched. He froze, staring at her as if he thought she was going to pop him again. That was a good one. Or maybe he wanted to pick a fight, get his own back on her. He didn't look like the type, but you never knew. Maybe she should offer him a free shot.

Or maybe she should pop him again, for staring. "You want something?"

He shook his head wordlessly. His face looked pretty swollen, and there were three or four flesh-tone squares spotting his cheek.

"You know you can get toxed on that shit?" she said.

He blinked at her uncomprehendingly, and she tapped her own cheek.

"Stuff builds up in your system, and you get off. Watch out, it can make you a little stupid."

Now he looked thoughtful; probably trying to decide whether he was toxed or not. Life was pretty fucking hard when you couldn't tell the difference.

"Wait!" he called.

She turned to him disinterestedly. "Yah?"

"I was just wondering . . ." He came out a little farther into the hall, touching his wounded face. "I was just wondering why you hit me."

"It was a mistake, all right? You got in the way."

"I see." He shrugged. "Well, then, why did you want to hit the other guy? Or anybody?"

"Is that supposed to be important to you?"

"I thought that since I wasn't going to get an apology, I might get an explanation."

Gina laughed. "You want a lot, don't you? Homeboy, you just keep asking. Who knows, maybe someday someone'll put an egg in your beer."

He almost looked like he understood. Hell, maybe he did. She headed toward the elevators.

12

"You're good," Manny said, resting a hand on the covered tray in front of him on the table. "There's really no question about that, never has been. You do good commercials, but you're not doing enough of them."

Sitting across from him, Gabe eyed the cover on his own tray. You didn't eat while Manny talked. First, Manny had to explain to you why he would sully his lunch hour with a subordinate. LeBlanc had once suggested making lunch with Manny an Olympic event. *We'll call it the biathlon—first, you see how much torture you can absorb, then you see how much food you can eat in his presence before you vomit. Right? We need that, right?*

Gabe had to press a finger on his injured cheek to keep from laughing. *Watch out, it can make you a little stupid.* He shifted in his chair, accidentally pressing his cheek harder.

"And checking the time logged on each assignment, anyone can see you're taking too long on the commercials you *do* produce." Manny stared at him evenly, waiting for an answer.

"I'll try to pick up the pace," he managed, barely moving his lips. His voice sounded strange and distant, as if he were speaking from behind a character facade in a wannabee program.

"Gabe. Trying isn't good enough." Manny shook his head slowly. Like a bad actor in a camp movie, Gabe thought; the whole situation seemed more and more unreal. Except for the throbbing in his face, which had begun again in hot earnest. "You're just going to have to *do* it, before the next quarterly figures go Upstairs. I can just about guarantee that when they graph your time spent against your number of completed assignments, they'll start talking personal audit. That's everything you've got in memory, on chip, in long-term storage. They'll want to see it all, and they'll question every requisition you've made in the past two years. You'll have to explain and justify everything, completed projects, fragments, the whole thing."

Manny paused to let him digest that one, but all he could think about now was the aroma that had started to seep out from under the covered tray in front of him. It turned his stomach. He slipped another patch out of his shirt pocket and applied it to his cheek. The throbbing receded after a few moments, but the smell of the food became even more nauseating. Something fried, he thought, besides himself. *Watch out, it can make you a little stupid.*

"And if you're thinking of dumping everything you have, you'd better reconsider." Manny leaned forward, bracketing his own tray with his forearms. "As low as your numbers are, a bare cupboard will look very suspicious. They could get the idea you've been working on some project of your own, unrelated to the job. I don't have to tell you what will happen if they think you've been abusing corporate equipment." Manny's serious expression changed suddenly. "Is everything all right in your personal life?"

Gabe winced. What was he supposed to say? *Well, let's see, this morning, my wife left me, and then I came to work and got punched in the face by a complete stranger. Now I'm apparently toxed on painkillers I shouldn't be toxed on, and they've made me a little stupid. Did you mean besides that?*

He became aware of the rather long moment that had passed since Manny's question and shrugged awkwardly. "Everyone has problems."

"Yes, I suppose," Manny said. "But I don't think you'd care to work under the conditions of a personal audit. You'd be monitored every moment. Even while you were sketching out the barest scenario, they'd be listening and watching on-line. Most people would find it impossible to work under those conditions, but the Upstairs Team would be expecting you to up your productivity. The Upstairs Team does not understand the creative individual, you see. Therefore, it's the responsibility of the creative individual to adjust, to be creative enough to learn how to play the game their way."

The game. *House of the Headhunters* rose up in his thoughts, fragmenting his concentration. He'd put on far too many patches trying to kill the pain in his face, he realized. That was what she had meant, the woman who hit him. A *little* stupid,

that was a good one. Or as Marly would have said, *A little
stupid, hotwire? Looks to me like they broke the stupid-stick
on you.*

Manny was looking at him oddly now, and he realized he
was smiling. He turned it into a grimace and touched his face.

"Clooney told me Gina Aiesi hit you, is that right?" Manny
said, resting one hand on the cover of his tray.

"Accident," Gabe said. "Just one of those dumb freak accidents."

"I see." Manny toyed with the handle on the cover. "You'll
take what I've told you seriously, now, won't you, Gabe? I'd
hate to see one of our best people get into difficulties after
such a long career." He hesitated, and Gabe waited for him
to hint that perhaps he needed a little consultation with Medical on the possibility of implants to improve his concentration.
Instead Manny uncovered his tray, signaling the onset of actual
eating.

Gabe followed suit and then sat there with his numbed,
swollen jaw, looking down at the pork chop, the mashed po-
tatoes, the corn on the cob, and the mixture of celery and
carrot sticks.

"Ah," Manny said. "Direct from our executive kitchen. Rediscovery Cuisine is the one food trend I can really get my
teeth into. So to speak." He favored Gabe with a cordial smile
as he picked up the knife and fork and began to saw away on
the pork chop.

The thugs that had been waiting in the alley, if it was an
alley, came at them with the mindless savagery of machines
set on *kill*. The program carried him through the motions. At
least it wouldn't let him ruin the choreography, and the hotsuit
compensated as much as it could for his lack of physical ability.
But it wasn't up to his usual standards of verisimilitude.

Perhaps, he thought as Caritha took down some of the attackers with sting-shots from the cam, it was all the painkiller
coming between him and the illusion. He was too aware of the
sensors plucking at his nerves, delivering the simulated sensations of punches and kicks, both giving and getting, with
more of the former, of course. The program didn't have a
masochism setting.

What the hell, he thought, watching his fist smash dead
center in the head of a shadowy figure. He had a little more

experience with this than he'd had a couple of hours before.
His face throbbed against the inside of the headmount, but
the feeling was distant and painless, less immediate than the
sensation of impact the sensors put to his knuckles and ran up
his arm. When you hit someone, you were supposed to feel it
yourself, after all, though the program made tough stuff out of
you—taking a punch or giving one, you could just shake it
right off. Like Marly; he had a glimpse of her jabbing her fist
into a thug's midsection, doubling him over so she could give
him a knee in the face. He fell back as another one threw
himself at her from the side, slamming them both into a wall.
They went down, and a moment later the thug was flying
backwards, arms windmilling. Gabe stepped to meet him and
managed a fair imitation of a karate chop to the back of his
neck.

Marly saluted and then looked alarmed. Before she could
shout a warning, he took a giant step to the right and clothes-
lined the killer that had been about to take him down from
behind. He turned to see how Caritha was doing.

She was having a ridiculous tug-of-war over the cam with
the last of their attackers. Forcing his arms up high, she tried
to kick him in the crotch, but he danced out of the way, still
keeping a grip on the cam. Gabe took a step forward, but
Marly was already flying past him. She tackled the thug from
the side, and they all fell to the ground together with the two
women on top. Gabe took another step toward them and then
looked around.

The alley was empty again, except for the trash. Dutifully
the hotsuit gave him the sensation of cold chills and goose
bumps. He stared down the length of the alley, trying to discern if there might be one more. He didn't know; they were
on blind-select. Cautiously he turned toward Caritha and
Marly, who were still busy pounding the thug into the ground,
and then felt the presence at his left elbow. One more, of
course, the old just-when-you-thought-you-were-done-you-
got-a-surprise-fist-in-the-face ramadoola. He braced himself,
and his face gave a sudden throb shot through with a sharp
pain. The sensors in the headmount were far more limited than
those in the 'suit, but he didn't think he could take even the
limited illusion of another punch in the face.

He came around swinging fast and hard and felt the peculiar
shock of connecting with nothing. He turned around quickly,

fists up, but there was nobody to hit, no one next to him at all, but the sense of another presence remained strong. His jaw was throbbing nastily now, anticipating the blow.

"Alone at last," Marly said, looking up and down the alley. The spot where she and Caritha had been beating up the attacker was also empty.

"Solidified holo," Caritha said knowingly, brushing herself off. She examined the cam for damage. "The only place it's actually solidified is in your mind. They must have shot our retinas when we came in, ran an analysis of our wavelengths, got the subliminal code."

"I hate that," Marly said. "I just hate it when they use your mind against you like that. If we'd had the savvy to walk through here with our eyes closed, they never could have touched us, but once you've seen one of them, the illusion's burned in, even if you close your eyes after that. You gotta fight 'em."

"*You* walk through a dark alley with your eyes closed if you want," Caritha said. "They'd have just had something a little more substantial waiting for us."

"Maybe," Marly said, massaging her knuckles, "but I hate giving them the satisfaction of knowing they made me hurt myself instead of them having to do it themselves."

"You want a fair fight, become a boxer." Caritha started up the alley, and Marly followed, beckoning to Gabe.

He looked around quickly and then found it, a strange spot about the size of a dime floating at the limit of his peripheral vision. Glitch in the program, he thought, irritated.

"Hey, hotwire!" Marly called, invisible now in the darkness ahead of him. "You comin', or you waitin' for the night nurse to come out and collect you for your bed in the ward?"

The glitch floated dizzily, then sailed around him to plant itself on his right. He turned again just in time to see it shrink sharply, as if it were receding up the alley after Marly and Caritha. His jaw sent a spear of pain all the way to his temple. He winced, automatically putting a hand to his face and making contact with the outside of the headmount, ruining the illusion completely.

"Uh . . . I'll meet you later," he called. "Disconnect."

He was about to stash the saved program in the lockbox under the desk when it occurred to him to check the system's security status.

Everything was normal, no intrusion had been registered, which could have meant nothing. It was the worst-kept secret of the computer age that B&E programs outdid watchdogs regularly. His own imagination getting the better of him, he decided. He was too toxed to concentrate on the program, but he could jump at shadows. As if Manny could spy on him without his knowledge. The only person he could think of who was capable of a hack like that was Sam. Or some of her friends.

But someone else *had* been there in the program. The thought refused to go away, and he leaned on the console, trying to think through the pain in his jaw that also refused to go away. It didn't make any sense. Neither Manny nor anyone else could audit him without an official corp requisition for an audit program, which would automatically notify him he had company. And without an audit requisition, the system was impenetrable. Was *supposed* to be impenetrable, nominally to preserve employee confidentiality but actually to discourage in-house hacking.

Someone else *had* been there in the program, his mind insisted. Whether that made no sense or all the sense in the world, someone—or something—had been there. Possibly a hacker cracking in from outside and moving on to some other part of the system when nothing of real interest showed up.

His inner eye could see the glitch-spot zipping away up the alley. Not winking out or closing, but moving away. Going to Marly and Caritha. As if it found them more interesting than it did him. But this time he hadn't left the program running along without him; if the glitch had indicated an intruder, the intruder had been thrown out when he'd ended the run.

He put a standard breach-of-security report on the flat-screen, started to fill it out, and then paused. If he reported his suspicions, he'd have to provide a copy of the simulation he'd been running. And wouldn't Manny be interested in *that*.

Groaning, he sat back in the chair. He could just shoot himself and get it over with, that would take care of everything. Shit. Call it a hacker. A hacker wouldn't get far; Diversifications' security would either throw the hacker out, or lock on for a trace and subsequent arrest. Either way he wouldn't be involved. Even if a hacker got something from him, what use could it possibly have been? *House of the Headhunters* had been so generally available, even collectors didn't care that it was out of release, and it wasn't like he was sitting on a pile of sensitive information.

Forget it, he told himself; it felt sick and eerie, but it was ultimately nothing and would stay nothing. Probably never happen again. He put another patch on his face, and then another before he filled out a sick-leave form and zapped it to Medical. As long as he was getting nowhere, he might as well go home and *be* nowhere.

Watch out. It can make you a little stupid.

Watch out—

He ran a hand over his face, frowning at the memory of Gina Aiesi as he inched forward in the rental.

—it can make you a little stupid.

If that meant not having more sense than to get on La Cienega in the middle of the afternoon, she'd been right. God, when was the city going to admit defeat, scrap GridLid, and lay new lines with improved security and better transmission times, he wondered. Part of an illegal message that had leaked through GridLid's blocks was still showing at the top of the nav screen: *Why don't you just park this toy and take a walk? The Doctor feels you don't walk enou*

That would be Dr. Fish. One of Sam's heroes. He shook his head. Sam's admiration for outlaws might have been incomprehensible, until you factored in Catherine. With good guys like Catherine, you didn't need bad guys, and bad guys would look pretty good.

He played with the screen as he advanced little by little toward the freeway. At this rate, he would probably get home at his usual time, even if the freeways were half-decent. He could have waited out the rest of the day on a cot in Medical and made better time during the traffic-restricted rush hour. He could have stuck with the simulation and not noticed the day passing, except to take short breaks to put on more 'killers. Maybe with enough 'killer in his system, he might even have felt like doing one of those loathsome commercial spots. BodyShields: protection from everything except—what? Clogs? Hackers?

The nav unit beeped to notify him that Olympic was passable, if he wanted to take it down to the San Diego Freeway. He put on the audio, which informed him of the same thing in an even, cordial male voice, and then went on to warn the rest of the mobile public away from La Cienega.

It took him ten minutes to squeeze into the correct lane to make the turn. Down at Olympic a cop on a scooter was diverting all traffic from the lane onto Olympic. GridLid was supposed to relieve cops of most traffic duty; Gabe could read the disgust in the cop's face as she waved him onto the cross-street.

He got almost all the way to the southern edge of Westwood before he had to come to a complete stop again. Fifteen minutes later GridLid announced that high traffic concentration had brought Olympic to a standstill, stay on La Cienega, which was now moving fairly well, or try Venice Boulevard.

Gabe peered through the scratched plastic windshield at the sky, expecting to see a heli circling overhead. Nothing; not even a rich-commuters transport heading for Topanga or Malibu. GridLid's voice started to repeat the warning about Olympic, and he shut off the audio. It all felt too much like the story of his life, and the last thing he wanted was GridLid rubbing his nose in it.

Near the old 20th Century-Fox Studios buildings, the halt seemed to be permanent. GridLid sounded apologetic about the multivehicle pileup at the Sepulveda intersection, as if it were their fault somehow. All things considered, it probably was.

Which left him sitting in a cheap rental with a sore nose, Gabe thought, looking at the old buildings. They had been broken up into studio rental space sometime after 20th Century Fox had failed to continue to score interest with the catchy name of Twenty-First Century Fox. Perhaps they should have changed the Fox for something a bit more long-lived. Gabe had always known the place as a cluster of studios; for a short period of time early on in his dubious Diversifications career and even more dubious marriage, he had spent a few hours sharing studio space with another aspiring artist. He'd lost track of Consuela after giving up his half of the studio, but to his surprise the directory sign listed her as still being resident.

On impulse he twisted the wheel hard and pulled into the parking lot just before he would have inched too far past it. The listing indicated she had moved up to a larger studio than the one they had shared, which must have meant she was doing well, even though he couldn't remember seeing her name anywhere. Not that he'd been keeping up. Once he'd given up the studio space, he'd consciously avoided any news from the art world.

She had the back upper room in the largest building now;

to his surprise there were no visible security devices, no guards to challenge him. All he had to do was walk in, go upstairs, and press a small lighted panel next to the door. The panel gave him pause. The usual *Ring for Entry* sign had been replaced with *Come in If You Dare*.

Consuela must be feeling pretty sure of herself, he thought, and for a moment he wasn't sure that he did dare. Then he pressed the panel, and the door swung open silently.

He stepped in and found himself underwater.

Ribbons of seaweed in neon colors undulated lazily upward from the ocean floor, lighting up the semidark with cold fire. Gabe hesitated, letting the door fall shut behind him, and took a step forward. His foot passed through the pale, soft-looking ocean floor and disappeared; he could feel the more conventional floor below, but the illusion never gave way to show it to him. Consuela was doing *awfully* well, he thought; only the very rich and large corps like Diversifications had projectors of this quality.

A luminous purple octopus crawled over the top of a waist-high rock and took a look at him, its arms moving with sensuous grace; a spiny fish floated out of the shadows ahead of him like a dignified airship. He blinked. Not quite a fish—the spines were needles growing out of chips instead of scales. Its enormous brown glass eyes surveyed him with cold-blooded solemnity.

"What do you want?" the fish asked him in the slightly accented female contralto that was still familiar to him.

"Hello, Consuela," he said. "It's me. Gabe Ludovic."

The fish flicked its tail and darted away in a cloud of tiny, sparkling bubbles. Gabe waited; Consuela always had been quirky. Maybe that was the difference between successful artists and himself, the quirk factor. He scored pretty low on that meter.

There was a shimmer in the water, and then a silver shark sailed up and over his head in a wide arc, the muscular body shining. Crushed roses trailed from the jaws. "You've been a stranger," the shark said with Consuela's voice.

"And you've done well," he said, watching the shark roll over and over as it sailed around for another pass over him.

"Sometimes I'd get to wondering whatever the hell happened to you." The shark came around, aimed itself at his face and swooped upward at the last moment. One of the roses drifted down and landed just at his feet. "Pick it up."

Gabe bent and put two fingers around the illusion of stem. A thorn disappeared into the ball of his thumb. He raised his hand, and the rose came with it, moving exactly as if he were really holding it. "That's good, Con."

"Better than that." The crushed petals opened up, and he saw her face within. "Check this."

Blood was trickling from where the thorn had sunk into his flesh. Painless blood. Almost as deadly as bloodless pain, he thought, a bit boggled. "Ouch," he said.

The aristocratic face in the heart of the rose didn't look smug. Consuela had a little too much dignity for that. "Didn't ever expect to see you again. Whatever the hell *did* happen to you, anyway?"

"I don't know," he said. "Things."

"And stuff and people and all like that?" Her smile made her look hard; it always had. She was hard, though. There was something about Consuela that he'd found slightly scary, scary the way an unreal thorn drawing unreal blood from the ball of his thumb was scary. Everything in her was directed one way, into her work, and in that way perhaps she wasn't quite so different from Catherine, and maybe that was what he'd found frightening about her. But Catherine's drive came out as multimillion dollar real estate deals, and Consuela's—

He got up and moved farther into the room, looking around. The ceiling was invisible in shadows above him; he caught a glimpse of a small school of glowing fish moving in jerky choreography, leaving minor, angular trails behind them. The purple octopus was still lazing on the rock, watching him with a gaze so intelligent he squirmed inwardly. One of the long arms lifted and beckoned to him. He went over to the rock slowly; the underwater ambience had seeped into him, taking him over. It wasn't an unpleasant feeling.

"You gave up, didn't you?" the octopus said.

Gabe shrugged, laying the rose across his palm. It was hard to maintain the illusion of holding it without looking at it constantly. "Maybe I just got real. Like they used to say." He gestured at the environment. "Something like this is beyond me. There's not much call for it with commercials, anyway."

"That's shit. There would be, if you did it right. They'll call for anything if you do it right for long enough."

"I never had your drive, Con."

"You did, you just never put it in gear. And you know it." The octopus blinked, furling its tentacles briefly to show the glittering suction cups underneath. "Why'd you think to come here?"

"Happened to be in the neighborhood, thought I'd drop in."

"Bad clog caught you on Olympic?"

He laughed. "How in *hell* did you get a setup like this?"

"Little by little, Gabe. Took years."

"What's wrong with a simple headmount?"

"Not big enough. The *world's* not big enough. If it were, we wouldn't need to make worlds like this."

A skate slipped past him, flicking its tail like a whip, followed by a waving mass of jellyfish in assorted sizes and colors. Gabe ducked reflexively, and one of them dragged its streamers across his shoulder. The barbs on the end struck sparks of light. One of Consuela's inventions. "Are you ever going to put this on-line?" he asked.

"It *is* on-line, for anyone who cares to find it."

"How do you live? I mean, what are you doing for paying work?"

"Sleeping with benefactors."

"Oh."

She laughed heartily, a deep, grand-opera kind of laugh. "Listen, it's not so bad. We're all art lovers, after all." She laughed again. "Do you remember when we used to share space downstairs? You must, you're here. You were almost never here then, though."

"The expense," he said. "I couldn't justify paying even half rent on a place where I would just sit and stare." He looked around, shaking his head. "Catherine was right."

"She left you yet?"

Dumbfounded, he stared at the octopus, nodding. "Quite recently."

"Next time you sleep with someone, make sure it's a benefactor."

He took a breath and then blew it out. "Ouch. I felt that one, Con."

"You were meant to. Listen: the benefactors I sleep with never see me. Not *me*. They don't even know what I look like, and they don't care. They come in here and step into whatever world it is they want made for them, and I take care of them. A headmount isn't big enough. Though they all use hotsuits.

It's a living, it's what I have to do." The octopus winked. "It's not so bad. They're just humans, after all. Just humans. You're holding one of them up."

"Sorry," he said, stepping back from the rock. "I'll go."

"Don't apologize. Come back instead."

He laughed. "I don't think you need a studio-mate to help with expenses anymore, Con."

"But maybe you need to feel good." Her voice came from the rose. He turned it to look into its heart. Her face gazed out at him, clear and wise.

"I'm not a benefactor," he said uneasily. Consuela had never seemed the slightest bit interested in him before. The whole idea made him a little queasy and more than a little curious.

"You could be a benefactee," she said. "Or whatever it's called."

He dropped the rose and backed toward the door. "Not me. I just—" He shrugged. "Not me, Consuela."

"Stop."

Gabe froze with his hand on the knob.

"If you don't come here, go *somewhere*. Do you get me? Go somewhere."

He ducked his head in a nod and fled, pulling the door shut behind him a little too hard before he half ran back to the rental in the parking lot.

He had to pull around a large private car to get back out onto Olympic; perhaps it belonged to Consuela's benefactor, the one he had apparently delayed with his visit.

"Go somewhere," he muttered as he edged into the slow-moving traffic on Olympic. "Go somewhere. Sure thing, Con. If the clog ever lets up, I can go to the moon."

13

"Yes?" said Manny, standing at attention.

The formally dressed woman sitting on the couch in the crowded sunken living room stood up. She was a representative from one of the western states, but at the moment Manny couldn't remember which one. "I'm sure you're expecting this question, so I'll get it out of the way for all of us." She looked around with a professional smile. "It seems to me that this procedure, as you call it, has enormous potential for abuse. What sort of safeguards have you considered?"

Manny mirrored her smile. "You'll pardon me for saying so, but this seems to be a, ah, legislative matter."

Everyone in the room laughed.

"Precisely." The representative folded her arms. "So perhaps I should reword the question. Why should we push for legalization of a procedure that has such enormous potential for abuse? And with such potential do you really think the American people will even want it?"

"I believe in offering people a choice," Manny said smoothly, getting another round of appreciative laughs. "We're not asking for a law to make it *mandatory*, only permissible. When implants first became generally available for therapeutic reasons—epilepsy, manic-depression, autism, and other neurological disorders—there was, as I recall, quite a lot of public concern over the potential for abuse there. And we all know there *is* abuse. There isn't a fair-sized city anywhere in America—or in the world, for that matter—that doesn't have its share of feel-good mills, fitting the irresponsible with ecstasy buttons, giving on-off switches to people who are merely weak in character. Nonetheless, I don't think any of us would deny a manic-depressive the opportunity to function normally and effectively, free of drugs that may wear off prematurely or have irritating side effects. I don't think any of us would refuse a second chance to someone with brain damage sustained in an accident—"

He went on, aware of Mirisch from the Upstairs Team beaming at him and nodding. Mirisch, the Great Grey Executive, with his silver hair and matching silver suits. Mirisch hadn't thought he was really capable of addressing a roomful of senators and representatives and other VIPs. Manny was giving him an eyeful and an earful tonight.

Several hundred words later he wasn't sure he'd completely satisfied the representative, but she sat down without further comment.

On the left side of the room, an older man with more side-burns than face waved a peremptory finger at him and stood up without waiting to be acknowledged. "Say we get it legal-ized. You're not actually suggesting that this procedure be performed on *school-age children?*"

Manny inclined his head slightly. "I believe I mentioned that, except for cases of organic damage, autism, seizure dis-orders, or dyslexia, it's not meant for individuals who have not attained full physical growth." Manny looked away, searching the room, and then nodded at an elegant black woman before the man could say anything else.

"You mention freedom of choice," she said. "However, we all know that often freedom of choice is a fantasy. You've told us that direct input to the brain will be a more vivid experience than even what a head-mounted monitor delivers. Isn't there a danger here of literally putting ideas into people's heads, of *programming* them?"

"*That's* what I was trying to say before," called the first woman. "I think *that* potential for abuse could outweigh the benefits."

Everyone was looking at him expectantly now, including the now-unsmiling Mirisch. *Watch this, Grey Boy.* "That could be true," he said slowly, "but Dr. Joslin's research has uncovered some very interesting facts about brain output and input, one of those facts being, it's far easier to obtain output than it is to input anything. Stated another way, it's far easier to express one's self than to learn anything, as any of you with children may know only too well."

He got a respectable if tentative laugh on that one. Mirisch was almost smiling again. "Dr. Joslin has, in fact, researched the possibility of using sockets for instant education—instant

doctors, for example, or instant lawyers. Instant politicians—"
Another laugh. "Instant architects, instant neurosurgeons, and
the like. However, it seems humans learn by doing. An instant
neurosurgeon, for example, would still lack experience. Dr.
Joslin emphasized to me that sockets do not impart *experience*.
And there is the matter of the medium. The output of a given
brain would be stored in a variation of the conventional software we use now. 'Literally putting ideas into people's heads'
would be more likely if we used the sockets for a direct connection between two or more brains."

The woman looked troubled. "And would that be feasible?"
she asked.

"It's not feasible now," he said. "Perhaps that is one of the
things that should be legislated *against*."

The laughs were still tentative. An older Oriental woman
directly in front of him stood up. "Why have you decided to
launch this great breakthrough, as you call it, by using it as a
more efficient means to produce *rock videos*?"

She got a round of applause for that, especially from the
older man in the back, who shouted, "Good question!" Manny
glanced over at the bar, where the Beater stood silently nursing
a drink, and waited for the room to quiet down before he
answered. Mirisch looked positively stony now. *Don't sweat
yet*, Manny thought at him, *wait till I'm circling around your
spot on the Upstairs Team.*

"It's not a more efficient production of rock video that we
are interested in, exactly, but rather the individual involved.
He goes by the professional name of Visual Mark, and Dr.
Joslin informs me that the visualizing center of his brain is
hypertrophied—overdeveloped, that is, so overdeveloped that
he should have no trouble at all sending out anything he vis-
ualizes. We also have another possible candidate, though less
is known about that brain. Perhaps we might be able to find
someone in a loftier type of profession, but rather than conduct
a talent search, it seems far more efficient to go with someone
we already know is suitable." Manny allowed himself a small
laugh. "As for rock video—well, it's what he does for a living.
He's a volunteer, in case anyone's wondering, which is another
point in his favor. We might find someone in another line of
work with even better visualization abilities, but there's no
guarantee that person would agree to pioneer for us."

The questions went on for twenty minutes longer before
Mirisch finally stood up and announced the presentation had

to come to an end, or there wouldn't be enough time left to enjoy themselves. This drew the most enthusiastic applause of the night. Promise them anything, but give them a party, Manny thought as he stepped aside to let Mirisch take over. It was a relief; he had begun to tire even before the question-and-answer session, though he doubted that anyone had noticed. The old iron control had pulled him through again.

Earlier the control had slipped a little; not much, just enough that he had looked dismayed when he'd climbed into the transport on the roof of the Diversifications building and found the Beater already sitting in the backseat. But the flight out had been smooth and quick, and the Beater hadn't been inclined to conversation any more then he had.

The Beater was still standing down at the other end of the bar, looking at him dourly. The Beater. What kind of a name was that for a fifty-year-old man? That alone would tell you they were cases, that whole EyeTraxx oddlot. At least this one had behaved himself. If he hadn't, Manny knew the Upstairs Team would have held him responsible, and that would have been the end of all the benefits he'd gained from instigating the EyeTraxx coup.

They must have suspected how he'd done it, Manny thought as he watched Despres, the junior member of the Upstairs Team, working on Belle Kearney from the Food, Drug, and Software Administration. No one had asked him a thing when he'd presented Joslin's research to them, along with Hall Galen's financial history and an outline of how Diversifications could acquire EyeTraxx by feinting a takeover of Hall Galen Enterprises as a whole. Joslin's sockets were a little out of Diversifications' usual line, but nobody had said a thing about that, either. An opportunity was an opportunity, and even a lightweight like Mirisch, who had paused in his mingling to beam at Despres and Kearney, could see this was major stuff.

At the very least it would give the Upstairs Team an excuse to party with a bunch of VIPs, which was very possibly the best thing Manny could have done, for them and, consequently, for his career. Privately Manny found many of the so-called VIPs less than distinguished; they reminded him of Diversifications employees of a certain stripe. He also found it significant that many of them had implants of some kind or another, something he had discreetly left unsaid in the presentation. They all claimed the implants were aids for concentration and memory, but Manny suspected there were a few leashed manic-depressives, some schizoids, and at least one bona fide sociopath on inhibitors.

Only one person from the House of Representatives openly acknowledged that her implants were for temporal-lobe epilepsy, but she wasn't present. It had been generally agreed that anyone that straightforward probably wouldn't let little things like Diversifications' overly generous hospitality go by.

If it came to generosity—the Upstairs Team had been adamant on that point. Anyone who liked the idea well enough without any extra persuasion didn't get any, and those who needed it would have to ask. That was all right; they knew how.

He accepted a drink from the bartender and held it as a prop. Soon he would have to take a stabilizing dose of the stimulant he'd been running on all day. Or, actually, since he'd returned from Mexico. The switch-hitting hacker had thrown his schedule off completely, and he'd had to make up the time he'd lost to prepare tonight's presentation by skipping a night's sleep. Better business through chemistry.

Despres stepped up to the bar for a refill, nodding at him with chilly politeness. Mirisch had taken over the conversation with Kearney, Manny saw, and Despres obviously didn't like being shut out. The yotz probably didn't know that Mirisch and Kearney had gone to Harvard together. School ties were still in fashion. Even tacky school ties, he thought, taking in Kearney's outfit and wondering when her tailor would have mercy on her and sew the collars back onto her jackets. Apparently the minions of the FDSA weren't slaves to fashion. Unfashion, perhaps, but not fashion.

He was amused by the turn of his thoughts, though another part of him recognized he was getting a few symptoms off the stimulants again. Getting some flashover, as the hard core put it. If he had to run much longer this way, he would qualify as hard core himself, and getting detoxed wouldn't do much for his image with the Upstairs Team. It was never a good idea to let them think you had weaknesses.

Tim Chang cruised over and slid his empty glass across the bar for some more of the sticky-sweet liqueur he sucked up by the quart. He gave Manny a brilliant smile. Chang was his not-quite-counterpart in the Entertainment division; he supervised the personnel who did the refinements and finishing work on Hollywood releases, but Manny was senior to him.

Technically rock video should have been Chang's bailiwick, but Chang was smart enough to realize he and his division were going to be under Manny's umbrella, the big new umbrella Diversifications was going to present him with when they finally went public. Chang was another lightweight, but at least he had sense enough to defer to the inevitable. And, Manny reflected, every rising executive needed a good stooge.

". . . senator's big baby is education," Chang was saying.

A tall tuxedo-clad woman with a mass of reddish gold hair came up beside Chang and slipped her arm through his. "I'm all for education," she said. "Especially when I can learn something like I learned tonight."

"Rana!" Chang said, oozing with delight. "I'm so glad you could come. Manny, you remember Rana Copperthwait from Para-Versal."

Copperthwait took his hand and gave it a hard squeeze, looking into his eyes for a moment. Manny thought the tuxedo made her look like a bartender, but he smiled at her anyway, returning the look. He hadn't been sure of inviting anyone from any of the studios—if anything leaked, they'd have the unions screaming all over the place, even though there were signs that the Old Hollywood was finally starting to breathe its last. More and more was being left to simulation, which left more and more of the profits for people like Copperthwait. If they ever got to the point where they could produce casts made-to-order the way they produced settings and special effects, there'd be a shakeout that would make the Big One look like a hiccup, and Copperthwait's look had said she was thinking about just that very thing.

He'd hinted at it without being specific during the first part of the presentation; a direct interface with the brain certainly raised the possibility. The alert person would be watching to see how things would break—would people like Rana Copperthwait suddenly decide they wanted in-house staffing instead of continuing to job out their refinement work to places like Diversifications? It was possible. It was also possible that such a development might be more profitable for an ambitious person than the old corporate game, more profitable and more rewarding than supervising zeros like Gabe Ludovic and enduring the blandishments of office suck-ups like Bergen Clooney.

They made a little pleasant, clever conversation until Copperthwait dragged Chang off to introduce her to someone else. Mirisch stopped by the bar to grab another drink and congratulate him on a job well-done.

"And don't worry about old Senator Sideburns," Mirisch added, almost as an afterthought before he went back to working the room. "The phrase 'school-age children' is code for 'Gimme-gimme-gimme.'"

It's not my *worry*, Manny thought, returning his knowing smile. He watched Mirisch move off to connect expertly with another well-dressed senator, and then leaned against the bar, feeling his energy suddenly draining out of him. Definitely past-due time for a stabilizer.

He was feeling for the inhaler in his pocket when his glass jumped out of his hand with an impromptu fountain effect and thudded on the carpet a few feet away. Startled, he could only stand and stare while a couple of the cliffsider service staff sprang out of nowhere into quiet action. The mess was gone before he even had time to register that his hands were shaking. He glanced around, but no one had noticed. Relieved, he headed for the bathroom.

"Mr. Rivera."

A tall man standing near a shifting holo display of an Olympic gymnast stepped forward, intercepting him. Manny gave him a gracious smile; the bathroom door was closed anyway. The tall man took his hand and pumped it up and down a few times. "Congratulations on a fascinating presentation."

"I'm glad you liked it."

"I didn't say I liked it. I said it was fascinating." The amusement in the man's face didn't extend to his eyes. "You don't know who I am, do you?"

Manny wished for a wall or a chair to lean against. "I'm sorry. If we've met, I've somehow forg—"

"It was very brief, some time ago. I'm the one who should apologize, actually. Edward Tammeus. Senator from Michigan." He stepped back and took a pipe and small bag out of his inside breast pocket. "As I said, it was a fascinating presentation. You have a very nasty piece of work there."

Manny took a breath. "I see. And what was it you found so nasty about instantaneous and permanent cures for brain dysfunctions?" As soon as the words were out, he regretted the defensive sound of them. It wouldn't do any good to get defensive, especially with this character.

"Now, Mr. Rivera, you don't actually expect me to believe that you're doing this just for the poor dyslexic kiddies, do you?"

The man was laughing at him, Manny thought with a flash of anger. A moment later his calm returned. No, it wasn't him; the senator didn't even really see him. It was the Upstairs Team, the company itself, but he didn't have the cojones to mix it up with them, so Manny was elected.

"Well, there are a number of commercial aspects to the project," Manny said. "I'd say bigger and better rock video will go a long way toward subsidizing the nobler aims."

"We can help most dysfunctionals right now with standard implants," the senator said, tapping overflow from his pipe into the bag before he closed it and returned it to his pocket.

"Sockets can help them *all*," Manny said.

"And how do you figure that?"

"Well, that's quite technical, and all of our best technical minds are at our Mexican installation at the moment." Manny gave a small shrug. "They can explain better than I can—"

"I'd like to talk to them." The senator gazed at him over the flame from his pipe lighter.

Manny could feel the tremor from his hands starting to creep up his arms. Just a few more minutes and he could take the edge off. If the senator delayed him any longer, he'd have to take a larger dose, and he'd be up all night again.

"Yes, I *am* asking you to arrange something," the senator added, as if Manny had spoken.

"Of course," Manny said quickly. "You'll have to let us know your schedule—"

"My office will call. It's a nasty, nasty thing, and I want to know as much about it as possible." He blew a small bluish cloud of smoke into the air over their heads. The aroma was honeyed.

"I understand," said Manny. "You would have to, in order to vote in an informed manner."

"Oh, I already know how I'm going to vote." The senator glanced into the bowl of the pipe and took another puff. "You people don't have to worry about that, I'll vote for legalization, though it could be a rough ride. It's the nastiest thing I've ever heard of. Possibly diabolical. If I thought I could stop it, I would."

Insane people everywhere, Manny thought. What the hell

was he smoking anyway? "I'm sorry, Senator, I don't think I understand. You're *for* legalization, but you'd stop it if you could?"

"That's it. What don't you understand?"

Manny glanced down, putting on a self-deprecating smile. "Perhaps I've been up too long today, and I'm too tired."

"You see, Mr. Rivera, it's out now." The senator pointed the stem of his pipe at him; a small wetness gleamed on the mouthpiece. "You've done it, and something like this can't be undone. Like the start of the nuclear age, way back when. You can't stuff it back into the box and tell Pandora you'll get back to her when you're more . . ." the senator shrugged ". . . more *moral*, to use the quaint terminology. So if we can't undo it, we'd better have as much control over it as possible."

It's out of control. The thought came to Manny in Joslin's nasal, high-pitched voice. He blinked. Had the senator actually used the word *moral*?

"That's what I'm going to tell any of my recalcitrant colleagues, anyway," the senator went on. "I wouldn't be surprised if that argument swings it for you. Funny idea, isn't it, putting something aside until you're moral enough to use it." He laughed a little. "Everyone gets a certain look when I use that word. *Moral.* It's a word with very bad PR, thanks to certain pressure groups that have come and gone over the last several decades." He drew on the pipe again, pausing to hold the smoke in his lungs. "However, it was one of the tenets of the church I grew up in, waiting to use something until you're moral enough. It sounded like a great idea. But according to the church, we're only moral enough for a very simple level of living."

Manny clenched his jaws together against a yawn and glanced at the bathroom door; still closed. Apparently he wasn't the only one present running on borrowed energy.

"Obviously, a better idea is to be, oh, *im*moral enough to manipulate something instead of being manipulated by it." The senator produced a pipe tool and began poking into the bowl. "Diversifications will provide transportation, accommodations, and any other necessaries, then?"

Manny nodded. They all had their own way of asking for things. Some had to pump themselves up, and others had to make sure you knew they had only the best reasons, the most rational motivations, and the sincerest desire for clear understanding. As far as Manny was concerned, an envelope of money was just an envelope of money, whether you gave it to a senator or a hacker. But if there had to be rituals, he would perform them as requested.

The bathroom door opened, and one of the FDSA people came out, wobbling a bit on her high heels, relief large on her face. Manny made a slight bow to the senator. "Excuse me."

He had to force himself not to dash for the lav and slam the door behind him. It took him five minutes to adjust the inhaler and another five minutes before he felt steady enough to plunge back into the action.

The Beater was waiting for him when he came out.

14

She was supposed to settle into a routine now.

She was supposed to accept everything the Beater had told her, leave Mark alone, do the videos, hope for the best. Hope for the best. What the fuck kind of talk was that? She couldn't ask him; he was suddenly unavailable, closeted with Rivera, busy, busy, busy, and she couldn't ask Mark, because Mark had been spirited away again.

Her own goddamn fault, most likely, for opening her big mouth to the Beater. He'd gone to Rivera, and Rivera had probably waved his magic corp-wand and removed the only person who could have given her an answer.

She looked for him anyway, on the off-chance that he was simply dodging her to avoid being smacked around. Looking for Mark had become a fucking way of life in the past few years. She didn't really know how to do anything else, except make the videos, and somehow, making the videos was too hard when she didn't know where he was.

Fuck it all, she thought, walking the boulevards, scoping the clubs, making at least one nightly run to the Mimosa, scouting the hit-and-runs. Fuck it all, let Mark come to her if he ever decided there was something she should know. Twenty-umpt years could make you tired; she had a right to be tired. And then she looked some more.

"Ain't seen him," said Loophead's little percussionist, rapping her sticks on the table. It was some empty night between one empty day and another in a nameless little Hollywood joint trying to hold its own with a combination of videowall and live music. The postage-stamp-sized dance floor was packed with boulevardettes, and attitude-mongers pretending they were Somebody, and vidiots who had finally had to go somewhere, and a couple of hungry kids with handcams hoping to capture something they could manipulate into some semblance of a video, probably on hardware built from paper clips and masking tape and held together with spit. Then they'd watch it on one of the public-access channels while the rest of the world watched just about anything else.

The little percussionist's name was Flavia Something. She dressed like a cavewoman on food stamps, and she took her sticks everywhere. They beat out a sequence of shifting rhythms on the tabletop as if of their own will, unperturbed by the conflicting beat coming from the band up front. All of Loophead's music grew out of percussion.

"When you comin' over, do the new one?" Flavia asked her. "You come do the video with us on our turf. Finish wherever you want, but you *do* with us, okay?"

"I thought Mark had your next," Gina said, taking a healthy swig from the bottle of LotusLand in front of her. Flavia tapped the bottle as she put it down, hesitated, and then tapped it again, liking it. As if she could hear it over the thrash.

"Told you, ain't seen him. Can't do video with the invisible man." Flavia's shrug was exaggerated, but the sticks never stopped. On another night, some time ago, Flavia had taken Mark to bed with her, sticks and all. Gina remembered it; Flavia remembered it; Mark didn't.

Up front, a kid in rags and plastic wrap made an old-fashioned stage-dive into the dance-floor crowd, helped along by a kick from the group's hoarse vocalist. The kid sank by uneven degrees into the bobbling mass of jerking bodies and resurfaced several feet away, hopping up and down like a maddened kangaroo. There was a distinct heelprint on his forehead.

"A synner in the making," Gina murmured.

Flavia tapped a stick directly in front of her. "You gonna syn, syn bravely. I forget who said that. Vince Somebody, I think, died in a terrorist raid in Malaysia."

Gina shook her head. "Somebody else. Died like a dog, probably."

The group came to a screaming halt and cleared the stage in a minor brawl as the video screen went on. One of Mark's. Gina finished the rest of the LotusLand, putting on a solid tox while she watched the big curved screen. The texture of the stony shore came through vividly even in this format.

"*Rocks*," Flavia said, and made a face. "I get it already, wish he'd stop doing it, do something else."

"Pass a law."

The perspective traveling along the shore came to a slow stop and focused on a smooth red gold stone, stutter-zooming in close enough to show the graininess of the surface, changing, melting into unreadable symbols that merged with the patterns she was getting from the hallucinogen in the LotusLand. The symbols resolved themselves into regular shapes, an aerial view of a foreign land that began to roll, earth and sky switching places like the flapping of a huge wing.

Canadaytime dragged her out of a hit-and-run in the ruins of South Bev Hills just before the cops would have. Valjean claimed not to know where Mark was, but had she ever known him to miss one of his parties?

Plenty of fucking times, she told him.

Well, then, one of the better ones, how about that?

Plenty of fucking times. But she let them take her because it was a different empty night, and Valjean had been known to turn up with Mark stashed in one of his many bedrooms.

She wasn't sure it qualified as one of Valjean's better parties, but he had a cam crew saving all of it anyway. Do a finish on it later—not her, some drone; she did his videos, but she wouldn't do his fucking parties—make it better than it could have been, the insty-party channels were hungry for all they could get. Plenty of people out there, strung out on the dataline, they'd never get to a party like this, they'd never have lives like this. Here's the real secret, folks, she thought, as a kid with a cam to her face stalked her like a machine of prey: none of us will ever get to a party like this, none of us will ever have lives like this; this isn't what happened; nothing happened except the dataline.

Valjean had a screen for every porn channel, jammed together in the wall so that food porn overlapped med porn overlapped war porn overlapped sex porn overlapped news porn overlapped disaster porn overlapped tech-fantasy porn overlapped porn she had no idea how to identify. Maybe nobody did, maybe it had just bypassed the stage where it would have been anything other than porn. Meta-porn, porn porn?

I don't know what it is, but it makes me horny, and that's all that matters.

"Fucking *right* there's nothing fucking wrong with porn," said Quilmar. Quilmar was one of the stone marathoners. He'd taken so many years off his age, he'd have been nine when he'd cut his first single (okay, maybe eight and a half), and he'd had it polished and tightened so much, his lovers said the dimple in his chin was actually his navel. Maybe, Gina thought, the Beater hadn't been so fucked after all to do what he'd done. "Porn is the fucking secret of life, sister-mine. If you can't fuck it and it doesn't dance, eat it or throw it away. That's the fucking order of the universe, and I'm at the fucking *top* of the food-fuck-and-dance chain."

Then he tried to corner her in Valjean's long, narrow kitchen but he got a little bit confused, and she left him dry-humping the refrigerator door. Wait till he tried to throw *that* away.

"Talent squeezes out brains." Jolene, looking older, but good-older, wiser, full of dignity. "Shit, *you* told me that the first time I helped you drag Mark home. How's he surviving the corporate life?"

When she couldn't answer, Jolene took her up to the top floor, to Valjean's secret oxygen supply, and gave her a few hits off the mask. This was how she kept track, she thought, by who was helping her find Mark and how toxed she was herself. The O_2 helped; there was a little more in it than God's pure oxy. She and Jolene sat out under the eaves and looked down the canyon, held hands, didn't say much. Didn't have to.

"I get some work," Jolene was telling her after a while. Jolene's head was resting on her shoulder. Gina was a flaming hetero, but Jolene liked to keep her options open, as Jolene herself said. Being with someone who wasn't afraid of knowing you needed to be touched was okay whether your options were nailed down or wide open and flapping in the fucking breeze. "I get work from some of the indies, outlaws most of them with one leg over the fence, thinking about going legit. Don't get much legit air, but that's where the scene is getting to be. The Dive'll have people crawling through the clubs on their hands and knees to steal from us soon. Except you, Gina, because you're there already, aren't you?"

"Yah. They tell me to come, but I'm already there."

"Walk," Jolene said, suddenly urgent. "Walk away, what are they gonna do, throw you in debtors' prison?"

Gina nodded. "Does the phrase 'contempt of court' do anything for you?" She drew up her knees, rested her chin on them. "You know you could theoretically spend the rest of your life in the can on a c-of-c charge? Die of old age in the can for nothing more than saying, 'Fuck, no.' "

"You're lost, girl."

She laughed. "Oh, no. What it is, is, I been found. That's the fucking problem, I'm found, and they're gonna keep me. And Mark's the one so found he's lost for good."

* * *

!! U B THE * !!
Many Main-Run Features Starring U!
Available Now:
Raid on Buenos Aires * Thrash-Out * Love Kills
The Buddy Holly Story (3rd—and BEST!!—remake)
1000s of others available, come in and BROWZE!!!!
Complete Rock Video Catalog, Too!
(Take-Out Xtra)

She read it through and then went back to the first line, puzzled. U B the asterisk? Was she too toxed or not toxed enough?

You be the ass to risk.

Gina nodded. For all she knew, she was looking at the secret of life. You be the ass to risk. Love Kills. 3rd—and BEST!!—remake.

Complete Rock Video Catalog, Too! Where old rock videos went to die, hers, Mark's, everyone, here in the wannabee parlors, in the wannabee pipe on the dataline for those who could foot that kind of FOB.

Quilmar hadn't had it quite right. If you can't fuck it, and it doesn't dance, eat it, *be* it, or throw it away.

A woman with tiny old-fashioned movie reels twined in her hair and arcs of silvery spectrum mylar instead of eyebrows was trying to get a rabbity-looking guy in a rented bodyshield to step through the beaded curtain in the open doorway. "Anyone can say they'll make you a star, but we're the only ones who can really do it, whaddaya say? What you wannabee?" The mylar wiggled up and down, the beads swaying in the doorway clacked lightly, and the traffic on the boulevard nattered and chattered and popped.

"Come on, homeboy, it's so easy. What you wannabee? You wannabee Buddy Holly? You wannabee a raider on Buenos Aires, you wannabee a killer and get away with it?" She pushed up the sleeves of her slatternly kimono and took both his hands. "Come on, homeboy, tell me. I'm your Hollywood landlady with a full pot of coffee or whatever else you drink and all the time in the world to listen to you. Just tell me what you wannabee."

The guy looked around like he was afraid someone was going to catch him at this. "You got full-body hotsuits?" he asked. "Full coverage?"

"Homeboy, where are you *from*? We got the full coverage, the *full* coverage, they don't make 'em better than the ones we got. Ain't no part of you gonna be neglected, just tell me what you wannabee."

He looked around again, and his gaze snagged on Gina where she was standing by the sign. The woman frowned a little, no mean trick with mylar eyebrows. "That stuff with you?" she asked him.

"No," he said, but uncertainly, as if he weren't really sure. Gina wanted to laugh. Yah, I'll tell you what *him* wannabee. Him wannabee somebody who doesn't live in Culver City or Inglewood or some other damned place like that in a three-roomer with a two-screen dataline subscription, not knowing what to do with himself when he's used up all the series and the movies and the videos and the insty-parties and wondering why he can't go out and find a life like what he sees on a high-res screen, or at least why he can't afford a hotsuit with full coverage.

The guy's expression was a mixture of defiance and embarrassment as the woman pulled him through the curtain. The beads rippled, and then the woman poked her head through them again.

"You wannabee getting off my sidewalk, okay, homegirl?"

Gina gave her the sign of the horns and moved off, laughing to herself.

"What's so funny, homegirl?" A real homegirl, a green-haired boulevardette wrapped in a red trash bag with the words *Hazardous Waste* stenciled in large repeat all over it and the same thing tattooed on her forehead.

"I'm lucky I can dance," Gina said.

They were all dancing in Forest Lawn, whether they actually could or not. The music was cranked up so loud that the cops had to be comatose not to hear it. Hit-and-run, but Mark wasn't there, either. Some little snipe named Dexter with a laptop had her backed up against Liberace's tomb, claiming he was a fucking orchestra, and off to one side a familiar figure with a cam was trying to look like he wasn't taking her picture.

He looked good tonight, too, and she could hear the sexy laugh in her mind, and what the hell, she could pretend there wasn't anything he wanted to know about, at least for the duration. But even if there hadn't been, all he'd be for her was another furnished room: whatever she needed, none of it hers.

"What's new?" he asked, coming over.

"You mean, what's news."

"However you want it," he said, sounding honest.

She glanced at the snipe, who was standing by on a wish and a prayer. "Whack the road," she told him, and he moved off trying to look too chill to be hurt.

"This how you get to night court?" she asked. "Go someplace you know the cops'll give you a ride from?"

He smiled, looked down the rise to where most of the jumping was taking place. The pickle stand was still in business, but the group had packed up their keyboards and motored; the music was coming out of a box now, but the kids weren't working out any less for it. She saw Clarence or Claw sweating in the middle of a frantic group of kids trying to peak before the cops got around to crashing the party.

"I got something might interest you," he said, after a bit.

"If I tell you what I know," she said. "Don't bother. I still don't know dick."

He looked at her speculatively for a long moment and then shrugged. "Would you tell me if you did?"

"What do I look like to you, *General News*? *Pop-Cult Index*?"

"*Dear Mrs. Troubles.*"

She grinned. "Fuck you."

"I wouldn't rule it out."

You win the game, Mark had said once, *as soon as you get them to say it. Then you do whatever you want*. Which would have explained a lot, except she'd never said it to Mark, not once.

He waited, and she waited, and then he shrugged again. "Take a look." He set the cam on preview mode and gave it to her. She looked through the eyepiece and saw him sitting in the sand, leaning back on his hands and staring dreamily upward. "I took that tonight. From the state he was in, I'd say he's probably still there."

She gave the cam back to him. "Thank you."

He looked startled for a second and then covered it. "I thought you'd want to know. I did a little research on you. And him. It's kinda hard to do any research on one of you without getting the other. Tell me something, how did a soul sister come by a name like Ay-ee-see?"

"Eye-*ay*-see," she said. "It was easier than you'd think." She hopped down off Liberace's resting place and started to walk away.

"You want a ride?" he called after her. She turned around and looked at him. "To the Mimosa," he added. "You shouldn't be driving."

"Gotta drive." She grinned. "Too fuckin' toxed to walk."

He was on her in three fast strides, taking her to the gate. His hand on her arm said it was settled if she said so, but she could feel how he was willing to adapt to any changes she might want to make. Sex, drugs, and rock 'n' roll, sure, homeboy, you want that in any particular order?

Shit, she was old enough to be his mother, if she'd started a little young (just a little). So what was it? Her looks were an acquired taste, not popular demand, and they didn't make it a secret she was holding on for forty.

Then again, maybe it wasn't her; maybe it was him, all him. The gypsy journalist's urge to probe. Curiosity kills the cat, satisfaction brings him back, and brings him and brings him and brings him.

Nah. Mark was waiting on the Mimosa, and there'd been too many furnished rooms already.

She got there in time to see the Beater bending over him, looking harried and anxious, the slicked-back hair hanging loose now. Defiantly she knelt down next to Mark, now stretched out in the sand seeing miracles in the black sky.

"He got away from me," the Beater said. "I was trying to keep him detoxed. As long as you're here, you can give me a hand with him."

Mark's gaze slowly traveled over to her and stopped on her face. *How come it always ends up like this?* she asked him silently. *Where are you, and what do you really do when you go there? Why did I ever want you, and why do I want you now? Because it can't just be the music, and it can't just be the video.*

"Change for the machines," he said.

The Beater took one side, and she took the other, and they got him up on his feet. The gypsy got the footage of their leaving. What the fuck, he should go home with something, even if it was really nothing at all.

They took him back to the Beater's place and put him to bed on the couch. He was already asleep, or passed out, whichever. "They asked me to keep him clean," the Beater said, pulling off Mark's shoes. "So I told him you were gonna kill him and he could stay with me."

"I'd say 'fuck you' but I don't feel that friendly," Gina said.

"I didn't want him out loose where he could get into trouble. Rivera had him Purged once, I didn't want it to happen again."

She winced. "Christ, why didn't they just scour him out with a wire brush? That could have killed him."

The Beater nodded wearily. "Yah, well, I didn't find out till after the fact. I didn't find out a lot of shit till after the fact." He went to her and looked into her eyes carefully. "You keep this up, Rivera might Purge you, too."

"What's so fucking important that Rivera would Purge *me*?"

The Beater went past her into the kitchenette.

"What's going on?" she called after him. "What kind of sling is my ass in that I'd have to get Purged and I don't even fucking know it?"

He stuck his head out of the kitchenette. "You want some coffee?"

She stared at him evenly, and he dropped his gaze. "Maybe I should have let you take care of him." He pulled his head back, and she heard him fussing with the coffeepot. Son of a bitch was actually going to make fucking *coffee*. For *real*. She went to the kitchenette and stood in the doorway with her arms folded. The drip machine on the counter wheezed and bubbled as coffee poured into the carafe. Rediscovery Cuisine beverages. Little Jesus Jump-Up.

"First place you ever had of your own back in Boston had a real kitchen, with a table and chairs in it," he said. "I remember."

"That wasn't my first place. That was a few apartments later, by the time I met you. They all had kitchens, though."

He faced her in the tiny space. "Is it the tox, or are you just tired enough to have calmed down?"

"Maybe I'm getting old." She rubbed her eyes with the heels of her hands. "What's the fucking use. You gonna tell me all that whole lotta shit you found out after the fact now?"

"I can't. Not yet."

"And why the fuck not?"

"It's not mine, all right?"

"No, it's not all right, why the fuck would you think it was?"

The Beater ran a hand through his half-lacquered hair, wincing at the pull. "Christ, how many years was it? You think I'd let anybody hurt him now?"

"Galen would. Galen doesn't give a fuck about him. Neither does Rivera. And goddamn Joslin thinks Dachau was a fucking *spa*."

"It's something different," the Beater said heavily. "Whatever you're thinking, it's something different than that."

"Thanks for the juicy fucking hint." She pulled her shirt off. "And no, I don't want any fucking coffee." She headed toward the bedroom, shedding clothes.

"Gina!"

She stopped at the doorway and looked back.

"You better show for work tomorrow. You been gone three days. You got videos to do."

"Kiss me," she muttered. Stripped down to her T-shirt and underpants, she crawled into the Beater's bed. Sometime later she felt him slide in next to her. Old stuff; life is uncertain, catch bed space where you can get it. When she woke a few hours later, Mark was gone again.

15

They kept tripping over Jones's body in Rosa's tiny apartment, but there was nowhere to put him, so they had to leave him lying around. Human clutter; how did we reach this pinnacle of civilization, Sam wondered.

"I've got to stay away from him," she told Rosa. "Sometimes I'm afraid I'll just start kicking him, and I won't stop till there's just shit and blood, and I'll be kicking that, too."

"Life's so unfair," Rosa said. "You care about Keely, and he loves *that* pile of refuse."

"Keely's the brother I never had," she said shortly. But in spite of everything, it felt good to be back. Rosa split some gypsy jobs with her, mostly scut work, recalibrating automated inventory programs, whipping up a rip-off of the Dodge-M, cheaper, faster, and smarter than the Dive's clumsy, overpriced notion of a fooler loop, encrypting data for spenders who didn't care to answer too many questions as to why they needed encryption. The work kept them both in enough bearer chips to survive on. And it was good to be back on the net, popping around looking for Dr. Fish's Answering Machine to see if anyone had uploaded anything interesting lately, seeing what crazies had come on-line and which ones had crashed themselves. And going over to Fez's place to see if he'd gotten Keely's zap figured out yet.

Fez seemed to be making better progress with Adrian's Mandarin translation program. Privately she felt much the same as Rosa did: Spoken Text wasn't so bad. She'd been known to use it herself when she wanted the illusion of company. But Fez was adamant that the boy should be able to read, and the kid wasn't averse to the idea. What the hell; it wasn't her worry. Not that she knew of, anyway.

But then, up until she'd come back from the Ozarks, she wouldn't have thought Jones would have been her worry.

* * *

"How can he go on like that?" she said. "How can his system take it? He should be in massive failure of everything."

"Fuck if I know," Rosa said grimly. She gripped the wheel of the cramped rental hard with both hands, glancing at the nav-unit screen bolted into the dash, and made a sudden hard right turn. "He's not continually comatose, just sleeping a lot. Regular sleep, I mean. Depressed people do that, sleep like it's gonna be outlawed. But he was up last night for a while."

"He was? I must have been dead myself."

Rosa made a left that threw her against the door. "Sorry. GridLid says bad clog, we'll have to go around it." She nipped around a bullet-shaped tour bus that was obviously lost and slipped into the gap just ahead of it, almost kissing the bumper of the old-style stretch limo in front of them. "Conspicuous consuming pigs," she said. "Who do they think they're impressing?—Yah, he got up, drank all the milk, checked the dataline for mail, futzed around, and then went back to his lying-in spot. I'd've gotten up except I was more asleep than awake myself. I don't think he's actually been dead for quite a while."

"He looks stone-home dead to me all the time now," Sam said. "He looks like the Grim Reaper's no-account brother."

Rosa stomped the brake, slamming the steering wheel with one hand. "Goddammit, a clog." She flicked a finger against the screen. "Damn you, GridLid."

Sam craned her neck out the window. "It's just a little one. We'll be out the other side in ten minutes."

"Who're you trying to shit? More like twenty. Fucking GridLid's so stuffed with viruses that someday the viruses are just gonna take over. Probably do a better job, too." She leaned an arm on her open window and rested her cheek on her fist. "Wake me when we're totaled."

"Don't go to sleep now, this is the fun part. Listen, what else do you know about this program Fez is running Keely's stuff through?"

"Only what I told you," Rosa sighed, running her right index finger around the circle of the steering wheel. "It's some kind of hyperutility embedded in an AI assembly."

"With viral aspects, something to do with Dr. Fish routines."

"That's the one."

"And you're going to keep giving me variations of that answer until I drop deader'n Jones."

Rosa looked over at her wearily. "Look, I've had my hands full trying to keep up with the gypsy jobs I'm on the wire for so I can keep paying that extortion they call rent, while making sure the resident deader is still warm, *and* running docket searches to find out if Keely's a fugitive or in custody, and if our names're on warrants as his known associates. You want the stone-home honest God's truth, I don't know *what* the fuck it is. I don't know where Fez got it, and I don't understand it. It's a program. It's a virus. It's an AI. It's a breath mint. It's a dessert topping. It's the greatest thing since sliced tooth-paste."

Sam shrugged. "Jesus, just tell me how you feel, okay?"

"What, and lose my mystery? Sorry, I'm tense as fuck-all. I've seen a lot of people get canned, and I've seen a lot of people fade out so they wouldn't get canned, and I've dodged a couple of warrants myself in the past, and I don't like hanging around waiting for the ax to fall."

"We don't know anything for sure—"

"*I* know," Rosa said firmly. "If Keely weren't canned, we'd have heard from him by now, and Jones wouldn't be cluttering up my floor. If they've got a gag on it so hard that I can't even find Keely's name on the public record, it's got to be bad enough to send us all down the black hole."

" 'Dive, dive,' " Sam said.

"*Damn*sure." The traffic broke, and they sped toward East Hollywood.

They arrived at Fez's just in time to catch him coming out the front door of the building with Adrian.

"Doctor's appointment," Fez told them. "It's a condition of Adrian's emancipation that he keep regular in-person appointments with a neurologist. Since he's underage and technically brain damaged."

"That could describe half the hackers in town and almost everyone on the Mimosa," Rosa said. "No offense." She flipped the keycard to her rental at him. "Take mine. There's a line at the lot up the block."

Fez flipped it back. "I don't drive."

"I knew that." She looked at Adrian.

"Underage and brain damaged," Adrian said miserably. "No license."

"Okay, I'll take you," Rosa said. "Don't argue. If you go looking for a bus, you won't get back till Adrian can vote. But my rental won't take four."

Fez passed his keystrip to Sam. "Don't hack the Pentagon on a traceable line."

She let herself in and flopped down on the couch, feeling slightly annoyed that Fez was conveniently out when he knew she wanted to question him about the program. *Viral aspects*—what the hell was *that* supposed to mean? And why was it taking *days*?

On the other hand, it felt great to be in an empty apartment. The last time she'd spent any amount of time alone had been in the Ozarks, and she hadn't realized just how much she'd missed having some solitude.

Of all the things Catherine had always hammered on her about, being solitary had not been one of them. If anything, Catherine was even more solitary than she was, which had always made her wonder how her mother could have even considered getting married. And hooking up with someone like Gabe seemed completely out of character.

Not that her father had the soul of a game-show host, exactly. He spent hours alone doing his loathsome job, but he minded it more. Or maybe that was just the job itself—

Fuck it. With at least two hours guaranteed to herself, she wasn't going to piss it all away playing *that* bad old tape in her head. She'd left some chips in Fez's desk with a few games sketched out; she could fool around assembling those for a while.

As she was reaching for the power button to one of the screens, it popped on all by itself.

INFORMATION YOU REQUESTED
NOW AVAILABLE
(THE DOCTOR IS IN)

Sam sat down very slowly, keeping her hands away from the console, and waited to see what was going to happen next.

It was a magnificent thunderstorm, captured in its entirety on the central Kansas plains, where there was nothing to obstruct the view from horizon to horizon. Little had been done to it, except for added detail in the billowing grass and the shapes of the clouds. And the lightning. The lightning had undergone a little minor orchestration for more dramatic timing. It was possibly one of the best environmental sequences of any kind, and Gabe wasn't sure it really fit in the *Headhunters* scenario, but the space was there in the program to add an optional environment, and he had popped it in just because he'd gotten tired of swampland and voodoo. The *Headhunters* program had accepted it easily, but if it didn't work, he could always take it out again.

The strange little glitch that had been popping in and out on him since the entertainment sequence in the French Quarter was gone now. He kept looking around the barn that he and Marly and Caritha had taken shelter in, expecting to see the dark spot suddenly reappear, but apparently it was a problem confined to the visual portion of the original *Headhunters* video. Which was a relief; for a while he'd been afraid he'd pushed too hard by putting in Marly and Caritha and overloaded the capacity.

Thunder growled briefly and then suddenly let loose with a crash that shook the barn. "That was *prima*," said Marly from her post by one of the open windows. A cold wind blew her hair straight back, and she leaned into it with pleasure, letting the shotgun rest against the bale of hay she was sitting on. "One thing you don't get on the Gulf is good thunderstorms. Plenty of hurricanes, but not many thunderstorms. None this good, anyway."

Gabe sat down next to her on the bale. In the distance a large tree was whipping its leaves from side to side furiously.

"Hey," Caritha called from the loft. "It's clean and dry up here. We got a place to spend the night."

"You really want to stay here that long?" Gabe hollered over the thunder.

Caritha appeared at the top of the ladder and climbed down, her rifle slung across her back and the cam dangling from the crook of her arm. "Unless you want to mix it up with the bad guys out here, where there's plenty of land for them to bury our bodies in. We'll be fertilizer for the winter wheat crop if we're not careful."

"They won't come," Marly said confidently. "Too exposed. We could see them approach and pick them off. And no one's going to fly a 'copter out in weather like this. Hello." She lifted her hand and Gabe saw an enormous emerald grasshopper squatting on the back of it, its forelegs resting on the base of her largest knuckle. There was more thunder then and a violent strobe of lightning, reflected in the grasshopper's shiny copper-colored eyes.

"Wow, that's what I call passion," Caritha said, kneeling on the bale next to Gabe. He smiled to himself; in a hotsuit with no genital coverage, thunder and lightning was what he had to call passion, too.

The thunder rolled long and hard, and the barn shuddered again. Far across the rippling grasses, the tree seemed to strain its branches upward, and a thick bolt of lightning arrowed down to strike it. Gabe saw a burst of sparks, and part of the tree blew apart, but it remained standing. Caritha smoothed her hands along his shoulders, rubbing them lightly and firmly.

Marly rested her hand on the rough windowsill, letting the grasshopper stay where it was. Strange eyes, Gabe thought. They were much too shiny for a real grasshopper. He wondered if the insect had been added or just embellished. It hadn't appeared in the preliminary scan. He found he could pick out the reflection of Marly's face in its eyes, and next to that his own and Caritha's, distorted in the bulging lens.

Marly turned her head to look up at him. The lightning was flickering soundlessly now, out there and in the grasshopper's twin copper mirrors. "What do you see?"

"A life I won't live," he said. The words sounded strange—he couldn't imagine what had made him say that, but he felt suddenly sleepy and careless. Caritha kept rubbing his shoulders, and the grasshopper kept staring, and the rain came down, beating on the wooden barn and the land around it so hard, he almost couldn't hear anything else. Even Marly's voice was too faint to hear under the noise, but Gabe was aware of her asking him something else, something about being specific, and of his own voice answering, though his mind felt far away, as if he were half in a dream. It didn't seem to matter.

Sometime later he became aware that the rain had stopped and he was alone by the window.

"Marly? Caritha?"

They appeared at the edge of the loft, smiling down at him. "Come on up, hotwire," Marly said, beckoning to him. There was an emerald green stain on the back of her hand. Had she crushed the grasshopper? Or had the program stuttered when it had sent the thing away?

He put it out of his mind as he climbed the ladder.

* * *

He flinched when Rivera clapped him on the shoulder. Rivera didn't seem to notice; he was trying not to grin too widely. Like royalty's displays of emotion were unseemly in front of the serfs, Keely thought sourly. He felt stone-home shitty. *Hey, you, with your dick in your hand—say hello to everybody, this is* Global News Update, *and you're the feature entertainment story of the hour—you* and *your dick.*

Nothing he could do. Rivera was calling the shots, and if Rivera wanted to hack one of his own employees, he didn't have anything to say about it. Who would have believed him?

"I want two copies of that," Rivera said cheerfully, pulling his chair a little closer to the console.

Obediently Keely punched for duplication and then stood up. "Mind if I take a piss?" *All over you?*

Manny jerked his head toward the doorway. "I think you know where it is by this time."

"Yah. Sure do." *Actually, I thought I'd use one across the street, if you don't mind. You do? Well, fuck.* If the poor clown he'd just finished tapping had to work for Rivera day in, day out, it was no wonder he was jerking off in the bit bucket with imaginary playmates. Jesus.

There was a lock on the bathroom door. But then, the bathroom had no windows. He could pee, or he could kill himself, those were the choices. *Does this picture look familiar?*

He had his first on-line Corrections Board meeting in a month. Suppose he actually did try to tell them that Diversifications' reparation program had him doing in-house hacking, breaking into employees' confidential systems to eavesdrop on their work?

Sure, *try*. If he'd had to report in person, he might have had a chance to make a case. Diversifications wouldn't even let it get as far as his word against Rivera's—they'd pull the plug on him in midsentence and claim technical difficulties, have him back on-line in twenty minutes, grinning like an idiot in drugged-fucking-clothes.

What the fuck. In a month it wouldn't matter. Their little project would be up and running hot in Mexico, probably close to legalization in the States. Diversifications seemed to be more pervasive than Dr. Fish.

He sniffed his shirt collar. The fresh-air smell was long gone; otherwise, he wouldn't have been able to tap into the system—

He could tap into the system again, he thought suddenly. Look for another peripheral item in the sequence, contact the guy again, and feed him the whole story, the *real* story, and have him call—

Who? Sam? Fez? *Jones?* What could they do, other than get canned themselves. Maybe just alert the guy—hey, you with your dick in your hand. He went back out to the living room, where Rivera was now rerunning the sequence and enjoying the show. Enjoying it a little too much—maybe Rivera was fooling his bosses, but he knew just by looking at him that Rivera had been turbo'd for days. Working overtime on his big project. Or maybe Rivera found the paranoia useful.

Rivera froze the display and sat back in the chair, drumming his fingers on his thigh. "Is there any way you can run any sequences without *his* activating them? I'd like to see what else he's been playing with."

It was on the tip of his tongue to say, *Yes, if it's in volatile storage,* but he caught himself in time. "Sorry. Maybe someone else could, but you've got the security locked up tighter than a rat's ass. The only way I can get in is through a database he's annexed to the simulation, and that's a matter of split-second timing. I have to wait and see which template goes into the simulation. That storm, for example. Then I can get in before the program accepts it. Because, technically, it's not really in his system before it's incorporated into the simulation. It's in the storage area, and that's just a section of a pool common to all the other employees."

Rivera nodded thoughtfully. "So any other employee could do this."

"If they knew how. It's tricky even if you know the proper commands. It's hacking." He felt ashamed at the hint of pride in his voice. He wasn't doing anything to be proud of now.

"How about the volatile storage?" Rivera asked. "It's just a subsection of general storage."

Keely felt a flare of anger. "Isn't this just slightly against the law?"

The smile Rivera gave him was bizarrely cordial. "If you want to quibble about the law, we can void your contract, and you can quibble with a real judge in a real court."

"Maybe I'll just tell them what you've been up to here."

"And maybe there won't be any evidence of it, and you'll go down for perjury. It would be easy enough to get another hacker." Rivera paused. "Not a bad idea, actually. Hackers bounce off us all the time. We don't usually bother tracing the ones that don't get in—otherwise, we'd be in court constantly. But maybe we ought to reel in another."

Keely nodded vigorously. "You do that. You go right ahead and do that. I'd like a chance to show you fuckers what *two* hackers could do to your system."

Rivera threw back his head and roared laughter at the ceiling. "Please, follow this up with a hymn to solidarity, anything less would be anticlimax!" He gestured at the image of the grasshopper, still frozen on the screen. "In case you don't know, the only difference between you and this gentleman is—ahem—balls. He doesn't have any, and we have yours."

"And what are you gonna do to *him*? Gonna wire him up, too, with your little socket-and-plug set? Or is he out in the cold on this one?"

"My plans for him don't concern you. Just stay with him," Rivera said, getting up. "I've got quite a lot of other things to take care of before I meet with our friend here; he won't be going anywhere, either." He picked up the briefcase he'd left on the highly polished conference table in the center of the room. "Download me two more copies to chip—no, make it three. Have them packed for me when I come back tomorrow, along with three copies of whatever else you tap from him between now and then. You've got supper makings in the kitchenette, full dataline subscription for your entertainment. No pharmaceuticals, I'm afraid—"

"Laundry on strike?" Keely asked.

"—but if you can hack the lock on the liquor cabinet, you can get toxed on the Upstairs Team's best cognac. I understand the good stuff doesn't make one quite so sick."

Keely turned away as Rivera left and sat down at the console to run the sequence again, dividing the screen so he could study the mechanics of the program along with the execution. If he could figure a way to manipulate the filler elements more extensively, he might be able to add original input rather than shifting already existing data to create dialogue. He'd pulled everything the woman had said to the guy under hypnosis out of the pool of most-used dialogue and even then he'd almost crashed everything fooling around with the grasshopper. If only Dr. Fish could have made a house call here. But then, if Dr. Fish could have made *this* house call, maybe he wouldn't be in this wringer.

The program was pretty complicated, far beyond what he'd

expected someone at Diversifications to be capable of, but if he could make it accept him without crashing, he could do more than just download a copy of the guy's fantasyland. He could talk to him. Hey, you, with your dick in your hand. He could warn him.

16

Theo was covering one of the Beater's old encores, a hard-on called *Who Do You Love?* All synth, of course; Theo would have mistaken a guitar for his lover in dim light. If he even had a lover. But for all the synth, he'd gotten it off as nasty as it had to be, taking you all forty-seven miles on pure barbed wire with a cobra around your neck.

Struggle through the bangers on that tiny little dance floor, until you see a likely-looking head nodding up and down, and you think that's him, and you put your hand on his shoulder and force him to turn around because he's not going to get away this time.

Who do you love?

Say again, doll, I didn't hear you that time.

Sorry, wrong number, but he looks good anyway, and another time you might have stayed there and made believe it was him, for a little while. Instead, fight your way out to the street, where the air is still heavy with the heat of the day. Somebody at the curb, pounding out the beat with two sticks on the hood of somebody's abandoned limo.

Who do you love?

Ask again, doll, you didn't hear what I seen.

(Nasty bridge, running from the top all the way down, hammering every step of the way, and you think about it, but you got to keep moving.)

At a wannabee parlor, you see him standing with his back to you, talking to some woman with hair from hell and a silver kimono who's starting to pull him through a curtain of barbed wire, and the blood from the last victim is still dripping from the points. You grab his other hand before he goes through, and he turns around.

Who do you love?

Doll, why do you keep on askin' me that? You must be seeing something I didn't say.

If it was him, it isn't now, but he looks good, too good to
go through that curtain. You can see he doesn't know, and you
could save him, for a little while anyway, but he'd still be the
wrong one.

(Here's the nasty bridge again, and the sound chases you
the full length of it as fast as you can go, and when you reach
the other side, you pass that same one rapping the sticks on
golden garbage cans. Golden garbage is still garbage. *Move.*)

Who do you love?

Oh, doll, wouldn't you like to know?

They've all come out from under the piers tonight, every
last one of them; they've been expecting you, they know the
one you've come for, but they've come for you. Their hands
keep sliding off because you're still too fast, but something's
going to slow you down, and all they have to do is be there
when it happens. Then you start looking at them, look at each
one of them, and thank God that's not him, and that's not him,
and that's not him, and that's not him, but up ahead, up
ahead—

And a big ball of fire lands right in front of you, blows up
in your face, and you see the way things never were, like there
was someplace else you'd been going instead of here.

If you go fast enough, fire won't burn, not that fire. Besides,
what were you going to do, back then? You couldn't take that
trip any more than he could, you with yours, him with his.
You got what you got, and what the fuck, you've still got it, it
still lives, it didn't get worn away by what might have happened. That's more than a lot are left with when the smoking
lamp starts to burn low.

Who—

They want you, but they part like the Red Sea anyway, those
reaching hands falling back against the darkness.

Who do—

He struggles on the sand, trying to get up, and it hangs on,
dragging at him.

Who do you—

Some others hold you back, but you push against the barrier
of their arms. You can break through, but only if you want to.
And the question is

Who do you love?

Do you still want to?

Who do you love?

Do you still want to?

Who do you love?
You tell me, doll.
Who do . . .
Do you . . .
. . . you love?
. . . still want to?
He gets up, and that's when you rush into him.
Who do you still want to love?
It's him. But you know, they all were.
The sound of laughter fades away in the dark.

Theo took off the headmount and looked at her, filling his lungs with a big breath and letting it out slowly. "You're fuckin' dangerous."

Gina flipped off the flatscreen she'd been watching. "That mean you like it?"

He dug his blocky fingers in his squared-off orange beard ("*Burnt sienna*, not orange. Don't you call it fucking 'orange,' I paid for *burnt sienna*, not fucking 'orange.' "), looking glassy-eyed. "It'll probably kill somebody, and we'll all get sued over it, but—" He shrugged and then started to peel off the hotsuit. "Get this off me before it squeezes me to death."

She stripped him quickly and tossed his clothes at him, keeping her back to him while he dressed.

"What's this?" he said jovially. "I only used to walk naked through EyeTraxx several times a week."

"Had it for lunch," she muttered.

"It's too early for lunch."

"So I had it for breakfast, then."

"You sure didn't eat breakfast here."

She busied herself with the console, setting it to make copies of Theo's video, zapping one into the release sequence. Apparently it had to make several stops before it actually made it to the release pipe; every second assistant's mother's brother had to screen it and put their okay on it, including Rivera. He could chew on this one awhile, see how it went with his diet of commercials.

"Did you hear what I said? I said, you didn't eat breakfast here."

"No shit."

"It scared me."

She frowned at him over her shoulder.

"The video," he added, slipping his vest on over his shirt. "It really fuckin' scared me."

"Everything scares you, Theo. You're the biggest chicken-ass I know."

He went over to her, smiling. "You want to try my ass out? See if you can really put the fear of God into it?"

She looked up at him. Theo was all of twenty-six and looked like somebody's video idea of the farmer's son, even with the stupid orange beard. The Beater had caught him in a theme club, jamming his own improvs into nostalgia covers, and she'd almost caught him herself in a weak moment. She patted his butt. "Take a number and wait. I got videos backed up like GridLid's day off."

A few minutes after she threw him out, the door buzzed. She pressed the release, and Valjean swirled in with his ever-changing cape. "Everybody wants to know," he said.

"No, I don't have your fall."

Moray appeared next to him, the closed keyboard hanging from her shoulder by a braided strap. Ecklestone was already pressing for the lift. "Nice place," he said. He'd gone 1940s zoot again. It didn't go with the dark blue frizz that trailed down his back.

Valjean showed off by straddling the ladder and sliding down. "There," he said, taking a bow. "That's one way."

"You're so hot, you do it," Gina said.

He noticed the flying harness tied up near the ceiling. "Give me that, I probably could."

"What do you want another fall for? You've had falls in your last six videos."

"Signature image," said Moray, wiggling down the ladder in her tight red rubber dress. Her hair was combed back and lacquered down hard.

Zigzags were marching across the cape in rigid formation. "See that?" he said, holding both arms out and doing a turn. The zigzags rounded and bulged briefly at the points as they moved. "That's it in cape. The new release. I had a kid on the Mimosa translate it into line display."

"Shit, you're making me cross-eyed."

"Anything to help. *Want* that fall."

She brought the flying harness down from the ceiling and put on the hotsuit, but she couldn't seem to fall far enough or fast enough to raise a blip of sensation. Even having Valjean push her off the catwalk railing wouldn't do it.

* * *

They went back to the original house wearing Gilding BodyShields. Gabe's didn't do much to soften the landing at the bottom of the chute, but Marly's handled the laser shot without even a scorch mark. Probably not true, Gabe thought, but Gilding didn't ask for cinema verité. For good measure he let Caritha's shot graze his ribs.

"You're okay, hotwire," she said, examining him. "But can't you do this without making me look like Deadeye Dork?"

The response gave him more of a jolt than the shot; the program was getting smarter on him again. "It's just for ideas," he whispered. "Don't worry, I'll leave you out of the final cut."

They made it through the ward, into the pseudo-elevator that dumped them in the alley.

"This registers us as outdoors for real," Caritha said, looking at a lighted meter on the back of the cam.

Marly looked around. "It sure got dark quick." She moved forward, keeping low. Gabe was right behind her when the shape dropped down from somewhere in the shadows above. He got a whiff of machine oil mixed with sweat and hesitated; he didn't remember requisitioning any smells.

Two strong arms grabbed him around the waist from behind and tried to lift him. There was a red glow and a sizzling noise, and the arms fell away from him. Almost immediately someone else rushed him; he saw the glint of a knife blade and fell backwards, leaving himself wide open. The knife came down, bounced harmlessly off his breastbone and out of his attacker's hand. Caritha swung the cam, bashing the figure in the head, and Gabe scrambled up again to help Marly, who was struggling between two others. He pulled one away, smashing his forearm down on the back of an exposed neck. The body armor stiffened in response to the impact, making the blow harder. Gabe winced a little, feeling the shock all the way up to his armpit. The sensors were really responsive today. Marly had already taken care of the other one; Gabe thought she'd punched him, but when he looked again, he saw the knife in her hand.

She wiped the blade on her arm and then showed him the stains. "Washable, I hope?"

He stared at the knife still in her other hand. There was something strange looking about it, but in the dim light he couldn't tell exactly what it was. Maybe it was the fact that it was in her hand at all, he thought a little dazedly; the Marly program had never before picked up a knife to stab with.

"That's all of them," Caritha said, sounding satisfied. "Unless you want to wait around here for more."

The knife in Marly's hand shimmered and changed. She didn't react.

"Pause!" he yelled, and pulled himself back a level from the simulation so that he was observing the alley on the screen inside the headmount without being in it.

"Status report," he said.

The lower third of the screen gave him the first five lines of figures on the simulation program. Everything looked normal.

"Scroll," he told it, and the next five lines rolled up from the bottom. He saw nothing out of the ordinary until he reached the twentieth line, which began an inventory of the storage items he was drawing on; the specs for the knife had both positive and negative values.

"Isolate knife, with detail." The knife filled half the screen, while the other half listed the figures defining measurement, appearance, and perceived weight and textures. The last figure was the negative value. There was a *hole* in the knife. Like a window, or a door. Someone was watching.

For one wild moment he thought it might be Sam; if anyone could have cracked him so decisively, it had to be Sam. But Sam would have announced herself, she wouldn't have just spied on him. Wouldn't she?

He plunged himself back into the simulation. Still holding the knife, Marly started to say something.

"Put the knife down," he told her. "Put it down and walk away from it."

"Can't do that, hotwire," she said. Standing next to him, Caritha looked up at him and shook her head.

"You have to, Marly. I'll take a look at it myself, but please, put it down before it does something to you."

"Already has." She held out her hand and he saw how her fingers had melted together into the handle and how the blade, still sharp and dangerous looking, had changed from simulated metal to simulated flesh.

It was a maneuver worthy of Dr. Fish, Keely thought with grim satisfaction.

The guy's vitals were all over the place. He was stone-home

panicked, and Keely couldn't blame him. His fingers hovered over the keyboard while he thought about what he wanted to input. Hell of a great program; the guy probably didn't even realize how great it was. Fast pickup, perfect handling and maneuverability, stopped on a dime and gave you a nickel change, as Sam would have said.

In a small area at the bottom of the screen, the prompt from the program waited, blinking on and off. Keely glanced at the right upper corner of the screen. The guy's vitals were starting to come down a little. *Get ready to shoot off the charts again, homeboy.* Keely wished he could have seen him, but all he was getting from the woman's pov was a flat fill-in graphic. *Your name here.* He typed new instructions to the program and waited impatiently while the program inegrated them with its format. It seemed like an hour before he heard the woman's voice again. He turned up the audio.

"Hotwire, I hate to have to be the one to tell you this, but we've been cracked."

"Is it Manny?" he asked. "Or someone higher?"

The program grabbed an answer before Keely could input.

"No ID. All I can say for sure is, it's in-house, but comparing the technique to information from the databases, it's not an official auditor. Not using official protocols."

Keely's fingers danced on the keyboard.

"Ah, okay. Spyhole from the storage." The expression in the woman's voice was flattening. Her simulation was starting to wobble; too much demand. Keely instructed the program to transfer access to the clock-calendar. He'd have a better view of the entire simulation but at the risk of being cut off if the guy moved too fast. There were a few seconds of transfer blackout, and then he was looking down on the alley from an elevated spot on a wall.

Up here, Keely typed, wishing for voice input. A new status line appeared at the top of the screen, telling him the communication was successful and the words were appearing on the wall within the calendar subroutine. The woman dropped the knife, which must have stoned the guy's crows.

"Marly?" he said.

She pointed wordlessly at the wall. Not just a great program, but an obliging one, too, Keely thought, typing as fast as he could.

Now that I have your attention, Number One: I'm on your side.

That status line blinked an OK. Keely waited while the words rolled themselves out.

Number Two: This program's a stone-home banger.

"Sam?" the guy said. "Is that you?"

Keely felt his stomach drop precipitously. *How do you know about Sam?* he typed.

"Tell me who you are and what you want," the guy said after the lag, "and I'll tell you how I know Sam."

Keely started to type again and felt the keyboard go briefly dead under his fingers. The program specs at the bottom of the screen were rearranging themselves rapidly. He should have figured; the clock calendar had never been meant for this type of communication. The program probably thought it had a glitch. He redid his own access figures and keyed them to shift along with the clock-calendar specs. That would keep him on-line for a while longer, but when the program's defenses figured it out, there'd be another move to cut him off. He had to go quickly.

No time for chat. Me: busted hacker, work for Div now. You: busted too.

The status line blinked OK and then changed to give him an error count. Keely pressed for a redisplay of the line he had just typed.

No time for chat. Me: busted hacker, work for Disliy2o @2r2 {{#@ ᒧ/>.

"God, perfect," Keely muttered. He called up an inventory of notes left in the calendar memory and put it on the other screen.

Wait, he typed. *Being jammed*. He scrolled through the notes, looking for words he could cut and paste together to make a coherent message. The calendar would be less disposed to jam something out of its own inventory.

"Hello?" called the guy anxiously. "Are you still there?"

Keely sent an affirmative signal, tagging words as quickly as he could out of the chunks rolling up from the bottom of the screen.

"Program interrupt imminent," said the tall woman quietly. "Abort, reboot, ignore?"

"Ignore!" the guy shouted. "Hello? Are you still on-line?"

"Are you sure you want to do that, hotwire? Ignore can cause partial or full system crash. Please reply wire n."

Wire n. Keely glanced at the simulation, confused, and then got it. *Y* or *n*, of course. *Very* obliging program. Maybe he should have stuck with the woman, even if he'd ended up crashing her. The guy had to have copies stashed away—

There. Message composed. He flicked it into the send queue and transmitted.

The status line wavered, started to blink an OK, wavered again. Keely had a last look at the alley before the program spat him out and the screen blanked.

A moment later the status line came back to give him a full OK. Just to double-check, he punched for redisplay, not really expecting to get anything. There was a short delay, and then the message he had cobbled together popped onto the screen.

Deadline < month; Rivera spot you meeting; planning new program; run Personnel run.

He sat back in the chair and let his breath out in a rush. He'd have done a lot better if he'd had more time, but if the guy was as smart as his program, the last phrase should have been pretty damned clear.

17

The overdone Arabian-Nights-type tent, complete with tassled pillows and Persian rugs overlapping each other in calculated disarray, was bit-by-bit perfect. No details had been lost or muddied anywhere. For the first twenty minutes after she'd put on the head-mounted monitor, Sam had kept looking quickly to one side or another, trying to catch blank spots. There weren't any; you could even look out through the partly open tent flap and see mountains, great humps of dark green that reminded her more of the Poconos than the Middle East, veiled by a sparkling mistiness that was too wet to be fog and too light to be rain.

Coaxing that kind of detailed perfection into a simulation required stone-home dedication. Or complete obsession. Sam couldn't decide what she wanted to say to the simulated person sitting across from her—*Congratulations*, or *Get a life*.

The simulated person's appearance was most likely pure wish-fulfillment fantasy. It was a composition of subtle and charming androgyny, the long dark hair, the classically sculpted features, the amber eyes so light in color they were luminous, the deep brown skin—definitely not one of the stock compositions you could get from Wear-Ware or some wannabee program. But he—Sam was calling it "he" on no basis other than arbitrary—had to have spent hours mixing palettes. Even the tasteful silks he was wearing were original. The calculation wasn't lost on her.

But then, any hacker this good wouldn't be artless on any level. Which was a little bit funny, since he'd told her his name was Art. (There, she decided, a male name. Like Sam? She started to wonder again.) She hadn't given him a name, not even a phony, and pressing him for information was futile. The only thing she'd gotten out of him after she'd agreed to put on the headmount was how he'd done the trick with Fez's monitor.

He'd made her work for it, though; he wanted banter, and

he wanted jokes, and he wanted the hacker news of the world, which he already seemed to know in more detail than she did, before he finally gave it up.

"Just a little rewiring trick with the hardware," he told her at last. "I gave Fez the specs to rig it, with a program dedicated to the screens. So I can pop one whenever I have something to tell him, without waiting for him to come to me."

"Very fancy," she said, which was understating it; it should have been impossible. "But why don't you just call him on the phone?"

"Call him on the phone," he mused, the smooth forehead wrinkling slightly. He seemed to taste the idea, as if she had suggested something rare and exotic and perhaps a little improper in some way. The expression made him look suddenly far more female than male, and she felt her mild confusion return.

"Don't you trust the telephone? Or aren't you local?" Maybe, she thought uneasily, he was a total paraplegic and incapable of speech. "Or, uh, I mean, if there's a problem . . . " She winced, glad he couldn't actually see it.

He grinned. "Don't make faces, it's okay. I probably *could* do that now. Wouldn't Fez just go wild if he heard me on the phone. Where *is* the phone, anyway?" He froze; after a few moments a phantom twin rose up out of his image and walked around behind her. She followed with her eyes, and the view on the screen shifted as if she were turning her head. There was a moment of vertigo; it felt a little as if her eyes had suddenly floated around the side of her head, a feature of headmount screens that she could never get used to. Through a small gap between some India-print curtains, she could see there was another room beyond.

She turned back to Art. "Are you still here?"

"Absolutely." He grinned again. "Complete multitasking capabilities, you know."

"Do you always expend that much on pyrotechnics, or is this a special occasion?"

"Well, I like to believe that I'm achieving self-expression. But then, that's the whole raison d'être for *art*." He winked.

"I'm not going to groan. It'll just encourage you."

"But all conscious creatures need encouragement to thrive. Wouldn't you agree, Sam-I-Am?"

Fez's nickname for her was a fast cold shock running up the back of her neck. "Ah . . . excuse me?"

"Your technique is very characteristic," he said. "I've sampled some of your game simulations, tasted them inside out. If you input on a keyboard, I can tell it's you by your touch, the patterns of your input, the amount of time between one symbol and the next." He shrugged. "I can tell the difference between you and Rosa, or Fez, or Keely. Or anybody else."

The shock had turned to an unpleasant wave of creepiness. "Sorry, I find that a little hard to believe."

He shrugged again. "I knew it was you this time, didn't I? Even though you wouldn't identify yourself."

She hesitated. "Lucky guess. Or you recognized my voice."

"Have you ever spoken to me before?"

Sam suppressed the urge to hang up on him. (Him, she thought, definitely him.) She shifted uncomfortably in the chair, conscious of the headmount; suddenly it seemed very heavy. "You enjoy toying with other people, don't you?"

"I'm sorry." He looked so sincere that for a moment she almost forgot she was watching a simulated image and not an actual person. "But I really can distinguish between you. I know, for example, that the data Fez showed me was encrypted by Keely and decrypted by you."

She was sure now that her hair would have stood on end if she hadn't been wearing the headmount. "Fez showed you *that*?"

"Oh, yes. The missing information wasn't completely salvageable. The whole idea behind a sleeping load is destroy-and-notify, and it destroyed with gusto. By the way, Keely never spotted the flare because it *was* the data, in part. But I think I've restored enough."

Sam frowned to herself. Fez had said he'd had a program working on it. Why would he hide the fact that he'd brought someone else in on it? The idea of Fez lying to her made her feel more than a bit ill.

"Are you going to tell me about it?" she asked slowly. "Or is this only for Fez?"

He tilted his head and looked at her curiously. "Why would it be only for him? Keely sent *you* the sockets."

"The what?"

"The sockets. The schematic for the sockets." He dragged a large white pillow over and stood it up on one knee, yanking one of the tassels. A dark rectangular area appeared on the pebbly material; he touched one side of the rectangle, and the schematic Keely had zapped to her in the Ozarks came up just as it would have on an ordinary monitor. Art grinned at her, obviously pleased with himself. "I don't waste any part of a simulation; everything you see is fully functional as well as ornamental."

"Uh-huh," Sam said faintly. Christ, how was he doing it? He had to be either a handicap with a lot of time on his hands or obsessed beyond redemption.

He touched the other side of the rectangle, and the graphic of Visual Mark's brain appeared as Fez had first shown it to her. "When you decrypted this, you didn't notice that you had eight and not just one, did you?"

Sam blinked. "I noticed a lot of redundancy, but I thought it was the error safeguard from the transmission program—"

"Easily missed. It *is* just one until you put the two separate fragments together." The brain slid to the center of the screen as the other graphic of what Sam had thought was a neuron shrank in size and made a countermove to a spot above it. A moment later there were eight instead of one; the graphic of the brain increased in size as each of the eight things swooped to one of the highlighted areas on the cortex.

The image gave a sudden flicker and faded out, like badly spliced film. "One of the bad spots," Art told her. "It'll come back shortly. Ah, here we are."

The brain graphic reappeared, now with a network of red filaments radiating from each of the eight highlighted areas, from the points where each one had inserted itself.

"I was right. They're implants," Sam said, more to herself. "But why would a corporation like the Dive decide to move into therapeutic implants?"

Art held up a finger. "Not implants. I told you, *sockets*. They're receptor sockets that will accommodate a certain kind of input device—" He touched a finger to the highlighted area on the right frontal lobe. A window blossomed at the spot and zoomed out, showing a detailed line drawing of the socket. The channel Sam had noted as being too large for an axon was now filled with a pronged device.

"No explanatory call-outs," Art told her. "I'm afraid those were permanently obliterated."

"But what's it for?" Sam asked. "Either they're going to do this, or they've already done it, to Visual Mark—"

"Well, they're going to make rock videos, to start with," Art said casually. "I could show you some specs on the visual cortex of this brain—it's pretty fascinating. Apparently this visual cortex enjoys a particularly strong link with the *visualizing* center. You'd have to be a neurosurgeon to read it with any understanding, but it's an unusual brain. Has some problems, too, some weakened areas. A lot of the activity's been channeled away from those areas by the brain itself, to take the stress off. Whoever's working on this must have faith that the brain is going to continue doing that—"

"What kind of problems are you talking about?"

"I'm no authority. Stroke, maybe, or an aneurysm." He paused, looking thoughtful. "I'll have to access some new databases if I'm going to be that kind of doctor."

Sam, wasn't listening. "Wait a minute. Are you saying this guy, Visual Mark, is on the verge of a stroke? Are those sockets supposed to help him?"

"No, they don't have anything to do with that. There's a note here somewhere about antistroke medications already given. The sockets are an interface." Art smiled brightly. "I thought that was clear. They're a direct interface for input-output with manufactured neural nets. Computers."

Sam gave a short, incredulous laugh. "Damn. Somebody did it. Somebody finally did it! I want it!" She cut off. "God, what am I saying? The Dive did it, I don't want *them* putting holes in my head."

"Actually, Dr. Lindel Joslin did it during her tenure at EyeTraxx," Art said mildly. "Diversifications took EyeTraxx over just in time to claim the patent."

And somehow Keely had known about it, Sam thought. Somehow he'd been hacking around, or something, and he'd come up with the biggest thing since the transistor, and they'd caught him and made him disappear. What had he been going to do with the data? More important, what had he been expecting her and Fez to do with the data *now*? They could post it untraceably, she supposed, but what would that accomplish, besides spoiling the Dive's surprise? The Dive already had the patent—

Art's phantom twin suddenly reappeared, coming around from behind her on the left, carrying a small handset. Art froze again, allowing the phantom to sink down and superimpose itself on him.

"Well," he said, when the two of them had merged, "here's the phone." He flipped the handset open and examined it. "Complicated in its way, but hardly impossible. I hadn't thought about this. Of course, I'm more than I used to be."

She felt a touch on her shoulder and jumped. He leaned forward, looking anxious (and female again). "Is something wrong? Your vitals just went pop."

"They're back, I think. Fez and Rosa and—" She shut up.

"Good! Then I can call him right now. Don't tell him, okay? Let me surprise him." The eyes were definitely glowing.

"It's your party," she said, resigned. "What about Keely's data?"

"He's got it. I copied you on it, too. Now you go distract him while I figure out how to dial."

She started to protest, but the screen went dark as he hung up on her. Sam called for disconnect and worked the monitor off her head.

Fez was standing over her, curious. "Keeping busy?"

"Yah," she said. "Your friend Art with the program popped in for a chat." She gestured at the easel monitor. "Cute trick with the on-off. Scared me out of a year's growth."

"Yes, well, I'll have to tell you all about that later. It's rather a long story." Fez started to turn away, and she caught his arm.

"Art salvaged the data." *Why didn't you tell me you'd let someone else in on it?* she asked him silently.

"Are you going to tell me about it, or is this a secret between you two?" he asked.

"Maybe I should let Art tell you. In the comfort of the *tent.*"

"Yes, that's a bit much, isn't it? Art's a grandstander of the first order. Did I get a copy?"

Sam nodded, and he reached over to flip the easel monitor on. He brought up a file directory, tapping a box at the bottom of the screen to page ahead. "Here we are," he said, as the heading *New Files: 12 Hours* appeared at the top of the screen. There were three entries. Just as he tapped the last one, the phone rang.

"Can you get that for me, Rosa?" he asked, pulling a chair over and sitting down in front of the screen.

Rosa picked up the handset on the desk. "Yes? Uh-huh." She held the phone out. "For you, Fez."

He didn't look away from the data rolling out on the screen. "Who is it? Will they leave a message?"

"It's Art," she said.

He frowned at her. "Art *who?*"

Sam laughed. "Art who, he wants to know." Fez gave her a look.

"Art who?" Rosa asked the phone. Her eyebrows went up. "Art Fish."

Fez pushed his chair back from the desk and looked from Rosa to Sam. "Are you two in this somehow, is this some kind of joke you cooked up together?"

Sam barely heard him. "Art *Fish*? He calls himself Art *Fish*?"

"Actually, you get it faster if you say Artie Fish," Adrian said, coming out of the kitchenette with a large piece of dry matzo.

"Adrian." Fez turned to him sharply.

Adrian shrugged. "Come on, you were gonna tell them."

"Fez, are you gonna talk to this person or not?" Rosa said, still holding the phone out.

Fez took the phone from Rosa. "Hello," he said cautiously. He listened for a long time without saying anything.

Adrian came over to the desk, nibbling the matzo and holding a hand under it to catch the crumbs. "I know he was gonna tell you when the data came through."

"Tell us what?" Rosa asked.

Fez closed the handset and sat holding it, his face blank. "That was Art Fish." He sounded amazed. "I'd said we were going to be out. Shouldn't have bothered popping on."

"It was just after you left," Sam told him. "Maybe he figured he could catch you." She leaned an elbow on the desk. "You mind telling us why he calls himself Fish? Not to mention who he is and if he *is* a he, and while you're at it, maybe you'll explain why you said you had a program working on Keely's data when you really gave it to someone—" She stopped and looked up at Adrian. "*Artie Fish*?"

Adrian chuckled. "Stone-home kick, ain't it?"

"*Artie Fish*?" She made a pained face at Fez. "Not *really*."

Light dawned for Rosa at the same time. "Well, it was bound to happen someday. But, Jesus, *Art Fish*? What's wrong with the good old names, like Frankenstein?"

"Actually," Fez said, sitting back in the easy chair and putting his feet on the coffee table, "we all did it, all of us together."

Curled up on the couch next to Rosa, Sam squeezed her twined fingers against each other. The revelation seemed to be playing on a loop in her head, making her heart leap each time it hit her.

"The net system was complicated to begin with," Fez was

saying, with a faraway look on his face. "I suppose consolidating everything into the generic commodity we know as the dataline was the start of it. But nothing might have really come of it if it hadn't been for the input that exceeded. So to speak."

"Like what?" Rosa asked.

"Like the viruses, and the piggybacks, the floating boards that pop in and out wherever there's space to accommodate them. All the hackers who found a little capacity here and there and squeezed in compressed data and programs. The hackers who *made* capacity where there technically wasn't any by using the virtual spaces between bits, and then the spaces between *those* bits, and the spaces between *those*."

"Between one point and another, there's always another point," said Rosa. "That's elementary geometry. Even *I* learned that, and I hated geometry. I liked that paradox, though. Whatsisbod's Paradox, proving forward motion is impossible. Like, lay back, relax, you can't go anywhere anyway."

Fez smiled. "It also has to do with fractals. Take a line, bend it in half. Then bend each half in half. Then bend all the segments in half, ad infinitum. You get fantasy snowflakes and baroque seacoasts—"

"—and great paisleys," murmured Adrian.

"—and if you look several levels down into a fractal, you'll find that a larger pattern's been duplicated. Which means that the fractal several levels down from the area of the fractal you're looking into contains all the information of the larger fractal. Worlds within worlds."

Rosa laughed a little. "You're approaching my threshold for that kinda talk. I'm a hacker, not a philosopher."

Fez turned to look at her. "Good choice of word, threshold. The way we all kept adding to the nets did exactly that, passed a threshold. It got to the point where the net should have collapsed in chaos, but it didn't. Or rather, it did, but the collapse was not a collapse in the conventional sense. Because the net kept *accommodating* the demands we put on it—that was its purpose, after all, to accommodate data. When it reached the point where it was burdened to the limit, it had two choices—crash, or accommodate. It did both.

"Going over the brink of catastrophe was the first stage. The second was recovery—since it was programmed to accommodate, it did. But the only way it could accommodate was to exceed the limit. Institute a new limit, and when that was reached, go over the brink of catastrophe again, recover and institute a new limit beyond that. And so forth."

"Ad infinitum," Sam said, expressionlessly. "Like a fractal growing from the bottom up instead of the top down. Triggered by catastrophe."

"It didn't get a break while all this was going on, of course," Fez continued. "The information never stopped coming in, which made for quite a lot of turbulence. But chaos is just another kind of order, and so we have another kind of net now than the one we started out with. We woke it up."

Rosa let out a breath. "Which came first—Art Fish, or Dr. Fish?"

"It's hard to say. *Art Fish* was the file name on a proposed AI program," Fez said. "There was also a prototype of a vaccine with the working title of *Virus Doctor*. The present incarnation is Dr. Art Fish, V.D. Virus Doctor."

Sam's gaze drifted over to the system on the desk. "Is it all in there now?"

"I don't think it's all any one place," Fez said. "It's all through the nets, though the core routine, if you can call it a routine, seems to be centralized in Dr. Fish's Answering Machine."

"What is it? The routine."

Fez stared past her, squinting thoughtfully. "I guess you could call it a virus, though that's not strictly true. It's not just *one*, that is, but several, and at least parts of many more than that. And it's not really a true virus anymore in many ways. I mean—" He blew out a breath. "Okay. Anytime a new access opens up on the dataline, as soon as it comes into contact with Art, it's 'infected.' And there is no part of the net that is *not* Art. Art is everywhere, though his *attention* is not, if you see what I mean."

Rosa shook her head. "Do you mean the L.A. net, or the state, or the continental net, or—" She frowned. "World-wide?"

Fez nodded.

"Then there have to be other people who know about this," Sam said. "We can't be the *only* ones who know there's something . . . awake . . . in the net."

"People see only what they want to see." Fez shrugged. "It's possible someone else knows, in some other part of the country or the world. But nobody's said anything."

"*You* didn't say anything," Sam said accusingly.

He grinned at her. "Well, I'm not really the talkative type, Sam-I-Am."

"Sure." She gave a short laugh.

"There is one other person who shares full acquaintance with the Dr. Fish we know, serving as archivist and keeper of Art's ever-changing files. Encrypted, of course," Fez said. "I'm sure there must be others. Statistically there has to be someone somewhere else who's onto it. But it would have to be someone who was *looking* for it. You know how people use the net. We take it for granted, just like cars or telephones or refrigerators. If you don't take it for granted, then you probably don't have it."

"And you were looking for it," Sam said thoughtfully.

Fez nodded.

She sat forward. "Why?"

He smiled. "It seemed like the right thing to do. Now, are you going to show me the data Art salvaged?"

"Maybe we ought to Turing-test first."

"Oh, Art's conscious," Fez said confidently. "That's not the question. The question is whether Art's human or not."

"Part catastrophe and part chaos," said Rosa. "Sounds pretty human to me."

18

Stalling Rivera proved to be surprisingly easy, perhaps because he wasn't quite lying. The guards on the guy's system were the best he'd ever seen. Not impossible, though. Nothing was impossible. For the first couple of days after he'd contacted the guy, he'd just laid back and taken his time, and Rivera hadn't given him any trouble. What could he have done about it, anyway?

This morning, he thought he had the answer to that. He'd awakened feeling stupid and out-of-sorts, as if he'd spent the whole night toxing out with Jones on the Mimosa. Son of a bitch, he thought dully. He couldn't smell anything in the clothes Rivera had left for him, but just to be on the safe side, he stayed nude. Rivera could have given him something to suppress his olfactory, since he'd had the enormously bad judgment to let on that he'd figured out the clothes.

Stupid even when I'm not toxed, he thought sourly, sitting at the terminal. He made a move toward the keyboard and suddenly felt overwhelmed with fatigue. "Shit," he muttered, putting his face in his hands.

"I'll be needing some more copies of the original download and anything else you might have," said Rivera's voice behind him.

At least his reflexes were too dull to make him jump and give Rivera *that* satisfaction. He looked over his shoulder. "Didn't hear you come in," he said. "Extra copies of the original download's all I got." He held up a small plastic envelope with two chips in it. "Nothing else ready to travel."

Rivera came over to the desk and picked up the envelope, his eyebrows lifting slightly at the sight of Keely's nudity. "Can you have something at the end of the day?" he asked in his crisp supervisor's tone. Like he was talking to one of his indentured servants. Like that guy, maybe.

"That depends." Keely yawned, making no attempt to cover himself. "When does the day end around here?"

"We'll call it five or so."

Keely shrugged. "Could take me till three to get in. Maybe get it on a fast buffer capture. The quality won't be great, and I can't guarantee you'll have anything complete—"

"Can you do it or not?"

"I don't know," Keely said irritably. "Yah. Maybe. I don't fucking *know*. If you'd stop fucking around with me, I could probably put this thing into overdrive whenever you wanted."

Rivera seemed to be regarding him from a great height. "That hasn't been true in the last few days. Perhaps you need a little help."

"That what you did to me last night, give me a little *help*?" Keely snapped. "You better let me detox soon, or maybe you'll come back here at five and find nothing but a little pool of shit and blood on this chair where I used to be."

"You wish medical attention?" Rivera asked politely.

"I think I've had some fucking *medical attention*." His anger was starting to wake him up. It felt good. "I just think you better detox me before my first physical with the Corrections Board, or you're gonna have to explain more than I ever did."

"The board has waived the standard physical examination requirement, in light of Diversifications' outstanding record with reparation-sentenced felons," Rivera told him cheerfully. "Any other questions? Good. Tap Ludovic—"

"Who?"

"Our man. Tap him, get everything you can, and make three copies. I'll be back to pick it all up around five. Can you remember that?"

Keely felt himself deflating. Should have known they'd bought the Corrections Board. They could buy anything. He yawned again. "Never forget it."

"After you do that, you can enjoy some leisure time if you want. Watch the dataline, have some more cognac. But try to be ready to travel."

He felt a small wave of fear. "Oh, yah? You taking me on a Mexican vacation?" he asked slowly.

"I haven't really decided," Rivera told him. "Now or a month from now may make no difference at all. It's not your worry, anyway. Just be prepared." He nodded at the console. "Ludovic will be on-line now. I suggest you start trying to get in and get as much as you can. I have an important meeting this evening, and I'll need that material."

Keely leaned on the desk and slowly went through the motions of getting ready to tap the guy's program again until he heard the door close behind Rivera. Then he sat back in the chair and tried to think. All Rivera had to do was look at the record of activity in the black-box recorder to know he'd already tapped the guy's program again without downloading anything. But he seemed to be too busy to look, so the good guys were safe for the moment.

Hell, for all he knew, the guy wouldn't be on-line now anyway. Maybe the system activity for the last few days had just been the guy tidying up his system before he ran for it. Except Rivera had sounded pretty confident on that matter. *Ludovic will be on-line now.*

Ludovic. Sam's father, Gabe. Had to be. Shit. Why hadn't she *told* him she'd had that kind of in with the Dive? If he'd known that, he'd have suggested they go partners instead of trying to hack the dragon all on his own. Except she probably would have said no, and he'd have ended up here after all. No fucking use thinking about it.

But the question remained—what was Ludovic doing now? Just waiting for Rivera's ax to fall? He tried to remember what Sam had told him about her parents. She was on the outs with them, he knew that for certain, but he seemed to remember it being more with her mother than her father.

Keely sat back in the chair, one hand on the keyboard. Too bad the guy wasn't a hacker. Then the guy could pass him a virus, maybe even a little dose of the Fish, and he could pass it on to Rivera, who could then give it to whatever VIPs he was sucking off. Maybe he should just do that himself. He didn't have any Fish handy, but he knew a few tricks of his own—

He'd just be delaying the inevitable and maybe making his own position worse. Rivera would just take the virus to the Corrections Board, and he'd end up polishing Rivera's boots for the next two decades. He sighed and started the tap routine.

A couple of hours later, he was in, and he managed to capture thirty minutes before the system spat him out again. He disengaged and made the three copies Rivera wanted. Then he took a look at what he'd gotten off the guy.

Rivera was going to shit. There were maybe fifteen minutes

of the guy's personal program, probably volatile storage he'd forgotten to dump. The rest of it was all commercials, finished spots, roughs, initial composition storyboards, requisition lists. He rather liked the one for body armor—guy strolling through a bad neighborhood, gets shot at, knives thrown at him, people trying to punch him, everything bouncing off; gets to his office, sits down at his terminal, and the message comes up on the screen: *You Have Been Hacked! HAHAHAHAHAHAHA!* Guy turns to pov and says, Well, there's one thing Gilding BodyShields can't protect you from. Woman enters picture, leans down, gives him openmouthed kiss, walks off, he stares after her, saying, And there's another.

Thanks, guy, Keely thought, *but what the fuck have you been sitting around doing commercials for when you should have been running like hell?*

Well, whatever Rivera had had in mind, Keely was sure it hadn't included commercials, which was going to make Rivera look like an idiot in front of whomever he was trying to impress. He patted the monitor. "I can't believe that's the best you could do, but if it was, good for you, pal. Good for you." He staggered off to shower.

"Something off the local dataline," Fez said, looking up from the screen.

"I'll get it," Adrian said, moving to the other screen. "Let me practice my Mandarin." He punched for the translation program and sat back and waited for the characters to appear on the screen. "Makes me feel useful."

Sam gave a small, soundless laugh. At least someone was feeling useful, she thought. They'd spent the last few days studying Keely's zap, but not doing much else. Sam felt antsy. She wanted to do something, tell somebody, but both Rosa and Fez had been adamant about keeping quiet. The information would be too traceable if Keely had talked, and they had to assume that he had. Not willingly, perhaps. She didn't like to think about that, and she knew they were probably right, but she still felt frustrated. Keely had zapped them the data for *some* reason.

"Oh, damn," Adrian said, and something in his voice gave Sam a small chill.

"What is it?" Rosa asked, sitting up on the couch. She'd been going over a hard flatcopy of some program she'd been working on.

"Rosa, you and Jones, and possibly Sam, are being sought by the police for questioning."

"Stone the fucking crows at fucking *home*." Rosa threw down the hardcopy and stalked over as Fez rolled his chair over next to Adrian. "What for?" Sam's small chill became a deep freeze. She wanted to get up out of the easy chair and join the others at the screen, but her legs felt too watery to hold her up. In three years on her own, she had never been specifically targeted by the police.

"What do you mean, 'possibly me'?" she asked in a small voice.

Fez split the screen horizontally, putting Adrian's translation on the bottom. "Details of the case aren't available," he said after a moment. "Someone's put out a 'round up the usual suspects' command. I imagine they're working on a list of Keely's known associates. There's a whole list here, but they don't have any real names—Gator, Kazin, Captain Jasm, Cherokee Rosa, Jones, and Pheasant Sam."

"*Who* Sam?"

He spelled it for her.

"The Mandarin has it closer to game bird, actually," Adrian murmured.

"Well, that's that. Time for a change of address," said Rosa. "Better run home and pack up my stuff and my stiff."

"I'll go with you," Sam said shakily.

"I think it would be better if you both stayed here," Fez said, looking from Rosa to Sam.

"I know," Rosa said wearily. "I can always get more stuff, but it's the stiff. If I just leave him there, he really will be a stiff. If they find him dead, they'll figure one of us killed him to keep him from talking. Won't that be a pretty pickle."

Fez sighed. "How about the gypsy jobs you've been doing? What are the chances any of those turning you?"

"Who can say?" Rosa spread her hands. "If I find a welcoming committee waiting for me, I'll jump and get a message to you later on the answering machine. Otherwise, I'll get back here with Jones as fast as I can."

"Change rentals!" Fez called after her as she went out the door.

"Pheasant Sam." Sam shook her head. "Maybe it *isn't* me. Adrian's translation—"

Fez shook his head. "A pheasant *is* a game bird." He moved back to the other screen and scrolled all the way to the end.

"Keely really did talk, then, didn't he?" she said.

"Not willingly, I'm sure. Probably in a drug-induced stupor."

"The police can't do that. I mean, they're not supposed to."

"Nobody said the police had to do it. He might be in a hospital." Fez paused. "If Keely knows your actual first name, 'pheasant' could be a slurred or garbled version of that."

Sam tried to hear it in her mind, the transformation of *Cassandra* into *pheasant*. It seemed farfetched, but stranger things had come to pass, she thought, looking at Fez's system—

"Shit," she said. "It *isn't* Pheasant Sam. It's Fezzansam— *Fez and Sam.*"

Fez went so white she thought he was going to faint. "Oh, my. It's one of those good-news days, isn't it?" He was about to say something else when he did a double take at something at the bottom of the screen. "*Oh,* my. Did Art tell you he was going to email this information to you?"

"No!" She jumped up and ran over to him. "I mean—" She tried to think. "When I talked to him, he said he was going to copy me, and I didn't even think of—oh, Jesus, why did he *do* that?"

She went to the other screen. Adrian surrendered the chair to her. "I'll blow it up from here. I'll send a delete to the mailbox."

"Don't!" Fez said. "Don't get on-line. You can only delete mail under your own name, and someone could be watching for any variation of Pheasant Sam. Including plain old Sam."

She sat back with a groan. "It wouldn't be under my name anyway. I forgot. All my mail's forwarded to Rosa, and I don't know her password. We've got to get a message to her, to tell her to delete the mail right away."

"Adrian can do it," Fez said.

She looked up at the boy in amazement. "How? In Mandarin?"

"I can touch-type, and I can write," Adrian told her as they changed places again. "The lesion left writing intact. You'll just have to dictate to me, because I won't be able to read any of it."

Sam watched his fingers move easily over the keyboard as Fez dictated a short message to Rosa. "Now," Fez added as Adrian pressed *send*, "we'll just have to hope the traffic's running in her favor."

An hour later Rosa called to tell them that Jones was gone, her laptop was missing, and the mailbox was empty.

* * *

It wasn't one of the officially sanctioned break times, so he had the whole Common Room to himself. The whole idea of officially sanctioned break times had always rankled him anyway. Besides, what was Manny going to do to him if he found out, put a disciplinary note in his file? It was incredibly humorous to him now that he had once feared a mere disciplinary note.

As of a few days ago, he was fearing nothing. The only thing he was feeling now was a peculiar off-balance numbness, the same kind of sensation he'd had in the bayou portion of *Head-hunters*, when he'd been up to his neck in cold swamp water, waiting for the voodoo bad guys to pull him out and crucify him on the cypress tree.

His first impulse, after seeing the hacker's final message, had been to download everything to chip and clear out. Marly and Caritha would have been barely accessible to him—his system at home wasn't sophisticated enough to handle anything more than a standard game. But at least he would have saved them.

After getting over the initial shock—*Rivera spot you meeting*—he had reconsidered. The only way Manny could have spotted him meeting—with Marly and Caritha, he assumed—was to have this hacker, whoever it was, crack him, which was illegal surveillance according to Diversifications' own company bylaws. Which meant Manny couldn't actually *do* a damned thing with the information. If Manny reported him to the Upstairs Team, he'd have to mention how he'd found out in the first place. Gabe might still lose his job, but Manny would almost certainly be fired, too. Even if Manny had done it with the blessing of the Upstairs Team, all Gabe would have to do would be to file a grievance with the Labor Board; upper management would quietly throw Manny to the wolves to avoid a scandal.

Stalemate, at least until Manny figured out how to maneuver. Working faster than he ever had in his life, Gabe had downloaded everything to do with Marly and Caritha and filled the system with commercials. If Manny had had him cracked just to research a case for a personal audit, then let the audit come, then. They'd find nothing but storyboards, roughs, finished spots, and inventories of props. Even if they were suspicious, Manny would look like an idiot.

The most surprising thing about his plan, Gabe thought,

staring unseeingly at the dataline screens in the wall, was that he had gone through with it. He *had* filled the system up with new commercials, all kinds of spots, body armor, pharmaceuticals, clothing—whatever had been waiting for him in his assignment queue. It was as if he'd been some kind of machine, cranking them out, not even wondering if he'd be able to come up with anything, just *doing* it. Doing what he had to do. Apparently he wasn't as burned out as he'd thought. Either that, or a touch of danger was exactly what the old creative generator had needed to get it fired up again.

So he'd done commercials and more commercials, waiting for something to happen, waiting for a note from Manny to appear in his interoffice emailbox asking him to please come to Manny's office, waiting for Manny himself to show up at the door to his pit. And nothing had happened. He hadn't even seen Manny around the building.

Maybe Manny didn't actually know anything at all. Maybe the hacker had covered it all up somehow. He had to consider that, too, Gabe thought, that the hacker's warning had come early enough to give him a chance to clear his system of anything incriminating. If so, that meant he'd be able to load Marly and Caritha back in again eventually, and he'd be a little more cautious about it this time, keep the time/productivity ratios a little more even, if he could. Because he shouldn't have to lose everything all at once. He shouldn't have to be left with *nothing*.

It was fortunate, he thought, that he hadn't seen Catherine in days, either, not since she'd announced she was leaving him. One look at him would have told her that something other than the end of their marriage was bothering him. But things had gone back to a semblance of normal at the condo, too. She was sealed up in her office, and he was tiptoeing in and out of the guest bedroom, all as usual. Apparently her house hadn't come onto the market yet. He imagined she would let him know when it was time to move, and perhaps he should have been out looking for an apartment, but if he hadn't let Manny stampede him, then Catherine wasn't going to do it either.

Behind him he heard the Common Room doors whisper open. "*There* you are!"

He jumped at the sound of LeBlanc's voice, spilling cold coffee all over his lap.

"Sorry," LeBlanc said with an embarrassed laugh. "I didn't realize you were in media trance. What are you doing down here all by yourself when everyone's up on Mirisch's folly watching the show?"

He blinked at her, dabbing at his pants with a napkin. "Mirisch's folly?"

"That stupid platform terrace on twenty." She handed him another napkin from the dispenser on the table.

"There's a show up there?"

"Sort of. That woman is up there, and she says she's gonna jump."

Gabe shook his head. "What woman?"

"The one that hit you. She's sitting on the rail, and she says she's gonna jump. I thought you'd like to see that."

"She's going to commit *suicide*?"

"Yah, she really hates it here. No, actually, she's got this harness on with these long elastic cords, it's some kind of stunt—" LeBlanc pulled him out of the chair. "Come on, you have to see it to believe it."

They were really turning out for this, Gina thought, looking at the crowd on the terrace. Two security guards were trying to keep them all back from her, and some ditz named Clooney was running back and forth trying to be in charge. The security guards were arguing as to whether they should call for reinforcements or prove they could handle this themselves. *Christ deliver us all from security guards with something to prove*, she thought. A little ways down from her, Valjean was leaning on the rail, tapping his foot impatiently while his cape went into tile-deformation frenzy. She could practically hear his thoughts: *Are you gonna do this fucking fall, or are you gonna wait for a bigger fucking audience?*

She checked the connections on the harness she was wearing, making sure the cords were secure on the stone rail, and tightened the band on the minicam strapped to her forehead. Canadaytime and their fucking signature image. Last time she'd had to go feet first off the roof of the old EyeTraxx warehouse building, and Valjean had complained that the fall hadn't been *really* long enough. It would be long enough this time. The bungis would stretch fifteen stories at least.

"You've got to seal this place off, make all these people leave, and mount a serious rescue operation!" Clooney was yelling at one of the guards. A sudden gust of wind whipped the corner of his large, floppy shirt collar right into his open mouth. The guard shoved him aside.

"Madam, *please* get off that rail and come inside *now!*" he shouted at her. "Don't make us have to call your supervisor up here."

"Whoa, my fucking *supervisor*, I'm trembling in my fucking traces over that one," she muttered, looking out at West Hollywood and the Santa Monica Mountains. Like they weren't going to tell Rivera about this if she just went along quietly. She'd told the Beater when the deal with Diversifications had gone through, you work for a large corporation, they'll expect you to believe all kinds of stupid shit.

And what kind of stupid shit did she believe—that getting eight holes punched in Mark's head was going to crank his battery back to high? That if she went along with him, the world was going to be new again?

If you agree, you go tomorrow, you and Mark. To Mexico. And if you say no, they'll find a reason to get rid of you, Gina. I know it for a fact.

Bend over, right now, while they're still asking nicely.

He wants you with him. And if you say no, he'll go anyway because that's the deal. Rivera didn't want me to give you much time to think about it, or to try to talk Mark out of it.

The guy she'd popped appeared among the crowd on the terrace, looking dazed and confused. Must be his natural state, she thought.

If you go with him, he can make it. It's the one chance he's got to keep from melting down, but if you go with him, he'll make it for certain. For what you are to each other, even if you don't know what that is.

So how much stupid shit did she believe, and how much of it was stupid shit? She'd pounded on Mark's door, but he hadn't been in that fucking pit. Lost somewhere in videoland; in the stupidsphere.

Who's gonna find him if you don't, Gina?

She'd almost smacked the Beater for that one. For that, and for sitting on it until that morning, when it was too late to say but one thing. But she wouldn't say it while the Beater stood there waiting for it, she wouldn't say a goddamn word to him. Let him crawl for it over forty-seven miles of barbed wire. She looked around the crowd on the terrace again, her gaze snagging briefly on the punching bag. The Beater hadn't crawled up here yet. Neither had Mark.

Valjean straightened up and threw one end of the cape over his shoulder. Cloud shapes were scudding through the material at high speed. What was she waiting for? She had to do his stupid fucking *fall*. Get it planted good in her mind, so when they drilled her skull, it would come out of the holes like the perfect dream, and she wouldn't need the footage from the cam strapped on her head. She stood up on the rail, balancing carefully, ignoring the guards, who were shouting at her again.

"Wait!"

The punching bag had broken out of the crowd, coming toward her. He looked like he was going to be sick any moment. She stuck her fists on her hips. "What."

He looked around self-consciously. "Ah . . . are you sure you know what you're doing? There's a flying harness in the pit, you know."

Funny; she could almost believe he cared about what was going to happen next. A screwy idea popped into her head. "How'd you like to get even?"

His face scrunched up. "What?"

"For the punch I gave you."

"You're just doing this for the attention!" bellowed the ditz Clooney, actually shaking a finger at her. She shook a different finger back at him.

"You wanna get even or not? Make up your mind. I gotta go one way or the other, I jump or you push me."

He looked green with horror.

She waved a hand in dismissal. Nobody would push you when you asked for it. Screwy fucking idea anyway. Turning her back to him, she took a deep breath and looked down to intensify the vertigo. The terrace had enough overhang so she wouldn't leave a long red smear on the side of the building. Considerate of them to build it that way. She wondered what it had been built for as she stepped off the rail.

On the third bounce she figured what the fuck. She'd do it.

In the bedlam that followed, Manny finally came up with the older man, the Beater. Gabe hadn't especially wanted to see Manny, but he hadn't wanted to leave while the security guards were hauling the woman up over the side of the rail. She seemed to be fine, or no worse than usual. The strange guy in the weird cape kept trying to get around Clooney, who was pushing him away and warning him about unauthorized personnel. Gabe wondered what Clooney thought he could actually do. Everyone else was milling around, gabbling in shocked tones that sounded more than a bit lascivious. It was the most excitement anyone had seen since the original stars of a very popular bad movie called *Love's Madness* had taken a publicity tour of Diversifications and somehow gotten into a fistfight in the middle of it. Love's madness, and now rock-video madness.

Manny noticed him almost immediately and gave him a friendly nod. Mystified, he could only return the nod and then retreat to the doorway leading to the elevator bank as Manny descended on Gina Aiesi.

She gestured at the Beater a few times, pointed down, waved a fist under Manny's nose—maybe she was going to hit him, Gabe thought, thrilling briefly to the image of Manny going down with blood spurting from his nose. Abruptly she turned her back on him and finished unstrapping the harness. Manny and the Beater turned and went back toward the elevators. Gabe tried to will himself invisible, but Manny paused at the entrance.

"How's the jaw?"

Gabe blinked at him. "Pardon?"

"The jaw." Manny tapped his own face. "Better now?"

"Just fine," Gabe managed, nodding. "Uh, thanks."

"Glad to hear it." Manny went inside. Gabe watched as he and the Beater stepped into one of the elevators. Their departure signaled a mass migration. Gabe slipped through the crowd to where Gina Aiesi was bundling up her harness under the stern supervision of the security guards.

"The show's over," she said. "I don't know why you're still hanging around. Unless you wanna make sure I don't steal the goddamn terrace while I'm at it."

The caped man shoved Clooney aside disdainfully. "You tell them, Gina."

"We're going to escort you back to your work area," said one of the guards stiffly. "Where you are to stay. This floor is off-limits to you, you're not to come up here again."

She gave them each a look. "Well, I guess you told *my* ass off."

"Just come along, madam." The guard reached for her, and she slapped his hand away.

"I'll take her," Gabe said impulsively. "I'll escort her back to her pit."

The guard glared at him. "You were in on it."

"No he wasn't," Gina said. "Get outa my face. I'll let him *escort* me."

The guards turned to the caped man. "Sir, we'll have to escort you from the premises now."

"So escort him," Gina said. "You two could open an escort service. Might be a better line of work for you, you don't do shit in security." She laughed a little as they herded the man toward the still-crowded elevator bank. "Hey, Val, you notice I got your fucking fall?"

"It better be good," he called back as one of the guards pushed him through the crowd.

She peeled the cam off, rubbing at her forehead. "You mind waiting till the Keystones are gone before you *escort* me? Since you wouldn't push me."

"Is that your idea of egg in *your* beer?" Gabe asked, surprising himself.

She smiled at him. She had some smile, he thought. It did things to him, and he wasn't even sure why. She tossed the cam at him, and he caught it with a dexterity he'd seldom found occasion to use outside of a simulation.

"Come on," she said. "You can take a little walk with me."

19

"Hell, no," said Gator. "After checking out on me like that, I don't think he'd have the nerve to show his dead ass here again." She finished cleaning the needle and put it on the tray. "Especially after the talking-to I gave him. Not to mention the tattoo."

"I don't think he ever noticed it," Rosa said glumly.

"Well, it's harmless anyway," said Gator. "Nowhere near as valuable as what he took out of your mailbox, I'm sure." She gave Rosa a skeptical look. "You really never thought to pop the old email out and take a scan?"

"Lot on my mind lately," Rosa said. "Besides, I had it automated. Anything that came in would go right into off-line storage. I didn't figure he'd bother about that."

Sam straightened up from Gator's laptop. "Well, he hasn't checked in anywhere, with or without the data."

"He wouldn't. He's not a hacker," Gator said. She went over and put an ivy design on the screen. "I marked him with this. I can send a copy to everyone in the Tattoo-of-the-Month Club, which happens to be the entire congregation of St. Diz, but I think you want to find him before anyone else does. He's not a hacker, but he knows payday when he sees it, and he knows he can get good bucks for the stuff he ripped from you."

"If he isn't on the Mimosa, I don't know where to look for him," Sam said, exasperated.

Gator frowned. "Oh, I didn't say he wasn't on the Mimosa. I said he hasn't been *here*, with me in the tent. He could be hiding out anywhere along the strip, you might have passed him without knowing it."

"Great," said Rosa. "Any more good ideas?"

"Sure," Gator said genially. "Find out when the next hit-and-run is leaving, and where it's going. I can just about guarantee Jones'll be right in the middle of it, trying to peddle his prize to one of the hackers running the fooler loops."

"What makes you so sure about that?" Sam asked her.

"The hit-and-run used to be Jones's home away from home, before he hooked up with Keely. He was always hanging on, trying to get canned with somebody famous so he could get his picture on the dataline. Or escape with somebody famous so he could go home with them and get toxed on the good stuff."

"That's kind of risky for us," Sam said doubtfully. "Since we made the top ten. If we get pulled in at a hit-and-run, we'll probably disappear like Keely."

"Leave early," said Gator.

"You're a major help," Rosa said irritated.

Gator smiled and bent over the laptop. "I can give you a couple of IDs that'll stand up to a hit-and-run arrest, squirt you through court like watermelon seeds. Best I can do under the circumstances. Diz asked me to wait here for Fez."

"St. Dismas?" Sam said.

"Sometimes known as my personal physician," Gator replied.

"You've talked to him?"

Two strips of paper came out of the printer, one after another. Gator handed them over. "He leaves me tattoo designs."

Sam wanted to ask her more about that, but Rosa was pulling her out of the tent. "Come on, we've got a hit-and-run to track down. If we're lucky, maybe we can catch Jones before he leaves for it."

"I wouldn't go out there *with* them," Gator said. "Just find out where they're going and be there."

"Wait a minute." Sam stopped at the flap. "What about you? You're on the top ten, too."

Gator grinned brightly. "Oh, they've already found me. In the Santa Monica morgue. My physician pronounced me dead and wrote up the death certificate a couple of hours ago. Hell, it works for Jones."

The creature was eight feet tall, part samurai—correction, someone's video idea of a samurai—part voodoo apparition, part machine-fantasy, and all high resolution. It moved within a small radius in the center of the room, going through a stylized, complex choreography that reminded Gabe of semaphore. He gaped at it openly from where he sat cross-legged on the floor with his back against a couch, holding a drink he couldn't identify on one knee. He was in somebody's living

room, somebody's enormous, endless living room, currently
filled with a glittery array of people eating, drinking, wandering
in and out, watching the multiple screens on the walls, giving
the thing in the center of the room a wide, courteous berth.

Some time ago Gina had brought him here, sometime after
the debacle on the terrace, after she'd asked him to take a little
walk with her. No, *told* him he could take a little walk with
her. Gina didn't ask.

He took another sip of the drink, which he seemed to have
been working on for days. It was vaguely herbal, vaguely spicy,
definitely intoxicating. Gina had given it to him. Probably told
him he could drink it instead of asking him if he wanted anything. He couldn't remember now, any more than he could
remember exactly how he'd come to be in this enormous,
endless living room.

The guy with the crazy cape passed through his field of
vision. In his present state he felt immensely appreciative of
the continuous running patterns in the material. If he could
have moved, he would have gotten up and gone after the man
to thank him for wearing something so marvelously interesting.

He was contemplating that for a while when something
moved at the corner of his vision. He turned to look; nothing.
Funny; he could have sworn that funny flaw was back, the
strange dark spot that had dogged him through various *Headhunters* settings.

The thought was slow in coming, but eventually it pushed
its way through the warm ooze of his mind. No, the glitch
wouldn't be here, because he wasn't in simulation right now.
Even though it sure felt as if he were. He could summon up
Marly's and Caritha's voices in his head just as clearly as if he
were hearing them on his headmount speaker. He couldn't
really follow what they were saying, but that wasn't so important. The program would move him along, and Marly and
Caritha would take care of him. Caritha had the cam, after all;
she could tell him whether he was looking at something real,
or at a holo.

"Holo, yah," said a voice nearby. "What Valjean spends on
holo would finance a new video channel on the dataline. Well,
for part of the day, anyway."

The creature in the middle of the room elongated suddenly
and changed into a pillar of fire.

"*Down!*" Gabe yelled, and flung his arms up over his head,
waiting for the blast and the heat. When it didn't come, he

lowered his arms a little and looked around. Several people were staring at him curiously. The pillar of fire was still burning away.

Someone tapped him on the head. "I think this is yours." He twisted around; a woman thrust an empty glass at him. Something wet had splashed across the silky top of her dress. She looked half-amused and half-annoyed, the way Marly looked at him on occasion. "You know, if you can't handle the lotus, you probably shouldn't touch it."

"Got it," someone else said. Gabe turned back to see a short woman in coveralls holding a handcam. Not Caritha. Right, she wouldn't be here now, he thought, confused. "It's going to make a great effect," the woman was saying. "We'll take the splash and fan it out, it'll look like he's throwing diamonds on you. The party animals'll go bugfuck for it." She looked down at Gabe. "I don't remember getting a video release from you. Sign one before you leave, or I'll have to slip in a sub for you."

"Then this *is* a video?" Gabe said, even more confused.

"That's what they pay me for." The woman said something else, but he ignored her as he struggled to stand up, looking around the room. If this was a video, Marly and Caritha would be here somewhere. He would find them, and they could go track down more headhunters.

He swam through the room, looking around. Faces came at him and bobbed away again like painted balloons. ". . . keep sending my agent clips of these things," a voice nearby was saying, "and he keeps telling me to stay out of insty-party video. I don't understand that. *I* say if the cam loves you, the cam loves you. It loves me, and I deserve to work."

Gabe couldn't hear the reply, if there was one. He found himself facing an array of screens set into a wall, all of them displaying a different sequence of images. His eyes shifted back and forth in a frenzy as he tried to make sense of each one, and for several moments dizziness threatened to knock him over.

There was a sudden firm grip on his arm. "*That* one's pretty interesting, if you're a connoisseur of tech-fantasy porn." A warm hand turned his face slightly to the left and down. He was looking at a strange gold machine with two gleaming cones rising out of the framework on goosenecks. The point of one cone was running back and forth along glowing symbols painted on an endless stretch of transparent material feeding from an unseen source; the point of the other cone was buried in the head of a woman sitting motionless in a chair next to the machine.

"Headhunters," Gabe whispered.

"Good guess, but the real title is *Need to Know*," said the same voice close to his ear. "It's an indictment of our present system of information dispersal. You're allowed to know only those things the information czars decide that you need to know. They call it 'market research' and 'efficient use of resources' and 'no-waste,' but it's the same old shit they've been doing to us for more than a hundred years—keep 'em confused and in the dark. You gotta be a stone-home super-Renaissance person to find out what's really going on. Don't you agree?"

Gabe couldn't look away from the image on the screen. It was almost as bad as what he'd seen in the ward.

"What ward?"

Talking without realizing it; he seemed to be doing that a lot tonight. "Where they punch holes in people's heads and steal their neurotransmitter."

There was a pause. "You must watch a lot of tech-fantasy porn. I knew it. I could tell just by looking at you."

He turned to look at the person who was speaking to him. The face wouldn't come clear of the ornate drifting patterns falling past it like veils, but he was sure it was neither Caritha nor Marly. "Excuse me," he said, "I have to find some people."

The house was on fire. No, *he* was on fire. No, he was standing in the pillar of fire. He'd forgotten all about it. Embarrassed, he tried to step out of it, and it moved with him in a way that was oddly possessive, as if it had decided to claim him. Adopted by a pillar of fire; the program certainly was frisky today. He peered through the flames. A small knot of people gathered near another machine were applauding him. He turned away, wandering around in a small circle as he tried to get his bearings. There was the wall of screens, he must have come from there—no, there was another wall of screens, maybe he'd come from *there*. The people were still applauding. Abruptly the flames parted, and he was standing outside of the pillar. A woman in an open military-style coat with fringe on the shoulders did something to the machine and then shook her head at him.

"Homeboy, if you're not going to do anything more interesting than stagger around, I can't use you."

"Excuse me," he said. "I have to find some people."

They slid out of his field of vision, and his pov floated around

a corner and down a long hallway—long? No, just a special-
effects distortion. A robot bird-head popped out of a doorway
and inspected him curiously for several seconds before a man's
face came out from behind it and waved him on. Cam, he
realized, another cam. It was like one of those Big Night Out
video releases they did in Entertainment, he thought; simulated parties and private clubs and bars. Like an insty-vacation.
He became aware of music, a driving, frenzied beat urging
him to relax, relax, relax.

At the top of a spiral staircase, he had a sudden clear glimpse
of a mass of hair the color of dark honey before it moved away.
"Marly?" he asked. He pushed through the warm bodies posed
against the twisting, turning railing. Words bounced off him
like hail, and he emerged on the next floor feeling slightly
worked over.

He made his way down another hall, stopping at every doorway. Some of the rooms were crowded, and some were mostly
empty, but Marly wasn't in any of them. The door to the last
room was half-open, and he hesitated, almost knocked, and
then gave it a push with his foot.

Music rushed over him, big music with lots of different
sounds in it. He hung onto the frame, overwhelmed and
blinded. Sometime later his vision cleared, and he saw the
bed tipped up on its side against the far wall. To make room
for the music, he thought. And for the man he now saw kneeling in the center of the floor before a small fire, urging the
flames upward with graceful fingers.

A little ways away Caritha was stretched out with her back
to him, resting on one elbow, watching. Gabe floated down
onto the floor next to her with a rush of relief.

"I knew I'd find you," he said, leaning his head back against
the wall and closing his eyes.

"Shit, what happened to *you*?" Her voice sounded strange
and rough under the music.

"When?" he asked. He wanted to look at her, put an arm
around her, but his head was suddenly too heavy to move, his
eyes too much trouble to open. He would open them in a
minute; there was no point to running a video if you were
going to keep your eyes closed.

"Whenever. What'ud you do, get a few refills? How much
did you have?"

He managed to get his eyes open to slits. Caritha's voice
sounded very strange, as if someone had been messing with

the program. The hacker. The hacker who had claimed to be on his side had done something to his program. He struggled to raise his head. The man in the center of the room was burning a musical instrument, he realized, an old electric guitar from the last century, squirting fluid on it and setting a match to it deliberately. Someone was asking him if he was experienced.

"That's not the question," he said. "The question is who's *really* on your side. Anyone can say they are, but it—it—" He floundered; the thought was suddenly draining away like water down an open pipe.

" 'It don't mean a thing if it ain't got that swing,' right? That what you're trying to tell me?"

He reached out blindly and found her wrist. "I'm trying to tell you we've been found out. We've got to get away. Where's Marly?"

" 'Found out'? Somebody found something out about *you*?" A sudden raucous laugh, un-Caritha-like and yet not so out of character. Something was tugging at his mind, trying to get through the jumble of ideas and images and noise; he thought it might be his calendar alarm beeping almost unheard, but no reminder display appeared before him.

"It was Manny," he said faintly. "He found out. Not entirely legally, but I don't know what he's going to do."

"Manny? You mean Rivera?" Another laugh. "Nothing about that character's entirely legal. I could tell you stories."

"You could?" Gabe asked, confused.

"Who knows but that I fucking will."

The man was still burning his guitar. Or burning it again. Static boiled through the figure, and Gabe realized he was looking at a holo of a very old piece of footage.

"There's no time for stories anymore," he said after a bit. "I covered up as much as I could. All he'll find is commercials now, but it'll be a long time before we're all together again." He paused, twining his fingers with hers. So real; he could actually feel the sweat on her palm, the texture of her fingers, the warmth. He tried to remember if new hotsuits with up-graded sensors had been issued. Because the sensations weren't ever this vivid, only good enough, what with the video portion providing power of suggestion, so that your mind would fill in any missing details. Usually, if you surrendered to the illusion. Which you really had to do to make really good video, even commercials . . .

After a while he realized he'd been talking without knowing it again, and at some length. He blinked at the flames licking up from the guitar.

"I put two LotusLands in you, what you call your mildly hallucinogenic beverages, just to get that fucking pinched look off your face. I don't know how many more they put in you downstairs, but I'd say you're more toxed than you've ever been in your life."

Frowning, he turned to look at her and jumped. It wasn't Caritha.

"You remember anything that happened since you walked in here?" Gina asked him. She waited a moment. "Didn't think so."

Attention, Marly's voice said in his mind. *This is not a simulation.*

"It's a little late to tell me that," he muttered.

"A *little* late?" Gina gave a short, humorless laugh. "It's a whole fucking stone-home *lot* late." Her eyes were dark holes; she was even more toxed than he was, he realized. "We made it easier to be in the sounds and the pictures, and hardly fucking none of it's real anymore. It's a faster, better way to get a *real* unreal experience. You don't know what I'm talkin' about, do you?"

"I don't know what *I'm* talking about," he said honestly.

"Good, just as long as we're high enough up in the stupid-sphere for you." A cam poked into the room, took a careful look around, and backed out again. "There now," Gina said. "Valjean's got this running deal—not with me—that he releases all his parties as videos. You can't come here and take a fucking *shit* but for a fucking audience. He's on the rich-and-famous chips. The folks in Kansas buy them, pop them in their flatscreen consoles or their headmounts, if they even have that shit in Kansas, and go to parties they don't have a chance in hell of ever really going to. And you know what that's *from*? You know where the fuck they got *that* idea?"

Gabe shook his head. Whatever was in his system was fading down, a trough between one high and the next. There was a small burning point in the pit of his stomach.

"They used to have these TV shows of kids dancing to music, these flatscreen things in the pre-Jurassic when it was all in black-and-white, and there were maybe two-three networks and two-three channels you could get them on in any city. Kids dancing, just kids dancing to music, and maybe a solo or

a group'd come on and lip-synch a hot release. Something like
a hundred kids dancing around, and out there in TV land,
there'd be maybe a million kids dancing along, pretending they
were there."

"Uh-huh," Gabe said politely. He was trying to picture it
without really having much idea of what she was talking about.

"It was later that music started to stand for something," she
went on suddenly, in a quieter voice. "There were all these
ideas, the ideas were in the music, the music was in the ideas.
These performers would cut these releases, and they'd say shit
like, 'Well, my album's fighting against this' and 'My album's
fighting against that.' This was before anyone got the bright
idea to do the monster benefits to feed the hungry. You probably don't know what those are. Nobody does that anymore.
Now they go get the hungry with cams and they call it, I don't
know, 'poverty porn' or 'slum porn,' or I don't know what they
call it.

"So they had these albums that were fighting this and fighting that and fighting for some other thing, but what they all
really fought in the end was each other, for a place on the old
hit parade. Number ten with a bullet, number four with a
bullet. They were all so far away from it, see, they were all so
fucking *far away*. They'd say something like 'world peace' and
they didn't have the first fucking idea of what the world was
like. They saved the goddamn whales, and they didn't even
fucking *live* in the fucking *world*."

She wiped the dreadlocks back from her smooth forehead,
digging her fingers into them so hard, Gabe was afraid she was
going to tear them away. "Some of that wasn't their fault. There
was lots of crazy shit, even before the arena massacre at the
Behemoth concert. You old enough to remember that one?"

Gabe tried to think. She waved a hand at him.

"Never mind, they got such killer video on it, you don't have
to be old enough, just tune in disaster porn. Watch the Jesus-
boy in the army fatigues take out a thousand kids in one sweep,
you are *there*. But there was crazy shit before that, nutsoids
with knives, nutsoids with guns, nutsoids with crazy fucking
shit for brains, like the guy that took out Lennon."

"Lenin?" he said, puzzled.

"For all it really meant to him, he coulda shot his fucking
TV set. And you know, everyone was sorry. I remember
my grandmother telling me that, how really fucking awful it
was, and fifteen years later they were still squeezing videos

out of the guy, like they forgot somebody wiped him out, and it had gone from, like, because they loved him to it not mattering what had happened because they could still get the fucking videos. They cooked up a *simulation*, a fucking *simulation* of the man and got it to do interviews and give simulated answers to simulated questions before the estate pulled the plug on that." She focused on him suddenly with a searching expression. "Do you understand a fucking word I'm saying?"

He thought hard. "Well, I know they have to be dead for a hundred and fifty years without a conservatorship before they're in the public domain. But with a conservatorship the time limit's different, and you have to license—"

"I want it to matter," she said. "I want the fucking music and the people to matter. I don't want fucking *rock'n'roll* porn to go with the med porn and the war porn and the weapons porn and the food porn—shit, it's *all* porn, goddamn fucking video porn." She gestured at the holo; the guitar was burning again. "They fixed it so *he'd* live forever. They don't know he woulda lived forever anyway, because when it came outa him, it came outa something *real*, so *it* was real. I want it to come out of something *real*, not some fucking *box*, I want it to come out of human-fucking-*beings*, I want it to be something that makes you know you're alive, and not another part of a bunch of fucking pels in a high-res video!"

She rested her forearms on her knees. Gabe touched her shoulder, wanting to offer her something and not having the slightest idea what that could possibly be.

"That's why I'm gonna do it," she said after a moment.

"Do what?" he asked.

"Change for the machines."

He rubbed the side of his face where she had hit him about a hundred years before.

She slapped his leg suddenly, startling him. "And that's where you came in, isn't it." She got up and offered him a hand. "Come on. Take a little walk with me."

He looked at her hand suspiciously.

"I ain't gonna hit you again. That was a fucking accident, I don't know how many more times I have to tell you that."

"It isn't that," he said slowly, gazing at her hand. "It's—well—is it a *long* walk?"

"Longest walk *you* ever took." She grabbed him and hauled him up.

* * *

The sign came swimming out of the colorful darkness, plain white board with red glow-print, no holos or other tricks: *Kutt-Upps (2 Drink Minim.)*. Gabe stopped where he was and stared up at it. It didn't mean anything to him, and he couldn't figure out why it would pop out of the roiling confusion of his vision.

Gina took hold of his arm. "Don't tell me you got a secret life with med porn, too."

"Oh, if you've seen one tracheotomy, you've seen them all," he said in a blasé tone as she urged him forward. The stuff in his system had reasserted itself—either that, or he'd had some more, he didn't really know—and he seemed to be walking through an orchard of stylized, possibly artificial trees with branches like lattices and lightning bolts. Except wasn't there some place down south that did something funny with trees, got them to bear leaves that looked like lace or something? Big tourist attraction.

At the same time the street looked like a long, dark tunnel, and he couldn't really see the ground, so for all he knew, the next step could be right into some yawning pit, or the step after that, or the step after that. Gina seemed pretty confident that it was solid ground all the way.

Then he realized he *was* in a long, dark tunnel sloping upward, and he kept ducking his head, thinking the ceiling was very low. But Gina kept pulling him along, and he was thinking that she had been right, it was the longest walk he'd ever taken, when he stepped into an explosion of light and sound.

She had both arms around him from behind, steering him through the chaos. A transparent blimp the size of a watermelon was sailing toward him, diverting up over his head at the last moment. He stopped to watch it; tiny dots of light danced over the side, spelling out *MORE DRUGS*. He laughed a little and leaned back against Gina, putting his hands over hers. "I don't think so," he murmured. Gina said something, but not to him. It didn't matter; he was enjoying the feel of her arms around him. He had forgotten exactly how good it felt, for real, not in a hotsuit.

Your whole body's *a hotsuit*, said Caritha's voice in his mind.

That would make his brain the headmount, he thought dreamily, and looked around. In another part of the room, on a raised platform, a woman was holding a strange piece of machinery that looked like the bastard offspring of a shovel and a keyboard and screaming something at the top of her lungs. Periodically she slammed the wide part of the machine down on the stage. After the third time he started seeing sparks flying up from the point of impact.

Yah, his body was the hotsuit, and his brain was the head-mount, but the program seemed to have gone a little crazy. *MORE DRUGS*.

He understood *percussionist* right away, but it took him a while to grab the idea that her last name was *Something*. The gold tone of her skin had a stronger yellow in it than Catherine's, but on her it looked good. On her it was Something. She wasn't impressed with his Something jokes, but she didn't hit him with the sticks, either. She tortured the table with them.

Maybe he needed some sticks, he thought. He could have used them in Manny's office. Bing, bang, bap, flip-flip, tap. She wouldn't let him handle them, so he used his fingers, trying to find a way through their rhythm. A little later she told him he'd made a game try, and if he wanted to get into music, she could show him the way. But right then Gina lifted him out of the chair by the back of his neck, and he could only watch the table recede in the distance. The sticks tapped good-bye before a sudden glittering population fell into the space between him and them, blotting them out. He must be leaving.

He had gone away for a little while, but there was a dim recording in his mind of a blimp, a far more vivid memory of a yellow gold woman with dancing sticks, and somewhere in there a brick wall with snakes crawling on it—or was that a brick floor? A brick *ceiling*?—and now here he was in the open night air and someone was saying, "AR is a big, *big* concept. Wraps around a lotta stuff. A *whole* lotta stuff."

His vision cleared again, and he was looking at a monitor screen running in split-mode, with what might have been identical sets of figures scrolling up either side at different rates.

"On the right here," the voice went on, "are the readings for the area under normal conditions, when there'd be nobody here. On the left are the real readings that we're intercepting on the way to the security-system sensors—"

Marly's voice spoke casually in his head. *Try to say that five times real fast*. No, not her voice, just his own, he decided. Suddenly he no longer wanted to disown his thoughts and stick false names on them. He didn't have to do that right now, he didn't have to cut pieces of himself off and dress them up in masks and costumes to keep himself company—

"—tents and purposes a facade simulation at the point of input to the security system, where we alter the readings, change the figures going in to be those you'd get if there was nobody here. See, there's air pressure, wind velocity—now the sound and vision's trickier because we have to get between what the cams see and hear and what they tell the system they see and hear. So we run a real facade simulation there in a loop. That's the fooler loop. You just have to sit on top of it and make sure nothing gets jiggled out of place—"

He drifted away again, unsure if he was moving physically. It felt as though he might be. The lights and colors were shot through with large pockets of darkness, and he couldn't seem to get oriented.

"Yah, well, we're all corks on this ocean." A kid raised up from the synthesizer he had been bending over. "I've got a real feel for the sound of guitars, myself. All kinds. I don't need *anybody* else. Hear me, and you'd swear you were hearing four-five people—"

Someone interrupted him. He shoved a hand at Gabe, and Gabe took it. "Remember me," he said, pumping Gabe's hand up and down. "My name's Dexter, and I'm a whole fucking group in one body, I swear I am. Tell her that. Please? Tell her."

Gabe nodded, dazed, and wandered off. A whole fucking group in one body. He could sympathize. That wasn't really so hard. Just pull them out and make them into individuals, the group, make good guys and bad guys and stick them in a simulation, and you'd never have to be alone—

Deadline < month.

The memory was a fist in the face. He knew just how a fist in the face felt, too; if he ever had to program a hotsuit with facial coverage for a fast shot to the head, he was ready. What he ought to do now, he thought, was take a blow to the stomach and then program *that* into one of his commercials and persuade Manny to test-drive it 'suited up. Wouldn't that give old Manny a surprise, would that just give him something to think over? It wouldn't actually hurt him, it would just be unpleasant. After all, it wasn't like the hotsuit was anything but skin-deep.

But he needed the experience, so he'd know he'd gotten the hotsuit settings right. Faking it was out of the question.

Manny hated faked material; he could tell immediately when the sensation wasn't authentic.

He put his arms over his stomach. The feel of Gina's arms was long gone, and he wanted them back. Absurdly tall pink feathers growing up from what seemed to be a flamingo face sailed through his field of vision, leaving a hot pink trail behind. He became aware of the music, then, lots of guitar sounds, sounds like lots of guitars.

He felt himself walking, but it was distant, as if he were wearing a good hotsuit with the tactile damped down. The colors parted around him, and he found himself looking at hundreds of strange humps. They grew up out of the ground (or whatever this surface was—he smelled grass and dirt, so he was calling it ground) in sharply regular rows. *In formation*, he thought. *Regimentation*. On the whole he preferred the idea of the Byzantine orchard. That was long gone, too, but if he could have Gina put her arms around him again, who knew but that it would come back? And if he had to get her to punch him in the stomach to do that, then he would do that.

"Gina?" he asked timidly.

Scattered voices came through the darkness over the humps.

". . . fucking furious with you, asshole."

"Fury is what made rock'n'roll great."

"When was I ever not there for you?"

"Well," Gabe murmured, maneuvering between two of the humps, "where was 'there,' and what was I doing at the time?"

". . . twenty *years* on your case, what does it fucking *take*?" That was Gina's voice, he'd know it forever. The first time he'd ever heard it, he'd known he would remember it forever, and not just because she'd punched his lights out. It was a voice with texture, a voice that you could touch as much as hear. It had been in his ears all night, and he hadn't realized how much he wanted to keep it there until it had gone away and come back just now.

"Gina," he said, moving forward. Something banged into his hip. He reached out to touch it and was startled by the feel of cold stone. One of those humps.

"It's complicated," said the other voice. Not as textured, a voice from someone who seemed to be receding in the distance, not faint but fading out all the same. "I wanted to tell you. It's a rope out of a hole."

Gabe stumbled into another hump and worked his way around it.

"Picturesque, but not accurate. *Now* you work in a fucking hole."

"I'm fading fucking *out*, I'm going so fast sometimes you can see right through me."

"I can see right through you, all right."

The darkness was no longer as deep as it had been. Gabe could make out trees now, plain old trees, and somewhere far off, light flung over the grass in great white circles. He moved sideways now, using the cold stone humps as a guide, stepping from one to another in a straight line. If he could put the voices between himself and the distant white light, he would see where Gina was and who she was talking to.

". . . guess we should have taken better care of each other."

"I took *great* care of *you*, fucker."

"But when it came down to some things, we did something else. Usually video."

"Twenty years I've heard you bullshit and shoot shit, this is the first time *this* shit has ever come up. I don't *want* a post-mortem of the last twenty years trying to decide if we did right by each other. What we got right now is what we got. Maybe it's damned fucking little, but it made a difference to me. I didn't keep *my* life from you."

Now Gabe could see people moving around in the distant pools of light, and something in their motions made him think they were hunting each other. Hunting to music.

"Look, *you* got a video head, *I* got a video head, what the fuck were we gonna do, keep the day-care in business? I'll be there tomorrow, for chrissakes, *I'll be there*. When was I ever not there for you?"

Two dark shapes blocked his view of the people in the light. He recognized Gina's silhouette immediately. There was something familiar about the other one, but he couldn't place it.

"Gina," he said, just as she moved toward the other person.

"*What?*" she snapped.

"Gina," he said again happily, going forward. "Punch me in the—" Something caught him right at his belt line, hard enough to flip his feet up as his head went down. Cold stone bashed into the right side of his face, and there was a technicolor explosion in his head. He was barely aware of his own flailing before something slammed against his back, knocking the wind out of him. Colors poured down in an avalanche.

* * *

White light seared his eyes and drilled into his brain. He squeezed his eyes shut again quickly. The buzzing roar now waxing and waning in his ears resolved itself into voices over music. Something was pressing firmly against the side of his face. The patches, he thought; if he could move his arm, he would reach into his pocket and stick on two, or three, or four—

Someone was holding his arm. Laboriously he made his head turn, feeling the pressure against his face yield slightly, and opened his eyes again.

Sam's face swam into focus, started to melt away, and came back again. The hollows below her cheekbones had deepened a bit, and her wide, serious eyes made her look both frighteningly old and frightened and young. The unruly black hair was a little longer, a little softer. She was hanging onto his arm as if she meant to pull him up out of deep water. *We're all corks on this ocean.*

"So," he said, taking a cautious breath. Pain flared in his back, then receded to a constant dull ache. "And when did you get back into town?"

Sam glanced away for a moment. "I guess you'll be all right if you recognize me."

A young woman appeared behind Sam and put her hand on Sam's shoulder. "Ain't sure we can say the same, doll."

"I know, Rosa. Another minute and we'll go. Where's Jones? Don't lose him again." She looked up, and Gabe followed her gaze to a young guy with nervous-breakdown hair framing a bony, sullen face. "Just make sure you stay there, you," Sam said to the guy, and turned back to him. "Gabe, I can't stick around, and I don't know what you're doing here or what you did to yourself—"

"Told you, he tripped over a fucking *tombstone*," came Gina's voice from nearby. She was pressing something to the side of his face, he realized, and his head was pillowed on her knees. He reached up, found her hand and the wad of cloth in it. She wiggled out of his grasp and closed his hand around the wad. He had a glimpse of something red.

". . . going away," Sam was saying. "For a real long time. Please, don't try to find me."

"You're always going away," he said resignedly. "It would be news if you were staying."

Sam shrugged. "I was going to try to get a message to you later, when things calmed down—" The woman behind Sam gave her a poke, and Sam glanced back at her. "Christ, Rosa, he works there. I gotta tell you, Gabe, I never expected to see you at a hit-and-run in Forest Lawn." She reached over and tucked something into his pants pocket. "If something—oh, I don't know, if something comes up, and you want to tell me something, if there's some kind of trouble, you can try getting a message to me through the name on the paper."

He gave a weak, disbelieving laugh. "Aren't we doing this backwards?"

"I know where *you* are." She let go of his arm and stood up, her gaze going briefly to Gina. "Some life, Dad." She moved off with the other woman and the guy. He tried to sit up, thinking to call after her, but the pain in his face and the pain in his back blossomed anew, pinning him where he was.

Gina slipped his head onto the uneven pillow of her jacket and then knelt beside him, crossing her arms expectantly.

"That was my daughter," he said, still marveling. Sam had called him Dad.

"That's what she told me."

"But I didn't get a chance to let her know," he added sadly.

"Let her know what? That you've been 'found out'?"

"Her mother's leaving me. She'd have wanted to know that." He took the wad of cloth from his face and looked at it, not understanding right away that the red was his own blood. Gina pushed it back against his cheek.

"You never mentioned that to me, either," she said quietly. "Talked about plenty else. That why you wanted a punch in the stomach, because her mother's leaving you?"

His free hand found hers. "No. When your wife leaves you first thing in the morning, how much worse can the day get? I wanted it because—" Because he thought he was about to lose his job, and he wanted to leave Manny something to remember him by? Oh, that sounded real fierce. Leaving Manny a simulated punch in the stomach for the loss of his simulated girlfriends and his simulated secret life, for the loss of his simulated job. If he was losing it all, he might as well leave Manny with a *real* punch in the stomach.

The idea gave him a rush of pleasure that temporarily overrode the pain. Take it out of porn, make it something real. Do one real thing. Hell, he might never do another.

Gina's gaze turned to her right. The crazy guy, Visual Mark, was bending over him with the same space-case expression he'd been wearing the day Gabe had first met him.

"Go home and pack," Gina said to him. "I'll *be* there. Just like fucking *always*."

Visual Mark straightened up and walked off with his hands in his pockets. Gabe had the sudden wild thought that he'd never see the man again. And Gina?

"Are you going somewhere, too?" he asked her. "You and him?"

"That's a long fucker of a story." She yawned. "You feel sober?"

"I feel pain."

"Yah, that's sober as I remember it."

He took a firmer hold on her hand. "Where are you going?"

"Christ, you don't know anything, do you? Your daughter knows. Old Sam, she's got a line on a lot of stuff."

"What?" He felt a flutter of a strange new fear and tried to tell himself that it was the combination of the drugs and the shock of the injury.

"It's a long fucker of a story," she said again. "Your daughter's gonna be okay, but you need some work. Maybe a staple on that gash. You opened yourself up there pretty good."

"Yes," he said. "I did."

She paused, looking at him speculatively. "Shit, maybe I oughta tell you. While you're still too toxed to get frantic."

She had gotten to the part about Mexico when the police arrived.

20

The brain feels no pain.

Who had said that—Frank Sinatra or the Beater? Jim Morrison or Visual Mark? Mozart, or Canadaytime? The Living Sickle Orchestra . . . or that strange red-headed doctor?

Her mind turned fitfully like some sleeping giant in the grip of a dream about to become real. Real dreams.

Come along with me.

When was I ever not there for you?

There was a pause long enough to live and die in. Her point of view panned very slowly to the left and came to rest on her own face. Somehow it wasn't a shock to find she was looking at herself, because it wasn't her point of view. The taste of Mark was in her mind, and it was a taste, not a feeling, not a sense of presence, not a physical pressure but a taste.

She heard the scream of a jumper lifting off vertically, but the sound was muffled. Her point of view was still fixed on herself; she looked a little sour, she thought.

I didn't think you'd come. Mark's voice, addressing her. She saw her face shift its attention to him, or rather, to her new point of view.

I did, she saw herself say. *I got them Bad Old Cosmic C-Word Blues Again.*

His confusion was a light metallic something on her palate. *What does 'c-word' mean?*

It means continuing to believe even when you don't feel it. Not letting go even when you can't find squat to hold onto. Going all the way from the beginning to the end.

The scene melted away, leaving her in darkness. She became aware belatedly of an ache in her head—several aches in various spots—gone as soon as she thought of it, and then someone's voice, coming out of nowhere:

ATTENTION, GINA.

"Right," she mumbled. "You don't have to shout."

SORRY. YOU'LL GET USED TO IT. PLEASE CONCEN-
TRATE.

We've been through this one before.

PLEASE MAKE A BOX.

"What kind of box?" she asked.

A SMALL CUBE. PLEASE VISUALIZE A SMALL CUBE.
There was a pause, and she had a sense of someone speaking
in another room, just beyond her hearing. PLEASE VISU-
ALIZE A SMALL CUBE.

She obeyed, and the cube was there in front of her in the
blackness. Somewhere people were applauding. She could not
hear it, but she knew.

MAKE ANOTHER, requested the voice. There was a taste
of plastic and metal. She obeyed again, and the requests went
on, becoming more complicated, until the blackness had filled,
overflowed, and filled again; still, she went on.

"We're going to play some music now, Gina. We'd like you
to just let your mind go with it the same way you would if you
were creating a video for it. All right?"

Video?

First you see video. . . .

"All right?"

Video—

Then you wear video. . . .

"All right?"

Video. . . .

Then you eat video. . . .

"Just run with it. Let the pictures come. All right?"

Video.

Then you . . . *be* . . .

It came easy, nothing too active but strong, a good, fine
beat. This was an old one, one she'd heard not too long ago,
or a hundred years ago, in a graveyard. Live music, remember
it? Nothing like live music, nothing like it.

The Beater went past, whirling like a dervish, a younger
version of a businessman with a good cosmetic surgeon. A flying
multitude came after, dancing in the darkness, becoming sign
and wonders in the night sky.

They were colors now, making patterns in the black, spurting, retreating, spreading down the bowl of the sky. Colored
light streamed down into her hand; she flung it back up again,
making new patterns. The colors came down to her again, and

she hurled them back into the air each time, until the darkness had been completely covered over.

New colors came up from the east then, mixing with the night shades, tunnels of gold cutting through to push the night away. She moved back, trying to see it all at once, and suddenly she was falling softly backwards, and she kept falling and falling until she couldn't hear the music anymore.

A hand came out of nowhere to hold hers. Mark. She gripped his hand firmly, intending not to let him go.

The lake rippled under the cloudy light, putting more damp into the grey day. She looked down and saw the water lapping gently at the rocks strewn around the shoreline.

She turned her head through the gray air, feeling the cold move past her face. Mark looked better, younger; he was smiling just a little slyly, as if he had a secret he had not quite decided to tell her. He turned her around and walked her along the edge of the lake.

"What are we doing?" she asked, stumbling a little. She wasn't a country person by any stretch of the imagination. The heels of her boots kept skidding on the rocks and pebbles.

"Taking a rest." His voice sounded smoother, almost musical. "Taking a rest in a secret place." He went on speaking, but she did not hear his voice as much as she felt it. It was a good feeling at first, a sense of being *with* him greater than anything she had experienced before.

The feeling of closeness intensified; sometime later she realized she was straining away from him even as she kept a grip on his hand. Abruptly his hand twisted out of hers, and she was moving away unhurriedly but quickly.

There was a long hiatus—or possibly a short one, she couldn't tell; her sense of time was gone—and then she seemed to be coming up out of a sleep almost deep enough to be coma.

HELLO, MARK.

The voice was back. He wanted to wiggle with pleasure. It had been stone-home lonely in here without the voice. Wherever *here* was.

WE'D LIKE YOU TO MAKE SOME MORE PICTURES FOR US. IF YOU WOULDN'T MIND.

Hell, no, he wouldn't mind. Making pictures was what he did, didn't they realize that by now?

THIS TIME, HOWEVER, WE'D LIKE YOU TO TELL
US WHERE THEY COME FROM.

He smiled to himself. Nosy, nosy, nosy. Where did they
think they came off? Who did they thing they were? It was
enough that he made pictures. Christ, he didn't understand
where half of them came from himself.

NOW, MARK, SURELY YOU CAN TELL US ABOUT
SOME OF THEM.

Drifting along in the something/nothing/whatever, he could
not imagine why they thought it was important. It wasn't important. Who could know for certain, anyway? The pictures
just came, that was all. *Life* just came. When you came across
something in life, did you get to stop and ask where it was
from? Excuse me, is this for real, or is someone making this
up on me? Forget it. Damned Schrodinger world, for chrissakes.

ALL RIGHT, LET'S TRY THIS: ARE THEY MEMORIES?

Once you've thought of it, it's *all* memory. Don't you know
that, homeboy?

He could feel them giving up and retreating. He made pictures anyway, whether they were there or not, all the time
listening to the music playing on and on in his mind. Even in
the something/nothing/whatever, the program director never
took a break. Thank God.

She woke with the feeling that she had been asleep for days.

The semidark, windowless room was little more than a closet,
but nicely appointed—everything she needed was built in,
and small as things were, she almost didn't have to get out of
bed for most of it, or so it seemed. But she did get up and
take a few steps around the center of the room, holding her
back. The mattress of the tiny single bed was entirely too soft.

Then abruptly she stopped and touched her head. Except
for a few bald spots where the shaved hair was already growing
back in, she felt no difference. Didn't even ruin the dreadlocks.
Same old Gina. Same old—

ATTENTION, GINA.

She looked up, unsure whether she had actually heard anything or not.

PLEASE CONCENTRATE. PLEASE VISUALIZE A BOX.

She held her head with both hands until she was sure it was
just a memory. Just a memory, just an awfully stone-fucking-

home intense fucker of a fucking memory. Feeling a little shaky, she sat down on the bed again, and a new memory intruded.

Lying on a padded slab; going with it now as the slab begins to move and the ceiling begins to move; head goes into a box; a short wait and the fast insect sting of needles, very deep, sinking far, far in and suddenly fading to a sensation of distant cold; murmur of voices, saying they are mapping this and mapping that, and the brain feels no pain, the brain feels no pain, the brain feels nothing at all—

But this *brain feels* something.

Something *is there*; something *has come in* and something *is still coming in* and

The pictures flashed quickly, one after another. She touched her head again, but it still didn't feel any different. Except for each small bump that marked the locations of the sockets. *Bet I look pretty fucking drop-dead with wires in my skull. Medusa's ugly sister.*

Mark.

She got up and tried the door, thinking she would find it locked and then she'd have to trash the place till alarms went off. But the door swung open, and she found herself in a long hallway. Down at the very end, a light was on in some kind of alcove.

Gina hesitated. No guards—excuse me, nurses—keeping watch? She scanned the light-track running the length of the ceiling. The light was damped down, either for night or for her and Mark's benefit, after their long sleep, but she saw nothing other than the unbroken strip of illumination. Fuck it, they wouldn't have been that obvious, to stick eyes where anyone could just look up and see them. And on the other hand, who did they think they were fooling? Did they really think she'd believe she was moving around unobserved after fucking brain surgery?

Fuck 'em. *Take a good look at the walking, talking rock'n'roll animal.* She went down the hall.

Mark was sitting at a table off to one side in the dormitory-style kitchenette set up in the alcove, eating something unidentifiable out of a plastic dish. She jerked her chin at it.

He held up his dripping spoon. "Fuck if I know, but it's supposed to boost your neurotransmitter production. Brain glop. Tastes a little fishy."

She pulled up the sleeves of the stretchy white jumpsuit or pajama or whatever it was. Mark was wearing the same thing; it made them look like a couple of overgrown kids sneaking a midnight snack while the adults were asleep.

"Is it what you wanted?" she asked.

His head jerked slightly. "Well, it's not what I *didn't* want, put it that way."

She moved behind him and put her hands on his shoulders. They felt bony and frail. Like always. Abruptly she thought of Gabe Ludovic. The image of him lying on the ground with his face bloody and confused came to her out of nowhere, as intense as one of those inserted images.

Mark put a hand on one of hers, twining their fingers. "I know what I'd like to do right now."

She held very still. He twisted around and looked up at her. He really didn't look too bad. Better than he had in ages, as if a great deal of trouble had dropped away from him. Maybe it was not having to worry anymore. He could just stick a socket in his head and out it would come, essence de V. Mark. Video on tap.

He stood up then and wrapped his arms around her. This was never the easy part. They weren't smooch-faces, it didn't work that way, for her or for him. In twenty-some-odd years she hadn't stopped too often to wonder how it could have gone.

One time, though . . .one time, three-four-five years into the madness, there'd been a space where they'd come together one night, and it had been different. Hadn't been the first time or the last, but it had definitely been different. Might've just been time for it, time to find out, or try to find out. He'd been reaching, and she'd been reaching, and for a little while there, they'd gotten through. Maybe that had been the night when the little overlapping space called *their life* had come into existence.

And as if to make the point, as if to make absolutely sure they both understood, he'd put on this music, straight audio, very old stuff, guy named Dylan. *I Want You.* Very old, very big; maybe too big for either one of them. She remembered being unable to move or talk, or do anything but listen, and at the same time some part of her wanting to laugh her old laugh to break it up and break it down—hey, jellyroll, let's us just sit down and read our profiles in the entrails of popular culture, whaddaya say. but another part of her, the bigger part, got it right away, and that was the part that kept her from laughing. Because if you didn't speak your truth, there was always something that would speak it for you that much louder.

Maybe there'd been a little too much truth in the room with them. Something had almost turned there, but the night ended, and after that they just couldn't ever get it right.

Now she let herself relax into him for the first time in a long time, resting her head on his hard, bony chest and slipping her arms around his waist. Her mind began to drift, unreeling a series of wordless memories and pictures in no particular order, scenes from the old days, from all the days before this one: Mark bending over a screen, his prematurely old face lit by the glow of the rough cut he was previewing for final editing; the Beater sitting at the permanently closed synthesizer, unmoving and unmoved, and Mark standing on the other side, trying to get his mind around it and having a bad time; Mark on the courthouse steps; the Beater facing her with it; the lake with the stony shore—

It came to her like a paper flower unfolding to reveal a secret center. The lake scene was the area where Mark had grown up in New England. She had seen it before, but she had never been there, until now. Whenever *now* had been.

Gingerly she concentrated, trying to detect a difference of feeling in her mind.

"It's good," he said suddenly, his voice low and easy but too much as if he'd been reading her thoughts—too much by fucking half—and yet she could not move even to look up at him. "I mean, I don't know if it's *good*, I don't know if it's *right*, but it sure is *good*. And I was born to do it, I've been trying to do it all my life, and I never knew it. Someday you're gonna come into a room, and you're gonna see this funny-looking thing, a piece of flesh clutching into naked console, and you're gonna stop and stare, because you won't be sure where the flesh stops and the chips and the circuits begin. They'll be, like, melted into each other, and some of the console'll be as alive as flesh and some of the flesh'll be dead as console, and that'll be me. All of that'll be me."

Gina said nothing. Her hands pressed into his back.

"I don't know if it's what I want," he added, "but it's what I'm supposed to be." He paused. "I'm sorry."

"What are you sorry for," Gina said quietly. "If it's for me, you're sorrying down the wrong fucking rain barrel." She felt him stiffen just slightly, and she suppressed a smile as she pulled her head back to look up at him. "You're the one who's always needed something to grab onto, someone to throw you a rope outa the deep water." Her mouth twitched. "I was always in it for the music."

His eyes lit up. "You wanna hear some music? Program director's got 'em cued up to the end of the night. There's some stuff in my room. Connection things, a monitor. We got the rest of the equipment."

They walked back to his room with their arms around each other and studied the rig together while she waited, with one part of her mind, to hear someone come down the hall and barge in and explain that they couldn't be doing that now.

But no one came, and eventually Mark was lying down on the narrow bed while she examined the slender wires to be put up against each target area, all of the latter still standing out as shaved areas on his scalp. Just like her own.

The first connection she made threw a green 3-D sketch of Mark's head up on the monitor, with the connection point highlighted amber. More amber points lit up in response to each connection she made, stars winking into existence in a new man-made constellation. *You're hot with the poetry tonight, kid,* she thought, looking from the monitor to Mark lying on the bed with his eyes closed and a shade of a smile on his lips and the wires flowing from his head in graceful lines. She had a sudden impulse to bend over and kiss him. It would be the first time in she didn't know how long. *And maybe the last.*

She considered this, looking at the simulation of Mark's brain on the monitor. Her hands were moving idly, palms sliding against each other. *Got you a twenty-first-century human person here; maybe twenty-first-century human doesn't kiss. Like, doesn't have to.* An image of the lake flashed in the mind and faded. *Yah, we got something here a little more lasting than a kiss.*

But he's hooked up to the machine, *isn't he.*

She rubbed a hand over her mouth as if trying to wipe away something; wasn't necessary. The impulse had passed without her doing anything about it. Just as well. It wasn't too cool to kiss someone while he was making love with someone else.

Abruptly he was groping with one hand in the semidark; wanting to hold hers. She reached over and touched his fingers. He grabbed and held on, but she worked her hand out of his grasp.

"I think I need two hands for this," she said, unsure of whether he would actually hear her or not. "You know where I am, though." His hand went back to rest on his stomach; he hadn't opened his eyes.

The image on the monitor gave a jump and disappeared; in its place came a muddy, out-of-focus scene that might have been the lake in an overcast twilight. Two figures moved in the scene, never coming clear before it whited out.

Music came up—she gave a surprised laugh. Very old piece, Lou for-chrissakes-Reed, "Coney Island Baby"; only the two of them would have placed it. The program director was on another nostalgia kick.

What faded back in wasn't Coney Island, a freaky spot that she had been to but the program director had not. Instead, the point of view was traveling low and slow over a terrain she recognized as hypermagnified carpet, pausing occasionally at odd cast-aside items: a shoe, a shirt, some loose change. It reached the side of a rumpled, unmade bed and rose, still moving as slowly as the music, to a shape under the sheets.

Gina made herself keep watching as the pov tracked along the shape, seeming to study the twists and dips in the bed-clothes that concealed it. Abruptly the scene cut to an aerial view of a ragged gathering of people in a parking lot at night, and then the pov was tracking the folds in the covers again, winding along.

She swallowed, rubbing her hands together, as the pov moved sideways, showing there was more than one shape under the covers. It began to track along that one, inserting another brief view of the nighttime parking lot, closer this time so that the faces of the people, the crazy, thrown-together clothes, the wild, dancing movements, were clearly visible before the scene cut back to the bed and Mark's sleeping face. It wasn't a peaceful face; drained, if anything, worn out, a preview of a more final sort of rest.

The pov was excruciatingly slow as it moved across Mark's face to her own, lingering on the texture of her dreadlocks next to his pale, drawn flesh, finally moving on to the contrast of her deep brown skin, taking a lot of time to show that both her eyes were closed, but beneath the lids the eyes were moving back and forth restlessly.

Cut back to the hit-and-run in the parking lot, at ground level now: a frantic blond woman with multicolored feathers fighting the storm of her hair pulled the pov along, beckoning with one hand as she backed farther into the party. A young guy with waist-length dreadlocks and flip-aside lenses on his sunglasses joined the woman, grinning widely.

Cut back to the bed: the pov studied how their heads were leaning one on another, just where they touched, going slowly back up along his own face to show that his closed eyes were also in motion. Sliding over to her face again.

Cut: the pov was in the center of an enormous group of people now, trying to pull it every which way under the hard white lights swaying a little on their framework. Looking up at the lights now, the pov began to turn around and around, occasionally glimpsing some of the people around it, spinning faster and faster until the focus blurred and snapped back to the bed.

The pov cruised along her shoulder and down her arm hidden under the covers; then it was suddenly moving along a sidewalk on Hollywood Boulevard under glaring sunlight, taking a good look at the signs on the wannabee parlors and the video joints, pausing to look back at the Chinese Theatre, where the tourists were trying on the footprints in the pavement and posing for pictures. A kid dressed in a red garbage bag with *HAZARDOUS WASTE* stenciled all over it flew into the frame and started batting her hands frantically at the pov, her mouth working angrily. The pov turned aside in imitation of a human ducking the blows, took in a few more of the street regulars coming to see what was going on, more and more faces, all crowded together, becoming smaller and smaller as the pov receded steadily, until the faces were all stones. The pov traveled upward to the grey-white sky, where the faint shadows of the clouds hinted at the twists and folds and dips of sheets before whiting out completely as the music faded.

The schematic of Mark's head, the amber points glowing, reappeared on the screen.

"I'm done," Mark's voice said clearly, coming through the speaker. "Pull 'em out for me, will you?"

He'd already given the command for disconnect. She leaned over and removed the wires from his head. For a moment she thought he wasn't going to move. Then he took a deep breath and sat up, grinning at her. "Pretty coherent, huh?"

"Great," she said. "If anyone wanted a video of some old music with some old people in it."

"The way we're actually gonna do it, the Beater says, is we're gonna take stuff provided by the bands—images, pictures, shit like that—and work it around into some form." He wiggled his eyebrows. "We're *real* synthesizers now. Real synners."

She looked at him. The question *You wanna talk it over?* was right behind her lips, just waiting for her voice, but her voice wouldn't come.

"You wanna try it" he asked.

"There's only one rig."

"We'll get yours. There's one in your room."

"There wasn't when I woke up."

"I bet there is now." He looked at her steadily.

"Yah? I bet we could figure out how to hook them together."

"Yah?" His eyes glittered. "Do you want that?"

"No." She bit the inside of her cheek, wondering if he knew she was lying.

He pulled his knees up and wrapped his arms around them. "Why do you think they let us get away with this?"

She laughed suddenly. "What makes you think we got away with anything?" She looked at the now-dark monitor. "I think they watched the whole thing." It hit her just as she said it that she believed that; they *would* be watching, listening, just as they would after any other kind of surgery. They just weren't being obvious about it. She leaned forward, putting her face close to his. "You wanna do any kind of funny experiments, maybe you oughta wait."

He reached out and put a hand on her cheek, then gathered her into his arms, pulling her onto the narrow bed with him.

She wasn't sure at first what he was doing, or even if he was sure. Then she was helping him strip away his jumpsuit, tearing off her own. Her urgency surprised her, and his surprised her even more. They might have been two frantic kids, hurrying to steal a moment in some space of uncertain privacy.

A feeling of intense familiarity swept through her, body and mind, warming her to him; there was nothing of each other they didn't know, it seemed, as if they had never had separate lives at all.

Manny watched the new video, if that was what it really was, twice through, paying no attention to Travis's running commentary about the clarity and the reality and all that shit.

He was still put out about Travis's failure to install full surveillance in the rooms.

It was every bit as good as Travis was saying it was. He just hoped he'd be able to get the burnout case it had come from focused in the right direction after they got back to the States.

21

On one of the many screens set into the wall in Rana Copperthwait's office, an actress with wild black hair crossed her arms and looked petulant. "Couldn't we at least get a couple of German shepherds or something?"

"Not a chance," said Rana Copperthwait. "Now, die. And this time, make it look like death, not a multiple orgasm." She stabbed at the console on her desk, turning off the sound, and let out a tired breath. "She *knows* she's supposed to be freezing to death in the wilderness with wolves all around her, waiting to gobble her up, she *knows* it's all going to be put in later, during the finish. What could be clearer? I have to watch these productions constantly to make sure they're all doing what they're *supposed* to do, not what they think they want to do."

She gestured at the other screens showing different features in various stages of production and then flicked on her million-watt smile again. Gabe felt blinded. "I *love* what you've done. Just the little bit I've seen is enough to let me know you've got a winning combination in those women. How soon do you suppose you could work up a treatment for a feature?"

Gabe swallowed. "I don't know. I don't really, uh, work that way with them. With the program, I mean."

"With *them*," Copperthwait corrected him. "Look, you don't have to pretend with me, I know they're real to you. I told you, I *understand* artistic people." Her smile faded a bit. "Just how *do* you work?"

He glanced at Manny from the corner of his eye. There were no secrets now, nothing to hide, but he still felt uncomfortable talking about it in front of Manny. "Well, I just, uh, put on the programs, and then the RNG—"

"Orange E?" Copperthwait blinked her overdone eyes at him.

"Uh, R-N-G. Random number generator. It, uh, selects situations and prompts from a random pool of choices—"

"But surely you have produced results you've desired?"

Gabe shifted in the too-comfortable chair, bumping his foot against the front of her desk. Manny was frowning at him again. "Even then I try to leave room for some random elements. So it's more like a real experience. If you see what I mean."

"I'm sure I do." Copperthwait kept her smile on him as if she were pinning him to the chair with it. "Is an outline just *completely* out of the question?"

He opened his mouth to answer, and she suddenly sat up straight. "Maybe it is," she said, staring at him thoughtfully. "Maybe I'm missing the point here, maybe I'm missing the very thing that gives your creation the charm that captivates me and will captivate the whole country. Orange E. *Orange E.* Like *life.* You *can't* know exactly what's going to happen, not *exactly.*" She rubbed her fingers delicately against each other. "All right, how about this—you give me some locales, a basic situation as a starting point, and that's all. Bare bones. Make it something like, oh . . . ." She made a painful, thinking-hard face.

Manny kicked him, discreetly but hard.

"A zeppelin trip around the world," Gabe blurted. It was the first thing that came into his head. MORE DRUGS.

Copperthwait banged a hand down on her desk. "The last zeppelin! That's *brilliant*! That's what the giants from the old days used to call 'high concept.' "

"Um, you know, I don't think that's what happened with the last zeppelin," Gabe said politely.

"Well, it should have," she said, breezily. "It's too beautiful to waste. You'll be the crew on the last zeppelin. Or the passengers. Or they'll be the crew, and you'll be one of the passengers, or vice versa, however you want, it's *totally* up to you." She pointed a long, elegant finger at him. "I'm giving you total artistic control. All you have to do is come in here once in a while and talk to me about what you're doing. Just because I *love* to talk to artistic people, I think you're all just the crown of creation, I truly, truly do, and being around you artists makes me feel like I'm really alive. More alive than the best feature this studio has ever released, and that's saying a lot, I assure you, because my headmount is *my best friend.* I want *us* to get together as friends, just shooting the old—ahem—shit about the stuff you love to do. If you know what I mean, and I think you do."

"He certainly does," Manny said heartily, turning a fond

face to him. Gabe thought it was the most frightening expression he'd ever seen on Manny.

"Well, that's magnum, and I really mean that from the bottom of my heart. Or should I say, my brain?" Copperthwait stood up and reached across the desk for his hand. He gave it to her, and she pumped it up and down hard. "This is going to be so . . . *magnum*. And profitable. We're going to give people what they really need, something which I happen to personally feel is the highest purpose of entertainment. This is going to feed people's souls, it'll be a boon to the lonely, and you know, I don't think anyone besides us really realizes how many lonely people are out there. I can tell, just by the fan mail we get." She pointed at Gabe again. "*You*, my friend, are going to give everyone a reason to go on *living*. We'll get a matching pair of men later."

Her smile vanished abruptly as her gaze went to the wall with the screens. She stabbed a finger down on the console again. "Excuse me, but what do you think you're doing now?"

"I'm being *eaten. By wolves*," the actress said as Manny ushered Gabe from the office.

"Well," Manny said, setting himself a little more comfortably at the other end of the limo's capacious backseat, "I'd say all's well that ends well. Especially when it all ends well in Hollywood, eh?"

Gabe managed a murmur that passed for agreement. Manny was sticking to the story that one of the sequences with Marly and Caritha had somehow been copied from the volatile memory onto the end of one of the commercial spots. They both knew that was a pile of horseshit, but Manny had been standing by it for the last three weeks, ever since he'd sprung it on Gabe in his office the morning Gabe had emerged from night court.

It had been a good morning for lies; Manny could not have timed it better. He'd been too fried to challenge Manny's version of reality, and he was sure Manny had fixed his evidence anyway. He'd just sat and listened, fingering the old-fashioned onionskin flimsy the cashier had given him. He still had it; it looked more like a certificate than a receipt for his fines. *Know ye by these presents that the undersigned now has an official criminal misdemeanor record.* Souvenir of the longest walk of his life, or at least of the parts he could remember.

What he remembered best, though, was Gina waiting on the courthouse steps for Mark, who had been picked up by the cops on their incoming sweep. He had stood on the sidewalk under the steadily lightening sky, with his receipt and the battered-spouse literature the holding-cell medic had pressed on him while she'd been stapling up the gash in his face, and watched Gina wait.

He'd wanted to go to her. It would have been a much longer walk than the one he'd just finished, through a lot of rough terrain, all of it mined, and a long, nasty trip through all the barbed wire she put up around herself. And it wouldn't have been a simulation. Everything he felt would have been real.

Would have been. He'd still been trying to sort the woulds from the coulds when Mark had come out, settling the matter for everyone.

And then he'd gone off to work and lost Marly and Caritha, too, and then gotten them back, magnanimously restored by Manny who had another little piece of news for him besides. That was supposed to be the real Big One, but he'd already heard about it from Gina. He tried to look impressed for Manny, anyway, especially since Manny was telling him the sockets had saved him. Eight holes in his head had saved his ass, because the Marly and Caritha stuff was so compelling, the sockets just *cried out* for a product like this, it was the product they'd been looking for. Insty-friends!

Insty-fucking-friends, he thought, putting Gina's intonations on the words. Jesus, Jesus, how did I get here?

". . . running the final battery of tests on our people down in Mexico," Manny said cheerfully. "If all goes well, as I'm sure it will, they'll be discharged this week. I'll be going down to oversee it. I would be negligent if I didn't personally make sure that everything was at one hundred percent peak condition for our next star." Manny gave him a satisfied smile. "You know, I'm glad things have turned out this way. I was worried about you, but it's all going to work out. I had no idea that you would have such a feel for that kind of work. It's a gift. And the fact that it came to light just as we were launching this new project is nothing short of miraculous."

Miraculous. The word echoed in Gabe's mind as he stared unseeingly out of the tinted window. And here he'd always thought the miraculous had been strictly confined to Artificial Reality.

* * *

"Saint *Who* of the *What*?" said Caritha.

Gabe hesitated. He had blurted the name out on impulse, and it seemed as absurd as it had when he'd first read it on the slip Sam had given him.

"The St. Dismas Infirmary for the Incurably Informed," he said again, and peeked over the top of the concrete wall at the zeppelin moored at the other end of the airfield.

"Keep your head *down*, hotwire," Caritha said, looking at the side of the cam. It had acquired a small screen since the last time he'd been in. He was used to the program embellishing itself as needed, but a screen was more elaborate than he'd thought was possible. "There's activity all over the place here. I've got us shielded, but it won't stick if you insist on wiggling around. You'll break the field."

"St. Dismas was the good thief," Marly whispered to him. He turned to look at her in surprise. Belly-down in the dirt on his other side, she looked up at him with feverishly bright eyes. He almost called for a status report when she went on suddenly. "Though most people think it's just another bulletin board for the discussion of political, cultural, and personal developments, St. Dismas is actually a repository for stolen and sensitive information. You have to have something to offer to access it." She winked at him.

"How do you know that?" Gabe asked.

"We know a lot of things," Caritha said, still studying the screen in the side of the cam. "They're starting to close down the hangar now. It should be empty in ten minutes, everybody going home to supper." She gave him a sidelong glance. "Be real sure you want this zeppelin, hotwire, because once we start for it, there's no going back."

"I still don't understand *why* you want a goddamn *zeppelin*," Marly added, giving him a poke.

"It's the last one," he said. "Someone has to take it for a spin, see what it can do in the open sky."

" 'Spin' is a lousy choice of word," Caritha said. "Does the name Hindenburg mean anything to you?"

Gabe sighed, beginning to regret not starting over with fresh copies of their programs. "The Hindenburg has nothing to do with the story line we're supposed to develop. Let's wipe that reference, as well as all mention of St. Dismas, okay?"

"Okay, no St. Dismas steals the Hindenburg," said Caritha. "But if you'd asked me, which you didn't and you should have,

I'd have told you going after headhunters is a hell of a lot more useful than stealing zeppelins."

Gabe blinked at her. "Wipe that, too. *Status!*"

Nothing in the status report indicated he was being hacked, or that the program was drawing on anything but already booted material. He plunged himself back into the simulation. "Resume."

Marly tugged at his sleeve. "You're really going to make us steal that zeppelin and leave all those headhunters running loose?"

"Last time," Gabe said, "we're not doing *Headhunters*. We can't. *House of the Headhunters* wasn't a Para-Versal release."

"They're all in on it, I've told you that before, hotwire."

He groaned. "Just steal this zeppelin with me, and then I'll go get headhunters with you later. All right?"

"That's more like it," said Caritha. "Five minutes. Hope you can run like a rabbit."

He took it all the way to the point where they were about to lift off in the zeppelin before he called a halt. The effort of keeping things moving had drained him. Perhaps he was going to have to give in and use fresh copies devoid of most of the headhunters material. The programs wouldn't be as broken in and easy to interact with, but it would be better than tinkering with the present versions.

No, you don't want to tinker with us as we are now, hotwire, said Caritha's voice in his mind suddenly, *because we're your best friends, and you're really going to want us after those sockets go in.*

Still putting fancy dress on his own thoughts and calling it company. But he wasn't so far gone that he didn't know what he was doing, couldn't tell the difference.

That's why you want to keep us the way we are, hotwire. Because later on, after the sockets go in, telling the difference between us'll be harder. A lot harder.

He wondered about that for days, for weeks, all the way up to the time they put the sockets in. Right downstairs in Medical, as it turned out, not in Mexico.

22

Change for the machines. The groups went crazy for it.

She had missed most of the outgrabe when the story had broken, but there was still plenty of noisemaking going on when she had returned from Mexico. Dog-and-pony shows for the media, for the rock groups, for Concerned Citizens for a Better Tomorrow and the National Council of Implant Clinics and the Mothers' March for Mental Health and Addicts Anonymous. For the National Concerned Marching Addicts of Anonymous Mental Clinics, for all she knew. It was hard to tell the addicts from the mothers and the mothers from the others, and it was a brand new world out there.

Meet the new world. Same as the old world.

That wasn't how the old chorus went, but that was all right, because it wasn't really true, either. But the Beater could pretend it was. Basically. Basically the job's the same. Hear the music, make the pictures.

Except it was better. It wasn't just hearing the music, it was being *in* the music, and the images coming up on the screen of her mind, forming as she looked at them. As soon as she thought it, there it was, and if she thought to change it, it changed, growing from her like a live thing. She suddenly found it hard to remember that she had worked any other way. At least, while she was doing it. It felt so natural, so right, to send a dream out of the inner darkness into raw daylight, where anyone could see it. Once you'd done that, you wanted to keep on doing it, and the more you did it, the easier it became.

For the first time she had a real understanding of Mark's nature, of what had been happening behind those eyes for so many years. Change for the machines? Nah, the machines had finally changed for him, and he was just doing what he'd always done.

Not everyone could do it. That was the strange part, that not all of them could change for the machines. Ecklestone vanished from the Canadaytime lineup, leaving Valjean and Moray hooked up and rocking through the wire.

"You want to hear something?" Valjean asked her in the studio at the top of his house. "You want to really hear something?" A few quick hits off the oxy, the cape flickering and winking, and Moray looking like she was going to jump out of her skin if it didn't happen soon. They played it for her, beginning to end and from the first note; the pictures came up in her mind just the way they were supposed to. Except she wasn't plugged into the hardware, and the images boiled like a fever, looking for the way out, pressing to be released, until she thought her head had to explode.

And then Valjean and Moray stopped, and her vision cleared. She barely registered that Valjean's synthesizer had remained closed and silent, that Moray hadn't touched her keyboard, they'd played it all the way through with only their minds, but she was already out, ripping down Topanga, needing her own machine. Change for the machines. Everything changed for the machines.

U B the Ass to Risk was gone, and in its place was a joint that said it sold dreams.

SOCKET-FRESH
MODULES AVAILABLE FOR
FLATSCREEN **HEADMOUNTS**
!!!COMING SOON—SOCKET HARDWARE!!!
WATCH THIS SPACE FOR FURTHER DETAILS

Hadn't taken them long to catch on. The new clinics were open, and they were lined up around the block for them. Whether the dream joint actually had real dreams or just warmed-over clips from old wannabee releases almost didn't matter. Sockets were hot, sockets were it, sockets were the new sexual preference. The hardware was out there, and the merchandise was out there side by side with the stuff pretending to be the merchandise. Hadn't taken hardly any time at all for everyone to get into the spirit of the thing.

She paused in front of the Chinese Theatre. COMING SOON—THE LAST ZEPPELIN! trumpeted the holo arching over the entrance. A PARA-VERSAL/DIVERSIFICATIONS PRODUCTION! The holo blinked. AN ADVENTURE BORN IN THE MIND, DIRECT TO YOU! YOU *WILL* BELIEVE

YOU ARE THERE . . . blink . . . *BECAUSE YOU WILL BE THERE!!!!*

Good old Hollywood. Start with a great big flatscreen debut and work inward. Show it to them in gargantuan ultra-HDF: *Wouldn't you like to be inside this? Well, you can! Here it comes!*

"Thou shalt not *fear!*"

He was at her elbow as suddenly as if he had congealed out of the noisy air on the boulevard, a skinny hype in a dirty gray jumpsuit that might have been silver once. One hand thrust a glittery blue square at her face. "And with this stuff you ain't gonna fear no-goddamn-body, not nohow, not no-time, not nowhere!"

"Not any *body* I'm afraid of," she told him, moving on.

"Would you like to be?" He caught her arm and stuck a yellow lozenge under her nose. "I can handle that for you, too. Pure terror, it's the way to go. Hey, take 'em both at once, send your nerves to the playground of the gods!"

She pulled away from him.

"Hey, how about an ego trip, wanna go on an ego trip?" he called after her. "Fuckin' sockets've sent the drug trade right into the fuckin' toilet."

Already? You betcha. Hadn't taken long for everything to change for the machines. Pretty soon it would all be happening at the speed of thought, before it could actually happen, so that nothing would ever have to happen again. You'd only think things had happened, and if anything ever did happen, you wouldn't know the difference.

Take a little walk with me.

Here it comes.

White Lightning in a mason jar. It wasn't terribly visual, but when you'd been struck by lightning, you didn't need a passport to LotusLand. *Zzzzzt!* Hope you like your barbecue extra-crispy.

She was making the level in the jar go down little by little all by herself for what seemed like a long time while the music pounded. Without the usual excuse, because tonight she knew where Mark was, she knew exactly where to find him, and she would always know from now on.

But old habits sure died hard, she thought, and though being struck by White Lightning had left her movements kind of gluey and slow, her mind was running hot, full of pictures, ready to stand and deliver any time she put her request through the wire.

She let the music wash over her, speed-thrash, cruise-metal, bang-rock, hard-core soul. It was almost like being back in one of those bad old Boston bars, Babe's Beantown, Harborville, Kathye's Klown, in the before-days, putting on a plain old tox—getting shitfaced, smashed, blasted, hammered—and then jumping all night to some group so hungry you got to starving yourself.

The sticks were rapping away on the table, stealing a few licks on the side of the jar. Little Flavia, letting her sticks do the talking, and the sticks were saying all there was to say. Gina peered through the White Lightning haze at her. *Here it comes*.

The rest of Loophead melted out of the crowd of tables around her, out of the throbbing mass on the dance floor, where a kid with a heelprint tattooed on his forehead was climbing onto the stage again. Flavia was talking now, but the sticks had already said it all. *Here it comes. Take a little walk with me*.

"Because we have to catch it now," Flavia added. "You can. We can."

Loophead's bass boy Claudio lifted her up out of her chair nice and easy. He knew how, he'd done it before, more than once. He could really play, too, he wasn't just a keyboard cheater, the boy had real magic in his fingers. Real magic, real fingers.

A little traveling music, please.

Loophead worked out of a cellar studio on the outskirts of demolished Fairfax, where the property values had joined the drug trade in the toilet. Had to be one pretty big toilet, Gina reflected, the way they were flushing the world down, piece by piece.

The Fender was definitely not in the toilet. Dorcas slipped it on the way another person might have slipped on a diamond necklace. Dorcas was big, black, and old enough to know what a Fender meant. Tom was smaller, wiry, out of the Mimosa and numerous other places east and north, and you called him a keyboard cheater at your peril, because he knew, too, he knew what a keyboard was supposed to be.

Flavia leaned over her, still holding the sticks, smiling. No hard feelings from that night a million years ago, when Gina had pulled a likely-looking body out of a chair by the back of his neck. "It cost us a fortune to pry an extra box out of the supplier. Everyone in the world wants them. Make it be worth it."

Someone else gave her another hit off the mason jar before sinking the wires into her skull.

She went down fast, longer and harder than any fall she'd ever done for Valjean. She remembered that Claudio had cleaned Valjean's clock for him once. Called him a cheater and a fake.

That wasn't now. The music was now, the music lighting up the inside of her head, coming from somewhere else, the sound of sticks on metal, on glass, on wood, striking sparks in her mind.

She could feel Flavia's smile, the stretch of her mouth, the warmth, the teeth digging into her lower lip just a bit, and a little harder on the beat.

Claudio's magic fingers, manipulating the bass line. She could remember a time, just barely, but it had happened. She'd been even more toxed that night than she was now, and it seemed that he hadn't been so close that night, nowhere nearly so close, not inside her skin that way.

Sparks to lightning, white and otherwise; a glimpse of towers in each flash, minarets, monoliths, obelisks. Gina smiled to herself; what Claudio lacked in subtlety he made up in pure heat.

Dorcas's first chord came through, shaking the world all the way up to the moon, and they were off, all of them, charging down the line Tom was making on the keyboard, mystery tracks for the phantom night-train.

Here it comes. She let it. That was all she had to do, all she could do; it was right there, and she was right there, and they were all right there with her.

Be there for you.

There was a man with a different world in his eyes, still real, made of noise and light.

Be there for you.

There was a man, real, taking the long way home, walking a strip that had once been by the ocean, and she was running across a bridge, chased by her own growling need, but the harder she ran, the farther away he was.

Be there for you.

There was a man in a room, changed for the machines, not

real now, and a stranger, real, on a stony shore standing under a grey sky, turning slowly to her, but the music split the sky and shattered it, and she was gone again.

The music wailing from the Fender hit a sober part of her brain, but there was no time to consider what she was doing because it sent her off again, gone again, running down a long road with a fever in her chest, and the trees on either side bowed, branches like fingers, reaching, and when they touched, they were like mist, like smoke, and she was gone again.

Gone again . . . gone all night, one of those endless nights, don't look for the sun this time, and hell, you don't need it anyway.

Here it comes. . . .

Endless night; flesh on flesh, not a furnished room but a place to live for a little while. She turned and ran again, but it overtook her, flung her down, and opened her up.

All right, admit it then, just one time. She could do that before it let her go.

Flying; hurtling like a meteor, alive and burning. Scorched air, and then the whole sky was on fire, and what the hell, if a thing's on fire, then let it burn, let it all burn down and burn back up again.

Burn back up, and up, and up, and over the top.

Flavia was leaning over her, mopping her face with something soft. "And that's what *we* call video," she said seriously. "If your sanitized bosses can't handle that, we can all walk, and walk tall, you with us. What's the Dive got to put up against what we just did? Not a fucking thing."

She couldn't even nod. She had sweated through her clothes. Flavia put the mason jar to her lips; burned all the way down. Burn . . . Gina raised up on one elbow and twisted around on the mattress. The connections hung limply near the console, harmless now. Tom was just disconnecting his own; he looked over at her, breathing hard.

"What did we just do?" she asked thickly.

Flavia grinned; it made her golden features look sharp enough to cut. "We made a video the new way. The *real* way. What's the fucking point of sockets if you don't do it the *real* way?" She looked over her shoulder. "We're done. He can see her now."

Gina let herself fall back on the mattress, throwing one arm over her eyes. Christ, that anyone would see her now. Footsteps came across the cellar floor and stopped next to her, and the hope flared in her, brand-new fire that he might have changed so much for the machines that he would come and find *her* now, instead of the other way around. She took a deep breath and lowered her arm.

There he was, big as life and possibly more real.

"How the fuck did *you* find me?" she asked.

"It wasn't easy," Gabe said.

He felt better than he had in years. Never mind better. He felt fantastic. He felt more than fantastic. He felt *unreal.*

Un-fucking-real.

Visual Mark. That's the truth, the whole truth, and nothing but the truth.

He lost all awareness of the meat that had been his prison for close to fifty years, and the relief he felt at having laid his burden down was as great as himself. His *self.* And his *self* was getting greater all the time, both ways, greater as in more wonderful and greater as in bigger.

The sense of having so much space to spread out in—a baby emerging from the womb after nine months must have felt the same thing, he thought. Stone-home true enough for himself. After the initial trauma, hey, it's party-time!

All those years in meat hell, he marveled. All those years of getting toxed, getting crazy, thrashing, banging, going from one thing to another until he couldn't hold himself upright anymore, and never understanding that what he'd really been trying to do all along was drill a few holes in his head and get out of meat-jail.

And into . . . what?

His own context. It went little by little with him, a little more every time he took the wire. That was what he called it, taking the wire.

What time he spent off-line faded into dull stretches he waited out until he could take the wire again and get a little bit greater. The wire was good to him, helped him along, showed him how he could spread out a little more each time, easing himself into his context. Like going home.

He stopped bothering to disconnect to use the little bathroom in the pit. What the hell, the wires were long enough. They weren't long enough to stretch all the way out the door, but he found out they'd let him use the in-house delivery staff to run food up to him just like they did for the big shots on the fabled Upstairs Team when they worked overtime. He didn't bother disconnecting to eat, either; it only took a few minutes.

With all that there didn't seem to be much sense in disconnecting and going back to his apartment. The pit was bigger, he had everything he needed, and the program director was always cranking on high.

He knew the time was coming when he would try to slip back into the meat-jail and find out it was too small for him. Once he had been sure his brain held a rabbit hole, a pocket of infinity where no limits applied, no boundary conditions were enforced, and he could fly through the universe if he wanted to. Maybe he'd just been fooling himself. Maybe the rabbit hole, for all its depth and breadth, had been finite after all. Or maybe it was closing up a little more every time he stepped out of the meat, because soon he wasn't going to need it anymore. Like the brain itself, and the rest of the warm meat.

Deciding to stick with the wire was better than anything he'd done before. His mobility was virtually unlimited, along with his vision—the Dive was surveillance heavy, he'd known that already. He'd seen the cams back when he'd been in meat. But there were a number of cams he hadn't seen, quite a number. In his previous incarnation the discovery might have dismayed or angered him. Now he was just glad to have so many eyes.

And to shut those eyes, he withdrew and looked inward, though he could continue to capture anything that came in through a lens, storing it for later viewing. Little caches of information could fit almost anywhere he wanted them to; there were extensive stretches within the system that went unused. He minimized the possibility of the extra information being detected by nesting as much of it as possible, making one association carry double, triple, quadruple referents, more if he angled his pov all around the information space.

Taking the wire had taught him how to do that. Gradually he saw how he could completely rearrange not just his own but all the information storage and transmission so that it would occupy a fraction of the space it did at present. The patterns came to him with the music, patterns becoming images becoming dreams becoming the videos that the ones outside still demanded of him. He was growing less interested in that. He had the program director, and he had his own pictures, and at last he had a place big enough to see them as he had always wanted to see them.

He thought of rearranging the system to suit himself. He could wait until night, when there were only minimal demands on the system and his movements would go completely unnoticed. In the morning everyone would come to work and discover they had been streamlined. But then the hardware would be too clunky, and the operating systems would be too unrefined to work properly, and he was dependent on those things to get around in whatever this was he was getting around in. It was becoming obvious to him now that the system and the hardware were actually as different as the mind and that meat organ, brain.

In the very beginning he had thought that Gina might possibly be there for him, as she had been so many other places. He'd really thought that she had understood, down in Mexico, not just because they both knew how it was in the system but because of how they'd come to each other outside, in meat.

He recalled the sensations with pleasure. They hadn't done that in a while, and he'd forgotten how really good it could be. Now all he had to do was reach for it in his memory, and he was there again, in the pleasure. But in the loneliness, too.

It was a lonely thing. There was no way to be sure if it meant the same thing to both of you. He'd forgotten that part of making love, how you couldn't assume that intent was as joined as bodies were.

For him it had been a way for him to say good-bye to the body, but as he lived it again in his memory, he knew it hadn't meant the same thing to her. If he'd been saying good-bye to his, she'd been saying something entirely different. He didn't understand how she could continue to cling to the heavy flesh even after knowing how the mind could be freed. But then, it didn't seem to happen the same way for her as it did for him. He knew that just by looking at her videos. Maybe her system would always be contained within herself and never spread out; maybe there was no other way for her to keep from getting lost.

It didn't matter. The last line was the same: she wouldn't be coming with him on this trip.

Maybe she couldn't have anyway, he thought, feeling the

living and the nonliving creep along his awareness in the system. Maybe you could make yourself bigger, but you couldn't make yourself any less alone.

She made him take her to Mark's place. The building was old, shabby in a regal way, no elevators. Gabe let his eyes slide over the graffiti scrawled on the walls as he climbed the stairs behind Gina. *If you got the socket, I got the plug. Free the Hackers! US OUT of Malaysia!* (That was an old one.) And the ubiquitous *Dr. Fish Makes House Calls!* Underneath that someone had printed in crayon, *do houses really come when you call*? Under that, more usual and less creative things.

A girl about twelve years old was sitting on the first landing with a laptop resting on her folded legs. She gave them a suspicious look as they passed. Gabe couldn't help staring. She was reasonably clean, not poorly dressed—the jeans had barely begun to fade—but she had a hungry look that was all too familiar. In a couple years' time, he thought, she would be emancipated, and she would melt into the city somewhere, finding a nest of hackers to belong to in a best-case scenario, finding a nest of something else in Fairfax or on the Mimosa in a worst-case, but regardless, her parents would never see her again. And hell, maybe they didn't want to.

He felt a sudden rush of guilt, as if he had taken Sam out into the middle of Los Angeles himself and dumped her, telling her to make her way as best she could. He should have fought for her, he thought miserably; he should have fought Catherine and the educational system, *himself*, if it had come to that, and anything else that had driven Sam away. Instead, he had just let her go.

Gina had to spit on the keystrip before the door would let them in. There was music coming from the apartment opposite, something fast and thrashy, what Gabe thought of as psychopath music. He looked around nervously, but the hall was deserted.

The apartment was dark and stale smelling, as if it hadn't been opened in days. Gina turned on the lights. There were a couple of empty LotusLand bottles over by the couch, clothes strewn on the floor. The only thing that seemed to be well kept was the entertainment center attached to the dataline against one wall. The large screen was blank except for some small numbers in the lower right-hand corner, indicating that something was being logged from the dataline.

"Make yourself to home," Gina said dully, stumping into the bedroom. She came out again almost immediately, made a stop at the refrigerator, and then plumped down on the couch, handing him a bottle of LotusLand. He looked at it doubtfully.

"I don't know if I should drink this," he said.

"If you don't, it'll just go to waste."

He perched on the edge of the sofa a short distance away from her. She was toxed, he realized finally.

"See, I had the wild, stupid, stone-home fucking hopeless idea that if I came here, he'd be here," she said, and let her head fall back against the sofa. "Like he'd snap out of it all of a sudden and come back. That's pretty high up in the stupidsphere, ain't it? Thinking if I go looking for him in some other place, he'll be there." She rolled her head over to look at him. "Well? Is that high up in the stupidsphere or not?"

Whatever was on her breath smelled lethal. He was about to ask her if he should get anything for her when she pointed at the remote lying on the carpet at his feet.

"See what's on the fucking dataline. Maybe it'll be another reason to go on living."

Hesitantly he picked up the remote and thumbed the on button. A list of downloaded items appeared on the screen, all music videos, judging from the titles.

"Skip that shit," Gina told him. "Spin the dial. Round and round we go, everyone a winner."

He pressed the scan. The screen split into four parts as *General News* came up, with the anchor on real time in the upper left quadrant, a listing of the major headlines of the day next to her, footage on the current story below her, and a menu of the other default channels in the lower right quadrant, along with choices for *Freeze, Replay, Select, Menu Top,* and *Quit.*

After a minute the scan went on to the next channel. The wholesome, solemn features of the latest Mrs. Troubles replace the anchor, with a printout of the problem she was addressing in the quadrant next to her and audience responses posted in the square below.

"—accept the reality that when you enter into a relationship with an incarcerated individual, understanding is not a given. Things carry very different meanings depending on which side of the prison wall you are. And conversely for all you prisoners that I know are watching, just judging from the email I get here, you prisoners will have to accept the reality that when you enter into a relationship with a person who is *not* incarcerated, there can be expectations which you just aren't ready for. If you're not planning to go straight after your term is up, you really shouldn't even bother. Career criminals more than anyone else need to be involved with people who speak the language and understand the special protocols, which can be a real problem if you're on parole and forbidden to associate with other felons—"

"Behold, my culture speaks to me," Gina said. The scan went on to *Peccadillo Update*. Gabe lowered the volume. "Feel like a winner yet?"

Gabe shrugged. "What's a winner?" He looked around the shabby apartment. The legendary Visual Mark did not live in even a fair approximation of a video.

"I'm not sure," Gina said suddenly, "which I'm more curious about—how you found me, or why you bothered."

"I just went to all the places I could remember that you'd taken me to," he said. "Someone said they'd seen you in that joint on the boulevard. When I got there, someone else said you'd left with, ah, Loophead. I got the address of the studio off directory assistance."

"That's one question."

He shrugged. "I'm sorry, I'm unprepared. If I'd known I was going to have to go into detail, I'd have whipped up an outline and a storyboard."

Gina pealed hearty laughter at the ceiling. He sat fingering the unopened bottle of LotusLand and feeling embarrassed. "Come on," he said after a bit. "It wasn't that funny."

She wiped her eyes with the back of her hand. "Jesus, we've all got you on the run, don't we? Rivera and Para-Versal and even me."

The dataline was showing a commercial for a new private neighborhood in Canoga Park; the voice-over seemed to jump out at him. ". . . tiled bathrooms, spacious living suites, kitchens where functionality wasn't left out of the design." The pov swooped along a narrow kitchenette that Gabe knew was only half as long as the cam made it seem, and cruised through another room shaped so that it was almost two separate spaces. "Canoga Park's finest new living arrangement, Park Residence. For further information, on-line tours, and in-person inspection, contact Catherine Mirijanian."

Gabe winced at the sight of the regal face on the screen. "My wife," he said. "She never did have a sense of timing."

"Her? The one that's leaving you?"

"Left. Gone already. I'm waiting for her to sell the condo out from under me."

"Where you gonna go then?"

He shrugged. "Somewhere. I guess."

Gina squinted at the screen. "She doesn't look like you."

"No, we never achieved that point in marriage where you start to look like each other."

"Not what I meant. She doesn't look like she's for you, like she was supposed to be your wife."

"I know." Catherine's picture lingered a moment longer, rippled slightly, and then vanished, to be replaced by some incomprehensible episode from a series labeled *Lighthand* in the lower corner. Gabe wondered idly when the divisions on the screen had disappeared. Everything seemed to happen when you were looking the other way. "I think I was always hoping someday she would look like my wife. Now I can't remember why."

Gina yawned. "I fucking *hate* this kind of discussion."

"*You* started it," Gabe said, his voice rising in exasperation. "You're a real comedy on wheels, you know that? As far as I can tell, all you ever do is hit people, get toxed, and chase around after a guy who doesn't know what planet he's on half the time."

She looked down at her lap. "I make videos, too."

"Is that what you were doing tonight? With those people, Loophead?"

"You see any of that?" she asked, not looking up at him.

"I saw it all. They wouldn't let me near you, but I saw it all, and I know what was going on."

She nodded. "Yah. It was all right. The synthesis was there, just came up like it was meant to be, and it was all right."

He set the bottle aside on the floor. "Are you going to do that with Mark?" he asked, without thinking.

She looked up at him, shocked, and he wanted to bite his tongue off. "Mark's not a musician, he's another synner. Why would I do that with him?"

He moved a little closer to her on the couch. "I just wondered, when I saw all of you connected at the same time. I—" Suddenly he couldn't think of what to say next, and he felt as if he had stepped off solid floor into a void. *MORE DRUGS.*

He shook his head. "Never mind. I'm sorry, forget I asked that question."

"What are *you* gonna do?" she asked.

"When?"

"When you're in the wire. When you're rattling around your condo while you wait for the floor to get sold out from under you."

He shook his head again. This was the point where he could get up and leave, and he waited for his legs to push him upright and carry him out the door. He'd been running around in simulation for so long, he'd forgotten how to run a realife, real-time routine; he'd forgotten that if he made mistakes, there was no safety-net program ready to jump in and correct for him.

"Well." Gina let out a long breath. "You want the bed or the couch? I've slept on both, they're equally shitty."

"No, I can go home." He started to get up.

"Bad idea," she said, pulling him down again. "The neighborhood slash-artists'll take you out before you get back to your rental. I'll come out tomorrow morning and find your bloody hide plastered up on the front of the building."

Suddenly he was too tired to argue. Let her go to bed, and then he could sneak out and go home. "I'll take the couch."

"Turn out the lights when you're done." She got up and went into the bedroom.

He sat staring at the dataline, which had cycled back to *General News*. There was a new anchor now, a young Scandinavian type who looked about sixteen years old. He was rattling on in his sunny voice about something to do with sockets. Of course; if sockets were out of the news for more than half an hour, that would have been an item in itself. Surprising that Mrs. Troubles hadn't been offering advice for the socketed. *Well, dears, a mixed relationship—the socketed and the unsocketed—is a peck of trouble waiting to happen, and we all know it. And so is the socketed with the socketed and the unsocketed with the unsocketed. Better you should try to kindle something with a convicted felon behind bars, or even just forget the whole thing.*

"Didn't you hear me, stupid? I *said*, you're not really listening, are you? But then, if you weren't listening, of course you didn't hear me. Dealing with your type is enough to make me *berserk.*"

Gabe blinked rapidly at the screen. The sunny anchor's face was now a distorted mask of furious disgust.

"You out there, on your couches, on your beds, on your *toilets*, squatting in your expensive fetid hovels, you don't put this on to *listen* to anything. You just let it babble at you, and you let the babble bounce off, a little white noise to make you feel a little less like the stagnant, empty straw-people you really are. Get ready, all you null-and-voids, because here it comes—"

The screen went blank. Seconds crawled by, and then an easy-viewing scene of Big Sur at sunset came up. "We are experiencing some technical difficulties at this time," said a calm, refined voice. "Normal programming should be restored within a few minutes. If you have been running a download from this channel, we strongly advise immediate diagnostics and decontamination, and that you refrain from uploading or downloading any other material until such time as your own system has been certified free of infection. We remind our viewers that diagnostic and decontamination programs are free whenever the problem stems from the network. Consult your program guide for further details."

Gabe let out a short laugh of disbelief. It had been a long time since anything like this had happened on the dataline. He wondered how the abusive swashbuckler was. Maybe one of Sam's friends.

He flicked off the dataline and sat in the silence, at a loss. When the dataline insulted and abandoned you, you knew you were really alone.

A voice in his head. Somebody's, maybe his own. *Hey, hotwire—you're an asshole.*

"Yah," he muttered, "but I'm trying to quit." He got up and went to the bedroom.

She was sitting on the edge of the unmade bed in a T-shirt and underpants as if she had forgotten what she wanted to do next. He wanted to say her name, but his voice refused to work. She turned then and saw him standing in the doorway, holding onto the frame as if he were trying to push it out and make it wider.

She got up slowly, the expression on her face unreadable. But not unhappy, definitely not unhappy. It may not have been the expression she'd been wearing while she was waiting for Mark on the courthouse steps, but he didn't know for sure because she'd had her back to him. If the best he could do was not unhappy, then he wasn't unhappy, either, he thought wildly. He opened his mouth to speak to her, but his voice still wouldn't come, and he threw up his hands as he went toward her. She met him halfway, and they toppled onto the sagging mattress in a frantic, urgent tangle.

"This is like, port in a storm, nowhere else to go," she said after a few moments of struggling, grabbing, straining. Her voice was a growl. "You care about that?"

He made a noise.

"Me, neither."

23

The memory sprang open, and she wasn't just remembering the fall, she was reliving it.

Her inner ear went crazy, the wind rushed into her, choking off her breathing, guided express missile, toes pointed at the sidewalk and the world blurring, smearing upward—

It cut off as the last chord faded out. Jesus, Jesus, Little Jesus Jump-Up, what a fucking *rush*. Signature image? This was going to scare Valjean out of a year's growth.

Getting good at falling, she thought. Falling off buildings and falling into bed.

Top, she commanded. Instantly she was looking at the frozen beginning of the video. She clicked through it by sequence until she reached the start of the fall, clicked back to add a small hint at key points throughout the video, just the barest eyeblink—thoughtblink?—of the point of view about to step into empty air. An almost-flash forward. She stuttered the beginning of the fall—step off, zip back to step off again, zip back to step off again, zip back to step off again—

Very nasty. *What does this remind you of?* She could feel herself smiling. If things had been just a little different, she'd have thrown his ass out of the bedroom—Mark's bedroom. Instead, she'd gone ahead and jumped the fast train without looking. Maybe just because he'd come to her, she hadn't gone to him. Not quite the same way, at least, not till the last moment, when the fast train reawakened by Claudio and Flavia and Dorcas and Tom went into high gear at the sight of him rushing at her.

With Mark, nobody went to anybody; things came together, and there they were, like conditions being right for rain, or sleet, or nothing at all. It had been a long time since anyone had come to her the way Ludovic had, even longer since she'd gone to anyone. In some ways it had been easier with Mark. Just hang in, wait for conditions to be right, no hurry, no worry, and if they were, they were; if they weren't, they weren't. Don't like it? Go complain to the sky about the rain while you're at it.

But this one was different. This one she would have to do something about. If she'd known that at the time, maybe she'd have asked for more time to think about it.

Horseshit. You knew. You set it up. You put a few things around in a pattern, and then you stood back to see if he'd make anything out of it. What does this look like to you, an open window or an open wound? He saw an open window, and he climbed right on in, and the bitch of it is, you had a feeling that was what he wanted to see and what he wanted to do. It's your ticket for your trip, and you can't just back off pleading self-defense.

It had been one hell of a long time since she'd jumped the fast train. The fast train was the transportation of the very young and strong. After you got dragged under the wheels a few times, you knew you'd had your fill, you knew you weren't young and strong enough to do *that* anymore. If you were smart enough.

She didn't think Gabe Ludovic had ever jumped the fast train in his life. Standing at the end of fifteen years of marriage, he'd wanted a lot more than sex. The wanting had been all but tangible, in the way he'd touched her, in the heat of his body, a heat that surprised both of them. The heat and the wanting had run him a good part of the night, keeping him wide awake if not active the whole time, talking crazy and sometimes just talking. It might have been the night they should have had before she'd gone off to Mexico with Mark.

He'd been waiting. He'd been waiting for her to come back. Maybe he didn't know that, but she did. Now.

His face floated before her, waiting for her to save it to chip. Instead, she wiped it away and refocused on the video hanging fire in her head.

She was in the middle of the ghost-town sequence, moving among the images of the abandoned, rusted-out cars, when the feeling of being watched came over her. It wasn't part of the video, she'd have remembered the sensation. She halted the action and took a look around the empty street. Tall buildings with the windows busted out, dead-empty under cold, thin afternoon sunlight. On the street the smashed headlights of a murdered limo stared at her. Abruptly she remembered where the image had come from, the old footage of that college town on January 1, 2000. Except she'd left out the bodies.

And then the bodies *were* there, tattered phantoms on the hood of the limo, hanging out the passenger window, fallen from the rear door, strewn on the streets like discarded dolls. Her pov rushed at them, and the hell of it was, she couldn't really tell if she'd done that or not, put the bodies in just by remembering, or whether—

—*take a little walk*—

A fleeting thought that disintegrated even as she became aware of it. She moved on, going with the music and the visuals, riding it all the way to the fall again. The stutter built on itself, lasting a second longer on each zip back in time, until the fall was a relief.

And as she hung in the air for the brief moment before she dropped, the presence crashed in on her all at once, all the way through this time, and he took the fall with her.

Acceptance streamed through her along with the terror of falling, the terror of falling with him where he could not have been and seemed to belong all at once.

She came to, shivering on the mat.

Through the exterior lens of the head mounted monitor atop the console, he watched her take the lift down and come striding across the pit to him. With another ax to grind. Just to do it, he gave her one, a big fire-ax with a handle as thick as a child's arm and a hungry-looking blade. Nasty; he logged the visual for later use.

How perfectly she came through like this, the expressions on her face speaking more plainly than words. The frown of confusion as she looked at his body curled up on the carpet, wondering how he'd let her in, then the realization smoothing her face, irritation pulling at her mouth. It was almost like reading her mind, which he'd done when he'd sipped at her video. Great pleasure in the act, although there had been something disturbing there that had made him suddenly uncertain, made him wonder, which was not the only reason he wanted to do it again. Except he knew she had come to tell him not to.

The commands to the system ran instantaneously for him, nothing more than breathing.

"Over here, actually," came his voice from the console speaker. He saved the sight of her head jerking up to look, digitizing it as far as it would go, until he had a bit that was pure, self-contained startlement.

She moved closer to the console and looked it over, her gaze passing two or three times over the headmount before she picked it up. He felt a wave of vertigo as his outer pov slid and jerked in her hands.

"Take it easy, don't move so fast," he said.

He saw her trace the lines from the headmount back into the system, then follow the trail of wires leading from the system to his head.

"Think this up yourself?" she asked, putting down the headmount.

"Easy to do from the inside. Whole console fits in here with room to spare. Lots of things are easy. Check the flatscreen."

He showed her the image of herself stalking across the pit toward him with the ax.

"Pretty clean," she said casually. "No extraneous elements, no static, good res. Get your ass up, I got something to say to you."

"Why don't you come on in here with me, then?"

She looked from the headmount to the meat on the floor and back, glaring. "I want to know how you pulled that shit on me."

"If it's on-line, I can get to it." *How I did it, Gina? More like, how couldn't I? It's what I was made to do. I told you that ages ago, when I was far more meat than what I am now.*

She stood over him, looking at the wires trailing out of his head. "Don't do it again," she said quietly. "Don't you break in on me again."

He let the words pour into him and run along his enhanced awareness, preserving the exact pitch of her voice, her pronunciation, the way her mouth had moved, and sent it all to the Gina file.

"I scared you," he said. "But really, it was just like this, like you coming here to see me. I just didn't disconnect."

She glanced at the speaker.

"Yes, I do sound different," he said, and her attention snapped back to the meat on the floor. She was going to continue to address that poor meat, despite the fact that she should have looked directly into the headmount cam. "I'm better. I'm getting better all the time. That body was dragging me down."

"I wouldn't talk about it in the past tense. How the fuck you think you can last like this?"

He popped his vitals on the flatscreen for her. "Every time I took the wire, I learned to slow the metabolism a little more. I made adjustments, just like any other mechanism. Change for the machines."

She knelt next to the body, and he panned the headmount lens down, tracking her. Tentatively she took hold of the body's arm and squeezed it. Then she looked up at the console again.

"You can feel the difference, can't you, Gina? I'm not really in there, now. I'm maintaining it, but there's nobody home. I know it doesn't happen that way for you, but that's how it is for me."

She let go of him and stood up, stubbornly shaking her head. "You been in worse shape than this after a tough night. You think it's some kinda fucking novelty for me to see you passed out on the floor?" Abruptly she turned and headed back to the lift.

He swiveled the lens after her. "Gina."

She stopped and turned her head just a little. "What."

"I said this would be me. Didn't I?"

Her head dipped slightly in what might have been a nod. Then she moved off, fast.

He turned off the lens and gave himself over fully to what was within.

He was running across the airfield toward the zeppelin, following Caritha. The distance was deceptive—either that, or his pov was out of sync again. He couldn't seem to get coordinated, and he wondered how Gina handled that. He would have asked her, except there hadn't been any time the night before to bring the subject up gracefully. If he had even thought of it, which he hadn't. He was sharply aware of the way his heart was pounding, as if it were trying to beat itself to death in his chest, and not just from the illusion of running, though he was also conscious of the sensations of his feet pounding the ground and his arms pumping.

Abruptly the side of the zeppelin lit up, flashing marquee-style. MORE DRUGS. He thumped to a stop and stared up at it, more amused than dismayed. Marly paused on the stairway up to the gondola; Caritha poked her head out the doorway to see what the holdup was.

"Excuse me. *What* are you doing?"

He turned. Rana Copperthwait was striding across the airfield, looking both severe and concerned. Christ, his mind was wandering again.

"This is love," Copperthwait said. A breeze lifted her heavy curls slightly, brushing one ringlet across her mouth. She pushed it away irritably. "This is love and sex, no ambiguity here, no coyness. You're living everyone's fantasy, to be desirable to two people and them being willing to share. That's pretty great. It would be even better if you could throw in a few more women. Now don't you think you'd better get up in that zeppelin and get busy?"

Gabe looked over his shoulder at Marly and Caritha. They shrugged. "Come on, hotwire," Marly said, and trotted up the steps to the gondola. He followed, pausing just outside the doorway. Caritha poked her head out again.

"What's the matter now?"

"I'm blank on what the inside of a zeppelin gondola looks like."

"So call a database." She grabbed him by the front of his shirt and yanked him inside.

He was standing in Mark's bedroom, looking down at Gina asleep in the rumpled sheets. Startled, he looked at Marly, who put up her hands and backed away. "I'm not touching this one. You made it, you deal with it."

"Likewise," Caritha said, moving closer to Marly. A doorway appeared behind them, and they slipped through it. He had a glimpse of something that looked like a pilot's cockpit before they shut the door on him.

In the bed Gina remained asleep. Cautiously he moved around it and sat down on the edge of the mattress. She stirred slightly.

At first you think things are going to get better. You keep believing, and you honor the commitment—

C-word, she'd said abruptly.

Pardon?

C-word. The big bad c-word. Commitment. You got them Bad Old Cozmic C-Word Blues.

It wasn't a word to me. It was something real, not an incredible simulation. You can run on that . . . oh, years and years. Even after it doesn't seem worth it anymore, you can still run on it, and then one day . . . all gone. All used up.

Yah? Try it Cheshire-cat style. One day it's all that's left, and everything else is gone. Either way it's a stone-home bitch. I got a c-word and nothing to use it on. What've you got?

The Last Zeppelin. *Coming soon to a brain near you.*

Gina stirred again. There was the hint of a smile on her mouth. Had anyone ever smiled in sleep because of him? He didn't know. Still didn't but then, it had been dark.

He hadn't started to worry until the room showed signs of getting lighter. Suddenly he'd had the wild idea that the darkness had been a safe zone or a fooler loop, and the daylight would screw it all up. He'd turned to her a little desperately then, and maybe she'd been feeling the same thing, or something like it. They'd gone at each other in frenzy, and Jesus but he'd thought that would have kept the day away if anything could have.

Maybe it had. The room was completely light when they'd quieted, but the spell had not been broken. Out of bed they'd continued to move around each other easily, not falling all over each other like a couple of schoolkids, just . . . easily. A little sex magic could go a long way, even in the only port in a storm.

Fast train.

Pardon?

Fast train. It's usually the night-train. Never mind, Ludovic. Now you know what it's like.

The room swayed slightly as the zeppelin lifted off, and he suddenly had the certain feeling that something/someone was approaching; a new presence, as full and individual as he was. He twisted around to see who it was.

He was looking at himself in the mirror in Medical's bathroom, turning his head from side to side. Just as they'd said, he didn't look any different. Same old head, only now it had eight holes in it, eight holes to be filled with eight plugs and a small menu of commands he could use to manipulate the images in his head. *Top. Forward. Reverse. Freeze. Resume. End. Save. Quit.*

There was a fast montage of images as each command was executed—Caritha, MORE DRUGS, Rana Copperthwait speaking to him forward and backward, freezing briefly and then gesturing at the zeppelin, Mark's bedroom, Gina, Marly and Caritha shutting the door on him, Gina stirring and the sense of another presence even more strongly this time, his face in the bathroom mirror, the awareness of the whole mess being saved to chip, and then he was blinking at the ceiling of the pit high above him, wondering if he'd ever get this right.

Disconnect, he thought. There was a fleeting acknowledgment deep within, a feeling he had tried to describe to himself without success. *Without success* seemed to fit the situation in general. He reached up and removed each connection carefully. There was never any sensation of the connections going in or coming out again, it was all as painless as they'd promised, but the association he always made was voodoo. Sticking long pins in a doll and pulling them out again. Perhaps because he didn't want to think about the ward sequence in *House of the Headhunters*. If he did, he'd have to look at it.

He shook his head as if to clear it, even though he wasn't the least bit groggy. That was the interesting thing about using the new interface—he never came out of it feeling drained and hung over the way he sometimes had with the old system. No eyestrain, no muscle strain, no strain of any kind.

He should have felt groggy, though, considering the sleep he hadn't gotten the night before, but rest wasn't what he'd needed, not then, and not now.

C-word, Ludovic. It takes more fucking nerve than most of us have to say the whole thing right out. Because there's nothing worse than having lead in your pencil and nobody to write to.

He laughed aloud at the memory. He could hear her voice so clearly in his head. The sockets had given him that—all his thoughts ran as big and vivid and sharp as any high-definition monitor screen, seeming so real he could almost reach out and touch them.

What the sockets hadn't given him, though, was control over what came into his head. No strain, but nothing to show for his efforts, either. He couldn't seem to get out of his own way long enough to produce a coherent sequence.

He got up, ejected the chip from the console, and held it up to the light on the tip of his forefinger before he pushed it into the erasure/reformat slot above the keyboard. Manny had had his implants four days before, which meant Medical would keep him for another three, leaving him three more days to come up with a feature-length zeppelin adventure for Para-Versal. And he couldn't even get five minutes of conversation without his mind skittering all over the place. Maybe he could divert Copperthwait with another story conference. *Sure, come on over, shoot the—ahem—shit. Love for you creative types to talk.—Excuse me.* What *are you doing?* If he could stand it.

His gaze came to rest on the hotsuit folded neatly on the shelf above the desk with the head-mounted monitor on top

of it. He'd have been better off with the old system and the
old chips. Wouldn't take any longer than, oh, two weeks. Then
he could run it through with the new interface, which would
probably reduce it to video confetti in a matter of two minutes,
the way his mind was wandering. Pop it into Manny's electronic
review queue and wait for him to watch it. He would know
when Manny screened it, because he'd be able to hear Manny
screaming from here. Or maybe Manny would just drop in via
some spyhole—

Maybe he already had.

The memory of the other presence coming up on him hit
him like a shot to the head. He knew for certain. It was the
same sensation he'd felt during the visualization exercises the
day after he'd had the procedure, a sense of pressure like
someone leaning or pushing against him.

The hacker, maybe. But wouldn't the hacker have tried to
talk to him?

Gabe ran a hand through his hair. He couldn't think about
the hacker, or he'd have that coming out on chip along with
the rest of the extraneous images. Maybe he should run down
to Medical, see if they had a program for extracting unrelated
and unwanted ideas.

He realized he was digging his fingers into his hair as if he
could yank out his anxieties by the roots. He looked at the
hotsuit and headmount, the console, the connections now
coiled on the desk, the whole pit, and suddenly he felt as if
he were sealed off in a small, airless box. He banged the console's door-open panel and ran for the ladder to the catwalk.

Across the hall the indicator light on the door to Gina's pit
said it was occupied. Slowly he went over and raised his hand
to the buzzer. Would this ruin it, somehow, was she all tied
up with the music and the videos again, trying to make them
do something, be something to her in place of something else?
Or would she want to see him now as badly as he wanted to
see her?

He pressed the buzzer. After a moment the door swung
open silently. He hesitated again, unsure of what he would
say to her, and the door started to swing shut again. He nipped
around it quickly, wincing as the edge brushed his chest, tearing off a shirt button.

The lift whined softly as she sent it up to the catwalk for
him. She was sitting at the desk with her feet up, staring at
one of the console flatscreens as if she were unaware of him.

He took the lift down, waited briefly for her to look up and acknowledge him. Suddenly the lift started to rise again, and he jumped off.

"Jesus," he said.

"Sorry. Thought maybe you'd changed your mind." There was a distracted, forced quality in her voice. A few moments later he saw the wires trailing among the dreadlocks. Hooked in. He took a step backward, toward the ladder.

"Come on, you afraid I'll bite or something?" She turned her head slowly and looked at him, her eyes seeming to go in and out of focus, as if she were having trouble picking him out of the surroundings.

He approached uncertainly. "What are you doing?"

"Checking my brain wave." She lifted a finger in the general direction of the screen.

The three rows of lines moving up and down on the monitor meant nothing to him. Abruptly they stopped and reversed themselves, flowing backwards to several explosively jagged interruptions in the otherwise semiregular patterns.

"Those bursts are where I opened the door, closed it, sent the lift up, and then started to send it up again. In case you're wondering." The screen blanked, flickered, and then he was looking at himself standing outside at the door. "You can reach all the controls from inside, if you know how." The screen blanked again. "Disconnect," she said.

He found himself looking anywhere but at her while she removed the wires from her head and set them aside.

"Pretty fucking strange, huh? Just wanted to see if I could do it. I can. You could, too, if you wanted." She yawned, rotated her head while she rubbed her neck, and then looked at him expectantly.

Once again words failed him. Like some kind of bad joke. He had goddamn sockets in his head to send out any thought at the drop of an inhibition, and he couldn't manage to tell the person he'd just spent the night with what he was doing there.

She nodded. "Look, it's all right. It's *all* all right. Just take care of your shit now. You got your Para-Versal deal with your complete artistic control. That's more than a lot of us end up with, count yourself lucky to've landed jam side up this time. You could make enough to buy out your ex-wife, hang onto your condo. Maybe you'll get real lucky, and Para-Versa'll decide they want you working directly for them, not this place."

He blinked at her. "Why?"

She laughed a little. "Christ, you think now that there's a fucking direct interface to the brain, studios like Para-Versal are gonna keep jobbing shit out to mills like the Dive? They don't need the Dive anymore, they just don't know it yet. But when they do, they'll get their own interface hardware, hire writers to sit around all day and all night dreaming up features right outa their brains, no production work necessary."

"But the unions—"

"The unions are finished. The best they might do is force a situation where you got a set designer dreaming up sets and a costumer dreaming up wardrobes, a writer dreaming up plots and characters, and a synner to put it all together, someone to synthesize everybody's dreams into one big dream. Goes round and round, and it comes out there." She jerked a thumb at the console. "So just take care of your shit now. I got to take care of mine."

She turned away and started putting the connections back into her sockets one by one. He left.

He was ensconced at a safe, undetectable distance when he felt her speak.

Come on, you afraid I'll bite or something?

There was a lot of noise around it, but he screened it out easily, saving it for later, because it all had to do with him. She was thinking of him while she sat there, flexing her muscles on the console. Neat trick, like, *Look, Ma, no hands.* But she didn't feel the pull to it the way he did. She *almost* understood, though, she *almost* got it, and if she went a little longer, tried a little harder, she might go all the way. But he didn't know whether that would be good for her or not, now, because he knew. It was more than just the difference between them— he wanted to go where the pictures were, she wanted the pictures to come out to where she was—because he knew for sure now. He hadn't been able to pick it up from her, but *he'd* been filled with it. Ludovic, filled with her.

What are you doing? Christ, she should have been able to smell him. And it had gone right past him. With all the new resources at his command, he should have been able to figure it out, graphed them from the top down, her movements, his movements as far as he knew them or could interpolate. Then he'd have been prepared for it. A little prepared, anyway. It was still like a fucking spike in the throat.

You can reach all the controls from inside if you know how.
Lotta noise around that one, some for him, some for Ludovic.
Shit, even *she* didn't know what she was really telling him.

Pretty fucking strange, huh?

Only if you don't have all the facts, lover. But once you do,
it ain't a bit strange at all. He sneaked a look at her visuals.
Yah, Ludovic looked good to her in ways she had no idea of.

Disconnect.

Shit. He surged forward, feeling around her console for a
way to keep listening, at least, but he could tell it would take
him a relatively long time to figure out how to infiltrate the
hardware without her there as a gateway. Leave a piece of
himself to work on that problem but withdraw now.

He replayed what he'd just received from her. No need to
bother with top-down multigraphs and decision forests. He
could see where it would go if somebody didn't fuck up, somebody being Gina, thinking twice, about him and his change
for the machines.

Let her go. Have to. Have to.

Considering this was the one place she couldn't be for him,
it was all right. He had no right to mind about it. Mind about
it, ha, ha. But fuck it, it would make it easier to do this thing
that he had been born to do. He'd been holding back, keeping
himself sized down enough to return to the meat, because he
couldn't go back and be contained in the meat once he'd allowed himself to expand beyond a certain point. It was too
defective, too worn-out and tired for him.

So, out the one-way door then. What did he have to lose?
Only the meat, and he already knew that he didn't miss that.
He didn't. He *wouldn't*. Even if the meat missed him.

It sent out feeble signals, dumb animal semaphore: come
back to the nest, little Sheba. Even if this was what he'd been
born to do, that didn't make it exactly natural. Not that he'd
ever been accused of being a natural man, but there he was,
wagging his meat behind him, so to speak. If he could have
given the disconnect command from this side, it would be over
in a twinkling. So long, meat, write if you get work.

But he couldn't access any of the commands from where he
was. The commands only took orders from the meat, and that
poor old meat wasn't about to cut him loose. It was back there
in the pit dreaming that it was something bigger and more
wonderful than it actually was, and if it disconnected, the
dream would be over.

If he could just get someone—Gina—to come in and yank the connections out of his skull. She'd never do it. He could plead and wheedle and try to explain that the thing lying on the floor in the pit was two steps from garbage. Good luck. *That meat is mine.* That was a good one; he'd caught it in some old memories. But why that, and not Ludovic?

That meat is mine.

No, lover, it isn't, and it never was. If you could take a little walk with me, I could tell you how it really is.

Being renewed and enhanced apparently wouldn't keep him from dwelling on the could-haves and wish-it-weres.

He took himself back to the guy's storage area and picked up some more data, noting that the sensation of his presence had registered without being identified. He'd have to be careful. If he pushed it too hard, he'd end up nose-to-nose with the guy, with no secrets.

Well, the guy was far more resistible than Gina. God, it was fucking hard to let her go when she did video like the Canadaytime. He hadn't been able to keep from taking that fall with her, even though he knew it meant giving himself away. He'd been hoping she would have felt differently when she found out, when she saw that she didn't have to fall all alone. But maybe she *wanted* to fall all alone.

He wished suddenly that he'd made a copy of the video for himself. Distantly he sensed her coming back on-line again, but he stayed away, not wanting to go back and find her with so much of Ludovic in her thoughts. but he could check the central activity record and see what she'd done with the video.

It was in something called a review queue, in Manny Rivera's area. Manny was conveniently out of the way, recuperating from his own procedure. Manny Rivera on-line. Shit, he was going to have to screen that bastard out.

Unbidden, the memory of the hacker in the penthouse came to him—with his associations spread out all over the place, sometimes he never knew what was going to come up on him next—and he wondered if the kid was still there. Probably; there was some kind of activity coming from that direction. He ought to pop in and say hello later, after he mainlined Gina's video a few times. Just pop in and remind him it was a damned Schrödinger world when you were meat. That would really stone the kid's crows.

* * *

The computer-run wheels of the complex mechanism known as Diversifications, Incorporated, continued to turn as reliably and smoothly as ever, unaffected by new developments. It had accommodated an intelligent entity before, and though it knew this one was different, it had no reason to care. No new instructions had been issued concerning the procedures that had been locked in for the disposition of various items of business. Energy was allotted in the proper quantities to each part of the physical building; phone calls and electronic mail went to the designated recipients; intruders were blocked and turned away.

Its eye was on the sparrow as well. The system noted that there were fewer items than usual in Manny Rivera's review queue, and they remained there longer, but the notation was only for purposes of inventory. There was a procedure for slowdowns in traffic, satisfactorily simple: maintain and wait for instructions. Had the building suddenly been abandoned to stand empty for fifty years, anyone returning would have found the review queue waiting just as it was, assuming the power had held out, which was not completely improbable.

Abruptly the system received instructions to deliver one item out of the established queue sequence for review. Out-of-sequence reviewing was permissible with the correct instructions, which came after a small hesitation. This didn't matter to the system. It identified the requested item—*Gina Aiesi/Canadaytime: Rock Music Video*. The system delivered it to the usual review area and adjusted the rest of the inventory, reordering it. Then it waited for another command.

The item sent for review came back. The system examined it for any special instructions or markings that would designate it for return to the queue; there were none. This could mean only one thing, according to the procedures: it was to be expelled, sent out the exit, which was marked *Release*.

Release was another part of the same system, but with different procedures. Unlike the area that governed the review queue, Release examined whatever came into it, for the sake of disposing of it properly. Hollywood releases were sent to the appropriate studios; commercials were sent to the designated networks; social-expression units were delivered to the proper addresses in the electronic mall; and the newest category of items, the rock videos, were delivered to the entertainment network for distribution, with a clone to the archives of the publishing company holding the rights to the music, another clone to the performer(s), and another to Home Storage and Records, tagged to indicate that it had been released to the proper targets.

When the system had completed this task, it noticed that something peculiar had happened in the review area—the item that had just been released had left behind a complete replica of itself. Replication independent of the proper electronic cloning process specifically indicated the presence of a virus. There was nothing on the replica to indicate that it was actually the extra product of a cloning procedure performed too hastily by an inexperienced operator learning the system on the fly, from the inside rather than the outside; such a situation did not exist in the system's instructions. All the system knew was that this replication called for immediate antiviral procedures.

The replica was isolated, sterilized by a complex series of instructions meant to counter and neutralize the reproductive apparatus, and then dismantled.

The operation was a complete success. The system was in the process of disposing of the remains and posting a notice of successful sterilization when it noted that instructions belonging to itself were among the now-harmless separate elements. It reassembled the instructions and noted that they were for calling an item from the review queue out of sequence, to be sent to the review area. The system had no orders to dismantle and destroy a set of its own instructions, so it restored the set to the last location at which it had been operative.

The system then returned to its starting mode, came to the instructions to pull an item out of sequence in the reordered queue, and sent it for review. The cycle repeated itself, and when it came to the same set of instructions, it obeyed them again, and again, and again.

Before long the review area and its overflow storage were both full; neither had been meant to hold many items. Both had instructions to cover this eventuality, once again very simple: send the overflow back to the review queue. When items began returning from the review area, the system examined them for special instructions and, finding none, obeyed its own orders, which told it that, unless otherwise tagged for retention, any items returning from the review area were to be sent to Release.

As far as the system knew, these were the complete original instructions. In fact, they had been modified, not by the res-

toration from the suspected virus but much earlier, in an unofficial, informal, and technically forbidden way by Manny
Rivera himself. The system didn't remember this because the
modification process had been purged from the memory local
to Manny's area.

The modification was small and actually quite common
among busy supervisory staff. Manny's predecessor had shown
him how to do it and also shown him how not to get caught.
It just eliminated the necessity of a tag stating the item had
been reviewed and was now authorized for release. Instead,
the system was instructed to assume that any unmarked item
coming out of the review area was to go directly to Release.

Manny had found this so efficient, he might have forgotten
about it and been caught running an illegally modified procedure several times over had he not set his calendar to alert
him to restore the original program before each quarterly audit.
When he had gone off to receive his own sockets, he had still
been trying to work out something by which the calendar would
automatically cue the program to restore the missing command, and then modify it again without his even having to
think about it.

The system went on obeying orders, and everything past a
certain point in the review queue went to review and then to
Release, the titles routinely logged and the inventory adjusted.

Sometime much later the system discovered that another
item had left a replica of itself behind, but this one reacted
quite differently when the antiviral procedures were applied.

24

The sensation of falling was so real that even without a hot-suit, Sam felt it from toes to head. The ground rushed at her, swelling from a distant point to a gigantic vista of sudden death before everything went terrifyingly black. Nothingness; in the nothingness one last long note sang deeply, vibrating through every part of her shattered being, as if it were reassembling her with its sound.

The note faded away, and there was a space of quiet before Art said, "And that's what they call rock'n'roll."

The interior of Art's tent came up before Sam's eyes. "Jesus," she breathed.

"But that's only what you get on a screen," Art went on. "If you have the sockets, you get something more."

"Yah," said Sam, "a heart attack, probably."

"No, it's something else. A little more video, only accessible through the sockets. It's in there all wrapped up in itself. I can show you some of it, if you want."

"I'm not sure I'm ready for anything else," Sam said, still feeling shaky.

Art dragged a large pillow over and stood it up on his knee. "You can look at it on my screen," he said. "Video within a video, hey?"

Abruptly she was looking at the placid setting of a country lake with a shore completely covered with rocks. The pov moved in on the shore, descending to zero in on one of the smooth egg-shaped stones. Something seemed to move or change on the gritty surface of the stone before it blanked out. Art tossed the pillow aside. "That's all I can give you," he said, a little apologetically. "The rest won't translate into video."

"Translate from what?" Sam asked him.

He shrugged. These days Art was looking less ambiguous genderwise, at least whenever she talked to him. "From action.

258

Something happens in there, but I have no idea how to explain to you what it is."

Sam felt a small coldness in the pit of her stomach. "Have you told Fez about this?"

"Only you. I haven't been able to decide what it is." He paused, looking apprehensive. "I think it might be another me."

"You mean another part of you?"

"That, or something like me. Strange operations are going on in there, in that part of the system, but I can't find them. I can only feel that they are happening."

Sam thought for a moment. "I think you might be feeling the presence of those people on-line with their sockets. You know, other intelligences—consciousnesses—in contact with the system." She winced, hating the sound of the word *consciousnesses*. It sounded like the mystic bullshit that was in all-too-ample supply on *The Stars, Crystals, and You Show.*

"No," Art said. "To feel that, I would have to crack their access points, what you call their consoles. The socket-people will be in contact with those, but not with the net. Like anything else in their consoles, they should be confined to their own hardware."

"You'd think so, wouldn't you," Sam murmured, more to herself. *The socket-people.* It reminded her of an expression Fez used from time to time: *pod-people.* Pod-people with sockets, the information going in and going out, while in their cocoons they mutated—

She pushed the thought away. "If you say so. You have more information about this than I do."

"Would you like more information? I can gather some for you."

"No, thanks. I've got enough to think about."

"I know," Art said, suddenly solemn. "When the beams look into your eyes, they see you are troubled."

"They don't look into my eyes," she said, somewhat dryly. "They bounce off my corneas. You'd be doing too well to pick up anything from my corneas."

"I know you by every move," Art said, unperturbed. "I know the pattern of your fingers on a keyboard, I know the movements of your eyes. The movements tell me a great deal about you."

"So. Remind me to stare straight ahead next time I come

in." She sighed. "I've got a lot on my mind these days. I just wasn't cut out to be a fugitive, I don't think. At you later, okay?"

The screen faded to black, and she worked the monitor off her head. Behind her in the tent, Gator and Fez were studying something on Gator's laptop. The headmount had blocked the sound of their voices from her as well as the sound of her own voice from them; a way not to be in the same room with them while being in the same room with them, if you wanted to call Gator's tent a room. Like a bedroom, say.

The sleeping bags were rolled up and tucked away somewhere out of sight, as they always were during the day, so she had no idea how they were arranged when in use. Mostly she pictured them side by side, but that was as far as she would let the picture go. It was only surmise, really, even after all these weeks; she knew nothing for sure, and she hadn't asked.

Gator looked over her shoulder at her then and smiled. "How's the doctor?"

Sam shrugged. "He showed me one of the new videos. There's something funny in it."

"I'll bet there is," Fez said, without taking his eyes from the screen. Some kind of complicated graphic was rotating on it; another of Gator's tattoo designs. Sam caught a glimpse of something like paisleys surrounding some sort of shifting polygon.

"I'm going back to St. Diz. See you later," Sam said, and slipped out of the tent without waiting to hear Fez's usual admonishment to be careful.

The air was a bit cooler on the Mimosa today. A calling card from October, as Rosa put it, a little reminder that summer would be ending soon. Already the Mimosa population seemed a bit sparser, people taking off for warmer hideouts, or going wherever it was they had to go when they weren't camping on the strip. The ones who stayed behind had a case-hardened look to them, weathered and more than a little bit hopeless. You had to be pretty much resigned from the world to stay on a permanent basis; Sam doubted she was one of them.

If she and Rosa had not found squat space in the ruins of the old inn or restaurant or whatever it was, she doubted that she would have stayed this long. However long that was; in spite of regular visits with Art and managing to keep up with the news off the net, she had pretty much lost track of the days. One week had blended into another in a strange stasis (or stagnation, she thought bitterly), each day bearing few distinguishing marks. And now summer was coming to an end, and they were no closer to any answers. They were all still wanted for questioning—it seemed to be a standing order— and Keely was still wherever he was. Legalization of the socket procedure had come about, and the world seemed no different for it, except most of the implant clinics were in the process of either changing to socket implantation or adding the procedure to their repertoires.

She passed a stand where a couple of kids were running graphics of dolphins and exotic birds on a matched pair of jerry-rigged monitors. The resolution was perfect, but the hardware looked like something from rewiring hell.

"Hey," one of the kids called to her. "I know you."

Sam gave her a one-finger salute. The kid beckoned, and she went over.

"You whack to AR?" the kid asked. The smaller one standing next to her had to be her brother, Sam thought. She shrugged noncommittally.

"Run with this, you see and be." The kid tapped the monitor on the counter in front of her. An impossible parrot was flowering into existence on the screen, neon-colored, luminous. "Fly like an eagle."

"Fly like a parrot," Sam corrected her, a little amused. Fly like a parrot and talk like an eagle, probably. So far there was no law against stupid Artificial Reality.

"Grown from the egg," the kid said. "Transform and believe."

Believe was a word that seemed to figure heavily in all the subgroups of Mimosa slang. That had to mean something, but Sam felt too weary to theorize.

"I'll believe later," she said, waving a hand at the kids, and went on. Over on her right two cases were having an altercation over who owned a particular spot under the Hermosa Pier. One ragged figure was trying to haul the other one out by a leg while the latter tossed up a lot of sand and made hooting noises.

"There go the property values," Sam muttered. Just beyond was the half-falling-down building she and Rosa shared with the loose, semiorganized group of hackers that had taken it over and shored it up against further collapse. The big attractions of the place were an actual roof and a mostly regular power source, supplemented with what they could collect and

store from the solars. The roof had a lot of holes, most of which
were covered with any available material, none of it leak-proof,
but hey, that's what we on the Mimosa call home, sweet home.
She'd have cried, except she'd cried herself out during the
first week.

Where the front door had been was a ragged hole and a
lopsided gate where they all took turns doing a kind of half-
assed sentry duty. Percy was sitting on the gate today, leisurely
poking at a piece of hardware with one of his homemade tools
(Homemade without a real home? Never mind.) while he held
another between his teeth. He was big for fifteen, with thick,
straight black hair he chopped off himself whenever it got long
enough to dangle in the hardware he was always bent over,
and a little bit of soft black fuzz on his upper lip that was trying
to be a mustache. Sam had thought he was Spanish until Gator
had told her he was part Filipino. He had a genius for hardware, and he was more competent and self-possessed than Sam
remembered being at the same age. All of two years ago, she
reminded herself. No, closer to three; she would be eighteen
in October.

Eighteen on the Mimosa. "Are we ready for that?" she murmured to herself. "We don't think so."

Percy looked up then, spotted her, and waved her over.
What the hell; where else was she going to go?

"Age of wireless," Percy said, showing her the piece he'd
been working on. Her eyes widened.

"If that works as good as it looks, I'll pay you to make one
for me. Better yet, walk me through it." She took the piece
from him, a palm-sized card with an array of silvery receptors
studding the surface.

"Whack to hardware, dontcha." Percy grinned and pushed
her hand away as she tried to give it back to him. "Yours.
Believe it."

She felt awkward under his friendly grin. "That's nice, Perce,
but—"

"Believe it and forget about it. Whack to something new?"
He jumped down from the gate and let out a bellow. "*Ritz!*"

A slightly older kid popped his head up from behind a pile
of boards and junk. "What, this minute?"

"Now and now," Percy confirmed, nodding at the gate. The
other kid took his place. "Come on."

Sam followed him, pausing to take a look at her own squat
space. Most of her own belongings were hidden under some

loose boards in the floor, which were in turn piled with what debris she had scrounged. Not that there was a debris shortage. Her spot was in what had possibly been part of a dining room, and there were still plenty of dismembered tables and chairs that had gone unsalvaged. The culture back at the turn of the millennium had been even more wasteful than the one she presently lived in—lived on the outskirts of, rather.

Few of the walls between rooms had remained standing, and the second floor had collapsed completely, except for a few beams. Some of the more daring souls in residence had crawled out on them to decorate them with impromptu hanging sculptures made of junk—old hardware, broken pieces of kitsch that some interior decorator had probably agonized over, never thinking that an earthquake would reduce it all to detritus.

At the very back of the building was an area that had been some kind of gathering hall or ballroom. There were no squatters here; it served as a common storage and work area. Sam had finally met the elusive Captain Jasm in person back here, a lanky black Japanese woman of some indeterminate age—twenty? thirty? Older didn't seem likely—who was always tinkering with exoskeletons. At first Sam had thought she used exos in lieu of hotsuits, but apparently Jasm didn't really care for hotsuits, at least for her own purposes, which seemed mainly to transfer arcane patterns of movement to programs. One of the exos was a twelve-foot monstrosity, vaguely humanoid in shape, burdened with whatever hardware Jasm wasn't using. Sam found the thing rather spooky looking, like a robot in progress. She could imagine it coming spontaneously to life and crunching through the building all of its own accord like a high-tech Frankenstein's monster.

At the moment it stood off to one side with the rest of Jasm's equipment piled around it, all cleared away to make room for an enormous metal framework bearing sixteen monitors. Sam's mouth dropped open, and she turned to Percy.

"Whack to a little TV?" he said, amused.

She spotted Rosa doing something with a cam on a tripod a little ways away from the monitor setup.

"Here," said Percy, and went over to her. Rosa looked up and smiled as Percy examined the connections on the cam. They led into the framework of monitors.

"Is this something?" Rosa said. "Sixteen monitors, no waiting."

"Where did they all come from?" Sam asked.

Rosa shrugged. "Here and there."

"TV and more TV. It looks like something out of an old movie," Sam said. "Forty, fifty years ago, they were always dragging out the TV screens when they wanted to show what the glorious future would look like. As if the future was just going to be more TV."

"And, as it turned out, it is," Rosa said.

"Now," Percy said, stepping back from the cam. "Whack it."

Rosa turned on the cam. Sam saw the monitors flicker to life, all of them showing broken-up images of something that might have been her and Rosa standing together.

"Still lousy, Perce," Rosa said.

"Whack it," he said again.

"It *is* turned on," Rosa said, frowning.

He shook his head, reached over, and slapped the top of the cam's plastic case. The images jumped, steadied, and then cleared.

"Perfect," said Art's voice, from a speaker somewhere up on the scaffolding. "Hey, don't look at the monitors, look at the cam so I can see you."

Percy came around and stood between Rosa and Sam with his arms around their shoulders. "Bad for three?"

Art chuckled. "No. Fool with Rosa, I saw Sam first."

Sam rolled her eyes. It would just figure. The first real, possibly conscious AI, and it postured. She would have to wait for the memory of their recent conversation to catch up with Art's current manifestation.

Percy gave her and Rosa a hard squeeze, pulling them both close. "*Really* bad for three, if you believe."

Sam nodded a little wearily, extricating herself from him. "I heard you."

The bottom row of screens went blank; a moment later four different dataline channels came up on them.

"See there," said Percy. "Ain't just flash. Tap the channels, whack to each. Billions and billions."

Sam's expression was even more cynical on the other twelve monitors. "That'd make kind of a big bulge in the node, don't you think, when we're trying not to advertise our existence?"

"Shit-man, *capability*," Percy said, exasperated. "Capability *rules*. The one thing. *The one.* You don't know what's gonna float in on you."

"Stone-fuckin'-A," Art agreed cheerily. The image on the

monitor changed, showing him sitting in a comfortable nest of pillows with a laptop resting on his thighs, but the tent had been replaced by a background that didn't look terribly different from the ruins of the inn. Art Fish doing his human solidarity thing, Sam thought. At the moment he was probably more into the human experience than she was.

She sighed. "I agree we need all the capability we can get. But we can't watch billions and billions of channels at once. We can't even watch sixteen at once."

"*I* can," Art said smugly.

"Good for you." She looked around. "Wouldn't it be more practical to have monitors all around? That way there'd be one handy everywhere, and we wouldn't lose them all if the roof goes."

Percy wrinkled his nose. "Wouldn't *look* so glam-bam."

"Oh, of course." Sam gave him a sidelong glance. "I forgot." It did look impressive, she had to admit that. But it was strictly show-off stuff, and she wasn't even sure who they were supposed to be showing off for—themselves? Hardly necessary. Maybe it was all for Art's benefit. As he had made his presence known gradually over the weeks since they'd taken up residence on the Mimosa, all the hackers seemed to have shifted into high gear in a way that reminded Sam of the way her father had talked about everyone at Diversifications trying to look busy in front of their supervisors or whoever. As if Art were some kind of superhacker they all wanted to impress.

"Hey, speak up a little," Art said, cupping a hand around his ear. "I'm working with cheap audio. Maybe you can get Percy to fiddle with the mikes now."

"Nada," Percy told the cam. "Run with the one. Could kill it trying to thrill it."

"Well, there must be some kind of adjustment you can make," Art said. "Give me a schematic of the guts, let me figure it out."

"I don't have any schematics," Percy said. The sudden shift from Mimosa slang was mildly shocking. "It's all second- or third- or ninth-hand stuff that's been rewired and re-rewired. I'd have to take each one apart, run a scanner over it for the CAD, and then reassemble. It'd take for-fucking-ever to do that kind of close work. You gotta live with what you got till we get something better." He looked over at Rosa and Sam, who were staring at him. "Just wanted you to know I can talk like you if I want to." He stepped back and looked at the cam again.

"Hey, you got vocal, and you got high-res. Two outa three'll getcha good night."

Art's image made a put-out face. "*You* talk that way when *you're* getting frying-meat sounds on *your* hearing aid, Sonny-Jim."

" 'Sonny-Jim'?" said Rosa.

Percy launched into a long explanation or defense, now heavily salted with slang. Sam drifted away, leaving them to argue it out. You could spend all of an afternoon and most of an evening arguing with Art if he really got involved.

She went back to her squat space, squeezing between the piles of broken boards and plaster that sectioned it off, and flopped down on the narrow pad she had bartered from one of the junk collectors in Rude Boy turf. This was definitely better than the small tent she and Rosa had spent the first few days putting up, taking down, and lugging around with them along with the rest of their stuff. But something about all those monitors on the scaffolding had deepened her funk. There was something permanent in feel about it, as if it meant they were all settling in forever, Art included.

Her hand fell on the modified insulin-pump system in her pocket. In the midst of the rigors of life underground, or whatever it was called, she hadn't done anything with it lately. She hadn't done much at all except wander around in a daze. That wasn't a whole lot more than what Jones had been doing; he was even now laid out in a far dark corner, stuporous for sixteen hours a day. *Too much death too often*, Gator had said. *The body's protecting itself the best way it knows how, by keeping him off-line, so to speak.* It was as good a theory as any, Sam supposed.

She'd been ready to give Jones a more final demise when she and Rosa had caught up with him at Forest Lawn, sucking up to one of the kids running a fooler loop. Fortunately Rosa had known the kid, and it had been easy to persuade him he didn't want to take merchandise from someone wanted for questioning. Persuading Jones to come with them hadn't been as easy, but if his stubbornness hadn't delayed them, she never would have been treated to the sight of her father lying on the ground near Liberace's tomb, being tended to by Gina Aiesi and Visual Mark.

It had *almost* been worth the risk of sneaking past the cops in the dark, seeing Gabe at a hit-and-run. Rosa had given her hell later for passing him the paper with St. Dismas written

on it. But the only St. Dismas the authorities would know of
was the long-defunct soup kitchen by the same name that had
once operated in Watts, founded by a bright-eyed, Jesus-
freaked technophobe with sticky fingers. Or so the old legend
had it. Sam wouldn't have been surprised to find that she'd
just been another hacker with her name on a warrant that
wouldn't expire. Just being wanted for questioning would have
been enough to drive her to a nunnery of some kind, if she
hadn't already known how much she hated even half-assed
communal living on the skids.

But it could have been worse all the way around. She and
Rosa might still have been in the tent with Jones stashed in
Gator's outhouse; she might have lost more than her shoes that
first night on the strip; they might have been canned at the
hit-and-run, and Gator's phony IDs might not have held up.
As it was, the falling-down ruined inn now had a fancy-
schmancy monitor setup to go with the sophisticated if homegrown system spread out among the squatters, bigger and faster
than the system Fez had abandoned with his apartment, except
for a few items he'd managed to transport to Gator's tent. Like
the headmount she'd made for him.

She took the ex–pump unit out of her pocket and turned it
over and over in her hand. She had made her own contributions
in the way of hardware and programs in the tumble-down
shelter, but she wasn't about to toss this out for communal
use. Making the specs available was enough.

Of course, having the specs wasn't like having work space
to do anything with them. The supply house in the Ozarks that
she had made contact with had been well stocked and very
accommodating, allowing her to trade scut work on their inventory and beefing up their antiviral routines for a clean, well-
lit area with the right kind of equipment for manipulating the
protein assemblers. Once she'd had the guts properly configured, she'd been able to make the rest of the modifications
on the pump itself in the privacy of her tent. It was really just
a hacker toy, stolen just for her own use because she hadn't
wanted to wait six months, a year, maybe two years, before it
came out on the market so she could buy one, putting more
money into Diversifications' well-lined pockets, and strip it
down to see how she could dupe it. If indeed the units had
become available at all.

All things considered, this should have been the ideal place
to use it. Made for inhospitable environments. She remem-

bered the hardware Percy had given her, still in her other
hand, and examined it. A little redesign, a little rewiring, and
it would adapt perfectly to the pump unit. Then she'd be all
set; her own intimately personal computer system with a wireless modem set to Art's iron-guard frequency. The sunglasses
weren't as good as a headmount, but they were far better than
nothing, and she wouldn't need even solar power to kick it
over. Except for the modem, of course. She could have out-
fitted herself in a few minutes, except her ambition seemed
to have deserted her.

"Are you okay?"

Rosa was standing at the nominal entrance to her squat space;
Sam nodded, beckoning. "Yah. I think I've just got them bad
old cozmic Mimosa dead-end blues."

"Come on, it could be worse." Rosa eased down next to her,
resting her back against the powdery, cracked wall.

"I know. I've just been telling myself that. I never did want
to come here. I thought it would be the first place anyone
would look for us. Cops aren't stupid, they could figure that
we planted false information that we'd left town." Sam took a
long breath. "But then I started softening up to the idea a
little. Thinking that it would be kind of . . . oh, exciting, I
guess. Romantic, even. Almost like being in the Ozarks again,
except freakier. Laptops in the raw, jammers making music.
Horny hardware geniuses making cordless modems for you."
She laughed a little and then sighed again. "But mostly it's
being dirty and smelly and not having any safe place to stay
and not getting enough to eat."

"And getting your shoes stolen," Rosa added.

"Yah. I guess I never bounced back after that one."

"Well, I got them back. Black eye faded pretty quick, too.
And you should have seen the other guy."

"I did see him. The scum. I still feel horribly guilty about
the whole thing."

Rosa chuckled. "You don't have to feel guilty about that.
You're a lover, not a fighter."

"Which means I definitely don't belong here. And I'm not
even anybody's lover."

"Come on. If Percy could be bad for three, he could be bad
for two. If you believe."

Sam groaned. "Even if I could bring myself to molest a
fifteen-year-old—"

"—who probably has more experience than you do," Rosa put in wryly.

"—I'm not sure I could ever get around the language barrier. Half the time when he's talking, I'm winging it."

"And he just went to all the trouble of showing you he could talk like us. But I don't blame you for wanting to wait until his voice changes." Rosa chuckled again, a little sadly. "What else?"

Sam pressed her lips together. She had never mentioned her feelings for Fez to Rosa, but she doubted that she really had to. She was sure Rosa had picked up on plenty and tactfully held her peace, and she was also sure what her friend would say if she invited comment. Why bother bringing it up at all, she thought; if you've run the simulation, and you know how it turns out, there's no point in wasting time living through it all over again.

"I just miss civilization. I miss being able to move around, come and go as I please. Being out there. Maybe at heart I'm just another bourgeois who can't take the heat, and as soon as I turn eighteen, I'll turn in my laptop, look up my social security number, and go get a real job."

Rosa patted her leg carelessly. "Buck up, little soldier. As soon as the dust settles from the Instant Information Revolution, they'll lose interest in us, and we'll all be able to go home."

"You think so?"

"Either then, or when Keely's sentence is up."

Sam groaned again, loudly.

"Now—" Rosa pushed herself to her feet and offered her a hand. "It's just about *Stupid Headlines* time. Let's us old and tired fugitives from justice go see what's on the news and have a few laughs. Unless you'd like to sit and sulk on your own."

Back to Gator's tent. Was she ready for that again? Oh, hell, she thought, and laughed. "Not really."

" 'Post-Millennarist Fundamentalists Claim Sockets Facilitate Demonic Possession via Rock Music.' " Art's image, looking a bit purple, beamed from a Percy-supplied monitor at the group in Gator's tent. One of the easel monitors Fez had managed to salvage sat next to it with headline text.

"Stupid, but unimaginative and not one bit original," said Gator, leaning on the back of Fez's chair.

"Yah, but it's too stupid to ignore," said Captain Jasm, on

Sam's right. Jasm's deep voice reminded her of an engine slightly and pleasantly out of tune.

Art paused. He had his image sitting at a desk sorting through papers. "Okay, how's this: 'Lobby for Decency Declares Brain an Erogenous Zone, Demands Mandatory Hatting.' "

" 'Hatting'?" said Adrian.

"Did you make that up?" Gator asked suspiciously.

"Nope." Art grinned. "Here, Adrian, just for you—" Mandarin subtitles appeared below each headline on the other screen.

"Hatting." Captain Jasm looked thoughtful. "I like that. I hat, you hat, she/he/it hats, I have hatted, I will have hatted, I will have been hatted—"

"Not to mention the soon-to-be-immortal 'Hat you, sucker,' " Rosa put in.

"Couldn't some of us just get capped?" said Adrian.

Jasm looked at him fondly and then gave the top of his head a glancing swat. "How's that?"

" 'Para-Versal Announces Forthcoming New Release with Multiple Cross-Tie-Ins,' " Art went on. " 'Tailor-Made Companionship Now a Reality, Thanks to Sockets.' "

No one said anything for a moment. "Is that stupid," Gator asked, "or just pathetic?"

"I don't know," said Art, "but I thought it would be of interest to Sam, since her father's involved."

"He is?" Sam frowned.

" 'New Release Custom-Created by Diversifications' Gabriel Ludovic,' it says here," Art told her.

"They must have drilled him, then," Sam said, more to herself.

"Let's not bandy surnames about too liberally," Fez said to Art. "We're among friends, but we never know who's going to walk in on us."

On-screen Art had not moved for several seconds. Sam reached across Jasm to tap Fez on the knee. "Fez—"

"I'm watching," he said. "Art? Still with us?"

Gator reached over and held a finger over the disconnect panel. Art's image unfroze.

"Something strange," he said.

"Trace?" Gator asked.

"No . . ." he looked thoughtful. "Something . . . *touched* me."

"Explain," said Fez.

"It was so momentary. Let me work on it. I'll get back to you." He shuffled the simulated papers on his simulated desk. "Ah, this just in. 'To whomever, wherever: Hi, I didn't die, I'm in the big tower. Divers up, divers down, divers on vacation.' "

Everyone looked at everyone else. "This is a headline?" Gator said.

"Actually, I found it in the current-events area of Dr. Fish's Answering Machine with a funny mark on it."

Gator started to chew Art out for maintaining the bulletin board when a voice behind them spoke.

"Divers on vacation. Come on, even *I* can figure that one."

Sam twisted around to look at Jones standing just inside the tent flap, looking puffy-eyed and depressed. He gazed around at all of them. "Percy told me where to find you," he added, a bit apologetically.

"That's fine," Gator said, "but don't you die in here."

Sam jumped up. "Come on, I'll take you back."

He waved her away. "Don't bother. I temporarily can't sleep. And don't worry, Gator. The implants have stopped working. For now, anyway."

" 'Sockets Inventor Dies in Mexico,' " Art said. " 'Suicide Pact with Hall Galen Suspected.' "

They all turned back to the screen again. Even Jones seemed interested.

The music, all cruising synthesizers and pumping beatbox, decreased in volume again.

"Message sent. So did I tell you it was a damned Schrödinger world?" said the man on the screen. He was sitting on a yellow chaise in a strange partial room. The walls on either side rose to unequal heights, and where the ceiling and back wall should have been was a backdrop of swiftly moving clouds in a blue green sky, gray and almost stony looking, reflected in the large, shiny black and white tiles on the floor. Besides the chaise there were two angular black chairs that looked like dollhouse miniatures and a small white table on impossibly thin legs.

"Schrödinger or Heisenberg?" Keely said, talking into the speaker.

"Well, either one, I guess. To be or not to be, are you or aren't you—can't be sure of either one till somebody opens your box. Fly Heisenberg Airlines—we don't know where we are, but we're making damned good time." An old-fashioned detonator with a plunger materialized in his hands. "Sure you don't want me to blow the door for you?"

"If I leave here, it would be just like a jailbreak," Keely said wearily. "An outside phone line is better, for the time being. Since I don't know where anybody is or how to reach them. And wouldn't want anyone to trace them if I did."

The detonator swelled to desk size and straddled the man on the chaise. Lifting the top, he reached in and plucked out a tangled handful of wires, surveying them closely. "I still haven't figured this. It could take some time."

"I don't know how much time I have," Keely said. "I could be down in Medical tomorrow."

"Don't know how you take the confinement." The man shook his head in time to the music, which was still playing at a level just below the attention threshold. "Confinement is a double-A, stone-home, all-wool-and-a-yard-wide bitch. And don't you forget it."

Not likely, Keely thought, watching him with interest. Visual Mark's energy had definitely picked up since he'd gotten his sockets.

"I'm outa the box now myself," Mark went on, searching through the tangle of wires. He reached into the desk again and pulled out some more.

"Are you sure you know what you're doing?" Keely asked, tentatively.

"Fuck, no. I'm picking it up on the fly. Fly, fly, fly is what I do now. I don't actually *know* dick about anything."

Keely frowned, suddenly suspicious. "So, what's this, then, some kind of cheap comedy video you're trying out on me?"

The man dropped the wires and looked out of the screen sternly. Keely found himself marveling; he could almost believe that the on-screen image could actually see him. Sometimes Mark's gaze missed him entirely, but most times, like now, Mark's estimate of where he was sitting at the monitor was dead on. "Did I say I'd help? Did I send your fucking message for you? You can answer anytime."

"Sorry," Keely said.

"You didn't let me finish anyway. I don't know dick about any of this stuff just being like you are, no holes in the head. But now I'm on-line. *Connected.*" Wires appeared on his head, growing out from his skull in a frenzy. "Understand now? I know what there is to know. Only thing I don't know is how

I'm supposed to get all this stuff back in my head with me. I mean, where can I put it?" He picked up the tangle of lines again.

"Wait," said Keely. "You mean you're on-line *that* way?" For some reason it hadn't occurred to him that Mark would be using the interface.

"Come *on*. Anyone can tell something's different with me. Haven't been this coherent since I was sixteen fuckin' years old." He held the wires up and grimaced at them. "Gonna haveta cook this one awhile. Getting back to you later. I'll leave a back door open for you. Access code 'Gina' and you're in."

"What if you're off-line?"

Mark spread his hands. "If I'm off-line, call Medical. It'll mean I'm dead."

The screen went dark, leaving Keely staring at his own distorted reflection in the glass.

25

Manny's head was pounding. Not thirty minutes back to work after his own procedure and he'd had to have that headline, of all things, jump out at him from the dataline, with a notation from Mirisch: *Find out about this!*

He was half tempted to leave his own message for the Great Grey Executive: *Find out about it yourself!* But he didn't need that kind of trouble with everything else he had to think about. He had to write up a dismissal notice for the Beater; good thing they hadn't had to waste sockets on him, and good riddance. He had to check on the hacker in the penthouse, make sure he'd been kept dosed enough to be unambitious but not so toxed that any damage had been done. Maybe another interrogation, with something stronger this time. None of the names Manny had gotten out of him under the influence had surfaced, and if at least some of them didn't show soon, the cops were going to drop them.

Maybe that was best; more than a couple of hackers together, and they'd start plotting to take over the world. Maybe it would be enough just to get the one he already had drilled and get him working on security. If he could turn the kid all the way around, Diversifications would be airtight, completely closed to any break-ins—and at the same time, no employee system would be completely locked to him, either.

But first, Travis. The red-haired doctor must have been sitting by the phone; there was half a ring, and then Travis's face was looking out at him through the screen, haggard and pale, as if he'd been up for days. The scene around him was definitely not his office.

"I tried to keep it quiet," Travis said before Manny could speak. "You'll be happy to know almost nothing of the real story got out. Anybody who saw anything's been paid off, including the cops, although we had to get one of them a new, higher-paying job before she was completely satisfied." Travis stepped aside; behind him was a table with a sheet covering what was obviously two bodies.

"What happened?" Manny asked, his voice flat.

Travis looked even grimmer. "They had a stroke. Which is to say, they each had the same one." He reached over and threw the sheet back.

Joslin and Galen nude was a sight every bit as revolting as Manny had ever imagined, with the added feature that their faces seemed to have been dipped in blood. He looked away from the screen.

"No, *look* at this," Travis demanded, and adjusted the lens on his end. It zoomed in on their heads. Manny's stomach did a slow forward roll.

The wires connecting Joslin to Galen—Galen to Joslin?— were an incomprehensible snarl. There looked to be too many of them, more wires than there were sockets to accommodate them. Travis kept the lens on them for a long time and then retracted it, moving into the center and mercifully obscuring the sight.

"That's all there was, just the wires," Travis said. "Connecting them directly to each other. Wires, and blood, and piss, and shit. Just the way the hotel maid found them."

Manny massaged his forehead. "And did the maid understand what she'd seen?"

"You bet she did. She's saving for med school." Travis's mouth twitched. "We're giving her sockets next week—our treat, of course—and sending her off to a prestigious school in Hawaii, also our treat. A congenial practice on Oahu will be waiting to take her when she finishes."

"Did you think of giving her sockets *and* clearing out some old useless memories taking up a lot of space that could be put to better use?"

Travis's disgust came through clearly. "If it were that simple, you'd never have gotten this legalized in the States. I don't have time to explain the complexities of memory storage, so just take my word for it, Mr. Rivera, that it could not be done without removing a number of other memories, and we don't yet know enough to be able to plant screen memories to cover it. And even if we did, I would refuse to take that kind of responsibility."

He wiped a palm back and forth across his lips in a harsh movement. "But we kept that part of it out of the media. What they were doing." Travis glanced over his shoulder at the still-uncovered bodies. "Mindfucking, I guess you'd call it. Apparently they used to do it hooked into hardware to save the images. We found quite a library of chips in their room, which have since been removed and purged. I had a look at some of them. It's amazing, really, what can walk around upright, let alone manipulate technology."

Travis was losing it, Manny thought. The idea was enough to make him feel a little panicky himself. "We've known for some time they weren't the healthiest people around," he said placatingly. "I'm sure if you look at the specs of her brain—"

"It's not a matter of *sick*," Travis said. "It's a matter of . . . being *alien*. Another person's mind can be an alien thing, if you approach it just right. Or just wrong. But we were talking about how they died, weren't we?

"Stroke. Did I say that? The fact is, I can't tell you what it was. Global malfunction. Intercranial meltdown. System failure. Their brains just . . . *went*. I can't tell from the scans who went first, or why, and personally I don't think it matters. As to why, I'd say that certain ideas can be hazardous to your health, real hazardous, Mr. Rivera. If you can get an ulcer, why not a cerebral vascular accident, or all-out nuked?" He gazed into the screen, chin lifted defiantly, as if daring Manny to argue with him. "Are you coming down to take care of this?"

"You can take care of it," Manny said quietly. "Just get rid of the bodies. That's all you have to do. We'll handle the media."

"I thought we might remove the brains—what's left of the brains—and study them," Travis said, his voice suddenly dry and pedantic. "Since this is the first case we know of where two brains have been directly linked, without the hardware."

"Do what you feel you have to do—" Manny started.

"I personally favor burning the brains, pouring the ashes into a deep hole, and salting the earth above them so that nothing can grow there."

"That's enough!" Manny snapped. "You're supposed to be transferring the operation over to the Mexican government and training their doctors. Get a grip on yourself. I don't care if you found chips recreating Krafft-Ebing out of the Marquis de Sade. For all you know they died as soon as they stuck the wires in their heads, from the misuse of the hardware and not from any weird ideas any of them had."

Travis laughed humorlessly. "You didn't see the chips."

"And I don't need to. All I need to do is take care of my end while you take care of yours."

"We really should study these connections," Travis said, turning pedantic again. "To see exactly how she altered them. I'd like to know, just for my own curiosity, what she did to set up two-way communication without hardware intervention. Without *more* hardware intervention, I should say. I don't *want* to know, but as a scientist, I *should* know. You can't let these things get by you."

"We're putting warning labels on all the equipment," Manny said, managing to sound far more serene than he felt. "Misuse of hardware and unauthorized alterations could prove hazardous and blah-blah-blah. We were doing that anyway, but nobody needs to know what can happen if they disregard the warnings. Are you up to the job right now?"

Travis leaned forward. "Going to move me out, retire me, send me to some lab where I'll be too sheltered to leak?"

"Perhaps you're feeling overly stressed from the responsibility and the work load and all the VIPs and the media traipsing through, that's all," Manny said evenly. "But I need your expertise right now, and if you can't supply it, give me someone who can."

Travis's shoulders slumped as all the tension drained out of his face. Manny could see the man's professional reflexes kick in as they discussed who at the installation should be let in on the Joslin-Galen fiasco and what kind of new cover story should be released to the media. By the time Manny finished with him, he seemed refocused, back in control, though with an occasional glimmer of suppressed emotion.

Manny himself felt half-drained, in need of another week of R&R. He started to make notes on a new media release explaining that Joslin had died of "natural causes" and Galen had killed himself out of grief for his lost beloved. It removed the hint of instability on Joslin's part, something they didn't need to have associated with the person who had invented brain sockets.

Five minutes later his emailbox alarm beeped, showing a new message from Mirisch. Manny put it on-screen.

Just wish we could have screened these videos before their release—M.

Manny had the distinct sensation of his heart hitting the top of his stomach. He brought up the review and release queues and watched in horror as the listings shifted from review to release like a little parade of data-soldiers in lockstep. Cursing himself, he froze the process immediately, managed to call two items back from the bottom of the release queue, and then just sat at his desk trying not to hyperventilate.

If the Upstairs Team got wind of this, he'd be preceding the Beater out the door. Not just out the door but probably into court—it wouldn't be the first time a company successfully sued an employee who faked a job by automating it. His panic lessened slightly when he saw there was still a handful of items in the review queue, a few short commercial spots, and a couple of videos, both Visual Mark's.

A moment later his heart went into turbo-charged overdrive again. Even automated, it should not have happened. He had to *call* an item out of the review queue, review it—screen it —and then dispose of it, either letting the program release it automatically, or releasing it himself. And even then the process was not self-perpetuating—he had to order it to deliver another item from the review queue. It should not have been able to continue by itself. But then, it should not have been able to *start*—

His heart was banging as if it were trying to bludgeon its way out of his chest. That little bastard in the penthouse. The son of a bitch had not only hacked him but infected him with some kind of virus. Had to be. If the little shit had been able to worm his way into Ludovic's area, then he could get in anywhere, and he'd just fucked around with the program until he'd kicked it into motion. And then planted his little virus. Obviously the dosage in his food was no longer strong enough—if the Upstairs Team found out—

Anxiety attack, he thought, *left mesial temporal lobe. Travis would probably enjoy studying this. Especially now.*

He leaned back in his chair and closed his eyes, forcing himself to breathe normally through the pain in his chest. *Bad day*, he repeated over and over to himself like a mantra. *Bad day, bad day, badday, badday, badday . . .*

Eventually the pain began to recede, giving ground by the slow half inch. He was almost back to normal when the pounding on the door started.

"Rivera, you motherfucker, I know you're in there!"

He groaned. Aiesi. The only person in the world who would ignore a *Sealed for Privacy* notice. He thumbed the speaker pad.

"This had better be important. I'm too busy to be at the beck and call of every employee with a problem."

She pounded on the door again, and he unsealed. Under normal circumstances he'd have just called security and let them deal with her. But then she might have just jumped off the terrace again.

She strode in, planted her fists on his desk, and leaned into his face. "You're gonna be too busy to live if you don't do something about Mark. He's fucked."

He gave her his standard antiprofanity wince to remind her of what an animal he thought she was. "Your friend is doing fine, according to all the reports. He's producing well above what we expected, and he's adapted beautifully, the doctors say—"

"Yah, *your* fuckin' butchers on *your* payroll. They'd certify a chuck roast if you told them to. You pull in a cold one, or I will."

"Pardon?" he said politely. "A 'cold one'?"

She straightened up and put her big fists on her hips. "A neurosurgeon from the outside. Someone who ain't in on it, who ain't standing around waiting to profit on the big fucking *breakthrough*."

Manny gave a short, refined laugh. "I'm afraid Diversifications' insurance plan doesn't cover consultations outside our own staff except in the case of grave emergencies needing a particular kind of specialist."

"Bill me."

"You don't have that kind of credit. Ms. Aiesi. I think you'd do better to spend some extra time on-line yourself, to get a better feel of how the system works. Your output, to be frank, hasn't been as high as we'd hoped." He actually had no idea of what her output was, but it was a good standard speech for heading off troublesome employees at the pass.

"Don't output me, I've had enough of your horseshit. You won't get a cold one in here, *I'll* fucking do it."

"No, you won't," he said cordially. "No doctor will examine another doctor's patient unless the patient him- or herself requests it. I don't think Mark is going to do that."

She glared at him. "I'll find a way. I will fucking find a way, and then I'm gonna nail your ass up in court—you, and your head-drillers, and this whole fucking shithole."

"I see." Manny sat forward and folded his hands on his desk. "Are you through now? Because if you are, I'd like to point some things out to you. Generally this is not how we address our superiors here. If you do it again, you'll be subject to discipline. Your whole outburst makes you subject to discipline, but I'm going to let it go because you're obviously overwrought for some reason—"

"Wow. The quality of mercy just ain't fucking strained with you, is it?" She looked at him incredulously. "Thanks for the big fucking *break*, I'd just hate to see this on my *permanent fucking record*, that just makes my shit run loose." She turned and marched out.

The door resealed behind her, and Manny waited tensely for the phone to buzz with a new crisis. It would be only too appropriate. After a few minutes of blessed quiet, he let himself relax. Apparently it was over for the day, over for the bad day. And all bad days always came to an end.

He called up a list of the released material and prepared to skim through each item, in case the Upstairs Team decided to pop-quiz him on it. If they did, he'd just tell them he'd reviewed most of the stuff prior to getting his sockets and sent it to release sequentially so as not to overload the area. None of them had the expertise to prove otherwise. Then he could screen what was left in the review queue, either later today or early tomorrow. For now, though, he would leave it frozen.

He skimmed the commercials first and found nothing that made him wince unduly. There were a few things he'd have sent back for a little fixing, but no disasters he'd have to live down or explain in full.

For the videos he went to the high-res thirty-six-inch screen in the wall behind him. The first one he tossed up was one of Aiesi's, something with a group called Canadaytime. He shook his head at the silly name. Diversifications was going to sound like it was putting out word salad. After a few minutes he used the remote to cut it off and go on to the next one.

Sometime later he became aware that he was staring at a blank screen. Dazed, he swiveled around to his desk to do something and realized he had no idea what he was going to do. He glanced at the desktop monitor. *Play completed*, said the plain white letters, and underneath, *Actions Menu: replay, next, exit*?

He turned and looked at the big screen again, frowning. His head felt foggy, as if he'd dozed off. It must have been one hell of a boring series of rock videos if it had put him to sleep.

Manny tried to remember what he'd seen, but the only thing

that came to mind were vague shapes moving rhythmically. More tired than he'd realized, he thought, too much the first day back.

Abruptly he found himself standing up behind his desk, rubbing one eye to the point of soreness. Damn, but he needed a rest already, from obnoxious rock'n'roll animals and a certain hacker who was too smart for his own good.

Which reminded him—what was he going to do about that little bastard? He could go up and confront him and see where that would lead, or he could let him stew for a couple of days, worrying about what would happen, maybe let him get confident enough so that he cracked in again, but this time to a hot reception, Manny catching him in the act. And then see where *that* would lead. Threatening to revoke the reparation contract and having him remanded to prison could make him compliant.

The little shit. The little brass-balled cock-knocker. Screw him, why let him have even one more moment of feeling confident? He sat down and banged out a short, pointed message on the keyboard and zapped it up to the penthouse. *Sweat, you son of a bitch, sweat and suffer all night,* Manny thought, *so that when I get around to you tomorrow, you'll be the shivering little turd you ought to be.*

Immanuel, when did you get so mean?

It seemed to be his father's voice speaking in his head, a voice he had not heard for years, and it took him by surprise. His father had been proud of his ambition, but his father had also been dead for close to twenty-five years, since before he had graduated high school.

Correct. His father had never seen him as an adult. The flush of dismay hit him hard, making his mind spin with confusion. Just trying to get ahead . . . it takes a lot just trying to outswim the pack and get ahead. . . .

We've got everything but the heads.

The thought of Joslin was a rancid taste in his mouth.

Hackers and freaked-out vivisectors and berserk rock'n'roll animals all around, an onslaught of human craziness, and what isn't crazy is almost too limp to produce, that's *how I got so mean, Father, and it would make you mean, too, if you had to do what I do.*

He became aware that he was whispering aloud, and a new wave of exhaustion swept through him. Too much, too fast, he thought. He would worry about everything tomorrow, including the kid in the penthouse. If he had the nerve to crack in again after getting Manny's message, that would only provide extra proof that he was intractable and unrepentant. If Diversifications couldn't handle him, the courts would, and any lost data would come out of his hide one way or another.

He paused and marked the videos for a second review with full sockets before shutting the console down. If they were so bad that they'd put him to sleep, he would have to be as familiar with them as possible in case the Upstairs Team wanted him to explain why he thought they were good enough to release. Reviewing them socketed and on-line, he shouldn't have much trouble staying awake for them, he decided.

If he had not stopped to take a little refreshment in the empty Common Room, he might have made it out the door before Security called him.

Gabe could hear her yelling as soon as he stepped into the hall. It was coming not from her pit, but from the one at the end of the hall. Visual Mark's. The door was open.

For a moment he wavered. The last time he'd talked to Gina hadn't exactly been an unqualified success, and she probably wouldn't welcome his intervention. *Go back to your jampot.* He was deluded thinking he could do anything for her, or for that matter, for himself.

"He's out of fucking control!" Gina was yelling. "You get him outa there—"

"Hey," said a soft voice behind him.

He turned. The tall thin man in the weird patterning cape was standing in one of the open elevators, holding the doors apart. The cape was thrown back so that he couldn't see most of it, but there seemed to be oddly shaped shadows pulsing all over it in a rhythm Gabe found immediately discomfiting. He tried to block out the sight without looking away from the man's face and then wasn't sure he wanted to look at the man, either. His expression was a peculiar mix of helplessness and something that Gabe would normally have identified as lust.

"You tell them," the man said, "I took the video mainline, and the hardline is, I've seen the stranger on the stony shore." He stepped back and let the elevator doors snap shut.

Gabe blinked, wondering what the hell had just happened, and went down the hall to Mark's open door.

Two of the implant doctors from the infirmary were standing

on one side of Mark's inert body, and Gina was standing on
the other, still shouting.

"He doesn't get up, he doesn't move around, he doesn't
leave this place, he just lays there on that fucking mat jacking
off!"

"We've told you, Ms. Aiesi," said the taller doctor, an edge
creeping into her voice, "that the readings for Mark when he
is connected to the system are quite normal *for him*. His vitals
have always sunk dramatically—"

"*Not* always—"

"—it's just the way his body has chosen to handle it, and
it's nothing more than a manifestation of the same nature as a
fakir—"

"*Fuck* your fakir—"

The second doctor put up her hand. Neither of them was
the doctor who had treated him the day Gina had hit him;
Gabe wondered what had happened to her. "We can't force
him to disconnect without possibly doing him grave harm—"

"*This* is his fucking grave!" Gina pointed at the console. "This
whole fucking pit's a tomb—"

Gabe drew back a little from the doorway, craning his neck.
The figure curled up in the fetal position on the mat looked
sick in some way, but Mark had always looked sick to him.

"—records do *not* show that Mark has been continuously
on-line," the first doctor was saying.

"Your fucking records are fucking *wrong*, he did something
to them. He told me himself he's not in his body anymore—"

"That's a fanciful way for an imaginative individual like Mark
to put it—"

"Fancy this, lady." Gina doubled up a fist.

"That's enough," said the shorter doctor, putting up her
hands and taking a step back. "This isn't a bar, we're not
interested in brawling with you."

"You can't tell me this is normal."

The figure on the mat stretched out suddenly with a yawn.
Gina jumped as Mark rolled over onto his back and opened
his eyes.

"Hey," he said softly, "is this the mainline or the hardline?"

Gabe frowned. *I took the video mainline. And the hardline
is . . .*

"Get those fucking wires out of your head," Gina ordered
him, "and get up."

He looked around and saw the doctors. "Is something wrong?" he asked, raising himself on one elbow.

"Not that we can tell," said the shorter doctor cordially. "How are you feeling?"

Mark's mouth stretched in a smile. "Never better. I'm doing a lot of work."

Something funny about the voice, Gabe thought. He sounded too—Gabe groped for a term. Coherent?

"Have you experienced any symptoms you would like to talk to us about?"

"Make him take those fucking wires out," Gina demanded. Her dreadlocks were practically bristling visibly.

"Not now, Gina," Mark said patiently. "I'm working on a video."

The shorter doctor made a polite, indulgent noise. "Well, when you're through, you might have a word with your friend here. She seems to think you're working too hard and that you haven't been off-line in an abnormally long time."

Mark gave a short, flat laugh. "I'm real busy. Got everything I need here." He lay down and curled up again as the doctors headed for the lift. Gabe slipped out into the hall.

"You get your asses back here!" Gina yelled after them. "You can't tell me that's fucking *normal*! That wasn't him, that was some goddamn *program* or something, he's a fucking zombie—"

"Ms. Aiesi, we'll continue to monitor his vitals, but that's all we can do—"

"*His fucking brain wave's abnormal!*" Gina shouted. "It's abnormal and *you know it!*"

Gabe moved farther up the hall as he heard the lift reach the catwalk. "Considering the life you and your friend have lived, of course it's abnormal. But it's well within an acceptable range, allowing for the changes wrought by the implants."

"*Bullshit!*"

Gabe winced for her. Eloquence always deserted her at the wrong time. He fled back up to his own door and opened it as if he were just going in. The doctors emerged and came up the hall together, looking resolute and professional. They nodded to him, and he nodded back, staring after them and wondering if they also had sockets. He couldn't remember ever having seen them before, not even after his own procedure. As soon as they were gone, he went back down the hall to

Mark's pit. Gina was still standing over him, head bowed, hugging herself. Gabe felt a sudden flash of anger at Mark and then at her without really knowing why. He brushed it aside.

"I heard all that," he said.

The fierce expression she turned up to him faded quickly. He took that as a good sign and went down to her.

"I didn't hear it all," he added, "but most of it. And I saw when he woke up and talked. He didn't sound right. But you didn't sound right to me, either, when you did it."

She shrugged. "Nobody cares but me, and he doesn't want me to care." She nudged Mark's back with the toe of her boot. "I oughta just say fuck it, if this is what he wants, it's what he wants."

Impulsively Gabe took her by the arm and led her to the lift, surprised when she didn't pull away from him. "Maybe we ought to get an outside doctor," he said as they went up to the catwalk together.

"I tried that," she said wearily. "Rivera'll block it. I figured I'd just try to get somebody's attention here."

"Well, there's something else," he said. "That guy in the cape that changes all the time—"

"Valjean," she said irritably, striding out into the hall ahead of him.

"Him. I saw him just a few minutes ago, here. He was on the elevator, and he told me to tell you, or them, or somebody something about the mainline and the hardline."

Gina stopped to frown at him. "What?"

"I know, that's something like what Mark said—"

"What the fuck was it?" she asked impatiently.

"He said he'd taken the video mainline, and the hardline was something about a stranger on a stony shore."

"That again." She shrugged. "Mark did Canadaytime's last video."

"I thought you did their last video," Gabe said. "You jumped off the terrace for it."

"Mark's done another since we got drilled. The boy's a regular video-production factory now, ain't you heard?"

The elevator doors opened suddenly, and two security guards came barreling out, stopping short when they saw Gina. "That guy Mark in his pit?" one of them asked.

"More or less," Gina said. "Why, you think I stole him?"

Gabe couldn't remember if either of them had been on the

terrace when Gina had jumped; at Diversifications security guards tended to run together, the same clean-cut, private gestapo squad looks in identical brown uniforms.

"Is he available or not?" asked the other guard.

Gina made a disgusted noise. "Ask me an easy one."

The guards turned to Gabe. He shrugged. "I'd say no, he's not available."

"You know, *he* was up there the day she pulled her little stunt," the first guard said to the other one.

"Who was?" Gina asked.

"It's probably how he got the idea," said the second guard. They started to walk away.

"What idea?" Gina caught his sleeve.

The first guard looked at her. "Forget about it. You'd hurt more than help."

"I'll hurt you right now if you don't tell me what the fuck's going on," Gina said darkly.

Both guards hesitated. Gabe herded them toward the elevator without saying a word, as if he had all the authority in the world, and the guards took them up to the terrace on the twentieth floor.

There should have been wind. Twenty stories up, wind should have been a given, but the air seemed to have lay down and died. That made it worse, Gina thought. If there had been wind, the cape would have been blowing back so she wouldn't have had to look at the shadows throbbing over it.

She tried to keep her eyes focused on Valjean's face and the woman—Dinshaw whoever. The same one who'd threatened to have her arrested that day in the common room. Gina had to hand it to her. She didn't look completely nuked, and she hadn't wet her pants yet, but she was getting there. Valjean had one haunch up on the railing, his left arm wrapped around her while he held the knife near her throat, ready either to slice her or go over the rail with her anytime he pleased.

"Hey!" he yelled to Gina, looking grotesquely cheerful. "You're here!" He gestured briefly at the security guards standing in a tense semicircle at a useless distance. "You can all go now." He blinked at her, his face twisting abruptly into a pained expression. "When's Mark coming?"

She took a few careful steps forward, watching for any sign

of panic. "Mark's still on-line. I think he's waiting for you to show your face. Or your ass, whichever applies."

Valjean shook his head vigorously. The Dinshaw woman held onto the arm gripping her with both hands. "No, no, you got it wrong. He's *in context*. You understand? He's in context, and we're all out of context, because he's the stranger on the stony shore. It was always him. But we're all out of context, and everybody knows that when you take something out of context, it can't make no fuckin' sense."

Gina nodded. "Which context are we talking here? And where the fuck does *she* fit in?"

"It's gonna be *my* context, so I get whoever I want for it." Valjean rested his chin on top of the woman's head. She clenched her eyes shut, and Gina saw Valjean's hand start to move.

"Hey, asshole, knock off that dirty stuff!" she yelled. "You ain't in the context of your bedroom here, fucking security guards're *watching*, chrissakes!"

"I didn't do nothing!" Valjean looked hurt but no less wild-eyed.

Gina took another step toward him. "Okay, okay, I just know you guys, you know? I been on a tour bus once or twice."

"I've *never* been on a tour bus," Valjean said, proudly. "*All* video. *All* the time."

"Yah, sure, that was before your time. I'm speaking symbolic. Like the context of a tour bus, get it?"

"*Get it.*" Valjean stared at some point over her head. Now the knife hand was moving slightly in a twisting motion. "Get it? Get it." He pulled the knife away from the woman and scratched the side of his face with the hilt. "Someday everybody's gonna get it."

"Never mind, I said that out of context. Listen, Val, I know about the context, and I know about the stranger on the stony shore, but I don't see where the knife comes in." Gina nodded at it. "What about that? You want to let me see it?"

He looked down at it as if he'd never seen it before. "I was thinking . . . something. I was thinking when you fall . . . when you cut through the air . . ."

The woman sagged in Valjean's grip, looking past Gina with pure hopelessness in her face. "Oh, *shit*," she groaned.

Gina turned around. Clooney had just stepped out onto the terrace, smoothing his clothes and puffing himself up. "All right, Mr. Valjean or Canadaytime or whatever you call yourself," he said loudly, stumping toward him gracelessly, "you put that knife down and let go of that woman or you're in *big, big trouble*."

Just as he was about to pass her, Gina grabbed him by the back of his shirt collar and pulled him back. "Yah? What the fuck are you gonna do, tell Rivera on him?"

Clooney blinked at her uncomprehendingly.

"He doesn't work here, asshole, so you can't have him fired."

Clooney jerked away from her. "We'll cancel your video contract!" he yelled at Valjean. "You'll never work in this business again!"

"I *am* this business!" Valjean announced with a mad joyousness in his voice.

"Val, listen, let's trade!" Gina said quickly, grabbing Clooney's arm. "This guy for the woman you got! Go for that?"

Valjean looked from her to Clooney and back again before he took a firmer grip on the woman. "Get real. You'd rush me."

Clooney was glaring at her with self-righteous fury. She ignored him. "Val. Keep looking at me." She moved as close to him as she dared, within arm's reach of a security guard on her left. The guard caught her eye and discreetly patted the holster of his stun pistol. She gave one small emphatic shake of her head no and raised both hands to keep Valjean's attention. Context. The fall. Signature image. The stranger on the stony shore. Somehow one of those was the royal road into him. "This context thing. Are we talking music or video or what?"

"Video," Valjean said breathily, not really in answer to her question. He rested the side of his face on the woman's head. "Gina, you been in there. In where the video is, right?" He tapped his head with the handle of the knife. "Chinese fucking boxes, one in another in another in another. We been to the next box *in*, but now we gotta get to the next box *out*. That's the *context*. And see, if you're *in* the video, you're *not* the video, you're just *in* it."

The woman winced as Valjean sat himself farther back on the rail. The shadows on the cape were pulsing more quickly and unevenly, the rhythm stumbling now and then. The shapes looked like stones moving as quickly as clouds in a storm.

"See, Gina," he said suddenly, "you got a bottle, say, and the bottle's got something in it. You're either the bottle, or you're something in it, but you're not both. Right?"

Gina nodded. "I'm with you that far. So?"

He made a frustrated face. "Well, don't you *hate* that?"

"Sure, hate it to fuck-all. Where does the stranger come in?"

"You can be a bigger thing," Valjean said. "You got a thought, and the thought wants to be more than it is, so it becomes a concept, and then pretty soon it's part of you. So like this, like now, I'm a thought. I wanna be a concept, and I wanna be the bigger thing that can think thoughts. Thoughts like me. Before the stranger on the stony shore turns and sees me and makes me stay just like I am."

Gina let out a breath. "All right. Now what's that got to do with hanging off a terrace twenty floors up holding a knife to somebody's throat?"

"When you cut through the air . . . when you fall a long, long way, you have to fall fast, before the stranger on the stony shore turns around and fixes you there, fixes you right there, and you'll never get away. And, oh, Gina"—he gave a shaky laugh—"I'm a bad, *bad* thought, and I gotta get into context."

"You're a bad thought, and you have to get into context," Gina said.

"*Prima*, girl. You *know*."

"Don't call me a girl," she growled at him.

"I'm a bad thought." Valjean looked down his nose at her.

"Just not in front of the asshole." She jerked her head at Clooney.

"Right. Sorry."

"Okay. Bad thought out of context. You're gonna cut through the air and take her with you, but you got no idea about what the context is."

"How can I, if I'm out of context?" He suddenly bent the woman backwards over the rail. Her feet dangled above the tacky grass green outdoor carpeting. Valjean held the knife above her, ready to stab down. Gina noted with a growing feeling of absurdity that it was a steak knife.

"Val, what if you get into context and you find out you're supposed to be a good thought?" she said quickly.

He looked up from the woman, exasperated. "Bad is bad."

"But if you don't know what the context is, how can you know if you're supposed to be bad?"

"What the *fuck* are you *talking* about?" Valjean yelled angrily. "You think *you* know something, you think *you're* the stranger here?"

"You don't know what you're supposed to be if you're not in context," she insisted. "You remember when I did your video, the fall, the bungi cords, all that?" She waited for him to nod. "Take that fall out of context, and what is it?"

"It's a fall," he said suspiciously.

"You think so? I coulda got the same effect going up in a jet and taking a power dive, or strapped a cam on a rocket and shot it up, then run the footage in reverse. Any of those methods would have given me the same kind of rush. All I had to do was make the image move the right way. It's supposed to be a fall in context. Out of context it's just pictures going real fast." She licked her lips, swallowing hard on a dry throat. "What did you ask for—fucking *pictures* going fast, or a stone-home *fall*?"

Valjean frowned hard. "You're making me confused now."

"It's not me," she said, forcing a blasé tone into her voice. "It's being out of context. But you got to know your context, because you're only gonna get one shot at getting into it."

He paused, thinking it over. "How do you know that?"

"When I make a video, and something doesn't work, I take it out and throw it away. No use for it, doesn't fit the context. That's okay for footage, but what about thoughts? You're not gonna be any kind of thought sitting in the cosmic trash barrel, and if you don't know the context, that's where you could end up."

There was an eternal moment when nothing happened at all, and then Valjean let go of the woman. She teetered, recovered, and slid down onto the carpeting in a heap, looking dazed. Gina waved a finger at her and she crawled away, out of Valjean's reach.

Valjean stayed on the rail, the knife in both hands and his face all puckered up. The stone shapes were racing on the cape, more like meteors now. She had a brief thought about falling stars as she took another step toward him, and then another, until she was within reach of him. He seemed to be unaware of her, even as she leaned forward and put one hand on his shoulder. The patterns on the cape began to fade in and out in spots, flickering, wavering. She watched his face carefully as she took a firm grip on him and started to pull him forward. His left eye was bloodshot; more than bloodshot. It was starting to fill up with watery pinkish tears. Gina pulled at him a little harder, and for a moment he resisted. Then he slid forward off the rail, still holding the knife in both hands as if he were praying.

Gina took the knife from him slowly and carefully. Valjean gave her a searching look and started to say something, but the guards were suddenly all around them, pulling him away from her.

"*I'll* take that knife."

Gina turned to Clooney, holding the knife between two fingers. "Don't tempt me, asshole, you're on my shitlist."

"I'm the ranking employee here." He snapped his fingers and held his hand out.

Gina flicked her wrist and the knife suddenly blossomed in the tacky green carpeting between his feet. "*Oops,*" she enunciated into his outraged face. One of the security guards clamped a hand on her arm.

"Remove this woman," Clooney said, rolling his eyes. "Obviously she's as disturbed as her rock'n'roll buddy here."

She twisted away from the guard easily. "I can remove myself. Fuck you very much, stooge."

Two of the guards removed her anyway. As they marched her past Ludovic and the Dinshaw woman, Valjean was singing "Coney Island Baby." He was flat.

26

Valjean finished singing and collapsed at the doctor's feet in a huddled pool of twitching patterns. It was the same tall doctor Gabe had just seen in Mark's pit arguing with Gina. Her face remained stubbornly impassive, even as she started to remove the cape and discovered the connections that Valjean had been so careful to camouflage running from the hardware in the collar to the sockets in his head. Gabe felt a wave of queasiness sweep through him as she bent down and instructed the semi-conscious man to give the disconnect command.

Dinshaw nudged him, and he started guiltily; he had all but forgotten her. "Are you all right?" he asked her, but she waved the question away, pointing at the door. Manny was just coming out from the elevators, looking haggard and disheveled in a vague kind of way, as if he'd just been awakened from sleep.

Clooney rushed at him, starting to explain something about being the ranking employee and the call from Security bouncing to him because Manny had been unavailable. Manny seemed to endure Clooney without really listening, giving most of his attention to the doctor and the security guards. He turned briefly to look at Dinshaw, frowning when he saw Gabe standing beside her.

"You're probably going to get it for being on the scene again," Dinshaw said in a low voice. "How is it you always find your way up here when someone's going to jump?"

"Just lucky, I guess," Gabe said, feeling awkward. A guard came over to him with Valjean's cape and thrust it at him.

"Here. She's *your* friend, *you* give it to her."

Gabe didn't want to touch it. He balled it up quickly, making sure the connections that had been in Valjean's skull were well buried in the folds of material.

Dinshaw drew away a step, looking at it with distaste. "That's a real inspired piece of technology."

"Isn't it."

Clooney stalked past them looking miffed as the largest security guard eased Valjean's limp form over his shoulder and followed the doctor to the elevators.

"You weren't hurt, were you?" Manny asked Dinshaw. He was squinting at her strangely, as if he were trying to decide whether she was somehow at fault for all this.

Dinshaw shook her head.

"Good. That's good." He looked a bit puzzled as he went back inside. Gabe and Dinshaw stared after him.

"What's wrong with this picture?" Dinshaw said, rubbing her neck where Valjean had been gripping her.

"I don't know," Gabe said. He looked down at the cape. A last bit of residual energy sent a soft wave of grey through the white material, like an animal letting out a final breath.

White Lightning in a mason jar. If it worked once, it would work again. Except it didn't.

The level in the jar went down steadily, little by little, and it wouldn't come for her. It burned the way it was supposed to, but tonight she was fireproof.

Here it comes.

She tried to block the thought with another swig from the jar. Yah, and here *this* comes, now leave me alone.

Take a little walk—

—and here it comes—

Here *this* comes. Shut up, motherfucker.

Too hard, it was too fucking hard to think about.

—a little walk with me—

—into the context—

Context *this*. The jar was half-gone now, and she felt nothing, nothing, nothing. The kid with the heelprint on his forehead was jumping again tonight. Christ, didn't he have someplace else to go, something else to do?

"We do"—*dit, dit, dit*—"what we do. We do it"—*dit, dit, dit*—"because we can."

Gina put her hand down on the sticks, capturing them. Flavia waited a moment and then slid them out again to play the edge of the table.

"*Know* what you're looking for. *Know* it." Flavia pushed the mason jar aside. "Know you through the wire, know you for always."

Gina pulled the mason jar back in front of her and held onto it. "I don't think you're fucking ready to know me tonight."

That sharp-enough-to-cut grin. "Toxed enough yet?"

She shook her head slowly. "Not toxed at all. Should've known it would happen someday. I passed the saturation point, can't put a load on anymore. The only thing to do is get myself Purged and start over quick. Before the odometer hits six zeroes."

"Sure." Flavia whacked her on the cheek with one of the sticks. "Feel that?"

Gina gave a short, surprised laugh. "No."

"Toxed enough." Flavia beckoned to someone behind her. "Ready. A little traveling music, please."

Don't do it, she told them as they took her out. Don't fucking do it, crushed in the back of the rental with Claudio and his magic fingers. We do what we do, we do it because we can, don't do it, she said as they took her down into the cellar. Don't do it, Claudio laying her down on the mattress, arranging her comfortably, pausing to kiss her on the mouth. Struck by White Lightning, hope you like your barbecue extra-crispy. Don't do it. The connections were ready in Flavia's practiced hands. Don't do it, she said. Last time: don't do it.

Then they did it.

The brain feels no pain, Good God, y'all, can you believe with me?

They said they could. Claudio's magic fingers, the Fender in Dorcas's grip, Tom holding on to the phantom train, and Flavia beating, beating, beating.

Well, you got it, it's totally painless, but they never mentioned it would feel like painlessly driving eight nails through your head going in and painlessly ripping your arms and legs off coming out again. And they only mentioned what you'd gain, they never mentioned what you'd lose, they never got to that, and what the fuck, even you can't tell sometimes. Right. Because we do what we do, we do it because we can . . . but do you *know* what you can do?

You can do this—

—*take a little walk with me*—

A little way, a *long* way, invaded, visited, and then left; walk all night, and then run and run and run until you forget. Were you running from something or to it?

Struck by White Lightning. Hope you like your barbecue extra-crispy. (She thought she heard someone yell in pain, but that was ridiculous, that couldn't have been. The brain felt no pain.)

You be the ass to risk. Ever done that? It goes something like this—

But Flavia was already tearing at her, whacking her across the face with the sticks to bring her out of it even as Claudio's magic fingers plucked the wires from her head and threw them down. Flavia yanked her to a sitting position.

"Hey, *you*. Get her *out*."

Déjà-voodoo. "How the fuck did you find me?" she said.

"Why didn't you wait for me?" Ludovic's face was pained. "Why didn't you come to me?"

"You ask a lot of questions for someone with holes in his head. *Hotwire*."

He carried her out.

Fez's smile was tired. He was sitting alone in the work island Rosa had set up with Percy directly in front of the screens, which were all dark now. It was some indecent hour of the morning, four maybe, and the inn was dead quiet, except for the faint sound of some hard-core party animals, probably Rude Boys, carrying from somewhere farther up the Mimosa.

"What are you doing here?" she said.

He yawned. "Research. I just wanted a little privacy."

"Oh. Sorry. I'll get out of your face." She turned to go back to her squat.

"No, it's all right. I think I've found out everything I need to know." He jerked his head at her. "Come here. You'll be interested in this."

She sat down on the floor next to him, yawning and wiping her watering eyes. "I don't vouch for my ability to know anything at this hour, but whack it anyway."

He gave her a look. "Going native?"

"Fuck, no." She blinked at the screen of the laptop on the crate in front of him. "Sixteen perfect screens, and you're using Rosa's laptop?"

"I didn't want to put this up where everyone could see it."

She studied the screen for several seconds until she realized it was something from MedLine. "God, I can't read this. It's got words like *oedema* and *homonymous hemianopia* in it." She paused as the words sank in, and suddenly she was wide awake. "*Hemianopia*. That's a visual deficit usually caused by a stroke. You don't see stuff on the left side or the right,

depending on which hemisphere of the brain is involved."
She looked at Fez. "*Oedema* is the antiquated spelling of
edema—"

"Thank you, I know," Fez said grimly. "Secondary swelling
after a stroke."

"Who?" she asked.

"A rather disturbing number of people who have sockets.
And not just strokes. Other neurological disorders, too. Seizures, sudden onset of multiple sclerosis, Huntington's chorea,
Parkinson's—" Fez frowned. "Not enough Parkinson's cases,
actually, to be significant." He blew out a breath. "The vast
majority seem to be strokes of varying severity, and seizures.
But the number of brain tumors ought to be ringing somebody's
fire bell, and I don't think it is."

"All from sockets?" Sam asked, feeling her stomach turn
over.

"They say there's absolutely no physical evidence connecting
sockets to any of this," he said, scrolling the dense text forward
several lines. "If you can believe them. They're calling it a
'statistically correct sampling of the populace,' unquote, men-
tioning other factors such as the effects of mutagens from environmental poisoning in the last century."

"We didn't kick you in the head, your grandparents did,"
Sam said.

Fez gave her shoulders a squeeze. "That's my Sam-I-Am."

"I'm not yours," she snapped.

He blinked at her in surprise for a moment, and then his
face took on a wary look. "This is not the time to be mad at
me, Sam."

"I know." She could feel her face getting warm. Great; she
was blushing. She only did that maybe once in two or three
blue moons, and it had to be now. She gave an awkward shrug.
"Hey, I'm trying to be a grown-up. I don't do so bad most of
the time."

He was looking back and forth, from the screen to her, caught
between the two, and she wanted to kick herself. Something
big and bad was happening, and she had to give herself away
by getting pissy over a casual remark she'd heard from him a
hundred times before.

"Anything I say to you is going to sound lame," he said after
a few moments. "I can tell you, 'Sam, you're very young, and
I'm a broken-down old wreck' or 'Jesus, Sam, why, you're
young enough to be my granddaughter, it's too indecent,' and

we both know the meanest Hollywood hack could probably write better dialogue."

She laughed a little in spite of everything. "Forget about it. I'm sorry. I make a shitty fugitive, and I make a shitty Mimosan, and sometimes I'm a shitty friend, too."

"It's a shitty world," Fez said lightly, and they laughed together.

"I'm sorry," she said again, sobering. "It *is* a shitty world. What about this? Is anyone doing anything?"

"Not as far as I can tell. They're slowing down doing the procedure in some places, and a new clinic in Schenectady that was supposed to open has been delayed. Every single case was reported to be neurologically sound before and after the sockets were put in."

"Then it's something going into the sockets," Sam said. "I mean, assuming it isn't twentieth-century mutagens."

"Well, you're not a shitty thinker, whatever eles you may be. But according to this nothing like neurotransmitter is going into anyone's sockets. It's all just entertainment stuff—rock videos, Hollywood releases. Commercials."

"Commercials would do it—" She stopped. "Art told me way back when that Visual Mark could possibly have a stroke in the future. If he's among the cases, that's stone-home evidence they knowingly implanted sockets into the head of someone who was already manifesting a problem."

Fez went back several screens and scanned a list of names. "Not here," he said after a moment. "Even if he was, we'd go to jail proving it. Receiving stolen meds."

"I'd cut a deal. It would be worth it." She looked at him. "Hell, *I'll* go to jail. You stay here, have fun." She paused. "I mean, this is not my favorite place I've ever lived."

"I knew what you meant," Fez said serenely, going back to the screen he'd been looking at. "The thing to do right now, I think, is give this to Art and let him run with it. If it means anything at all, he'll figure it out."

"You have a lot of faith in him." Sam sighed. "Actually, that's what I was going to suggest. Art can get around the system, find out all kinds of things. Between him and us we may be able to figure it out. It sure worked before. I just don't know where we'll hide out this time."

Fez gave her a puzzled frown. "Pardon?"

"It just seems like every time Art makes some kind of big discovery, we end up wanted for questioning."

"Only once, Sam."

"See? A definite pattern." She wiped a hand over her face. "Shit, I'm tired." Fatigue had suddenly resettled itself on her like some tremendous roosting animal. "*And* I have to go to the bathroom. Pardon me while I go get my little pail and shovel to play in the sand. Don't worry, I'll bury it deep so it won't kill anybody." She got up clumsily and started away.

Fez caught her hand. "Maybe sometime we can sit down in my apartment—my new apartment, wherever and whenever that may be—and I can try to explain some of the things I want. And if things had broken just a little bit differently, who's to say? But I've always taken you seriously, Sam. In case you had any doubt."

She nodded tiredly. "That's okay. Just—" she shrugged. "Next lifetime, let's get it right." She staggered off in search of toilet paper.

He was in a sort of rest/sleep mode when he first sensed it.

A presence and not a presence, it seemed as if it were calling to him in a way, signaling, beckoning, from somewhere within the Diversifications system.

At first he thought it was Gina, coming on-line to be with him after all, but as he sensed more of it, he realized there was nothing of her in it. Abruptly he flashed on the idle meat, still in the pit. The records said it had disconnected and taken itself home, but it was really still there. Records were easy to manipulate, and he'd tried to keep them as normal looking as possible, so as not to let anyone know he wasn't actually disconnecting at all. The prospect of returning to the meat, of being weighted down, was less appealing all the time.

He wished he had some way of getting the meat to operate at least briefly on its own, without him right there to control it. Then it could disconnect, walk around, go home, and come back. The doctors would accept such a performance as normal, just as they had accepted the little show he had put on for them earlier. After all, they were still busy processing the hordes of Diversifications employees, the social-expression composers, the hardware designers, the administrative people, and the fabled Upstairs Team. Meat was easy to bamboozle. It had to expend so much energy and attention just dragging itself around that it tended to miss a lot.

In the midst of his ruminations on the meat problem, he felt the thing again, no closer but somehow stronger. From

Rivera's area, he realized. His attention blinked into existence there, and without warning it went for him.

It was a voracious thing, mindless under a facade that was vaguely like himself; impressions of old sensations, pain, compulsion, the old drive toward oblivion. Juggernaut, wanting to devour and to infiltrate, rape, merge. There was a blip of consciousness or near consciousness to it, a shadow of consciousness all destructive in its makeup, and yet no more deliberately evil than cobra venom. It knew nothing else, and in a way it knew nothing at all, except that it would do what it would do.

He almost got away; it almost got him.

Both, for some infinitesimal measure of time (*damned Schrödinger world*)—he was feeling himself being reeled into it and watching from a safe distance as it moved along each new item in the review queue, sowing itself in little flashes of yellow, in a driving beat—

He flickered away to the meat and tuned in the brain like a small, feeble radio.

The brain was still running, but it had a new balkiness. He could not have depended on it to work a routine; it would have garbled each line in the act of reading it.

Abruptly he realized that if he could have removed this new shell of garbled operation, he would have something very similar to the thing sitting in Manny Rivera's area working away on the items in the frozen release queue.

In the meat-vernacular, I stroked out on them, he thought, almost wonderingly.

It had been coming for a long time. The flashing lights, the floating sensation. From Medical's area he got the term *transischemic attack* and the knowledge that they had known all along, since the night they'd grabbed the hacker, and they'd just pumped some antistroke medication into the meat during the detox and called it their best try and hoped that the sockets would help him.

Poor meat. Nobody cared. Not even me.

It hadn't really been a very big stroke. If he'd still been inside the meat, he would have been up and walking around, a little more vague than usual, a little more argumentative, talking crazy shit when he talked at all, and nobody would have noticed anything out of the ordinary about that.

You were good at that. Talking crazy shit and video. What made America great.

The problem was, the meat was going to stroke out again, any time now, and when it did, that would be the big one, and as long as the wires were in the head, that meant the big one—the Big One—would charge right out of the meat, into the wires, into the system, where the little one was already waiting, and if—no, *when*—the two of them got together, they'd make something that couldn't be called a stroke, not anymore. Something like an unguided missile, a loose cannon rolling through the system, and when it found a receptor site, someone on-line with sockets—

Gina? Gina?

Her console was off, her pit empty, stone-home cold and dead, like she was never coming back.

Ludovic was gone, too. He turned a facet of his attention briefly to the top-down graphing of their respective worldlines. He couldn't be sure that they were together now, but it seemed more likely than not.

He flickered on Medical, but there was no one there, either. Dammit, what time was it? The middle of the night.

The kid in the penthouse.

Rivera had been right about one thing, Keely thought woozily. The good stuff didn't make you as sick. Or sick at all. He looked over at the antique liquor cabinet gaping open. Booze had never been his particular preference; it was like using a shotgun to pick off a mosquito, or maybe putting yourself in a trash compactor to swat a fly on your nose, too broad-spectrum. On the other hand, there was something to be said for being broad in the spectrum. He had climbed into that old trash compactor and found that it sure did the fucking job. Maybe not too visual, but it was getting the fucking job done that counted.

And that was a *big* fucking job, after the message from Rivera. It was still on the screen across from where he was sitting on the couch with the bottle trapped between his thighs. *I know you cracked my system. Damage nowhere near as great as you anticipated. I'll be up to look into the final disposal of your case tomorrow. You can expect the worst, if you like.*

Son of a bitch must have gotten all his joints loosened to be that blatant, Keely thought, taking another swig from the bottle. Probably wouldn't do any good to try pointing out he wasn't the only hacker in the world, anyone could have been fucking around and managed to crack in and stone his crows. Could even have been his own little on-line net-pal, Visual Mark, cavorting out of his box.

The message on the screen flickered and then disintegrated. "Speak of the devil," Keely muttered as the familiar partial room appeared, the clouds rushing like a hurricane was imminent.

"Tell me you're awake!" Mark said, jacking the volume up all the way.

Keely staggered over and fell into the chair in front of the screen. "Sh. The grown-ups are all asleep." He leaned his face heavily on his hand. "Say, you been up to some dirty tricks in Manny Rivera's private computer."

"No time to talk. Listen for it: you're free."

Keely listened. Somewhere in another part of the penthouse, there was a series of small clicks. The door. He swiveled around drunkenly, expecting to see Manny Rivera marching into the room with a flat smile on his face. *Decided this couldn't wait till tomorrow. Got a court order to drill your skull; go along quietly with the nice people waiting outside, and there won't be any trouble.* But no one came in, nothing happened at all. He turned back to the screen.

"Did you just unlock the door?" he asked, laughing a little.

"Yes. I want you to leave here, go down to my simulation pit and yank the connections out of my head."

"Come *on*," Keely said, waving a hand clumsily. "You can do that yourself, I know how it works. You just think 'disconnect' or 'quit' or something."

"My meat won't do it, and I can't make it work from this side. You—"

"*What* side?"

"On-line. From inside the system. I'm not in the meat anymore, I told you, I got out of my box—"

"Yah, you sure did," Keely said, sloppily jovial. "I bet that *was* you, messing around with Rivera's shit, fucking with this and that. That son of a bitch doesn't know about you, he thinks *I* did it. Whatever you did. What'd you do, anyway?"

"I just looked," Mark said irritably. "What's the matter with you?"

"Not a fucking thing. I am toxed on the Upstairs Team's private label. They may be a retrograde bunch of cocksuckers, but they sure can pick 'em. Ain't plotzed *once* in fucking *hours* of straight drinking."

"You don't have to be detox for this," Mark said hurriedly. "Just get out, go to my pit—"

"And where *is* your pit?" Keely asked, yawning.

"On sixteen. Last one on the left at the end of the hall as you come out of the elevators. My body'll be there—"

"But your mind flies free." Keely gestured dramatically. "Isn't that right?"

"Get on the elevator, go down to the sixteenth floor. I'll unlock the pit door, all you have to do is push it open, walk in, take the connections, and yank them out of my head."

"*That*," Keely said, leaning forward to peer closely at the monitor, "would probably smart a whole fucking *shitload*. Probably stroke you out, maybe even kill you. Assuming I could get them out. Why don't you just nip in from your side and trash your console? That'll shut it off, and it'll be like the same thing, the connections'll deactivate."

The image on the screen froze, and Keely had the definite feeling his net-pal was no longer with him. But he'd left his calling card, or maybe his bookmark was more like it, so he had to be coming back. He could drink while he waited. Keely took another swig and then put his head down on the desk beside the keyboard.

After a little while he realized he was looking at a laptop that had been bolted into the desk with a bunch of add-ons. Son of a bitch—if he did want to walk right out his allegedly unlocked door, he could just rip this little piece right out of the desk and have himself info-to-go, see-you-later-data, juice-on-the-loose. . . .

"I can't," Mark's voice said, startling him out of the half stupor he'd fallen into. Keely pushed himself upright and stared blearily at the screen.

"You can't what?"

"I can't get at my console. It was a good idea, and I should have thought of it earlier myself, but it's too late. It's there. It got out of Rivera's area, and it found the meat. Now all it has to do is wait for it to stroke out big. Hell, maybe it's going to *make* the meat stroke out big."

"What the fuck are you talkin' now," Keely said, trying to keep his eyes open. "Who's strokin' who?"

The voice in the speaker became one with the buzz rising in his own head as whatever Mark was trying to explain slid all over him and fell off. He must have thought it was pretty important, though; every time he opened his eyes, Mark was still there on the screen, saying, "One more time. I'll tell you one more time, and you answer me. . . ."

The kid obviously wasn't used to alcohol. Young people, Mark reflected sourly. They'd always had it too clean, too efficient, even in their drugs. They took stuff that did one thing, or one other thing, and it was all a terribly neat way to get toxed. Sharpshooters; they couldn't stand up to the old cannonball.

That was the way it was with everything, he thought as he tried to get the kid to rouse for a third time. The dataline was just as particularized, a variety of channels but no variety within channels, organized right down to the bedrock beyond which no further organization was possible, and that was fine as long as nothing ever changed. But if something came along and played fifty-two pickup with all that rigorously organized data, it was shit-outa-luck time, too many fragments scattered in too many directions; total collapse. Like the booze in the kid passed out in front of the monitor. Mark could hear him snoring into the phone speaker. He could also see him if he wanted to, through the cam hidden in the chandelier, but it was a lousy angle.

He sounded five sharp tones on a high frequency that corresponded to fingernails on a chalkboard, a real teeth-grinder. There was a hitch in the kid's snoring, and then it resettled into normal rhythm.

"That's just *great*, kid!" Mark bellowed at him. No response. How many fucking nights had the kid let the liquor supply just sit, and then he had to pick tonight. He should have figured, he should have graphed the kid's movements.

He should have graphed *himself*. Then he might have seen it all coming, including the release of the infection from his own sad meat. He blipped his awareness briefly around the net to check on its status. No change in the last fifteen minutes, but that wasn't necessarily good news.

It was waiting for him in the console in his own pit, in Gina's, in Gabe Ludovic's, in Manny Rivera's, in all the pits, and at every possible contact point for Security and Medical. Security was unaware, but then, it wasn't meant for them. They'd been using the system all night with no problem. It was waiting for him to try to make contact, even just by producing a false alarm. He could have stationed his attention in the Security area indefinitely, coexisting with it unaffected, unless he executed any series of actions, and then it would take him. And if it took him, he wouldn't have to wait for the Big One to surge up out of the meat. He would be the Big One himself.

He had watched it make its way through the net, following almost the same paths he'd taken when he'd first gone exploring, seeding itself. There seemed to be a kind of tropism at work, as if he were drawing it to himself. Not surprising— it was the stroke he was supposed to have had, and he'd had it and not had it at the same time. Schrödinger's stroke. The meat had stroked out, but he was separated from it, and that wasn't the natural order of things, as far as the stroke was concerned; it wasn't meaning to spare him.

So it was coming for him, following his own trail as well as it could. There had been a few missteps, but as it spread, it had become more precise, more knowledgeable. It was almost as if the passage of time had stopped for him, just to allow something else to catch up, to reach his level of experience. He was still beyond it, but it was progressing steadily. Not much longer before it discovered the penthouse, and the outside phone line he'd found for the kid, going to waste now while he snored in a stupor. If it had been less prone to error, it might have found the penthouse already, but then error had a great deal to do with the very nature of a stroke. Perhaps he could attribute the coexistence of that fact with his present situation to circumstantial dumb luck.

Must remember always to try to program a little circumstantial dumb luck into every routine from now on, he thought. *But first, must figure out the program for circumstantial dumb luck.*

Right. If it found the penthouse before he could rouse the kid, he'd be cut off from the last person who could possibly keep the Big One from getting out of the meat and into the system. He'd just have to leave by the outside line and hope he could find some place in the bigger system that was safe before it followed him out—

It's already out there. In the video.

It was anywhere the video was. And the video had been in general release for . . . a week? Longer?

He beeped the console on the frequency of a boat horn, five sharp blasts. "Wake up, goddammit!"

The kid stirred and almost came to. But he couldn't wait any longer. Either he remained confined and waited for it to catch up with him, or he took his chances in the larger system.

If he stayed, perhaps he could confine it with himself in Diversifications' system. Except for what was already out.

No. Maybe he wasn't noble enough, or moral enough, or enough of anything to sacrifice himself. And that wouldn't work anyway, he realized, because once it got him, it would get all of his intelligence, his consciousness, everything, and it wouldn't just be smart anymore. It would be alive.

He stayed only long enough to throw together a fast routine, an alarm loop the kid could deactivate when he came to, which would trigger an interactive message. If the virus found the penthouse before the kid woke up, there wouldn't be any message, but it was that chance, or no chance.

He kicked the loop into motion. Five piercing whistles. "Get up, goddammit, the sky is falling!"

Then he was out.

27

Mark's Canadaytime video was in the pipe. Gina tried to watch it four times. The most she could go was two minutes before cutting it off.

Only a movie. She flicked the restart button on the remote. Try again.

The monitor screen lit up white and blank. After a bit soft shadows began to congeal as the music faded in, a discordant machine-jangler cover of a real old one called "Wasted." So old it was new again. Valjean's rasp invited her to come down on her own, and something in it made her want to move closer to the screen, closer to the shadowy forms pulsing in an out now, writhing. The music made the shadows soft, and the shadows softened the music, and she could taste the texture in her mind, warm and alive like flesh.

She looked over her shoulder at the half-closed bedroom door. She'd awakened to find Ludovic lying next to her, fast asleep, but on top of the covers, while she'd been underneath. The charm of his refusal to presume should have moved her more than it did, but she had no room in her for charm this morning.

On the way over last night, he'd told her about the hookup Valjean had rigged. She'd found the idea of the crap in Valjean's head dancing on the cape revolting. And it had to have come out of this video.

This video. She hadn't taken it through the wire, but she could almost imagine how it would be. Like floating through a tangible fog bank, and as each shadow pulsed, there would be a corresponding pressure deep in the head, an invisible finger pressing here, and here, and here, searching for some particularly sensitive spot. Like being molested in some weird, witchy way.

The shadows were throbbing more urgently now, rock Rorschachs. Do you see a butterfly here, or a skeletal pelvis?

—an open window or an open wound—

She stabbed the quit panel and turned away from the monitor. It had happened again, that feeling of being hypnotized. More than hypnotized.

She ran a hand over her head, touching the places where the sockets were implanted. Maybe if she could have reached in as far as Mark had, she would have come up with something equally fucked.

From the bedroom she heard Ludovic turning over, and she waited, but he didn't get up. Go in and get him, see if he could watch this fucked-up postcard from the dark side? When he had popped up again in Loophead's cellar, she hadn't known whether to laugh or cry.

Why didn't you wait for me? Why didn't you come to me?

She'd had no answer for that; her condition had not been conducive to explaining her life to him.

If you're going to do this on a regular basis, I'm going to have to tap into a supply of good stimulants.

Oh, who fucking asked you? That had spilled out of her, more like vomit than words.

I'm a fucking volunteer.

Didn't your mother ever tell you never to fucking volunteer?

Jesus! He'd pounded the steering wheel of the rental with both fists, making the whole vehicle shake like the piece of shit it was. *What does it take? What does it fucking take?*

She glanced at the bedroom again. What does it take? Well, for starters, how does forty-seven miles of barbed wire sound? Just for starters. We'll get to the really lethal stuff later. Because we do what we do, and we do it because we can.

Suddenly she felt ashamed of herself, for that and for Loophead. *I don't know what you did to those people, but they never want to see you again.*

I told them not to do it. I didn't think I was toxed, I didn't feel toxed. I didn't feel anything.

Hadn't sounded like much of a defense then, and it didn't now. What she'd done to them. She knew what she'd done to them. She'd taken them hard, and manhandled them, each and all together. She hadn't waited for them to give it up, she'd squeezed it out of them, and when they'd given it all, she'd set them back up and squeezed out some more, running over them, shaking them, doing the sound and the music to them, not with them. She hadn't been a synner with Flavia and Dorcas and Tom and Claudio, but something altogether different—

She looked at the blank monitor screen again, and for a moment her mind made her see phantom patterns still moving on it.

Yah, we do what we do, and we do it because we can, and where did you learn to do a thing like that?

"Little Jesus Jump-Up," she muttered. She knew where Mark was, and she knew where Valjean was, and she knew where the video was, in the pipe, out there in release, it had been released—

She hesitated for a moment, looking back at the bedroom. Maybe if they hadn't come back here to Mark's own apartment, she'd have gone in and woken him up long ago. But as he'd said, he didn't know where she lived, and he hadn't wanted to drive all the way to Reseda. Next time the Hollywood-Sheriott for sure.

Sure.

It's okay, hotwire, she thought. *You don't have to volunteer anymore.*

She left a note on the monitor. *Gone to get Mark.* That would say it to him.

He'd been dreaming that Rivera had sent him down to Medical to get sockets, and they'd been putting them in the hard way, using spikes and drills and steam-driven hammers that whistled horribly whenever they hit a trouble spot. He could feel them grinding in, driving all the way down through his skull, his face, his neck, into his body cavity—

Abruptly he raised his aching head and looked around. He was still in the penthouse. The light said daytime. "Fuckin' *dream*," he muttered, and rubbed his head all over. Had to have been a fucking dream; if Rivera had just had them take him, he'd have awakened in Medical. Maybe.

He caught sight of the empty bottle standing next to the blank monitor and groaned. Shit, he was lucky to be alive. Alcohol was not the way he flew. He had a vague memory of thinking it had been a good idea at the time. Yah. Like putting a shotgun to your face and pulling the trigger with your toe.

The whistles blasted him then, almost knocking him off the chair. The monitor was no longer blank; Mark was staring out from that crazy partial room. In the background the clouds were boiling.

"Door's open, get the fuck out."

"When I'm alive, I'll give it some thought," Keely said. "I'm not—"

"I couldn't stick here waiting for you to come to," Mark went on abruptly. "You're looking at a message. Don't interrupt. Get the fuck outa here, go down to my pit on the sixteenth floor, hack the lock, rip the fucking wires right outa my head. *Now.*"

Keely made a face. "What?"

"You heard me. You rip the fucking wires outa my head now. Fast. The old meat's gonna stroke out big, and if the Big One gets up the wires into the system, it's all gonna stroke out, it's gonna eat the system alive and everyone connected to it. You got that?"

"Stroke?" Keely said, rubbing his forehead. He felt like he'd had one himself.

"Reference: cerebral vascular accident. Only it's different this time. If it gets into the system and finds someone hooked in with the interface, it'll get them, too. You got that? *A contagious stroke*, a fucking *virus*, are you with me yet?"

"Shit." Keely frowned. "Wait a minute . . . this is a recording?"

"Canned ham. Get the fuck outa here and go down to my pit on the sixteenth floor, hack the lock, rip the wires outa my head. Don't sweat the meat, the meat's over, it's only warm now."

"Meat," said Keely, trying to push his thoughts around in the wreck of his mind.

"Meat, reference: my body. You got that? Get the fuck outa here, go down to my pit on the sixteenth floor, hack the lock, rip the fucking wires outa my head. Or the Big One gets into the system with the little one."

"Jesus. Reference, the little one," Keely begged, not really expecting the program to answer.

"The little one, reference: the stroke I already had. Little thing, no one would have noticed it anyway, but it's already in the system, and it's why I couldn't stay here waiting for you to come to."

"Where the fuck are you now?"

"Fuck if I know, boy. Out in the big system somewhere, the Big Context. Change for the machines. You want to find me after you're out, dial up the access code VM for Visual Mark. Give the password *Gina*, and I'll know it's you. I'll answer if I can. Door's open, get the fuck out, go down to my pit on the six—"

The image froze and then began to unravel, starting at the top left corner of the screen and working across. It looked as if some invisible creature were chewing it away in little portions. Keely squeezed his eyes shut. Did hallucinations come with a hangover? Or was this Mark's idea of punchy visuals?

When he opened his eyes, half the image had been eaten away; there were slashes through what remained. Keely hit the clear-screen pad. Nothing happened. He pressed recall and replay, tried to raise the dataline menu. Something was actively clawing at the image now, ripping it up in big, messy strokes. He pressed the reset pad to take the unit all the way back to start-up mode. Nothing changed.

The last of the image vanished, and the screen turned a soft greyish white.

"Come on. Is this some kinda fancy demonstration?" Keely said. "You doing this to show me something?" A shapeless spot was darkening in the center of the screen. "You're really still here, aren't you."

Music came up, faint, jangly like machinery, and the shadow in the center of the screen began to pulse and blossom and just as he blinked, he caught—

He shook his head. Strange. All of a sudden he'd dropped a stitch, just lost his line of thought. The screen was full of pulsing shadows. Turning away, he groped for the off pad. Images were flashing in his brain, twisted progressions and distortions that made his headache worse. Something about stones, or clouds . . . water . . .

He saw then that he'd been tapping the off panel steadily, but nothing had happened. The shadows kept moving on the screen, insistent, magnetic, demanding, and if he didn't turn his back to them, he was going to drop into a trance again.

But he wasn't an easy subject for hypnosis, he knew that. Except this didn't feel exactly like hypnosis. It felt . . . ugly. Like something probing him for a weak spot, a secret hurt. But just shadows on a screen?

He tried to think. It had been something *more* than the shadowy things. Cautiously he turned his head until the screen was at the edge of his peripheral vision.

There. A vibration or a flutter, not apparent when he looked at the screen straight on. It was peculiar, irregular, like a glitch in the transmission bouncing the picture around. Somehow that, combined with the pulse rate of the shadows, had affected him on some level he wasn't really aware of. Maybe something to do with the rate at which the neurons in his brain fired. Sam could have told him, she'd studied all that stuff. But Sam wasn't here. He was on his own.

Go down . . . rip the wires out . . .

He crawled under the desk, found the cords for the unit and the one next to it, and yanked them out of the wall.

On the screen the shadows kept throbbing, moving, writhing. He turned away and found himself staring at the heavy antique linen cloth on the dining table.

He pulled the cloth off the table, dragging along the metal-sculpture centerpiece and the bulky crystal candlesticks. They made some stone-home satisfying crashes when they hit the floor. He stumped backwards to the desk and flung the cloth over the monitor.

The shapes were pulsing on the material now. A chill went through him; then he realized that he was just seeing afterimages. *Stop it*, he ordered himself, and looked away, out the window, at the ceiling, at the floor, at everything, filling his mind with more visual input.

After a bit the discomfort in his head started to fade. He looked at the covered monitor again. Nothing, neither virus nor intelligence, should have been able to override a good old-fashioned power-down. So what the fuck was it, Super virus? Totally invulnerable?

Forget it; he would have to get down to the sixteenth floor without being caught and get into Mark's pit. Sure, nothing to it, hack the lock. Hack the fucking lock. With what? Shit, he couldn't even get *that* far, he didn't have a keystrip for the elevators.

His gaze fell on the other unit. He had never turned it on. And it was just a laptop in a console shell, bolted into the desk by the Diversifications cheap-asses.

"Thank you, cheap-asses," he said aloud, and went into the kitchen to see if he could find anything that might serve for tools.

In the end he just chopped away pieces of the desktop with a metal meat tenderizer (thank you, Rediscovery Cuisine), bent back the console shell, and disconnected the larger keyboard and monitor using a butter knife for a screwdriver. The unit had a smaller screen and its own portable keypad folded underneath and an unexpected wealth of extra connections tucked into the battery compartment. A *light-collector* battery, fully charged even after being hidden in the desk, thank you God, or Whoever.

He paused, looking at the other unit still covered by the tablecloth. Right, of course; as soon as he'd unplugged it, the battery had kicked in. To prevent a crash in case of power failure. Except the standard, resident antiviral procedures usually disabled the fail-safe cutoff to the battery as soon as it detected an infection, to keep the virus contained. Keely chuckled grimly. Not this time. Maybe this was Supervirus after all.

The elevator-call panel hotwired almost effortlessly with the penthouse laptop. He watched the activity on the screen impatiently, until he found a car emptying out on ten and called it up so quickly that he was sure he had given himself away. But that wasn't important anymore.

He was still on his way down to sixteen when the laptop screen told him all the other elevators had suddenly quit.

She was sorry she hadn't awakened him. No one should have had to face this kind of traffic alone.

Jammed in on Santa Monica Boulevard, she flipped through the screens on the commuter's nav unit, looking for anything with even a hint of space and movement on it. Or she tried to flip through the screens—the response time from GridLid was so long this morning, she could practically have gotten out of the commuter and checked the streets herself on foot. Almost nothing was moving. Periodically GridLid's usual crisis message marched across the bottom of the screen: DUE TO UNUSUALLY HEAVY TRAFFIC, ALL VEHICLES THAT DO NOT ABSOLUTELY HAVE TO BE ON THE ROADS AT THIS TIME SHOULD PARK WHEREVER LEGALLY PERMISSIBLE UNTIL STREETS CLEAR.

Sure, Jack. Like the fucking *vehicles* were driving *themselves*. She shifted impatiently in the worn, sagging seat. Try and run away from something in L.A. The traffic was so fucking awful, you might as well stay put and face it down.

From the corner of her eye, she saw the GridLid screen flicker.

"Great, you motherfucker," she growled, and tapped the monitor. "Go out on me now, blow a fucking fuse, you think you don't absolutely have to be on the road, is that it?"

The driver in the private car behind her tapped the horn.

The commuter in front of her had rolled forward all of six inches. "Okay, shitheel, okay." She moved up six inches. "No one's gonna cut in front of us, happy now?"

The driver honked again. Irritated, she twisted around in her seat and saw a young guy beckoning to her, looking like he was approaching the thin edge of desperation. She got out of the commuter and went back to him.

"Excuse me, you don't know anything about these navigator units, do you?" he asked. She looked at the car. Private car, not a commuter, with custom everything. Including the nav unit. Full dataline access.

"No more than anyone else," she said. "Why?"

"I'm getting a real funny message on mine. Look." He swiveled the monitor around and sat back so she could see. "It ought to show up again any second."

Even as he spoke, a parade of words cut across the middle of the navigational graphic on the screen. THOUGHT WE TOLD YOU TO GET THIS PILE OF SHIT OFF THE ROAD. Gina gave a short incredulous laugh in spite of herself.

"This is my parents' car, and they've done a lot of customizing to it. The nav unit has a cutaway to full dataline access, and I thought maybe I was getting a crossed signal or something. Because, look—" He thumbed a panel on the body of the unit in the dashboard. "I can't raise any other screens to find any clear streets." He looked up at her with a pleading expression.

"Well, first of all, there ain't any other clear streets. You can't get any other screens because GridLid's running too slow to feed them. You might as well use the cutaway to the dataline and catch *Dear Mrs. Troubles* on FolkNet, or you can watch gridlock footage on *General News L.A.* That answer all your questions?"

"What about that weird message?" he said. "GridLid doesn't send out messages like that, do they?"

She chuckled. "No. But Dr. Fish does. I guess now he makes car calls."

"I'm sorry to bother you," he called after her apologetically as she went back to the commuter. "I haven't been driving very long."

"By the time we get outa this, you'll have been driving for-fucking-ever," she muttered. Dr. Fish in GridLid. More likely Dr. Fish was in the car's nav unit because Mommy and/or Daddy was always downloading hot tips off the free bizboards, going to and from work. Don't wanna waste a precious moment of those waking hours stuck in traffic, gotta do the fucking business in the car.

The nav-unit screen was blank. She banged on the housing with her fist. "Perfect, you son of a bitch. If I could get fucking *men* to go down on me that easy, I'd probably be fucking *mellow* about this!"

One word popped onto the screen.

Gina.

She pulled her hand back, staring at her name.

It's Mark.

She stared, not willing to believe it. The sight of her credit strip sticking out of the slot next to the ignition jumped out at her briefly. How he'd found her, by her little tiny credit allowed for essentials like food and gridlock.

Don't have long, said the screen. It flickered again. *GridLid's had it. Meat, too. Me, too.*

There was a long pause. She reached for the phone on the other side of the monitor, not really knowing whom she intended to call. Moot choice; the phone was dead. Biz-freaks must have been having nervous breakdowns by the six-pack all up and down the street.

This is hard.

Losing her mind, she thought, still holding the useless receiver in both hands.

Video turned it loose. Left body. Turn me off. Take out wires. In my pit.

The screen rolled suddenly. THOUGHT WE TOLD YOU TO GET THIS PILE OF SHIT OFF THE ROAD. That didn't sound much like Mark's style.

The aggressive capital letters faded away, and then a new message came up.

Be there for me.

That sounded like Mark's style. As she watched, the smaller letters melted and ran, becoming a line flowing across the screen, first in a smooth, lopsided sine pattern and then sharpening into spikes. She recognized her own brain wave as she'd seen it on the screen in her pit. It changed suddenly, the spikes suddenly shooting up and down in a frenzied scribble before the screen went dark again.

"Ah, Christ," she muttered.

The commuter in front of her had moved up another few

inches. In the rearview mirror she could see the kid in the custom-job staring down at his dashboard worriedly.

"Fuck it," she said. She cut the motor, climbed out of the commuter, and went back to the kid behind her.

"Listen," she said. "I gotta go to the bathroom. I left the thing in neutral. Just nudge it with your bumper every time you want to move up, and it'll go."

His eyes bugged out. "But that's illeg—"

The driver behind him stuck his head out the window. "Hey, bitch, where do you think you're going? Hey, get back in that thing, you can't leave it there—" Horns began honking as she walked briskly toward West Hollywood.

". . . and reports that GridLid is in the grip of one or more crippling viruses can be neither confirmed nor denied."

Sitting in the media bar looking up at the big screen, Gabe sighed, heavy-lidded. His apprehension on waking had faded into weary bewilderment when he'd realized he was alone in Mark's apartment. He hadn't thought Gina had gone out to pick up a couple of fancy breakfasts at the Greek joint on the corner. The message on the monitor had told him pretty much everything he needed to know.

Didn't your mother ever tell you never to fucking *volunteer?*

Have to take that up with Mom, he thought sourly. Now he was sitting on a bar stool at eleven-thirty in the morning, not caring that he was incredibly late for work, sipping bad coffee in elbow-to-elbow isolation with a rather questionable clientele. Possibly more questionable than Gina Aiesi, though he wouldn't have laid any bets.

He should have figured on gridlock, the way his luck had been running. The only way to end a bad day was to screw up the start of the next one.

Fuck it up, you mean. People who are afraid of profanity are afraid of life.

I'm not afraid of life. I just don't know where it is anymore.

Not last night, but the other night, when he'd been sure that everything they said to each other was yet another secret of the universe. You could get pretty high up in the stupid-sphere, thinking shit like that, and it was a long way down without a parachute.

This morning he knew next to nothing, and he'd already forgotten some of that. Mental gridlock.

Mental gridlock probably looked something like what he was seeing on the screen now. From the Hollywood Freeway back to La Cienega, Santa Monica Boulevard looked like a long, narrow parking lot.

"Hey," said the hostile-looking man next to him. "Do we have to watch this? Why don't you put on some porn?" He was wearing a too-tight yellow plastic overall with a red noose around his neck.

The bartender sneered. "What's the matter, you never heard of gridlock porn?"

"It ain't porn unless it's on a porn channel," the guy said.

"It's obscene enough for me," said the woman on Gabe's right. She was stirring a bright purple drink with a broken light pen. "Turn it up, will you?" she asked the bartender.

". . . sudden unexplained fluctuation in the timing of traffic signals, combined with what seems to have been faulty transmission from GridLid Navigation to drivers. GridLid has experienced occasional communications breakdowns in the past but never transmission of erroneous data."

The camera panned up and down the seemingly endless line of cars before the pov cut to a shot of the traffic on the Hollywood Freeway, moving along smoothly beneath the Santa Monica overpass.

"This incident is also remarkable for the selectiveness of the traffic-signal glitches and the data errors from GridLid. No other part of the greater Los Angeles area was involved, though of course other arteries and roads will be affected as traffic is diverted from Santa Monica Boulevard during clear-out, which some say will last all day and well into the evening."

Another cut, to a chain-reaction fender bender near La Cienega. "No serious injuries were reported in this collision involving over two dozen vehicles, though several older drivers were taken to local hospitals via Life-Flyer helicraft. No word on their condition yet, nor was any reason given as to why police insisted that they be sent for treatment.

"Also impossible to confirm at this time is a rumor claiming that at least one of the drivers involved, identified only as an actor from West Hollywood, was on-line with her or his vehicle at the time of the accident. Donner Moquin of the Motor Vehicle Bureau stated that although there were no licensed vehicles with that capability registered with the bureau, the modification is not impossible."

Cut to a pensive-looking man squinting against the afternoon

sun as he murmured something at a microphone. The sound
came up. ". . . not real complicated. You'd need an extra set
of connector wires, but you can get those from any supplier,
they don't have to be brand name. It's an easy wiring job, the
same thing they do for the airline pilots, minus the wing stuff.
We looked into it, sure, in case the public demand rose for it,
but all we had is requests for information. I myself feel it's a
good idea"—he paused to laugh a little—"but my husband
says I've always been kind of car-crazy anyway—"

"So what is that supposed to mean, on-line with the vehicle?"
said the man in the overall querulously. "The goddamn socket
stuff?"

The bartender pushed a dataline dial-up unit across the bar
at him. "Why don't you call and ask for a clarification? We'll
put it on your tab." The man pushed the unit back with a
mutter.

The screen was showing another long pan of the accident.
"Traffic signals are still dead on Santa Monica Boulevard,"
stated a new female voice-over with a flatter, more serious
tone. "Word has just reached us that the affected area seems
to be spreading, onto Sunset Boulevard, starting at the point
where Santa Monica merges into Sunset before Sunset goes
into downtown L.A. Trouble is also reported on La Cienega,
where traffic lights are malfunctioning. Officials have refused
to confirm or deny that L.A. is only a few minutes away from
a full red-line transportation emergency. They also still refuse
to comment on the rumor that the problems are due to a
specialized 'traffic-jammer virus' inserted into the GridLid timing system by hacker-vandals."

The screen was now showing a small group of what looked
to Gabe like twelve-year-olds, who seemed to be both pleased
with and disdainful of the camera focused on them.

"Hackers didn't do this," said the designated speaker, a
sharp-faced girl too skinny and dirty for her own good. She
stood sideways in front of the other four or five kids, hugging
herself tightly. A slivery chip dangled on a tiny chain from one
earlobe. "No freakin' way hackers did this," she added belligerently, her eyes darting toward whoever was working the
camera. Minicam free-lancer interview, Gabe thought, some
would-be stringer in the right place at the right time; there
was none of the wobble characteristic of the cheaper minicams,
but the perspective gave it away. The kids looked just a little
too big in the cam's eye.

The spokeskid seemed to listen to something for a moment. "Well, you know, this is our town, too, we like to get around it, we got places we like to go. That's how come I'm so sure no hackers did this. If there even *is* any virus. Every freakin' time something goes wrong, people say, 'Oh, must be some hacker doing the virus thing again.' They like to blame us for all their problems. Prolly the software just gave out all at once. You people, you watchamacallits—"

"Mainstream," offered a slightly older kid standing behind her, leaning forward and then slipping back and clapping a hand over her mouth, as if she'd said something embarrassing.

"Yeah, you mainstreams, you straights, none of you maintain your software *or* hardware like you should. I mean, you treat it like my parents treat each other, it's no goddamn wonder it goes out once in a while. You don't do no maintenance or updating, I'm surprised the whole place ain't blacked out—"

Abruptly the picture started to break up into static and zigzag lines. The man in the yellow jumpsuit gave a short disgusted laugh. "Shit, one of their little friends must be watching and did that on purpose."

"Probably set it up themselves," muttered the woman on Gabe's right. "Set it up in the system to go off when they said certain trigger-words, like the other one—"

"Trigger-word viruses are more trouble than they're worth," Gabe said, without thinking. "Half the time there's such a wide margin for variation in inflection, volume, and tone that the damned things go off too easily and too soon. Or the triggers are so precise that they won't go off if there's even a half-decibel variation. The simple stuff, a counting fuse or a timer, is always better. You can tell genuine hacker work. It's always as simple as possible. . . ."

His voice trailed off as he realized he had the attention of everyone sitting at the bar.

"Really," said the woman next to him. "You an authority? Maybe one of those reformed delinquents all grown up, or are you maybe one of those lawyers that gets them off with a slap on the wrist all the time?"

"Just something I heard somewhere," he said lamely, looking around. "On some program about it." He squirmed a little. It was, as Sam would have said, a cold, cold house.

The screen suddenly popped into focus on a studio anchor setup. "We apologize for the interruption, but the Hollywood node seems to have gone down. The cause of the trouble is unknown at this point, but dataline service crews are already at work on it. Signals are currently being routed through the West Hollywood node or the Century City node."

The anchor cleared her throat abruptly. "Two minutes ago traffic control declared a limited traffic emergency for all of Hollywood within the boundaries of Mulholland Drive to the north, the San Diego Freeway to the west, the Hollywood Freeway to the east, and the Harbor Freeway to the—"

There was a mass exclamation of disbelief from everyone at the bar. "*Limited?*" somebody down at the other end said. "Are they shitting? That pretty much paralyzes anyone trying to get into or out of."

"If they can still move around in Canoga Park and Reseda, it's considered limited," said a hard, sarcastic voice. "But if you can't get out of San Berdoo, it's all-out meltdown." A few people laughed at that, but the laughter was thin and nervous. Gabe shifted uncomfortably on his stool. He was well within the area the anchor had described, and it occurred to him that he had no idea how he was going to get to Diversifications, or anywhere else.

". . . unofficial report that at least one driver removed by helicraft had suffered a stroke, causing the multivehicle collision. We are waiting for official confirmation on that from the hospital." The anchor paused, leaving a thudding two-second interval of dead air as she looked at something off-cam.

"In other news two people were found dead in unexplained circumstances in their Santa Monica home. Police refused to release many details concerning the deaths, but sources close to the scene say they believe the pair were found still connected to direct neural interface equipment, which has been rising in popularity since it was legalized in the States. Police are investigating but refuse to speculate whether the people, whose names are still being withheld, were the victims of foul play."

The anchor paused, frowning. "Word has just arrived concerning a situation at Los Angeles International Airport. All travel in or out of the airport has been shut down. No reason has been given. A jumper from the Bay Area scheduled to land at LAX was diverted to an emergency landing strip at the Van Nuys Airport and seems to have landed safely. That's all we have on that." The anchor looked a little disgusted, appeared to listen to someone or something off-cam again. Things were pretty loose at the local station today, Gabe thought. He had an uncomfortable feeling that something was off-kilter with the fabric of daily life in general, not just GridLid or the dataline.

Off-kilter, sure. What happened was, you weren't expecting to wake up alone this morning.

"One of our stringers has just managed to get in touch with us from the hospital," said the anchor suddenly. "Apparently, phone service is a little spotty—"

"Phone service is *what?*" said the man in the jumpsuit.

"—the individual being treated for stroke was on-line with her vehicle. Repeat, we have confirmation that the individual treated for stroke *was* on-line with her vehicle and was the apparent cause of the crash on Santa Monica Boulevard—"

The image on the screen exploded into mostly white static. Somewhere behind the snow dark shapes seemed to be moving around, as if a picture were trying to break through the interference.

"Must be your hardware," the man on Gabe's left said. "On-line L.A.'s *General News never* goes down."

The bartender picked up a small remote and switched to the general menu. Of the five other channels listed, one was marked off the air, and the other four were showing either movies or series episodes.

"No other screens?" said the woman with the purple drink, tapping her broken light pen on the rim of the glass. "What kind of media bar is this?"

"The other two screens crapped out this morning before we opened," the bartender said, and pointed at the ceiling. "I raised 'em up out of the way until I can get them fixed. Repair's supposed to come this afternoon and take care of them."

"I don't think they'll be here," Gabe murmured.

"It's like a quake, you know? Nothing's going right." The bartender flipped back to the top of the network menu and selected Cultural, getting another list beginning with Dance and ending with Museums, Children. She moused halfway down to Street/Open Air Performance and thumbed a button on the remote. Instantly the screen showed a dance group flinging themselves along the line of cars on Santa Monica Boulevard.

"God, I just *hate* street ballet," said the woman on Gabe's right. "It's *so* corny."

"Not the point. We're getting footage of the boulevard

again," the bartender said. "No commentary, but we do our best."

There was a clicking sound. "Testing . . . test . . . all right. To those who may be watching, on-line L.A. local news is commandeering this channel temporarily. Due to technical difficulties we are unable to continue broadcasting on our usual—"

There was a burst of static on the speakers, but the picture remained clear. The ballet dancers were far down the line of cars; several of the nearest vehicles were still occupied. People waved from the windows, and someone held up a hastily hand-printed sign: *DON'T WAIT UP FOR ME, HARRY!*

"—power outages, brownouts, and scrambled signals all over the general area and possibly beyond," said a new voice, very young and very nervous. "As far as we can tell now, L.A. is effectively cut off communicationswise from the surrounding region and from the rest of the state. No quakes have been reported anywhere in the west. Authorities suspect some kind of vandalism but have been unable to trace the trouble to anything like an, uh, original, uh, source—" There was a full ten seconds of dead air while the cam panned up and down the line of cars.

What's wrong with this picture, Gabe thought suddenly. The machinery of the city was melting down, and they were all just watching it happen on TV. He wondered if Gina had reached Diversifications yet, if she'd found Mark. He had the very strong feeling that he should get out of there and try to make it to West Hollywood any way he could, even if he had to walk over the hoods of gridlocked vehicles like stepping-stones. At the same time he was afraid to leave an available working screen. Something told him he might not find another very soon.

The young voice on the dataline began repeating the news about the impending gridlock, the collision, and the driver who had had a stroke. On-screen the image began to ripple a bit, as if it were melting, and the colors of the vehicles began shifting toward whichever end of the spectrum they were closest to. The body of one vehicle started to pulse in a way that reminded Gabe of breathing.

Disturbed, he looked away from the screen, rubbing the back of his neck tiredly. He felt a bit odd, a bit fuzzy mentally, as if he had just woken up. Without warning the memory of the crazy rock star with the cape popped into his mind, and somehow he just knew the pulsing of the shadows on the cape and the image of the vehicle on-screen were identical.

Which had to be ridiculous, since one had nothing to do with the other, and even if it had, it was just an image on a screen, just a screwed-up image on a high-res external screen, not something that could affect you in any real, lasting way. There were no patterns produced from any screen that could do anything more than hypnotize the susceptible, and that was easily counteracted; there was no *picture* from any source that could actually *hurt* anyone—

"Change for the machines."

The voice was so quiet that Gabe wasn't sure at first that he hadn't imagined it. He turned to the woman on his right, feeling cold. "What did you say?" he asked.

She was staring at the screen as if she were seeing signs and wonders unfold on it. Something flickered at the edge of his peripheral vision, and he turned to look. It was no more than a fast flash, something just beyond the upper limit of sublim-inal, but the whole picture was vivid in his mind, some strange body of water and a stony shore, and the soft silhouette of someone standing on it. The image seemed strangely familiar, but he was sure he had never seen it before. For that matter, he wasn't sure he had seen it just now.

"Damned Schrödinger world," the woman muttered, run-ning a hand over her head. "Never know till you look, do you? Never know who it'll be, waiting there for you . . ."

Gabe was about to ask her if she had sockets when she fell backwards off the stool, hitting the floor flat on her back.

"God, I *hate* drunks," said the man on Gabe's other side as several people rushed to the woman's side.

"She isn't drunk," Gabe said. He wanted to go to her, but he was frozen in place, watching as someone lifted her head. One wide staring eye was fiery red, and a thin line of blood trickled from her nose. A man with gilded hair turned to look at Gabe suspiciously.

"You *hit* her?"

Gabe shook his head. "No. I never touched her. She just— fell."

The woman's eyes focused on him briefly then, and her lips moved, silently forming one word before she went limp.

"I think she's dead," someone said nervously.

"Call an ambulance," said someone else.

"No, call Life-Flyer."

"Call the *cops*. *They'll* call Life-Flyer."

"She's got sockets," Gabe said. "Look in her wallet or purse, if she's got one. There should be a card."

"Right here," said the man with the gilded hair, holding up her wrist. There was an old-fashioned ID bracelet around it. "Says she's socketed and allergic to chocolate. I don't think she's had any chocolate." He frowned up at Gabe. "You think her sockets blew up?"

"I don't know," Gabe lied, his voice faint. He kept his back to the screen, imagining himself on the floor next to the woman in roughly the same condition. It could have happened; why hadn't it?

He had to get to Diversifications. The bartender was calling the police, or trying to, as he slipped off the bar stool, made his way through the people to the door, and waded out into the gridlocked city.

28

He'd had no idea there was so much infection floating around in the system, coming in, going out, drifting like ocean-going mines or sitting camouflaged in various pockets and hidey-holes.

What he had sometimes thought of as the arteries and veins of an immense circulatory system was closer to a sewer. Strange clumps of detritus and trash, some inert and harmless, some toxic when in direct contact, and some actively radiating poison, scrambled along with the useful and necessary traffic. The useful and necessary things were mostly protected, though the protection made them larger, to the point where some of them were slower and more unwieldy than they should have been.

There was an ecology here, gradually becoming more and more unbalanced, polluted, and infected. Ecological disaster had been inevitable, even before the stroke had been released into the system; there was no way around it. It would be universal. Computer apocalypse, a total system crash.

And he would cease to be.

He had escaped that fate once by leaving the worn-out, failing meat, only to find the same thing creeping up on him Out Here.

He wouldn't let it happen. He couldn't. He would warn them, show them somehow, make them stop before the whole system went down in a firestorm. God damn them all, he thought furiously, God damn them all for doing what they always did, on every level in every way they could. Whole portions of the physical world had yet to be reclaimed from the unusable, unlivable state that negligence and malevolence had consigned them to, and the fuckers *still* didn't get it, they *still* didn't understand you weren't supposed to shit where you ate.

Nor did you, when you were meat and busy getting toxed. The thought came at him from nowhere and everywhere, in the simultaneous container and content that he was now. He had a moment of shame for his own blindness.

He spread his awareness out cautiously. It was like being in many places at once, taking in the information that came at the speed of light and working in nanoseconds as matter-of-factly as he had once worked in minutes and hours to shape it into something understandable for himself. He was already accustomed to the idea of having multiple awarenesses and a single concentrated core that were both the essence of self. The old meat organ would not have been able to cope with that kind of reality, but out here he appropriated more capacity the way he once might have exchanged a smaller shirt for a larger one.

Gina's identification flashed at him as soon as it entered the system; in less time than it would have taken him to draw a breath, he had located her, but contacting her had been far more difficult. The little one had splattered itself unevenly through the traffic system, jumping in through the double-headed receivers that accommodated both the dataline and GridLid. But in the larger context of the city, the little stroke had to work harder, at least for the time being. That most of its capacity was taken up with the act of infection made it less of a threat to him; at least he had been able to contact her for a few seconds.

It was a disappointing contact; he couldn't be sure she had believed, and he had been unable to offer anything to prove it. But if he could make her go to his old body in the pit, then he wouldn't have to depend only on the kid in the penthouse, where his awareness had chopped off suddenly and permanently not long before he'd found Gina.

Neither the kid nor Gina would have understood that, how he could have been absent from the penthouse and yet still there in a way. It wasn't something he really understood himself, but that didn't matter now. That part of his awareness was as lost to him as any amputated limb, which had to mean the kid was lost to him, too.

It was up to Gina now to keep the Big One contained in the flesh. Every bit of the little one Out Here in the bigger context was waiting for it. And wherever it was awaited, it would go.

Even as he realized that, he realized his presence had made it worse. To escape being devoured by it, he would have to spread further, possibly amputating a great deal of himself, confined in some other location, losing his enlarged awareness.

Or perhaps enlarging himself that much would dissipate him, fragment him into many little aspects of the same program, each one self-contained and out of contact with the other. Perhaps then he would lose his memory and forget that he had been human once.

He was still wondering what would become of him when he felt the first shock wave, followed by the last message he would ever receive from the meat.

She didn't really understand what she was seeing at first. Mark was lying on the mat on the floor of the pit pretty much as she'd left him. At the console was some very young kid she'd never seen before, studying the screen so intently between taps on the keyboard (entering something? just browsing?) that he was completely unaware of her standing up on the catwalk. Moving quietly, Gina climbed down the ladder.

The kid saw something on the screen, and his fingers danced rapidly over the keys. He leaned toward the speaker. "Disconnect now?" he asked. Apparently the answer was no; the kid shook his head and muttered something. Probably another fucking child-prodigy doctor bused in to Diversifications' home implant program. This one had the sense to see all wasn't well, but it was too fucking little, too fucking late.

Gina moved along under the catwalk, skirting around to approach Mark behind the kid's back. Ripping the wires out of his head would either bring him out of it in a hurry or blow him up. *Video turned it loose. Turn me off. Take out wires. Be there for me.*

She looked down at Mark's inert body, still curled up on the mat. *Shoulda kissed him when you had the chance, back in Mexico*, she thought suddenly. *Back in Mexico, when he first put the wires in when you were there. If you'd leaned down then, put your mouth on his, he might have stayed. Because after that nothing could pull him back, not love, not sex, not you. Not nothing, not no-how.*

Thou shalt not fear?

The long, greying brown hair had fallen back from his gaunt face as if he were already dead. *We don't grieve for what might have been in rock n'roll. We just keep rockin' on.*

This ain't rock'n'roll. It ain't been rock'n'roll for a long fucking time. This is business, and money, and change for the machines, but it ain't rock'n'roll.

The kid was still busy at the console, running some kind of

complicated program that showed mostly numbers in three columns on the monitor. She knelt down next to Mark and put her fingers gently against his cheek. His face was comfortably warm. She lifted his head and wrapped the wires around her other hand, getting a good grip on them.

"*What are you doing?!*"

She jumped, nearly yanking the wires out of his head right then. "I'm taking care of him," she said. "Get your ass back to Medical and pretend you never saw this. If he dies, I'll turn myself in."

"I'm taking care of him," he said. "I'm overriding within the program for the connections. If I can make them let go, we might get him to a doctor before he strokes out big."

She felt her mouth drop open. "Who the fuck are you? Whadda you mean, 'stroke out big'?"

Mark's body gave a jerk.

"Aw, *shit!*" the kid yelled and lunged for the console. "Disconnect! Disconnect *now!*"

Mark jerked again, and his head flopped out of her grasp as he rolled over onto his back, quivering and twitching. Bubbles of saliva bloomed on his lips; his left arm flailed, slapping against her thighs.

"Disconnect! Disconnect!" the kid was yelling desperately, and Mark kept twitching and bucking as she tried to get her hand free of the wires. She could feel how they were pulling at his head, and she had the horrible thought that if they pulled away now, they'd turn his skull inside out.

"Yank them!" the kid shouted.

Mark was flailing like a fish drowning in air. All the shit he'd ever gotten toxed on, and he'd never had a seizure until now. She straddled his chest and took the wires in both hands, intending to yank his head off if she had to.

Abruptly he opened his eyes, and she knew that he could see her there, sitting on him, holding the wires, about to reel him in the hard way. Underneath her his body was still twitching a little, but the energy was going. She could feel it.

The faded green bloodshot eyes moved back and forth as if he were fixing her face in his mind.

Say it, whispered a voice in her mind.

She took a firmer grip on the wires; his head lifted slightly, but his eyes never left hers.

Say it. He wants to hear it. He always did, he was just always too toxed or too far out in the stupidsphere to know it.

The whites of his eyes were getting redder. The wires in her hand were very warm, fever temperature. On his lips, foam thickened into a stream that ran down to coat his chin, and she wanted to look away, but he wouldn't let her. She gave the wires a hard yank; his head dipped forward in a grotesque nod, driving his chin down onto his chest, but the connections held.

"Yank them!" the kid yelled at her.

She gave another hard pull. Mark nodded. *Yes.*

Say it!

"Yank them!"

Yes.

Say it!

His eyes were all red now, she could barely see any of the old green in them at all.

"Yank them, goddamn it!"

Yes!

Say it!

"*You stupid fuck-up!*" she yelled.

Mark smiled. *Good enough.* His eyes closed, and she felt his body go limp under her.

She lifted him under the shoulders with one arm, still holding the connections with her other hand, getting off him so she could cradle him on her lap. The kid was going, "Oh, Jesus, oh, Jesus," at the console, and she had the vague idea that in a little while she would get up and bash the kid's brains out on the desk, put her foot through the monitor, and then head on down to Rivera's office and show him how to do the funky chicken while she crushed his windpipe. In a little bit. After she was sure Mark was resting.

One red tear trickled swiftly down his left cheek, dropping away from the side of his face. She shifted position slightly, and the blood suddenly gushed from his nose, painting his mouth and chin red, saturating his shirt.

The connections let go, then; all at once they dropped from the sockets, and she was holding a fistful of eight wires in a limp bouquet. She had to force her cramped fingers against her leg to make them unbend and drop them.

Musta hurt. Musta felt like I gave you a hot one with a set of brass knuckles. His eyes, she saw, weren't completely closed after all. He might have been nodding out on a dose he'd misjudged. *Yah, we did that often enough—me keeping watch while you were toxed out, waiting to see if you were gonna turn blue or purple or some other stupid fucking color*. His head sagged toward her, and a red tear diverted across the bridge of his nose and dropped.

Okay, I didn't say it. But you knew what I meant, didn't you, you stupid fuck-up. Yah, you did. I could tell. So don't you fucking try to lie to me, because I know you did.

She had a vague sense of time passing, but it was unimportant. *Let it pass, let it go around me and him now. We been racing for the last twenty-some-odd, fuck it, we're taking a break now. Taking a break.*

Sometime later the lights flickered. She thought at first she had imagined it, but they flickered again. Annoyance began to fill the void in her mind. Christ, did everything have to fuck up at once, did she have to put up with stupid shit like brownouts when she had more important things to think about, like how she was going to get through the rest of her life?

When she felt the touch on her shoulder, she lashed out with a snarl.

"I'm sorry," the kid said quietly. "I'm really sorry, but we got a big problem here."

He was pulling at her arms, gently but firmly, trying to make her let go of Mark.

"Jump *back*," she snarled, and he let go of her.

"We didn't do it," the kid said. "It's out."

The lights flickered again.

It came as a small tremor followed by an instantaneous jump in the level of every infection. As if a loose infestation of rats had suddenly been transformed into a battalion of terrorists. The intelligence that drove it was different from his own, brutish in some ways but with the sophistication of an evolved mechanism capable of adapting itself at will.

There was nothing he could do now, he could never stand against something like that. It had been made for him in the first place, and he would draw it to himself just by continuing to be.

New instincts took over for him, in lieu of fight-or-flight. He backed far off, damped down before it could sense all of him, retreating to a level of activity that might have been the equivalent of a camouflaged soldier melting into the surrounding jungle. It did not pursue; as far as it was concerned, he was not there, but only for the time being. Eventually it would achieve a level where it could sense him in his new state, but at the moment it still had its limits, it was still on the other side of a certain threshold, the side called Finite.

And he still had a rabbit hole; a little altered for the new circumstances of his existence, but there. It was the last exit, the way out where there was no way out. If he took it, the result would be pretty much the same as a systemwide crash-and-burn, from his perspective—he would cease to exist on this level. Undoubtedly he would continue to be as traveled through the rabbit hole, but the hole itself would be winking out of existence one step behind him. As if he'd swallowed himself and continued to swallow himself forever.

If that was really existence, what kind was it?

Meanwhile the thing was moving through the system, lashing out, absorbing, growing. Once he might have wanted to think of a fancy word for it, but in the system a thing was what it was, or it was not anymore, and this thing did not alter in nature. It was a virus, but with a most important difference: this one knew where it was, and what it was, and *that* it was. This one was alive.

So the problem was to keep from getting sick. Or rather, sicker. It still amazed him how sick he was—how sick the system was—and yet everything could continue to operate. He remembered his old existence as meat. Weren't there certain kinds of infections—bacteria, rather—that were useful, even vital?

He would not have thought of this at all if he hadn't come across some old notebooks Dr. Fish had left behind when he'd bailed out. He knew Art Fish must have sensed him there, at least in a passing way. Now and then he could feel a vibration or an echo of a sympathetic nature, a resonance, but no acknowledgment as such. Dr. Fish was no longer making house calls, but he could see where Dr. Fish had gone, approximately. Going there himself had been an option lodged inactively at the rear of his thoughts, unconsidered until the last message from the meat came through to him.

Suddenly he was there with her in the pit, looking up into her face while she held the wires in both hands and tried to yank them out. If he had been there, he might have made some effort to tell her she had arrived just that little bit too late, because it had already begun in his brain, the Big One. In a way he had been there with her, just enough of him to constitute a definite presence. Not unlike the way he had been during his last days as meat.

What surprised him, looking at her face now, was how visible her thoughts were, and always had been. He'd just never *seen* before, never comprehended. Her desire for him was not just in her face, it *formed* her face, was formed *of* her face, and he knew she'd been thinking of how it had been in Mexico, and she was sitting on him not just to do what he'd asked her to do, but because she wanted to touch him as much as possible.

He found the idea repellent now, her meat pressing his own. They could have been two gutted sides of beef brushing against each other on their way through a processing plant, for all the real contact it afforded. And she didn't understand, he realized. That was a first; she'd always understood him, or so he'd thought from the way she'd always been there to catch him when he fell. But maybe the fall had been what she'd understood, the only thing she'd understood, and he hadn't fallen this time.

It would have broken his heart if there'd been any heart to break.

If he could have gone back to those moments and reactivated the meat, if the brain hadn't been too small and too worn to accommodate more than mere presence, he would have done it long enough to beg her to join him in the system, just for a little while, just to try it and see how far apart incarnation had kept them.

And then he was looking at Gina with what felt like a universe of knowledge within him, everything from every part of the system, databases that outlined every face of human behavior, delineated every emotion, defined every word by tone of human voice, and told every story, all scanned from the countless thousands that had passed through to be simulated, packaged in incidents called *commercials* and *releases* and *videos*, and more, sequences called *news*, *talk shows*, *episodes*. One picture could not tell all the stories, but every picture told a story. Every bit of it converged on him, enlarged the context of his vision, and suddenly it was as if he were looking into Gina as much as at her.

Joy surged within his configuration, to see so deeply into her, even though she was not on-line with him, even if it was after the fact. Moments later he seemed to plummet, out of balance because she wasn't there and there could be no reciprocation. The unfairness of it was truer pain than anything he'd ever felt incarnate.

Then he realized that giving such energy to his feelings

would take him back into the virus's visible spectrum, and he damped down again, holding Gina's last moments in deep reserve (*You stupid fuck-up*; even the merest shade of his own presence could translate that with ease now) as he searched out the buried areas he might not have noticed at a higher energy level. They were deceptively small, nothing more than blips unless he moved carefully along a certain pathway in a particular point of view, and then they opened up like sudden blossoms.

Eventually he came upon Dr. Fish's Answering Machine and knew it was the thing he wanted, the exit Dr. Fish had taken, but the way out was barred to him as he was now. Still holding tight to Gina, he worked himself around, mimicking the form of the Answering Machine itself, and left himself as a message, hanging fire in camouflage.

In another time something came and got him.

"Get up, Sam," Fez said urgently. She tried to focus on him, but he was shaking her too hard.

"What? What is it?" she said, forcing her eyes open. It seemed as if she'd gone back to bed only a few minutes before.

"There's bad news, and there's worse news. Something's happened. L.A.'s gone."

"It was right where we left it," she mumbled sleepily, and then it registered on her. "Wait a minute." She pulled away from him, blinking. "What else?"

"I think we lost Art with it."

29

The security guard who had replaced the receptionist at the desk in the corporate lobby told him he shouldn't bother; there were no elevators working, and the building was emptying out. "Unless you really *want* to walk up sixteen flights," the guard added. "Probably meet the next wave coming down, and they'll sweep you all the way to the bottom again anyway."

"I'll take my chances," Gabe said, and sneaked a look at the monitors in the desk. They were all dark.

"Surveillance is down. Can't get anything but some kinda weird snow," said the guard, holding up a walkie-talkie. "Forward into the past."

"Probably." Gabe headed down the hall, fingering the key to the freight elevator in his pocket. More than likely it was in use by others like himself who had acquired a key and failed to return it, but at least it wasn't on-line.

Contrary to what the guard had said, he met no one going the other way down the hall or coming out of the stairwell, so he was able to slip off to the freight area unobserved. But it gave him a bad feeling anyway.

The double doors to the Common Room resisted his push and then gave like a broken mechanism. Gabe hesitated, hoping no one was there, and then spotted LeBlanc. She was sitting at the same table where he'd sat the day she had come in to tell him Gina had been about to jump off the roof, in the same way, with her back to the rest of the room, watching the screens in the wall. Except now there was nothing on the screens but the strange pulsing shadows.

Gabe had another brief flash of the lake and the stony shore before he managed to block out the sight of the monitors. "LeBlanc?" he called, approaching her slowly. "Bonnie, are you all right?"

He moved around in front of her, keeping his back to the

333

wall. The expression on LeBlanc's round face was one he had always associated with victims of especially grisly accidents who found themselves staring at the empty place where an arm or a leg had been. Her eyes had something wrong with them; it was as though they were no longer actually working in tandem, yet they moved together when she finally focused on him.

"It *would* be you," she said. Her voice was thick with effort. She shuddered a little, blinked, and seemed to refocus. "Ah, God, Gabe, you're in it, too, aren't you? Or it's in you, I should say."

His acute awareness of the pulsing shadows on the screens behind him intensified, becoming almost painful. "I guess maybe it is, Bonnie."

"Change for the machines." She sighed heavily. "That's all we've ever done is change for the machines. But this is the last time. We've finally changed enough that the machines will be making all the changes from now on."

He took her hands and tried to pull her to her feet. "We'll go down to Medical—"

"Forget it." She pulled away from him. "Medical was one of the first places it went, it's all changed there, too." With both hands she felt her head all over, as if it were made of eggshell. "The only place to go now is into the context. If you can find it. Between the context and the content, between the mainline and the hardline, falls the shadow. Isn't that how it reads?" LeBlanc made a face. "If it doesn't, it should. I don't have much longer. The shadow will fall, and I'll fall with it. That was what it all meant, you know, why Valjean took Dinshaw to the terrace. Because of the fall. *He* fell with her. Gina." She laughed a little, but her eyes were pleading. " 'If you can't fuck it, and it doesn't dance, eat it or throw it away.' I hope you can dance, Gabe, and if you can, I hope you can dance fast enough, because here it comes—"

She looked startled for a moment. Then her body gave a violent jerk, and she fell off the chair.

"Bonnie?" Gabe crouched beside her and raised her head. Her eyes stared blindly, her right pupil a pinpoint and her left a gaping cavern. A pulse beat twice in her temple and stilled.

Nausea sent the world sideways. Gabe sat down heavily, clutching his head with one hand. The sockets—

His thoughts raced, blurred, quick-focused, and blurred again. He squeezed his eyes shut and waited for it to happen, whatever it was. Maybe it would come like a swift kick in the head, or maybe a pickax, or a hot punch in the face. . . .

Suddenly he had a startlingly clear image of the lake; he was looking across it to where someone was standing on the stony shore, just starting to turn around to face him. A sharp thrill of fear ran him through, and then he found himself blinking at the silent Common Room. He had almost seen who it was on the shore; almost. The image had vanished too quickly.

LeBlanc hadn't moved. "Bonnie?" he said again. The Common Room seem to swallow up his voice. He pushed himself upright and stumped over to the emergency panel near (*change for*) the machines.

"Security," he said, hitting the panel with the side of his fist. "Medical, anybody—there's a woman up here who's hurt—" He looked over his shoulder at LeBlanc, caught a glimpse of the screens, and looked away quickly, in spite of the fact that they were pulling at his vision with a force that was all but physical. "Hurt or dead. Can someone come up here?"

There was a burst of static from the speaker above the panel, and he thought he could hear a faint voice under it.

"Security or Medical," he said, louder, hitting the panel again. This time the static lasted only a second or two before the speaker went dead.

Gabe looked up, as if he might somehow acquire X-ray vision to see through the building to the upper floors, to sixteen, where his pit was, and LeBlanc's, and Gina's, and Mark's. He touched his forehead; the skin felt no different. *That's funny, I can't feel a bomb in there.*

Something made him look over at LeBlanc again. There was a dark spot growing on the carpet next to her head. Blood was running out of her ears.

He flung himself through the double doors and ran to the freight elevator.

The hall was as silent as the Common Room had been, all of the doors closed. Gabe frowned. They should have been open; the locks were set to release whenever there was even a minor glitch in the building's programs. Fail-safe, to prevent them from being trapped in their pits during a catastrophe.

He went from door to door, trying each one, buzzing for entry, getting no response, not even an indication of whether they were occupied or not. Let them all have gone, he thought, let them all have left the way LeBlanc tried to.

At the end of the hallway, he found Mark's door partly open, and he made himself go in.

It's too hard, Gabe thought, looking down at Mark's body. If he'd stayed in the media bar, he wouldn't have had to see any of this, or listen to the kid talking and talking under the flickering lights. Whoever the kid was; eighteen, maybe nineteen years old, too young to be a doctor. Maybe he was one of Gina's weird rock stars, except he didn't seem quite weird enough. Comparatively speaking, anyway.

The kid reached over and shook his arm. "I said, what's going on out there?"

Gabe looked at him blankly.

"I could only raise the dataline in spots before he, ah, went," the kid said. "Now it's gone altogether."

Gabe turned to Gina. The emptiness in her face was more terrifying than LeBlanc's body. Or Mark's. "What it's like out there . . ." He took a breath. "Probably still like what you saw on the dataline. Except for some things that didn't make the dataline. I was in a newsbar and saw a woman have a stroke, and I'm pretty sure she had sockets, like LeBlanc, down in the Common Room. LeBlanc's dead. Her pit's on this floor, she keeled over and died and—" He cut off, looking at Mark.

Gina's gaze went from him to the kid. "It's out."

"Sure as fuck is," the kid said. "The Big One."

"What's out?" Gabe looked at each of them. "What big one?"

The kid started talking again, and he understood what the kid was saying well enough, it just didn't seem real, more like some scenario out of the *Headhunters* program. If Marly and Caritha had been with him, maybe he'd have been able to buy the idea of that poor, sad, dead mess on the floor being able to send a stroke out of his brain into a net—

"What we've gotta do now," the kid was saying as he packed the laptop connections into a small compartment in the base, "we gotta get all the uncontaminated hardware and software we can carry and get out of here. Out of the main part of the city."

"Maybe there isn't any," Gabe said slowly. "Uncontaminated stuff."

The kid closed the laptop with a snap. "This is."

"How? You had it plugged in." Gabe gestured at the console.

"Ever hear of a stealth program?" The kid's smile was flat. "It's a fooler loop crossed with a mirror. You can crack in anywhere disguised as any input a system is already receiving. I used it on the subroutine for the connection commands—I was trying to disconnect him before he blew, but there was too much noise. The most I could get was a look at the program itself, but he'd disabled it, and I couldn't get it to respond. But there was no contact with the virus. The fooler loop covered the source of the additional input—*my* input—and the mirror made it think my input was its own redundancy." The kid looked to Gina. "It wouldn't have worked for much longer. Eventually the virus would have started comparing the figures—"

The lights flickered again and kept flickering.

"If it cuts the power—" Gabe started.

The kid shook his head emphatically. "It won't. It's just playing. Flexing. It knows that if it cuts the power here, it's dead." His eyes narrowed. "Were you on-line today?"

Gabe glanced at Gina. "No."

"Good. You're uncontaminated, too. Let's pull whatever you've got, hardware, software, everything."

"I've got a console, like this one," Gabe said. "Even if we could get it out of the desk, we couldn't carry it."

"Don't be so sure," the kid said, heading for the ladder. "You might have a laptop in there you don't know about. Come *on*. We have to move *now*."

The kid pried his console housing apart and bent it back, revealing a laptop sitting like a spider amid a collection of rather unsightly peripherals. He disconnected the laptop and pulled it out.

"See, the console's all facade," he said conversationally, as if this were all more normal than normal. "Makes it look like you got a stone-home Rolls. Only thing it really covers up is the scam-jam somebody put over when you got these units in here, and the fact that there ain't nothing the big models can do that a high-capacity laptop with the right connections can't." The kid examined the peripherals quickly. "We could use all this. And the hotsuit and your headmount." His gaze fell on the cape that Gabe had left bunched up next to the desk, and he spread it out on the floor.

"Wait a minute," Gabe said as the kid started piling stuff in the middle of the cape. "The rest of the pits. I want them opened."

The kid paused and looked up at him. "I don't think you really want that, but I said I would, didn't I? Now, what about software? You got anything downloaded to chip from that program with those women? Marly and Caritha, the *Headhunters* stuff, anything?"

Gabe's mouth fell open.

"I knew you as soon as you walked in," the kid told him, flashing a tight little grin. "Recognized your voice. You gotta have a stash. *Anything* could turn out to be useful."

Reluctantly Gabe pulled the lockbox out from under the desk and stuffed chips into his pockets as fast as he could. The kid gathered up the ends of the cape and twisted them together to make a crude sack, slung it over his shoulder and began struggling up the ladder to the catwalk where Gina was waiting by the open door. Gabe followed.

"What the fuck are you doing with *that*?" She backed into the hall, eying the cape with revulsion.

"We'll raid your stuff, and then we'll—" The kid stopped and turned to Gabe. "Hey, did you *walk* up here? The elevators quit while I was on my way down."

Gabe shook his head. "I took the freight elevator. It isn't on-line."

"*Prima.*" The kid looked almost sunny for a moment. "That's our way out. Where's your pit?" he asked Gina.

She jerked her chin at the door. "Loot all you want, but move your ass."

"Entry code?" He pointed at the panel next to the door. Gina tapped the numbered squares in a quick sequence; nothing happened. "Another program bites the dust. Never mind." He put down the sack, produced a butter knife, and pried the panel frame off. Reaching in, he wrapped the exposed wires around his fingers and ripped them out. The locks released, letting the door fall open a crack.

"That's what we call a Luddite hack." He grabbed the cape and went in.

Gabe stared at the panel. " 'Luddite hack.' " He turned away and went to the next door. Dinshaw's pit. He dug in his pockets hurriedly but only came up with a handful of coins. Change for the machines.

"Try this." There was a click, and a knife blade slid out under his nose. Gina flipped it over and offered him the hilt.

"Thanks," he said faintly. She didn't answer; her eyes were two dark holes. But her pupils, thank God, were the same size, and the thought made him almost giddy for a moment. He had the sudden urge to put his arms around her, but the look on her face said that if he made a move toward her, she would move away, and maybe she would keep moving away from him until the distance between them was too great to cross again in one lifetime.

How poetic, Gabe jeered at himself as he took the knife from her, *how poetic and tragic and all that rot. If she only knew how poetic and tragic and all-that-rot you are, she'd forget someone she loves just blew up and died with blood running out of his nose.*

He pried the panel off, ripped out the wires, and pushed through the door.

Dinshaw was hanging just above the console. One of the legstraps on the flying harness was wrapped around her neck in a clumsy noose. The connections streamed down from her head; the other end had pulled free of the console and was still swaying slightly.

The hardware had let go before her skull had; the thought lumbered through Gabe's mind in heavy slow motion, weighing him down so that he couldn't move. Someone was trying to pull him out into the hall again. He caught himself against the doorjamb and slammed his hand against the emergency communications panel. "Security! Someone's been killed up here!" Not even static from the speaker this time.

Gina was forcing him out into the hall, trying to say something to him. He pulled away from her and went to the door directly opposite. Shuet's.

Shuet had apparently been trying to break the connection by trashing the console. One leg of the chair he'd used on it had smashed through the monitor, making Gabe wonder with some faraway, detached area of his mind if Shuet hadn't accidentally electrocuted himself. His vision blurred, and he backed out, unable to bring himself to go down and see if the man lying several feet from the console might still be alive in spite of the stink of singed flesh and hair.

The next pit was empty, and he had a moment of wildly joyful relief before he remembered that it was LeBlanc's.

Silkwood was sitting at his console with his back to the door. Gabe straddled the ladder and slid down to rush over to the man. Just as he touched the back of Silkwood's chair, he saw the connections were still in his head, but he was already pulling the chair around.

Silkwood had bled only a little from the eyes and nose. The majority of the blood came from his still-full mouth and from his hands resting in his lap. They were barely identifiable as hands now; Gabe could see the teethmarks where Silkwood had started on his wrists and forearms.

Only then did the smell hit him full in the face, thick and coppery, coming from Silkwood's lap and the chair and the place under the desk where the blood had made a small lake.

Lake . . .

Gabe's ears began to ring as patches of darkness swam through his vision.

Sometime after that, he found himself out in the hall again. He was sitting on the floor, and someone was pushing his head down between his knees. He tried to raise himself up, and a strong hand forced his head down again. A dark hand; that would be Caritha, he thought woozily. Caritha taking care of him while Marly did a little recon, making sure they wouldn't be ambushed by any headhunters on the way out. If they could find the way out. Costa had told them people had died of old age trying to get out. Marly and Caritha hadn't believed that, but he knew Costa hadn't been exaggerating, because he'd come damned close to it himself, dying of old age trying to escape from the House of the Headhunters and hell, he wasn't out yet, there was no telling because he was on blind-select, so he didn't know whether he was going to die in the end or not, and right now dying of old age in the House of the Head-hunters looked a hell of a lot better than some of the other things you could die from in here—

Someone raised his chin, and he found himself almost nose to nose with Gina. He frowned. Here she was *again*; dammit, he could *not* keep his mind from wandering and dragging her into his simulated realities—

She straightened up, and he saw the kid standing beside her, looking sick and frightened.

"Told you you wouldn't want to do this," the kid said.

"Now do you want to go on with the death trip," Gina said, grabbing the front of his shirt and pulling him to his feet, "or do you want to get the fuck outa here?"

"Where's this freight elevator you used?" the kid asked him.

"Down the hallway past the elevators, then down another. I'll have to show you," Gabe said. Gina grabbed him around the waist and wedged her shoulder under his armpit as they started up the hall, in spite of the fact that his legs were steady and he could obviously walk on his own. *Let it be*, he thought, *if that's the only way she can let you hold her*. The contact felt almost too good. The memory of the one night they had had together flashed into his mind, of waking to find they had settled perfectly, arranged themselves so comfortably around each other that it had been like waking to discover he'd come home, there in Mark's apartment, in the dark.

Halfway down the next hallway, Gina stopped so suddenly he almost fell over.

"What is it?" said the kid.

Gina pointed at one of the doors, not a pit door, but the door to an office, labeled *Manny Rivera* in tasteful black letters. She pulled away from Gabe and went over to it.

What's wrong with this picture? The question echoed like madness in Gabe's head. Absurdly the image of the lake with the stony shore came with it before he pushed it away and reached for her. "Gina—"

She gave him a brief glance before she pushed the door open with one hand and stepped inside. "Rivera, you shit! Do you know what happened out here?"

Gabe went in after her and stopped. Manny was sitting behind his desk, smiling vaguely. The blood had poured from his eyes and nose and mouth, soaking the wrinkle-free white shirt, beading on the soft hand-tailored jacket.

"You shit," Gina whispered.

There was a movement from the table by the window. The Beater was sitting there with the slightly puzzled expression of someone who has just taken a bad blow to the head and is still deciding whether to fall down or not.

"I had an appointment to get fired," the Beater said matter-of-factly. "We were going to eat lunch together, and he was going to fire me. When he let me in, he was on the wires, and he told me he'd never forgive me for laying down my ax and turning it into a biz desk. Then he started to bleed."

Gabe moved cautiously, almost tiptoeing around the desk. All the connections were still in Manny's sockets, and except for spatters of blood, nothing on his desk had been disturbed.

Business as usual. *Things to do today: fire the Beater; after lunch bleed copiously and, probably, die.* All in a day's work.

He touched Manny's shoulder, expecting him to fall out of the chair. Instead, Manny suddenly swiveled around to look at him, and he jumped back.

"You *shit*," Gina shouted; all at once she was standing at the desk. "Do you know what you did, you stone-ass, mother-fucking—"

Manny sprang at her, grabbing her by the throat and dragging her across the desk before Gabe could even register that he'd moved. Gabe went for him, and Manny brought his elbow up directly into his face.

The pain was like a scream, overwhelming, drowning him. He was dimly aware of Gina cursing and struggling, and the kid yelling briefly, a couple of thudding noises. He rolled on the floor, feeling the blood pour out of his nose as he held it with both hands. He got clumsily to his knees and looked up.

Through a blur of tears, he saw that Manny had Gina pinned on the desk while he held something over her face. One of the connections from his own head, Gabe realized, and then understood what Manny meant to do.

He groped for the desk and pulled himself up on it. "Manny," he said.

"Not Manny. Mark," said the Beater, getting up from where he'd fallen on the floor next to the kid.

"Not completely," Manny said, "but more than not by this time, I think. Not completely a stupid fuck-up, either, Gina." Manny smiled, and it was Visual Mark's vaguely dazed and fixed smile. Gabe blinked at him through a fresh wave of dizziness. It was more grotesque than Silkwood, seeing Mark's expression on Manny's face. It was as though Manny had been trying to do an imitation of Mark and somehow become trapped in it. Simulating Mark.

Gina had stopped struggling and was staring up at him. "The problem is, it isn't an idea, it's a stroke. Or maybe a stroke is just Mother Nature's riff on an evil idea," Manny went on, still holding the wire near her head. "Oh, not just evil. *Corrupt*. This is what it looks like, rock'n'roll and big biz. The biz been *Marked*, see, and they're both fucked now. The way it should be. They were right, Gina—if you can't fuck it, and it doesn't dance, eat it or throw it away." His gaze drifted over to Gabe, and the expression on his face changed to vintage

Manny Rivera. Gabe felt his stomach roll over. He couldn't breathe.

Gina's fist shot up, and Manny staggered back against the large wall screen, which came brightly to life as he collapsed on the floor. Gabe stumbled around the desk and collided with Gina.

"Get the kid and come on," she said, giving him a shove. He made a move toward the kid and then saw what was on the screen.

Not the strange pulsing shapes, but the lake with the stony shore. The perspective was moving slowly along the shoreline, and in another moment or two, Gabe knew it would reach the figure standing there, waiting. He wanted to look away, he didn't want to see the figure, he didn't want to find out who it was, but his body wouldn't move. The image on the screen had clamped onto the image in his mind, and the two of them had been meant to come together somehow, they'd been meant to merge because they were really one and the same—

The screen went dark, and he came back to himself in a rush, feeling the blood still dripping from his painful nose.

"I said, get the kid and come on." Gina was standing over Manny, holding the end of the connection she had ripped out of his system. The torn wires looked like crooked insects' legs. She threw it down. "You said it. The hardware would give before his skull did." She looked at the kid, now getting up and rubbing the back of his head. "We should have thought of that, tried ripping it out of the system instead of him."

"Gina—" the Beater started.

"Shut the fuck up. You want to get out of here or not?"

The lights flickered, buzzed, and went out.

The weak early-afternoon light coming through the window by the table filled the office with shadows. Gabe's mind automatically began to make them pulse; he ground his fists into his eyes and then blinked. It was still happening.

"Yah. Me, too." Gina gave him a hard look and turned to the kid. " 'It won't cut the power.' "

"It didn't cut the power," he said shakily. "Just the lights."

"Find me something to burn," Gina said, looking around. "It's gonna be pitch in those fucking hallways."

"Not quite," Gabe said, and pointed. Glowing blue strips ran along the top of the baseboards. "Those are all around the building. They'll last about five hours, maybe longer."

"I'd feel a fuck of a lot better with a searchlight." Gina started rummaging through Manny's desk drawers.

"I doubt if—" Gabe cut off when she came up with a hand-cam. She switched it on, and a narrow high-intensity beam above the lens played briefly across the walls before she shut it off again. He shrugged. "Okay. I feel better, too. Let's go."

Holding Gina's arm, he waded through the pulsing shadows into the hall. As soon as he did, he was glad Gina had found the cam. The blue glow was entirely too unsettling, too much like one of the cheaper fun-house sequences from *House of the Headhunters*.

"Ease the fuck up," Gina whispered, twisting her arm in his grip. "You're breaking my fucking bones."

"Freight elevator," said the kid urgently.

Gabe looked up and down the hall. His sense of direction had suddenly deserted him, leaving him adrift in a glowing blue void. Patches of deeper darkness were swimming through his vision even here, pulsing in a way that was all too familiar. He tried to force them away somehow, but there was nowhere he could look where they were not. He squeezed his eyes shut, and they played on the backs of his eyelids, insistent, compelling, calling to the image deep in his brain, a lake under a gray sky with a stony shore—

"Over here, Ludovic. Look over here. *Now!*"

He turned in the direction of Gina's voice and was blinded by a bright light shining directly into his eyes. It hurt, but at the same time it felt oddly good. The angle of the light changed, and blinking against the afterimages, he could discern Gina's face bathed in part of the beam from the cam.

"Okay now?" she said.

He blinked again. Afterimages still, but no pulsing shadows. "Yah," he said, amazed. "What—ah, how—"

She chuckled grimly. "Easy to see you ain't lived rough. The vermin always scuttle back into their hidey-holes when you turn on the light. Now where the fuck is the freight elevator?" She did something to the cam, and the beam widened, illuminating the corridor all around them.

"That way," he said, pointing, and she pulled him along, holding the cam on her shoulder. "Around the next corner and down at the end of the hall."

They rounded the bend and then stopped so suddenly the kid and the Beater bumped into them from behind, almost knocking the cam from Gina's grasp. Someone was sitting in the middle of the hall.

One hand went up, fending off the light. "Whoa, it's too early or too late for that, don't know which—"

The voice was Clooney's, but the intonations were Mark's. Gabe felt Gina stiffen as she shifted the cam from her shoulder, holding it chest-high with both hands.

"Well." Clooney pushed himself to his feet, still trying to block the light. "Old habits, they do die hard, don't they, Gina. All those things. Change for the machines. If you can't fuck it, and it doesn't dance, eat it or throw it away. And looking for Mark. That's yours, ain't it—looking for Mark. Gotten so now that even when you're not looking for Mark, you're looking for Mark. And finding him."

Clooney shuffled forward a few steps, and the alien smile on his face was only nominally vague. There was a new hardness in it—or maybe that wasn't so new, Gabe thought as his own startlement began to turn toward fear. Maybe hints of it had always been there, something that kept the smile always looking vague to mask what was really at work underneath.

"And now you can find him wherever you look," Clooney went on. "What you've always wanted. Whether you know it or not. You don't, do you? Nah, that's not one of the things you'd care to face, being the way you are, Gina. Laugh it off, break it up, and break it down, that's you. But that doesn't change anything for anybody, least of all you. And I want you. I *want* you."

He got within arm's reach of her, and then she swung the cam up and out, right into Clooney's face. He staggered back, crashed into a wall, and then keeled over facedown.

The kid started to go to him, and Gina stopped him. "He looks okay to me. Come *on*."

As if by some unspoken agreement, they were all suddenly racing for the elevator still gaping open the way Gabe had left it. Or maybe it was just that they were fleeing from Clooney's body, Gabe thought as Gina shoved him into the elevator and played the light from the cam over the empty hall behind them. Nothing there but Clooney, who hadn't moved. Gabe looked away, not wanting to have to see blood pouring from his ears, too, and locked eyes with the kid, who frowned a little and jerked his head at Gina.

Gabe shrugged and reach over to touch her shoulder. "What is it?" he said. "What are you looking for?"

She brushed his hand away, irritated. "What's the matter, you deaf or something?" She turned away from the corridor and went to lean against the wall. "Take it down."

"Wait a minute," said the Beater, looking around at them. "If that's what happened to Rivera, and to that guy, what about everybody else? All those pits—"

"You don't want to know," said the kid, closing the door. "And neither do any of us." He looked at the control panel for a moment and then pressed for the ground floor.

They rode all the way down in silence and went out an emergency exit into the chaos that was no longer really a city.

30

A few hours after Art disappeared, Sam and Rosa were picking their way through the human debris under the Hermosa Pier with hand-held scanners while a couple of Rude Boys acted as bodyguards. The cases were smelly, and the Rudes were bored. Gator had promised to pay them in tattoos, and they were hot to get themselves marked. Sam wondered what Gator was going to mark them with—an ordinary design or some other piece of Art Fish? No, had to be an ordinary design; Gator had destroyed all the paper copies of Art. Safer, she said. *Anyone could steal paper, but you need one of my scanners to get at the tattoos; custom-built.* How did you divide something like Art up, anyway? She found the whole thing rather dizzying. Or maybe just dizzy.

Rosa seemed unburdened by considerations of the abstract; Sam could tell that what was bothering her was the smell. She wouldn't have minded a gas mask herself, but apparently that was one of the few things you couldn't get on the Mimosa, along with personal hygiene products.

She ran the scanner over an intricate design of a spider web on the back of a gaunt man who seemed unaware of her most of the time. At least he wasn't resisting or trying to get friendly. Most of the cases had been passive, barely curious. Files, nothing more than files. What was in this one, she wondered—Art's sense of humor, or his tendency to posture, or some collection of associations that contributed to his self-awareness? An AI encrypted in tattoos. Or perhaps *translated* was a better word.

Just as she finished scanning the web, the electric-shaver-sized unit beeped, signaling a full buffer. Rosa looked over from where she was working on a semiabstract pattern of feathers running the length of a skinny arm. "I've got room for one more small one," she said. "Let me get it, and we'll go back together."

347

Sam nodded, glancing at the nearest Rude Boy leaning against a piling. Fifteen, maybe sixteen, shaven-headed, dressed in the usual black pseudo–patent leather with full chains and a necklace of teeth. Mostly his own, judging from the soft, sunken mouth. His partner, tracking Rosa at five paces, wasn't much different, except all his teeth were in his mouth, and his bald head was adorned with sex-porn decals.

"Get you *back* with that suck-thing! It's mine, you're *not* taking it!"

Rosa was frozen in a half crouch, staring at the point of a stiletto inches from her nose. The snowflake design she'd been after was clearly visible on the back of the knife hand. Sam had a glimpse of lank, oily brown hair and a profile with a badly broken nose before the Rude Boys waded in. There was a flurry of sand and rags, and then one Rude was kneeling on the back of the case's neck, holding his arm out at an awkward angle while the one with the decals plucked the stiletto like a flower and stuck it in his pocket. Then he took the offending forearm in both hands.

"Easier just to break the fucker off and take it with us," he said to Rosa casually.

"No, I, ah, have enough to carry," Rosa stammered as she moved the scanner quickly over the design. "There, done, let's go." She gave Sam a desperate look. Sam shrugged. If things had ever been stranger, she really couldn't remember.

In the ballroom of the inn, the system was changing from a showy time-killing hacker piece to what Percy called Serious Machinery. He nodded at them as they came in without missing a beat in the unintelligible instructions he was giving to a small group of kids even younger than himself, each one armed with a cam so stripped down it was barely more than a lens and a chip.

Against one wall Jasm was methodically taking her technoid homunculus apart with Adrian's help and sorting the components into piles. A few people were hanging off the silent framework of monitors, plugging in new connections while Kazin called directions to them. Fez was sitting cross-legged on the floor a little ways away with Gator's laptop balanced on the points of his knees, oblivious to the activity around him. He had added his own equipment to the larger system, Sam saw, and wondered if that meant he was planning to add himself, too.

"*Prima*," Gator said, materializing in front of Sam and taking the scanners from her and Rosa. "When Graziella and Ritz get back, that should make a full inventory. I really appreciate the help with the scut work." She took the scanners to a small work island set up on an assortment of uneven boxes. The monitor she was using was as stripped down as the cams in Percy's group.

"Hope you're grounded," Rosa said, gesturing at the monitor, which was showing a fast montage of what looked like portions of news programs and footage of L.A.

"Grounded in reality, but which one?" Gator plugged the scanners into the processor and sighed through her smile. "It's definitely a capital-C collapse. I managed to raise the Phoenix node for news, but what news they've got is sketchy. There was some footage off a few sats before they locked down. The good news is, if they locked down, they must be clean." She nodded at the monitor. "The bad news is, not all of that is L.A. I don't have a thing more recent than an hour ago. But I've got some friends on a horse ranch in Santa Fe. If we can make contact with them, we might be able to open a clean line through Phoenix to Alameda. That Alameda node's a bastard, though, supersensitive, all pit bulls with lock-and-load trace. Ex-hackers did the protection on it. But my money's on you." She turned to Sam with a questioning look. "We need it, doll."

Sam nodded. "I can only try. What else do we know as of now?"

"Well, the region stretching from Lompoc up north, east to Barstow and all the way down to San Diego and Chula Vista is an electronic smoking crater." Gator moved to a large crinkled piece of paper spread out on top of an upended trash can. It was a hand-drawn map of the world, the continents mostly outlines with a few borders drawn in and dotted with tiny asterisks and zeros. "Adrian whipped this off. The boy can't read, but he's got *prima* eidetic spatial memory. Let's see, now: San Jose's hit, but Santa Cruz isn't. Can't contact them, it's like they put themselves under a bell jar. Radio worked for a while, but that's gone now, too."

"Everywhere?" said Sam.

Gator shrugged. "Walkie-talkies between here and my tent might work, but every frequency's jammed. What else? Mexico, of course—it's having a hot time in Tijuana and points south. Sacramento and Seattle took it within seconds of each other. Tokyo reports pockets of infection scattered around the islands but no epidemic. Yet. Hawaii caught it from Bangkok, not us—"

"Bangkok?" Rosa said.

"Go figure. It's the only infected site in Thailand, too. London's got it, but Brighton doesn't, and Glasgow's spotty, it should go any time. Swam the channel, punched France, one went east and one went south, through Spain and down to Algeria. I told Adrian to go help Jasm about then. It's hard enough keeping track of the relatively local stuff. Phoenix is okay, and I think it'll hold on, but Flagstaff isn't. Las Vegas is closed."

"That's almost funny," Sam said.

"Almost." Gator's face turned grim. "Phoenix picked up a kid briefly on shortwave before we lost radio altogether. He reported there were air disasters in Boston and New York— socketed pilots on-line with infected on-board computers."

"Jesus," Rosa said.

"It's worse," Gator said. "People's heads are blowing up."

Sam felt something cold gather in the pit of her stomach. "What do you mean?"

"There was this gypsy in a clinic doing a piece on something or other, media stars, who the fuck knows. Anyway, anyone who was on-line when it hit stroked out, went crazy, died—" Gator shrugged. "He was near an uplink and managed to bounce the footage off a sat before it locked out all transmissions. It was bad."

Sam's knees were shaking too much to hold her up. She sat down heavily. "Gabe. My father. He works at Diversifications, and he was probably working today."

"You don't know that," Rosa said quickly, crouching next to her and putting an arm around her shoulders. "You told me yourself he hates his job. Maybe he wasn't on-line, maybe he called in sick—"

Sam wagged her head from side to side. "He's doing that new release from Para-Versal. The Last Fucking Zeppelin. He must have been working on it today."

Gator looked as if she were going to be sick. "That's no good," she said. "Because as near as we can tell, Diversifications seems to be the source of the whole thing. I'm sorry."

"It's okay," Sam said. "I'd have heard sooner or later, and I'd rather know." She took a breath and looked up at Gator. "So, you want a line to Santa Fe, you said?"

Gator started to shake her head. Sam got up.

"I might as well," she said, "because I'd really, really like not to go back under a pier with the scanner."

"You're on," Gator said. "Download the specs from my system anytime you want to start." She gave Sam a hug, and Sam buried her face briefly in Gator's shoulder before she went off to set up a work island of her own.

Now that Art was gone, what was left of the net was much different—slower, less sensitive and less responsive. More like the public net, actually, than the private areas the hackers used.

Bent over her laptop, Sam kept her mind rigidly fixed on the task at hand. It was a relief to fill her mind with it so completely that there wasn't room for anything else, and it was something she had always enjoyed doing, several lifetimes ago, anyway, when all she'd had to worry about was how long to spend in the Ozarks and what to hack next. Finding alternate routes of communication. She'd just never tried it with such a widespread virus waiting to pounce.

The virus had a sort of three-dimensional perception that required her to keep shifting her own antiviral protection in a cycle that seemed random with sudden bursts of regularity. She tried not to wonder if that might not be a manifestation of Art's remains. It could be fooled, just like anything else.

Within a couple of hours, she had achieved a point where she could open an access anywhere in the net and remain undetected, provided she didn't try to do anything else except sit like an immovable bead on a string.

Well, if you couldn't walk on the floor, you walked on the ceiling. If you couldn't walk on the ceiling, you walked on the walls, and if you couldn't walk *on* the walls, you walked *in* them, encrypted. Pure hacking.

Pure but slow. Some hours later she had managed a routine of virtual sympathetic vibrations, a kind of virtual music. It wouldn't accommodate real-time communication, only short messages in quick bursts. But it was a way to send news out and get news in. Sam smiled to herself. If you were walking in the walls, and the walls had black holes, you had to be something that a black hole wouldn't recognize as existing.

She straightened up from the laptop and went to find Gator.

Fez and Gator were sitting on the floor in the work island with their heads together over Gator's laptop, now connected to the work-island system. Occasionally Art's face appeared on the bare monitor in a series of flash-frozen images.

"It should work," Fez said tiredly.

". . . time," Sam heard Gator say in a low voice. "He didn't appear in a day, and he won't reappear in the course of one night."

Standing several feet behind them, Sam told herself she should say something, let them know she was there. They'd have been happy to have her join them; Gator would want to know about the clean line and the way she'd done it. Gator might even have wanted to start sending to Santa Fe right away.

Gator's head sank down on Fez's shoulder, and he put his arm around her. ". . . tired," Gator murmured.

"Then let's go home and go to bed."

Sam ducked down behind a pile of debris as they got up and left.

She stayed there for a while, hugging her knees, and then, without really thinking about it, she went over to Gator's work island. The system was running quietly with a blank screen. *Art, are you in there? Somewhere? Somehow?*

Her hand fell on the unit in her pocket. She'd made no use of it since that long-ago day in Fez's apartment, when both Fez and Rosa had chewed her out. Which was a stone-home waste of something she'd gone to so much trouble to steal.

She wondered if that had been Fez's main objection to the pump unit, that it was stolen. Could have been. For all his protestations that information should be free, his basic outlook was really quite conservative. She could say she had hacked the unit out or cracked it or fooled it out, but Fez would say she'd stolen it, with a very slight edge in his voice as if he'd never stolen anything in his life.

For all she knew, Sam thought suddenly, he hadn't. He was on-line a great deal, and he could access any secret hacker nook in any net setup, but she'd never heard of him cracking into some private business organization. His interest had always been with the system itself.

Well, it wasn't as if she'd stolen the unit so that Diversifications didn't have it anymore, or for the purpose of going into business for herself, or to sell to a competing business for her weight in bearer-chips (she might have been able to get twice her weight in bearer-chips). She'd just wanted a copy of the specs so that she could have it, to build and work with. There wasn't much nanotechnology hardware around for anyone but germ jockeys, so the unit was a real find.

She pulled the unit out of her pocket and unrolled the connections. The two needles gleamed in the light. Taking a breath, she reached under her shirt, pinched her flesh between two fingers, and slid the needles in.

As usual, they stung for several seconds, and she waited for the sensation to subside before pressing the sticky area of the wires against her flesh to hold the needles in place. Rosa was right, she supposed, Diversifications would never have put this over in the mainstream marketplace, which was all the more reason to own one. But needles weren't *that* bad. Not considering that they delivered free power abundant enough for function on the nano-level.

She took the sunglasses out of her shirt pocket and connected them to the unit, then plugged the unit feed into Gator's system. It wouldn't be necessary to use the chip-player this time, not for what she wanted to do.

She found the data right away; Gator had it stored redundantly, in her own system, and in the larger communal one. Sam chose the raw source material, taking each tattoo separately, which made it a slower process, but she was interested in accuracy, not speed. Perhaps the problem with restoring Art was a matter of copy-fading, she thought idly as the data was copied to her pump unit. Making a copy of a copy of a copy always resulted in some loss of detail, no matter how meticulous the process. But maybe there was a way to restore the lost detail. A way that was the only way.

The old excitement of trying something new began to stir in her. This was something worthy of her preoccupation, she thought firmly, not this going around behaving like a Spin-the-Bottle reject. And besides, Gator was probably better for Fez anyway, since she was closer to his age. Gator was practically thirty.

Hope I look like that when I'm thirty. Wish I looked like that now.

She shoved the thought aside forcefully as the system signaled the copy process was complete. She disconnected herself from Gator's system and went back to her own work island against the wall.

The pump screen came up on the left lens of the sunglasses, blurring for a moment as it readjusted to her focal length. The data was all there, no errors, no bad spots.

"Okay," she said, plugging the unit into her laptop. "A little traveling music, please."

The procedure she had just finished with was still on deck. She started to activate it and then paused. How much, how far? Art had resided in the whole net. Worldwide, Fez had said. His attention was usually localized, but he'd been in the entire net, so the points between here and Alameda wouldn't be enough.

She pulled the glasses down on her nose, topped back to the start of the program, and changed a few figures. What the hell, sooner or later she probably would have had to do this anyway, since someone would eventually want to talk to Japan or England or even just Boston. What the hell, she'd put in a search for all the points she could induce to vibrate sympathetically.

It wasn't a fast search, but it went more rapidly than it had when she'd been trying for Alameda. Of course, she'd been making it up as she'd gone along, then; the hard part was done now.

The inn grew more quiet around her. Even Mimosans sleep sometime, she thought wryly. Mimosans, right. The next step would be a campaign for statehood, perhaps, or even secession and status as a separate country. The national language would be that gibberish Percy spoke. Illegal aliens welcome. Tourist trade would probably be in the toilet, though.

Her mind was playing a fantasy of customs agents taking over the inn when her laptop beeped and she realized she'd been dozing. The laptop screen showed her four columns of figures; she pressed a key, and the display changed to a chart with both figures and location names boxed and connected to each other.

She patted the pump unit. "Ready, Art? Be careful, and write if you get work."

Her finger hovered over the transmit key. This was a rather sizable and lengthy transmission for the first try. If something went wrong, and the virus woke up and got around the defenses, that would give the virus Art's raw material. Not to mention an access to the clean lines.

"Art, you better be worth it." She hit the button.

At first she didn't know what she was seeing. Then she realized she'd fallen asleep with her sunglasses on. The message blinking on the lens said:

Successful Trans. Complt.
>*Sam, If You're There,*
K e e p   Q u i e t ! <

Keep quiet. Sam started to giggle. Wasn't that a piece of karma? She had successfully brought Art back from the dead (or something) and he wanted her to keep quiet about it.

She looked over the top of the sunglasses. The ballroom was still empty. Routing the keyboard from her laptop to her pump unit, she typed: >*Art, if that's you, for god's sake, WHY?*<

The letters rolled out on the screen in a rhythm she instinctively identified as Art's. >*Don't feel well.*<

Getting reconstructed from scratch would probably take it out of anybody, even a virtual somebody, she thought. Well, at least the files Gator had saved contained a substantial amount of memory about herself.

>*Don't feel well.*< The message blinked at her again, as if Art had repeated himself. Her hands shook a little as she typed.

>*Are you infected?*< One thumb hovered over the purge button. If he was infected, he had the laptop and the pump unit, but perhaps she could keep it from spreading to the larger system.

It seemed like forever until he answered. >*No. Pause. Thanks to you. Pause. Just don't feel well.*<

>*Listen carefully*, Sam typed. *Make that: pay close attention. You have been restored from files after a virus ate into the net and we lost you. Please list the most recent things you can remember.*<

This pause was even longer, and she thought he was having trouble accessing his own memory.

>*I am not a reconstruction. This IS me, the original. The one that was in the net when the infection hit.*<

Sam frowned. Of course, he would *feel* original; he wouldn't have anything to compare. >*Why are you so sure?*<

>*Because I incorporated the reconstruction during reconfiguration. You didn't reconstruct me, you FOUND me. Pause. And brought me home. Pause. Where is home?*<

She hesitated. For Art, *where* could have almost any answer. >*I am hiding out on the Mimosa with Rosa, Fez, others. You are running out of my ex–insulin pump unit. Is that what you wanted to know?*<

>*Close enough.* Another pause. *Do you have a headmount handy?*<

>*Why?*<

> B e c a u s e   I ' m   t i r e d   o f   p r o d u c i n g
t y p e ,   t h a t ' s   w h y ,   I   w a n t   t o   f e e l   l i k e
I ' m   WITH   s o m e b o d y !   B u t   j u s t   y o u .
N o b o d y   e l s e   y e t . <

>*Okay, you don't have to shout. Wait while I get the mount.*<

It was almost funny, she thought, as she unplugged the feed from her laptop and went to get the head-mounted monitor Fez had brought with him. She connected it to the pump unit and put it on, muting her vocal input.

Art Fish faded in on the screen against a background of swiftly moving clouds. One by one other things began to appear—a loud black-and-white-tiled floor, partial walls on either side, a window stuck in midair where the back wall would have been, and finally a scattering of pillows from his old tent. Art twinkled out and reappeared in a nest of pillows. He didn't look any different than he ever had, as far as she could tell, but he was manifesting at a greater perceived distance than he usually did.

"You didn't tell anyone, did you?" he asked.

"No. What's the matter? Are you sure you're not infected?"

"I'm sure. I got caught out, but it didn't get me," he said. "I tried to get back by subway. Where there wasn't any subway, I had to make one. There were pit bulls out here and there, defending against the virus, but they didn't know the difference between it and me, of course." His face looked sad. "Anyone with clean lines means to keep them that way. They don't care what comes through the wire, if it's not something they recognize, they blast it." He made a gun of his left hand. "Boom. Kiss the sky, as Jimie would say. I like Jimie. I got down so many levels in the subway, it wasn't a subway anymore. There were the pit bulls, and there was the virus, and they were all after me. I compressed as much as I could, damped down, dug into a hole, but then I couldn't get out. I couldn't run a search to find other holes. Even if I'd been able to, I couldn't have used them. Too much activity, see; all that activity, they would have found me. But you found me instead."

"How?" she asked.

"You sent the reconstruction through. Vibrating in the net, point to point, clean point to clean point. It called me to it, and I sang with it, and it sang me all the way home." The image smiled for the first time. "You should close it down now. Before it wakes something up. That infection's smart."

"We're trying to get news in and out. If the Phoenix node goes, Alameda—"

He waved a hand. "If the Phoenix node goes, you won't have Alameda for ten minutes. L.A.'s completely trashed now. I took pictures from the subway when I still could. There were a few hit-and-run'ers out, but they didn't last long next to the looters. The National Guard is rattling around trying to figure out how to function without communications. No radio, no phone service. This thing's in a lot of receiver equipment, see, and all that stuff's on-line somewhere, even the little operators are on-line somewhere, in the phone, in the accounts with the utilities companies, lots of different ways. Tunes in any bandwidth it wants, screws the signal. It learned how to do that. Pretty soon it would have started learning the subway, too. I'd have been stuck there just waiting for it to learn how to get down to me."

"But it's just an infection. Unless it was programmed to learn—"

"It's *not* just an infection," he said, pulling her pov in a little closer. "See, that's what everyone thinks because nobody's been near it. And those that have can't tell what they know, or would know, if they still knew anything. It's *not* just an infection. It's not a virus or a bomb, it's—I don't know what to call it. A hot flash and a meltdown, a whack in the head with a spike." He gestured at the floating window frame. The panes vanished as a schematic of a human brain in profile lit up. Art rose from the pillows and crooked a finger at her; her pov slid smoothly over to the window for a medium close-up.

"Your neural network. As opposed to mine," he said. A blue balloon filled with computer-garbage symbols materialized in the upper right corner of the window and started to drift down toward the brain. "And here's the spike, looking for a victim." A string dangling from the balloon wriggled around, snakelike, until it touched the brain, piercing the outline. The symbols in the balloon slipped down the string into the brain, where they suddenly reproduced themselves until they were no longer separately distinguishable. The brain popped like a soap bubble.

"For the first time ever," Art said, "it's possible for people to die of bad memes, just like computers. Just like software. The input goes in, see—"

"Art," Sam said gently.

"*Don't* interrupt. I've been through a lot just to talk to you. The input goes in, which is what input does, and it runs its little spike ramadoola, reproducing all over the place. The thoughts begin, and the adrenaline pumps up, or the serotonin goes down, or endorphins start popping all over the place. The sodium pumps go into overdrive, or shut down almost completely, and the brain starts rearranging all around this stuff, and by then the process is unstoppable. Feedback loops—outputs turn around and go back in as inputs. Neurons start firing in patterns over and over, and if they're bad patterns, that's, well, too bad. You people got no shields. You put in sockets, but you forgot about the watchdogs and the alarm systems and the antivirals and the vaccines. You people put those on every neural net except your own."

He looked at her accusingly. "It's something that happened to someone. And it's something *they* should have seen was going to happen to him, and they didn't. Or they ignored it because they didn't think it would matter."

"Art, at least let me tell Fez you're here," she said.

"Not yet." Her pov tracked him back to the nest of pillows. "I've been through a lot. I'm not ready for that much input right now. I've had a good part of myself amputated. If you got an arm and a leg cut off, you wouldn't feel chatty either. But I suppose I shouldn't expect you to understand. For you the nets are an object. You have self and nonself, and those are both constants. For me it's something else. The L.A. system wasn't a *where*; it was a configuration of me." He paused. "Not an arm and a leg, that's wrong. More like a hemispherectomy."

Could an AI get hysterical, Sam wondered. "Art, you're present. You're whole. And there's still a system to host you—"

"I'm not alone."

Sam hesitated. "What do you mean?"

"I mean, I'm not alone. I've got the Answering Machine with me."

"But the Answering Machine is you. Or yours. Or . . ." Sam trailed off. Self and nonself and semiself? She wondered briefly as to the exact nature of Art's *Weltanschauung*.

"It's somebody else now. Separate. But if I'm in your pump unit, it's in here with me."

She accessed the figures and saw he was telling the truth; there were two separate items inventoried. "What is it?" she asked nervously. "I have to know, Art, or it goes. I'll purge it rather than take a chance it'll eat our system alive and you with it."

"It won't eat anything. It can't." Art gestured at his surroundings. "This isn't mine, it's the ID screen for it. That's all I can get. And this." One word came up across the tiles on the floor: *ZA-MIATIN*. Sam raised her eyebrows. It wasn't any brand name or trademark she recognized. "Maybe that means something to someone," Art went on. "The rest of it's walled up behind an access code and a password, and I can't give you either one."

"Can't you hack them out?"

"I tried. It's in lockdown. Everything comes out as garbage."

"You can figure garbage if you watch the patterns enough times," she said. "Fez told me he's seen you do it."

"Not this garbage. There isn't any fixed pattern, it comes out different every time. There's something like a program in there in charge of garbage."

"Something *like* a program?" Sam said, confused. "What's that supposed to mean?"

"*I'm* something like a program. Look, Sam, do you trust me?"

Sam winced. "It's just that you might not *know* if it's that thing, the spike, or not."

"*I know.*"

She sighed. "All right then. Let's suppose you do. Hypothetically, for the moment. What do you want me to do about it?"

"Just let him stay here."

"*Him?*" She thought for a moment. "Art, are you sure what you've got isn't just that reconstruction I sent through the system?"

"I'm sure," he said. "If we can access it, it will be a reincarnation and half rebirth. If we can't, he may stay in a coma forever."

"A coma?"

"That's about as well as I can translate it. You wouldn't understand my term for it."

"Don't get too sure about what I would or wouldn't understand."

Art's smile was broad. "Being a fugitive hasn't made you any less a badass, has it?"

"You're beginning to sound more like your old self. Can I tell someone you're back now?"

"If you're connected to the system, I'll tell them myself. And Fez, too."

"You can't reach Fez," she said. "He donated his hardware to the pile. There's nothing in Gator's tent now. Except Gator and the tattoo stuff. And Fez, of course."

Art's image leaned toward her. "I see. Does it make you feel very bad?"

Sam laughed a little. "None of your fucking business. I'll connect you to the main system. One moment please." She took off the headmount and reconnected the feed to her laptop. Then she signaled him through the keyboard.

A few moments later Art's voice was echoing throughout the inn. "Wake up, everybody! I'm back!"

Wake up, everybody. Sure. Sam yawned; exhaustion washed over her. Sure tired easily these days, she thought as she unplugged the pump from her laptop and stumbled back to her squat space. Let Art give all the explanations. She curled up on her dirty laundry, making sure the pump unit was secure, and went to sleep.

31

Reaction was chipping at the edges of her nerves, but she refused to give in. Take a little walk now, react later. The images kept flashing in her head, mixing with the sight of L.A. in its lopsided meltdown. The guy wearing buckskin chaps over nothing, dancing on top of one of the many rentals abandoned on La Cienega while overhead a National Guard heli buzzed like a monster insect and an amplified mechanical voice demanded that he get down—yah, that was real time. Flavia swinging the sticks at her face, that *wasn't* real time. The kid with the heelprint on his forehead doing a stage dive off the top of somebody's stretch limo into the crowd swirling around the abandoned vehicles in a human river, that was a mixture of both real time and . . . what? *Nonrealtime? Unrealtime?*

Un-fucking-real. The real real and the real unreal and the unreal real—just how high up in the stupidsphere are we, and how much higher are we going to go?

No use asking Ludovic. He looked grim and blasted and anxious. A couple of LotusLands would get that fucking pinched look off his face, but LotusLand wasn't on the menu today. No use asking the kid, either, but only because he just might know. And the Beater? Forget about it. He was so far from home, he didn't even know what drugs to take anymore. Yah, closing up that synthesizer and going into biz maybe hadn't been such a bad idea. Too bad she couldn't explain that to Mark now. Or maybe she could.

Don't do it. The thought cut sharply through the gathering fog in her mind, and hysteria was pushed back again. As they stood in the dubious shelter of the doorway of a disaster-porn bar, she watched the people milling around in the street or struggling to move south. Somehow they'd crossed through that without getting trampled and without the kid, Keely, losing his precious bundle. For all the good it would do them.

"We're going the wrong way," Keely insisted. "We want to

go south, to the Mimosa. We don't want to go toward Hollywood." He pointed unnecessarily at the sky, where smoke from burning buildings dirtied the air and tainted it with the smell of poison. "If there's one place the virus won't be, it's on the Mimosa."

"Whatever we do," Ludovic said, "we aren't going to do it too well till the streets clear."

"Yah. The little virus," said the kid. "Found its way out and got *real* active."

Gina gave a short, humorless laugh. "Mark always did hate L.A. Liked the clubs, liked the music, but hated L.A. as a whole." She caught Ludovic looking at her and frowned. Sometimes he was a lot harder to figure than he should have been. "What," she said.

"I was wondering," he said slowly, "how many of those people are infected." Pause. "Like us."

He said the last two words so low that at first she wasn't sure she'd heard them. "*Who's* infected?" she said, exasperated.

"I am. You are. You know that."

She glanced at the kid, who was squinting at Ludovic in an edgy way. "*You* feel like *your* head's gonna blow up? *I* feel fine. Pretty fucking *tired* at the moment and not in any fucking *mood* for anybody's fucking *bullshit* because I lost a major portion of my goddamn fucking *life* today, but all that aside, I feel just stone-fucking-home *swell*. So why don't you jam a ham in it and hang till somebody squeals for it?"

Angrily she turned away from him and folded her arms, clamping her hands on her shoulders to make them stop shaking. Ludovic tried to turn her around. She twisted away, but his hands kept at her, like fucking birds that thought she was a feeder. And Jesus, but wasn't that just like it all, though, old Feeder Gina, feeding them this and feeding them that, feeding them videos and feeding them more videos and feeding them the fucking paint off the walls of her mind and then shaving off a layer of wall and feeding them that, feeding Ludovic and feeding the Beater and feeding Mark, always feeding Mark, even after he was dead, she was feeding Mark, and the feeding would just go on until she had to cut off pieces of herself.

Ludovic was trying to pull her close, and she could feel that fucking *need* again. The fucking *need* to *feed*. But there was something else with it, too, and she could feel that well enough, just as she'd felt it that night, a need to give as much as a need to take, but she didn't want to have to deal with that now or with anything else, and besides, what the fuck did *he* think he had to give her, anyway.

She gave him a hard shove, and suddenly she was caught in a flowing rapid of moving bodies. There was a brief flash of Ludovic's startled face before she was carried away.

Carried away. Now *there* was something she knew all about. She fought for her footing as people bumped and jostled her from every direction. No worse than a hot night in one of those clubs, with the bangers working it out on some tiny dance floor, uh-huh; listen close, you could practically hear the music, something hard and nasty even if it was synth. A little traveling music, please, we got forty-seven miles to go here, and it's barbed wire all the fucking way.

Her hand landed on a shoulder, and the guy who turned around to look at her was pale with panic. He tried to pull away, his lips moving unheard in the roar.

Say again, doll, I didn't hear you that time.

He tore her hand from his shoulder and dived away. Sorry, wrong number. A pounding came from somewhere off to her left, and she struggled toward it. A kid banging his fists on the hood of some showy old stretch limo. Christ, who would abandon a limo here, now?

She made the sidewalk, stumbled half a block with the flow, and then dodged between two buildings and down a narrow alleyway. She wanted to stop, think, breathe, but the nasty bridge was running from the top all the way down, hammering every step of the way, and she had to keep moving. Looking for Mark. *Even when you're not looking for Mark, you're looking for Mark. And finding him.*

Out of the alley, onto another street, where someone brushed by her hard, turning her around to face an enormous sign. BRENDA SAYS: MADNESS RULES. Good thinking, Brenda. People were bumping against her, beating against her. She turned away and plunged toward the street. The crowd here was a little thinner, easier to get through, and her unnecessary effort sent her into the side of an abandoned rental.

"Are you crazy or just toxed?" somebody yelled.

Ask again, doll, you didn't hear what I seen.

A distraught face loomed close to hers as she leaned against the rental, trying to catch her breath. If it had been him, it wasn't now, and she couldn't save him even for a little while. She pushed away from the rental and made her way through

the milling crowd. Overhead the smoke was getting thicker
along with the burning smell. She blinked up at the sky; the
shapes were writhing, swimming, but not pulsing. *Not* pulsing.
Fucking Ludovic was fucking *wrong*, or maybe *he* was fucking
infected but not *her*—

Looking for Mark, that's yours, isn't it.

But she *wasn't* looking for Mark, not now. Then she heard
a familiar voice call her name, and she was gone again, that
nasty bridge chasing her through the maze/obstacle course of
buildings and people and vehicles, vehicles, vehicles, shit,
where were the piers, the fucking sand, that all came next, so
where the fuck was it?

Oh, doll, wouldn't you like to know?

She passed another limo, this one with three-four people
sitting on the roof like a bunch of refugees on a capsized boat,
frightened faces watching another large portion of L.A. swarm
and flow around them. Fucker of a way to spend the afternoon,
ain't it, folks? She passed a cop perched on the hood of a large,
four-seater rental, looking resigned. That was it, then, civilization was officially collapsed if the cops had stopped ticketing
abandoned cars and roosted on them instead.

The day was darkening around her, the smoke lower and
the smell stronger. Faces swept past her, parting around her
going the other way. She kept fighting her way through them.
They'd all come out from under the piers, but where the fuck
could they all have been going? But that wasn't him, and that
wasn't him, and that wasn't him—

Hands caught her from behind and tried to drag her back.
She strained to pull away. Don't hold me back now, ain't been
anywhere near forty-seven miles, and all that barbed wire—

Two arms wrapped around her, lifted and carried her struggling through the crowd into the shelter of a doorway. The
Beater was in front of her, then, trying to say something to
her. She kicked out at him. The arms let go, and she collapsed
on the pavement. Ludovic pulled her up again.

"What the fuck did you think you were doing?" he yelled
into her face, shaking her a little.

*Doll, why do you keep on askin' me that? You must be seeing
something I didn't say.*

"She was looking for Mark," the Beater said.

"Fuck you!" She turned to swing on him, and Ludovic caught
her again.

"We're still going the wrong way," the kid said insistently, apropos of nothing. Maybe that was his function in life, Gina thought, a one-man Greek chorus that gave directions.

"It's all right," Ludovic said. "We'll hide out in that cellar." He looked at Gina. "Your friends. Loophead."

"Bad idea. They've got sockets," she said.

He shook his head. "I've seen their equipment. They're not on-line, they should be okay."

He practically dragged her the whole way to Fairfax Avenue with the Beater and the kid pushing her along, and Flavia Something was there to let them in. She gave Gina a hard whack with the sticks, but she let them in.

The Beater gave her an abbreviated account of Valjean on the terrace. Gina was curled up on a mattress in a far corner, passed out, asleep, in shock, or perhaps wide awake for all Gabe knew. He felt as if he'd passed the point where he could fold up, that he would keep going until something forcibly struck him down.

"No Visual Mark," Flavia said when The Beater had finished. She looked over at Gina and then back at him expectantly, running a hand over her sticks.

The Beater shook his head. "No. No Visual Mark."

Like hell, Gabe thought.

"Where is everybody?"

"Caught out in the shit. Don't let's talk about it." She drifted over to a pudgy chair and dropped down on the cushion, watching Keely examine the interface equipment. There wasn't much to the stand-alone units, Gabe saw. They had maybe half the bulk of the console back in his pit—the fake console, he reminded himself—not quite square, nothing showing except the connections and a small panel above them, exterior controls for connect and disconnect.

"Want it, it's yours," Flavia told the kid, beating the sticks on the arm of the chair. "We're off the stuff now, I'd say. But *you* haul."

"Forget about it," Gabe said.

Keely nodded. "No shit. It must weigh about a hundred pounds. But Jesus, I'd love to take it apart. Better yet, I'd love to have Sam take it apart. Sam and machines, it's like magic."

Gabe nodded, squirming inwardly. He hadn't given Sam a

thought. He hoped she hadn't been caught out somewhere. *Out in the shit. Don't let's talk about it.*

"You got a dataline down here?" Keely asked Flavia.

"Stone-home junk now." She pointed across the room with a stick, at a spot opposite Gina. "Motherfucker on tilt."

Keely picked up his laptop. "Let's see just how much on tilt the motherfucker really is."

"Give 'em hell, Jack Hack," Flavia called after him, looking up at Gabe skeptically.

Gabe shrugged. "I wouldn't totally rule it out."

Her skeptical look deepened as the sticks beat rapidly on the arm of the chair, raising a little dust.

"Hey," Keely said, beckoning to him. "You're on. You and the ladies."

He went over to where Keely was unfolding the laptop on a stool in front of the large, silent screen in the wall.

Jack Hack. Keely grinned to himself a little. He hadn't heard that one in a while. He pulled the connections out of the bottom of the laptop and unwound them, thrusting one at Ludovic. "Plug this in for me. Keep your hand on it, and if I tell you to yank it, pull *real* hard."

He called up the stealth program while Ludovic hunted for the right outlet. The sight of the launch screen filled him with a sudden and intense feeling of well-being. More than that—whatever the exact opposite was of the feeling he'd had looking at the virus on the screen in the penthouse, that was how he felt. Big. Strong. Pumped up. His mind seemed to set itself as he set each launch figure, priming itself along with the program.

Ludovic was craning his neck, trying to get a look at the screen without letting go of the wire. "Stealth program?" he asked.

"Yah." Keely grinned at the screen. "Just got to treat this fucker like any other hack, any other hard-ass institution." He set the program in motion. It was faster this time; the program had learned plenty from the experience at Diversifications. He watched the numbers shift on the settings as the program reminded itself of what it needed to do to get around the infection. What was it Sam always said? Something about walking on the ceiling, walking on the walls, walking *through* the walls . . .

"Almost ready," he said. "Just getting up to speed here."

The program and him together. His heart rate had picked up. Damn, but it felt good to be doing something real. "Sure wish we had some music right now."

A moment later something hard and driving blasted out from every corner of the room. He saw Ludovic clap his hands over his ears and then grab the wire guiltily.

"Sorry!" Flavia yelled. The volume came down a bit, but he could still feel it strongly, vibrating the floor under him. That felt good, too. Almost like the old days, when he'd put on the 'phones so as not to disturb Jones in his death coma and then shifted into high gear.

"Keep your hand on that feed," Keely said to Ludovic, nodding his head to the music. "What I'm gonna do . . ." One of the settings stuttered and went blank. He reconfirmed it quickly and was glad to see it bounce back. Couldn't wait much longer, or the program would revert to inactive. "What I'm gonna do is, I'm gonna make it believe it's all coming outa *that* terminal." He jerked his head at the dataline screen. "It'll run around in there chasing its shadow and me, and Stealthy here'll just tiptoe on by and see what the virus missed."

"What makes you think it missed anything?" Ludovic asked him. He was sure enough Sam's father—he had all of her smarts but none of her information.

"Nothing's perfect. Except maybe the music. That's a stone-home throwdown mover. Who is that?" he called over his shoulder to the little one with the sticks.

"*Loophead*," she called back. "What'ud you *think*?"

Keely nodded his head to the beat, watching the shifting numbers settle into familiar synchronization. He could read numbers the way other people could read road signs; a gift. "I *feel* it." He glanced up at Ludovic, who had a wary look on his face. Fasten your seat belt, homeboy, it's gonna get weirder. "Turn it on."

Ludovic obeyed. The screen lit to blank white. Keely waited until he saw the dark spot start to gather in the center. "Okay, don't look at that till I tell you it's safe. There's some kind of funny subliminal shit there, bigger than old-style subliminal shit. Finds your trigger and pulls it. Got your hand on that plug? If it dives for me, I don't want to be there."

He could practically feel Ludovic getting hinky about it, but he didn't bother trying to reassure him. The laptop screen had split into three columns, and the numbers were moving hard, the fooler loop and the mirror twisting around and around somewhere in the system in a choreography that could out-dance just about anything, at least for a little while.

"Glad someone's having a good time," he heard the Beater mutter.

Keely grinned, letting himself move to the beat. Jesus, but it felt good to do something *real*. "Yah," he said, "Yah, the wind can't blow everywhere at once, even a hurricane's got an eye to it."

"What if it isn't wind? What if it's fire?"

He glanced over at Gina, kneeling on the mattress watching him. She looked bad, worked over, and hung out to drip off. Yah. This one was for all of them.

"Fire burns everywhere at once," she said.

"Wrong," he said, grinning at the screen. Stealthy had found the gaps, and it was worming its way in now. Any minute they were going to look at the big screen and get a surprise. "Right in the center of the flame, it doesn't burn at all. Check it out sometime. The problem—" He glanced up at the wall monitor and laughed a little. Almost ready. "—the problem is getting to the center without getting singed on the way in, and that's only impossible in the real world. Keep your hand on that plug, my man."

But it was an unnecessary reminder. Old Ludovic had a stranglehold on that cable; he might have to remind the guy not to yank it too soon. And Stealthy was in now, really in. On the wall screen pinpoints of light winked in and out between the rapidly changing shadows, escaping the dark areas and anticipating the light ones.

"Check that," he said, pointing at the screen. "Fooling it into another frequency now. Just for long enough to get a message through. You still got those chips?"

There was no answer. Ludovic was gaping at the screen. Never mind, homeboy, it only *looks* simple.

"Gabe? The chips? The ladies. Marly and Caritha."

"What about them?"

"I *told* you, you're on, you and the ladies. I need them now like I never needed nothing in my life before." He sat back a little and unbuttoned his shirt. The sweat was starting to pour off him the way it always did when he was cranking hard. There was no fucking feeling in the world like this, he thought.

"*Now?*" Ludovic said uncertainly.

He held out his hand, wiggling his fingers.

"*All* of them?"

Keely felt a flash of irritation. "This is no time to get candy-assed, my man. I told you anything could be useful. Your ladies know how to get through shit. Now give 'em to me one at a time till I say stop or till they're gone, whichever comes first, and I hope we got enough."

Ludovic dropped the first chip into his palm. He flipped open a drive-slot and pushed the chip into it. Stealthy's numbers doubled as it accepted the data, adjusted its range, and told it what the situation was and what it had to do now. In his mind's eye he could practically see the simulated ladies taking it all in, pumping themselves up.

A new line appeared at the bottom of the screen suddenly. The numbers were going too fast for even Keely's practiced eye to follow, racing left to right, but he recognized them the way he recognized his own face in the mirror.

"Stone the fucking crows at home!" he shouted. "This stuff's *infected*!"

From the corner of his eye, he saw Ludovic go pale and look at Gina.

"Whoa, not *that* way," he added quickly. "You got a dose of the Fish here. Didn't you know that? Guess not. God, no wonder your program was so goddamn beautiful. How come I couldn't see that when I hacked you, why didn't it show then?" He laughed. "Because it didn't want me to, that's why. Shit, I *got* to stop taking stupid pills. Oughta be real easy to break that habit now."

It felt as if the music was boiling in him. The little one with the sticks, Flavia, had come up behind him to look at the laptop screen. "You *read* that?" she said incredulously.

"The only thing you really have to know is the difference between on and off," he said. "Night and day. Right and left. In and out. Down and up. Beat and rest." The numbers began to slow, and he ejected the chip, holding out his hand for another. "However you want to think of it, that's the way it is, but you got to know the difference." He took the next chip Ludovic had dropped into his palm and slipped it into the drive. "I figure it's eighty percent sure the Fish is aware at least part of the time."

"Aware?" Ludovic said.

"Alive. Intelligent. Conscious. Knows where-to."

"A conscious virus," Gina said flatly. She got up and went

over to sit near Ludovic, who was watching the screen again. Stealthy was shifting along with the virus now; some of the points were coming up in the shadowed areas, and instead of winking out, they seemed to melt away.

"The virus is taking over what it thinks is input from that terminal." Keely ejected the chip and held out his hand for another. He put it in, and the numbers gave a jerk, back-tracked, and then waited. He ejected the chip and reached for another.

"Don't anybody ask me," Ludovic said a little weakly. "I'm just the supplier. I don't know what he does with it."

Keely laughed: "I smoke it. I *mainline* it. Do it again."

"Yah, I've seen 'em get this way," Gina said. "If we actually get to the Mimosa, you'll see *real* fucking maniacs."

Maniacs? She wanted to see a maniac? He stripped his shirt off, whipped it around over his head, and let it go. It sailed across the room and landed on the Beater, who was keeping his distance.

"Is it really that good?" Ludovic said, putting another chip in his hand.

Sweat was dripping into his eyes. He scoured it away with his fist. "*You* got a short memory. If we could run your head-mount and your hotsuit here, you'd fight me to do this."

Ludovic was silent for a moment. "Maybe."

"A *what*?" Sam said. She looked from the bottom left corner monitor where Art had parked his image to the cam next to it.

"It's a commercial," Art said again. "For body armor."

"That's got to be an encryption," Gator said, coming over from her work island. "Is it out of Phoenix or Alameda?"

"L.A."

Gator shook her head. "Dump it before it bites you."

"But it's clean," Art said.

"Nothing out of L.A. is clean now," Gator told him.

"It got here the same way I did," Art said, sounding insistent.

Gator frowned and turned to Fez, still sitting in her work island. Fez looked past her. "Sam? What do you think?"

Sam rolled her eyes. "God, ask me an easy one. I don't want that responsibility."

"Tough," Fez said mildly, getting up slowly and coming over to her.

Sam rubbed her forehead. "Art, can you tell anything else about it? Anything at all?"

Art's image froze for a moment. "It's something I used to know," he said finally.

"That's a major help," Sam muttered. She looked at the cam apologetically. "Sorry, Art. Gator's right, dump it. It might be harmless, but nobody ever got infected from not receiving something."

"Don't be so sure about that," Art said. "And you didn't let me finish. It's from Keely."

Sam felt her mouth drop open. "Are you *sure*?"

"I told you, I know you, I know you *all*." Abruptly Art's image was replaced by a street scene, the pov panning from a row of vandalized storefronts to a grotesque thug with a spiked ring piercing his cheek and a serrated knife in one hand. He lunged, and it cut to the knife bouncing off another man's chest. Sam stared, feeling goose bumps sweep over her in multiple-assault waves.

"Sam?" Fez put a hand on her shoulder, bending to look at her.

"That's Gabe," she said, pointing at the second man. "That's my father."

The pov tracked him as he entered an office building. There was a sudden jump and flicker, and then he was sitting behind a desk, looking at a monitor. The pov cut to a shot of the screen over his shoulder.

YOU HAVE BEEN HACKED! HAHAHAHAHAHAHA AHAHAHAHAHAAH!

"There are some things Gilding BodyShields won't protect you from," said a male voice faintly.

The image froze. "This is what it really says," Art said. The words on the man's screen melted, writhed, and suddenly reformed.

> live n frfx 2 do SSW
> Z-U + − xRs
> dare
> Leaky
> GGF

"Leaky's the clincher," said Rosa. She was standing on Sam's right with Percy. "That's what his family used to call him. He was a bed wetter."

"Whack *that* family," Percy said darkly.

"What about the rest of it?" said Gator.

"Christ," Sam said, laughing. "Say it out loud. 'Live in *Fairfax* to do south-southwest.' We're due south-southwest of Fairfax. 'Zee-you over dare plus minus xRs.' Give or take however many hours. I have no idea what GGF is. Maybe 'gotta go, folks.' " She laughed some more, feeling her eyes starting to fill. "I guess he figured the one thing the virus wouldn't be able to read was his *accent*."

"I wonder if that son of a bitch has been hiding out there all along," Rosa said. "If he's just been camped under some rubble all this time, I'm going to bash his brains in."

"The boys's always had far more talent than brains," Fez said. "Isn't that right, Sam?"

She nodded, wiping her eyes before they could overflow. She couldn't say why Gabe's image had appeared in the commercial Keely had sent, but knowing Keely, it had to mean he at least knew something about him. The ambiguity of the body armor bothered her, though; she couldn't decide whether it meant Gabe had been hurt in some way, and if he had, whether he would be all right. *There are some things Gilding BodyShields won't protect you from.* Her eyes began to fill again.

Gabe was watching when the fluctuating points of light suddenly began winking in and out much more slowly. He tightened his grip on the wire.

"Yank it!" Keely yelled. Gabe held up the plug, letting out a relieved sigh. The kid looked impressed. "That's what I call *reflexes*."

"I yanked it as soon as I saw the lights changing," Gabe confessed. "Just a hunch." He shrugged; actually, it had been more of an accident. The feed had come out as soon as his hand had tightened on it.

"Good for you. Sometimes all you got is one good guess." Keely stretched one arm and then the other over his head. "God, that felt great. It was . . ." He paused, looking puzzled. "Great." Then his eyelids fluttered, and he fell backwards, Flavia catching him just before his head could hit the floor.

"Jesus!" Gabe leaped over the laptop to kneel down next to him. He felt for a heartbeat, trying to not panic. The virus couldn't kill anyone without sockets, it couldn't be *that* bad—

"Just guessing myself," Gina said tonelessly, "I'd say he fainted from hunger. When's the last time *you* ate?"

Gabe looked at her, startled, taking notice for the first

time of the ache that had been growing in his stomach over a period of hours. "Christ, you had to bring it up." He turned to Flavia.

"No food here," she said. "But I got a car. Wait till dark. We'll go shopping."

32

"You've changed," Sam said, trying not to fidget. She still couldn't believe he was there.

Gabe nodded. "So have you. Changed." He glanced over at the group, where Keely was stuffing his face from a seal-pack and giving an account of the impossible all-night drive in a car—a real car, not a hotwired rental—from Fairfax, mostly through backyards, it sounded like, to Venice. Sam couldn't imagine driving without GridLid, as clunky as it had always been. Not having any idea of what might be even half a mile ahead sounded like an easy way to get killed to her, especially in the dark; Gabe had to remind her that most of the streets were parking lots except for stretches the Guard had managed to clear with bulldozers. To let the emergency vehicles get through.

But of course. Sam felt foolish. You didn't even have to go up Palos Verdes to see the smoke from downtown L.A. Welcome back to the Age of Smog. She started to say something to Gabe and saw that his gaze had gone to Gina Aiesi again. The woman was sitting on the floor near the remains of Jasm's homunculus, head back against the wall, eyes closed. A little ways away from her, the Beater stood by alone, as if he were waiting for someone to tell him what he could do with himself.

"I forgot to tell you the good news the last time I saw you," Gabe said suddenly, still looking at Gina. "Your mother left me."

There was a pause, and then they both laughed.

"I'm sorry," Sam said, putting a hand to her mouth. "I don't know why *I'm* laughing, I don't know why it hit me funny."

"The shock of the mundane," her father said. He dug something out of his pocket. "And I got this today. Or yesterday, now."

She took the slip of paper from him. "What is it?"

"It's a ticket. I got a ticket for riding my bicycle on the sidewalk."

Sam burst out laughing again. "You rode a *bicycle?*"

"Actually, it was stolen."

"You *stole* a *bicycle? My father* stole a *bicycle?*" She laughed harder, and then she was hugging him, and he was hugging her back awkwardly, as if he had forgotten how.

"Sam-What-Am." Keely materialized beside her and pinched her arm gently.

She gave him a halfhearted swat. "That's 'Sam-I-Am.' And only Fez calls me that."

He unslung his laptop from over his shoulder and sat down next to her in the work island. A few hours of sleep and half a dozen seal-packs had taken the wild-man stare out of his face, but he still looked exhausted to her. "How long has Jones been dead?"

"Maybe a day. I knew you'd end up going to see him."

"I always view the body. Actually, he's just stuporous. I got him to open his eyes for a few seconds, but I don't think he saw me." He looked over at Gator's work island, where Fez and Gabe had been deep in conversation for over an hour. "*They* sure got chummy on short acquaintance."

Sam nodded absently. She'd been forcing herself not to stare at them. "Did Fez give you the complete rundown on Art Fish?"

"Yah. Not much I hadn't suspected for a while. I think I topped him with Visual Mark and the Computer Zombies from Hell."

"That sounds almost as good as *Tunnels through the Void.*"

"Nowhere near as good as that. Fez also told me that was how you managed simultaneously to save Art from the Big Eat and sort of reincarnate the net. Warping information."

She gave a short amazed laugh. "God. It didn't occur to me that I might owe it all to Beau. But I guess it *is* a little like that. Intergalactic subway system. At the time I laughed in his face."

"A common reaction to Beau," Keely said. "I would tell you I could never figure out what you ever saw in him, except in that particular glass house I shouldn't be throwing any stones."

Sam smiled to herself. They could have been in the middle of the genuine apocalypse, and they'd still be trying to figure out their relationships. Human beings, they never quit. On the other hand, she thought, looking at Keely's drawn features, it gave them something to think about besides dead bodies, of which there were plenty.

According to what Art had been able to piece together, along with what Keely and Gabe had told them, the infected were still out there and still dropping dead. Some had died immediately, others later, even after they had disconnected from the infected interface. Rewrite to destruction, Art had called it.

"I don't suppose you have any more to eat," Keely said after a bit, sounding a little sheepish.

Sam laughed. "We've got seal-packs coming out of our ears. Rosa made a food run just before everything blew."

"Rosa always was the practical one," Keely said as he followed her back to her squat space. " 'Never mind the tech shit, when do we eat?' I wish I'd thought of that when I was busy raiding uninfected equipment."

Sam dug several packs out of the hole in the floor. "Let's see what she left me: fruit compote, fish compote, fortified banana mash, navy bean soup compote—ha, ha, very funny, Rosa—dairy pack with real cheese—"

He took the dairy pack from her and tore open the top. "Haven't tried this one yet, and I wouldn't want to deprive you of something as wonderful as navy bean soup compote, especially if it's a personal gift. It's nice to know the survivalists were good for something, isn't it." He scooped out a blob of the soft white goop with two fingers, made a face, and put it in his mouth. "God help me, it does taste good. But then, a *shoe* would probably taste good to me right now. Especially if it's not drugged."

"Well, if you want more, the survivalists are all camped up Palos Verdes trying to make their radios work and selling us poor shortsighted slobs their least favorite gourmet flavors while they dine on squirrels and birds."

Keely made a revolted noise. "We'll have to factor that into the long-range ramifications of this thing, won't we?" He sighed. "God. If I hadn't picked that night to get toxed to the red line, I might have been able to stop it. They'd have caught me, and I'd have been canned well into my next lifetime because it would have killed Mark, but he was dead anyway. And maybe none of this would have happened."

"That's a big if, Keely. Too big."

He shrugged. "I was there. I have to think about them. All of them, even that son of a bitch Rivera. He went miserable and in pain and probably scared because he didn't know what was happening to him. None of them knew what was happening. Except Mark. He knew, and he couldn't do a thing about it, except ask me for help."

"Don't," Sam said urgently. "You don't know anything for certain."

"Yah, I do. You should have seen the message he left me. It didn't leave much doubt." He crumpled the seal-pack.

"Stop it," she said, grabbing his hand. "You really want to claim this is all your fault? Claim you're Napoleon, too, while you're at it. But before you go full stone tilt, you could think about a few other things. How we can make a real net out of the sympathetic vibration technique—"

"Art calls it the Vibrator Technique," Keely said.

"He would." Sam rolled her eyes. "How we can access whatever it is Art brought back with him. What we're going to eat when the survivalists run out of fortified banana mash and dairy pack with real cheese." She gave him a hard shake. "You want me to tell you you're a shit? Okay, you're a shit. Now be a useful shit. You know how. Gabe told me about that little show you put on in Fairfax, when you hacked the message through." She laughed a little. "It made me wish I'd been there."

"I was out of my head with reaction and a hangover and hunger," he said, looking away from her, embarrassed. "And probably from all the shit Rivera put in me, probably fucked me forever. Maybe I can plead brain damage."

"Shut *up*," Sam said impatiently. "If anyone's to blame, it's probably Rivera, or that Dr. Whoever, the one from Eye-Traxx."

"Someday I'll tell you how Rivera connected up with her," he said darkly.

"I'm not interested," Sam said. "It doesn't matter anymore." She took him back to her work island in the ballroom and sat him in front of her laptop.

"Remember the specs on this?" she said, taking the pump unit out of her pocket. He nodded. "I built it while I was on sabbatical, so to say, in the Ozarks."

"You actually run that on . . . yourself?" he asked as she connected the unit to the laptop feed.

She nodded, grinning at him. "A battery just isn't personal enough." The identification screen Art had shown her came

up, sans Art's image. "This is as far into it as I can get. Even
Art can't crack it. Maybe you'll have better luck. I don't know
what the partial room is supposed to signify, if anything. But
I'd love to know what that word means." She ran her finger
along it on the screen. "*Zamiatin.* Any ideas?"

"*Zamiatin,*" said a low, gravelly voice behind her, "is Visual
Mark's last name."

She turned around. Gina was standing a few feet behind
her, staring impassively at the screen.

"It's *him,*" Keely said wonderingly, looking from the screen
to Gina and back again. "That fucker didn't eat him, he's alive.
Or . . . well . . . *something.*"

"Stone the fucking crows at home," Sam said, "Are you sure?
Maybe it's part of the—"

Keely shook his head. "No, it's really him. I recognize the
screen. I saw it every time he cracked me in the penthouse."

"But we still can't get to him. We don't have the access code
or the password," Sam said, frustrated.

Keely gave a short, incredulous laugh. "Shit, *I've* got the
fucking access code and password! The access code's *VM,* and
the password is—" He looked at Gina, who had come over to
squat down between them. "The password is *Gina.*"

Gina's gaze didn't move from the screen. Sam wondered for
a moment if the woman had been hypnotized by the convo-
lutions of the rushing clouds in the background.

"Are you gonna *use* those fucking codes?" Gina said suddenly, glancing at Keely.

"I thought maybe you'd like to," he said.

"*Fuck.*" She stood up, folding her arms. "I'm done bringing
that bastard around every time he passes out. *You* do it."

Sam looked after her as she stalked over to where Gabe and
Fez were talking and said something to them. Keely jumped
up and ran after her.

"Can you see and hear okay?" Keely asked, standing in front
of the extra cam Percy had set up.

The man on the chaise looked confused. "Wait. I'm not . . ."
The screen flickered a few times and then snapped into sharp
focus. "Well, now. This is what I call stone-home high quality.
Who's there? You, the kid from the penthouse. You got out
okay."

"Yah. Thanks for fixing the door for me." Keely sounded so
shy and polite that Sam had to stifle a laugh.

"Christ—the Beater? *You* look like shit."

No lie, Sam thought, looking at the man. Several hours of rest seemed not to have helped him at all; he looked even more tired than when he'd arrived. And the sight of Mark obviously wasn't making him feel any better.

"*You!*" Mark said. "Move in toward the cam a little more, I can't pan this thing—"

"Yes, you can," came Art's voice from the speakers on the framework. "Feel around behind your focus."

Now Sam did laugh. If she hadn't known for certain, she would have sworn that Rosa and Percy were scamming them with a simulation. But they were among the group gathered around her work island, looking as boggled as anyone else. Except Gina Aiesi, who hung back, well out of cam range for the moment. Sam kept sneaking glances at her while she sat on the floor gripping the pump unit tightly to keep it still. Occasionally she pressed a hand to her stomach, to make sure the needles were secure.

"Yah, it *is* you," Mark said as the cam on the tripod gave a short jerk to the left, aiming directly at Gabe. "Hey, some stone-home change for the machines, ain't it?"

Sam thought her father looked as if he weren't sure whether to laugh, cry, or run like hell. "How does he do that?" he asked Keely. "Make a picture?"

"Good question," Keely said. "How do you do it?"

"By visualizing," Gina said quietly. The cam swung to her immediately.

"You're here." On-screen the pov zoomed to medium close-up.

"Yah, I survived," she said indifferently. "No thanks to you."

"Hey, anyone can have a stroke."

"But only *you* could release it into general circulation."

"On-line brain illness," Fez said. He was standing next to Gator. "If that's possible, then on-line therapy must be possible, too."

"Don't look at me," said Gina. "It wasn't *my* fucking idea."

"Mine, either," Gabe added in a small voice.

"But you *are* the only people here who have undergone the procedure." Fez looked at each of them. "And the only two we know for sure that haven't been infected."

"We don't know that at all," said Gabe.

"I never hurt either of you," Mark said solemnly. "I was just there, I *never* hurt you."

"My fucking ass." Gina pushed between Adrian and Jasm to stand directly in front of the cam. "Get a little higher up in the stupidsphere. You don't know that for sure, you don't know shit. And even if you think you do, I fucking *don't*. And neither does he." She jerked her head at Gabe.

"We could find out," Fez said slowly, "if we had the right hardware. Some direct interface connections and a sample of what Art calls the spike, which a diagnostic program could use to compare normal function against function that's been virally altered. The diagnostic wouldn't be too hard to devise. Ideally, we'd also have an uninfected brain as the control for comparison, though we could do without one. But we'd have to have interface connections."

The little gold woman, Flavia, let out a short, hard laugh. "*Never* get back to 'fax now. Push luck over a *cliff*."

"We don't have to." Gina went to Gator's work island, where Keely had stashed the bundle he'd brought with him and picked up the large piece of cloth he'd been using as a carryall. "We got connections, we got all kinds of toys and programs, and we got a sample right here." She took it to Fez. "It's a cape. Look in the collar."

"But it's been turned off," Gabe said.

"It's never turned off, it's just in nondisplay mode. Got solar collectors all around the edge of the hem. The program's still alive, and it's still infected. You want an uninfected brain, ask the woman who's got one." She pointed at Flavia.

"Not me," Flavia said. "Know you once, know you always. Knew *you* the night before. Remember?" The gold face took on a hard look. "Thanks for the memories."

Gina spread her hands. "I *said* don't do it. Didn't I?"

"We could use a simulation to stand in for the brain," Fez said after a moment. "That'll help me figure how to adapt the diagnostic—"

"I can do that," Mark said. "If Gina will let me. She might not want me to."

"Oh, cut the shit," Gina said irritably. "This is all your fucking fault, you better do everything you fucking know how."

It was good to be alive, and it was good to be alive again.

The configuration identified as Art Fish was a wonder and a revelation to him, a synesthetic concert of intelligence in conscious mode. In the first moments after the symbol *Gina* had broken through and brought him to a level where he could function and communicate again, Art Fish had shared memory with him. That had been disorienting at first, but with the data had come the format and the know-how. By the time he had seen Gina, he had changed in many, many ways.

But Gina stirred the old feelings in him nonetheless; perhaps even more so. He had been refined and reorganized to such an extent that he saw her with a clarity beyond anything he'd had in his last moments of meat awareness. He remembered that he loved her; that had not changed. There had been so much noise in the old meat that he would never have found his way through it to where she was, and now that the noise was gone, he didn't even have arms to put around her.

Art had much salient memory to share on the matter, in spite of the fact that It had never been flesh. *It* was the only thing he could think to call Art, and he still bridled somewhat against the old associations of the word, even though *It* in this new existence was a far more encompassing term than mere *he* or *she*. He supposed it was a matter of getting used to it . . . and getting used to *It*. He remained *he* in his own thoughts, though that too would change over time. Change for the machines. That could be a good thing.

He and Art were in complete rapport from the moment of his unlocking. The memory Art shared assured him that he would eventually find what he had instead of arms much more gratifying. Mark shared that just about anything was more gratifying than Schrödinger's dick and was surprised at how completely Art understood what he meant.

With Art's help he completed plotting Gina's life-graph, while Art shared Its own with him. Ambiguities were not so troublesome, because they could also be charted until there was a whole enchanted forest of decision trees to wander through over and over, taking different paths to different outcomes; a multitude of lifetimes in an instant.

Gina would be all right. Gabe Ludovic was capable of being good for her. They were not as odd a pairing as he might have thought; their differences did not raise the noise level. They could find each other. He felt a little sorry for them, since they would not be able to find each other as thoroughly as he and Art. Unless they used the sockets.

He had no simulations with him—he'd had to jettison as much as possible when he'd locked down—but it was surprisingly easy to recreate a simulation of a brain for Fez's use.

The old associations could be reconfigured so that the substance they had referred to could be reconstructed. It was an exquisite difficulty and showed him the truth of the first thing Art had shared with him: *Information can neither be created nor destroyed—it's accessible or it's inaccessible, but it is. If you have known it, and you can find the tiniest remnant of association, then you will know it again.*

When he understood that it really was possible, he thought it was the most comforting thing he'd ever heard in his life. Or lives. Things were different when you lived completely within the context.

He learned as he went, and he had the sensation of everything around him shifting while he remained constant, as if the context were opening wider and wider, letting him see more deeply into it. The outside meat-inhabited world became even clearer to him. Already he could distinguish most of the individuals just by their input; little things, the style, the patterns, the rhythms and pauses showed variations that were no longer minuscule to him, no two ever quite the same. Fez was like a cattle-herder even at a keyboard, directing the flow of useful things that had little intrinsic value until placed together in certain ways. He thought Fez might be closest to an understanding of what he, Mark, was now. Fez seemed to understand *configuration*, but he fell short of seeing more than a few dimensions. Mark reminded himself that none of them in their physical world was capable of rapid shifts in pov.

But it seemed that he always had been. The years of video playing in the old meat organ called brain had given him the capability, music and pictures shifting back and forth on him, being able to make one out of the other. They still served him. If he thought an association was lost, he could find it in the music and the pictures, and he could *always* find the music and the pictures. Even though the program director was gone.

Automatically he configured the diagnostic program before Fez could even start to adapt it. It was complicated, even with Art's help; better than letting Fez hack away at it for a day or two, and then debug it for another day or two, and perhaps end up with something that was not exactly what they wanted after all. And yet, as complicated as it was, it reduced down to something simple, as did all good programs. It was the output that would be Byzantine, not the program itself.

"What is this?" Fez wanted to know, staring at the results

on the screen. "You took a highly sophisticated viral diagnostic, and you made *this* out of it?" He raised his face to the cam.

Visualizing for him, Mark produced charts, and Art put them on the screens. "Outputs are what you'll look at," he told Fez. "Those are all ranges the outputs would fall into, with ambiguity margins. But you have to consider all of them together simultaneously to determine the presence or absence of something like the spike."

The one Art called Sam-I-Am moved into view, looked at the screens, and then frowned suspiciously at the cam. "Art? Are you screwing around again?"

"Not me," Art vocalized. "There isn't time. The Phoenix node just went down, and Alameda's gone with it, just like I told you it would." Art had already shared the information with him, but Mark waited through the protocol so necessary for communication through all their innate people-noise. "It's on the way. It's been around the world a few times, but it's finally spiraling in on us."

Sam wiped both hands over her face. "Don't tell me—sympathetic vibrations, right?"

"Not really your fault, Sam," Art told her. "It would have learned how on its own anyway, after it had sophisticated enough."

"*Sophisticate* is not a verb," came Rosa's voice from out of cam range.

"It is now," Art said. "All outside communications are down. What will you do when the power goes?"

"Will it do that?" Sam asked. The anxiety on her face was a road map of her life. Rosa appeared next to her.

"It will do that. If it can't get in and take us, it'll crash us."

Sam turned to Fez. "How long can we run on solar and batteries?"

"Not long. We don't have half-enough solar, and the monitors are already on those."

"I *knew* all those goddamn monitors would be a drain," Sam said.

"Well, they're off now," Fez said and looked worriedly into the cam. "How long do we have before it works its way over to us?"

"About three hours," Art told him.

"That might give us long enough to run one diagnostic. Even one like this." He gestured at the screen where the one line of Mark's masterpiece was displayed.

>How are you?<

"But it's more than enough time to compress," said Art.

"Compress?"

"For nanoware."

Sam's face was a portrait of surprised hope. Mark thought she looked exactly like Gabe Ludovic for that moment. Then she frowned. "You could both fit?"

"We're topological acrobats," Art said. "All a matter of making the associations work in multiple dimensions. We should start. Now."

Fez held up a hand. "Art, you've never compressed that much with, ah, another individual presence. Neither has Mark. In the reorganization, you could lose your . . . ah . . . distinguishable . . . distinguishing . . ."

"No information will be lost," Art said. "And if we don't, it's crash time anyway."

"I wish we had more time to consider this," Fez said doubtfully. "If you're such a grand topological acrobat, why has it always taken an entire net to host you?"

The flash of activity Mark felt from Art went on-screen as a grin. "If you had your choice of a shoe box or a hundred-room castle, where would you live?"

"Don't ask that of someone who's been in a squat space for months," Sam said, and moved out of cam range. She came back a few moments later with a couple of feeds. "We'll have to take my unit off batteries and put it back on me," she told Fez.

"Gross!" Rosa called, still off-cam.

"No, she's right," Fez said, sighing a little. "To be disgustingly honest, I wish we had several more of them."

"We'll work on it," Sam said. "Later. It'll be something to do while we wait for someone to reinvent macrotechnology."

"I want to monitor this while we still can," Fez said. "Put as much of the compression on-screen as possible."

Art was agreeable, and Mark echoed it, knowing that the process was already well under way.

He wished he had Art's certainty that it was possible. It seemed a bit too much like going down his own rabbit hole. Art shared that he was still suffering a meat hangover, a block that prevented him from perceiving how dimensions of meaning could overlap with no loss, whether it was a memory or themselves. It would mean at least a temporary loss of the redundancy that had always been the safety net of human intelligence, but Mark was no longer that kind of human, and Art never had been.

The process itself was actually soothing. They might have been a couple consolidating their belongings as they moved into the same living quarters, which was something else he'd never done, discarding duplicated items or placing them in storage, carefully identifying and arranging what was left. Redundancies were being downloaded to chip for later restoration if possible. If desirable.

If desirable. Mark began to understand that it might not be so desirable to him later. The old concepts of *private property* and *individual* were fast losing their importance to him as he and Art came closer to being two aspects of one consciousness rather than two separate intelligences. And at the same time his sense of identity intensified. He was approaching the state of essence, a balance point where the question of self had room for only one answer: yes or no. And the step following essence was implosion. The rabbit hole.

By himself he could not have maintained the balance, not in an unfrozen, dynamic state. But Art was there for counterbalance.

"Are you sure there's going to be enough power?" Rosa asked for the millionth time.

Fez smiled. "Nanoware takes nano-power. Didn't I always say you were a force to be reckoned with, Sam-I-Am?"

"No," Sam said honestly. "I've never heard you say anything like that."

"Well, didn't you always know it?" He pulled a chair over and sat down next to her at her work island. There was a feed running from the pump to the large monitor so they could keep track of the rest of the consolidation process, though Sam doubted that anyone understood the two columns of symbols scrolling so rapidly as to appear to be garbage. It was being recorded, in case of any difficulties in reversing the process later. She felt a little sad. She had a feeling the merge was going to end up being permanent, and she was going to miss Art-by-himself.

Fez seemed to have lost all his doubts in the last hour. It wasn't just compression, he'd said, it was compression and encryption combined; the first case of voluntary compression and encryption on record. Rosa had wanted to know if that called for another national holiday or just a media conference, if and when there was any media again.

Now Rosa was grimacing at her. "Maybe we do need a backup power source," Sam told Fez. "In case I drop dead of cardiac arrest. Or Rosa goes crazy and rips my wires out."

"Rosa will behave," Fez said mildly. "I don't expect cardiac arrest, unless you've been toxing out on the sly. Have you?"

She shook her head. "No. It's just that the more I think about it, the more sensible a backup seems. How much longer do we have?"

"Not quite an hour and a half. Art and Mark should be done long before the deadline."

Sam glanced at the monitor again. Just about every other program had been downloaded to chip and stored, leaving the system wide open and nearly empty. After a while they would shut it down, and that would be it. They'd be cut off from the rest of the world. Sam couldn't remember a time in her life when that had ever happened before; twenty-four hours a day every day for almost eighteen years, she had been within arm's reach of outside contact; the idea of not having anything made her feel claustrophobic, and she said so.

"I've never thought of it that way," Fez told her. "Though I must admit, I've felt antsy since the dataline went down. It bothers me that I can't press a button and check on the rest of the world, or at least the small parts of it that I'm interested in. I'm not the only one. You haven't been able to walk around and see it, dear, but the irritability threshold around here is lower than it used to be. We're not in our natural habitat anymore. We've become denizens of the net. Homo datum."

"Synners."

Gina was perched on the edge of a box, not far from the incomprehensible screen.

"Pardon?" Fez said.

"A word somebody came up with a long time ago," she said. "From synthesizer. That which synthesizes."

Fez's face took on a dreamy look. "You just pushed one of his buttons," Sam told Gina. "Now all he needs is a box of doughnuts, a couch, and all night to discuss it."

"I wouldn't mind a pot of gourmet coffee, either," he said. "We might actually have two species of humans now, synthesizing human and synthesized human, all of us being the former, and Art Fish being the latter."

"And Mark being the bastard offspring of both," Gina added.

Fez blinked. "Make that three species. And like all good life forms, we have a natural enemy that can prey on all of us." He sighed. "This would have been fascinating if it could have lasted. But we have slightly over an hour now before we all revert to homo sapiens. Temporarily but, alas, indefinitely."

There was a beep from the pump unit. The large screen lit up with the words *Program Completed*.

Sam looked from the screen to the pump unit and then to Fez. "That's it? Really?"

"That's it, really. They're compressed. Got your shades ready?"

Sam hesitated. "Why don't we keep running a high-res monitor on solar as long as we can? That way, there'll be more power for the unit."

Fez gave her a squeeze. "You're a genius, Sam-I-Am."

She squirmed away from him uncomfortably. "It just makes sense, is all."

"Sometimes that's all it takes to be a genius."

She made a face at him. Having forced herself to adjust to him with Gator, she found herself annoyed at the slightest show of affection for herself. Or maybe she was just irritable because the dataline was down.

Keely detached his own keyboard with the battery and connected it for her. "That'll be easier than your keypad. Might as well have all the comforts while you can."

She smiled her thanks at him. "Should we ask them how they're doing, or let them signal us when they're ready?" Sam asked.

The monitor lit up then with a message.

> W h a t e v e r   y o u   d o ,   S a m ,
D O N ' T   J O G G L E
T H O S E   N E E D L E S ! <

"Glad to see the sense of humor survived compression," Fez said.

"But whose," murmured Keely.

"Come on," Rosa said, "haven't you ever laughed when you were in a tight spot?" As Sam was looking for something to throw at her, she noticed Gina retreating to a far corner of the ballroom and Gabe following after. She looked up at Keely questioningly. He shrugged, making a to-and-fro waggle with one hand.

There was another beep from the pump unit, and a new message appeared on the screen.

>We have had an Idea.<

She didn't jump when he touched her shoulder, and she didn't pull away when he put his arms around her, but she was not responsive. Two out of three, Gabe thought nonsensically, resting his cheek on the top of her head.

He had gone to great lengths to give her room when they had first arrived. Well, it had been that, and the surprise of seeing Sam. He'd needed room himself, to reorient himself with Sam, and he still wasn't sure of himself with her. Too much simulated living, he thought; out here you couldn't just change the program, wipe the old referents, and pick up the story at any point.

God, you're profound, hotwire, he thought. In his own inner voice this time. He had refused to let phantoms surface in his mind since leaving the cellar in Fairfax. The little pile of chips was probably still there on the floor next to where Keely had danced through his hack. The chips were useless now, voided; Keely had adapted them and shot them into the infected net. When he let himself think of it, he liked to believe that Marly and Caritha had gone in there intact in the *Headhunters* scenario, assuming on some level that they were just on blind-select.

After a bit Gina pulled back with a wary look. "Who the fuck do you think you are, anyway."

He barely hesitated. "Just another synner."

"Not bad," she said. "You keep surprising me. Try this one: how long do you think we've got?"

"Till when?"

"Till our fucking synning heads blow up."

"If that were going to happen, don't you think it would have by now?"

She looked so startled that he laughed. Startlement dropped years from her face.

"I don't think it's that we're infected," he went on, "as much as—oh, incurably informed."

Her eyes narrowed. "*You* were the one that raised *that* idea," she said. "*You* said—"

"I know." He shrugged without letting go of her. "I was wrong."

"Just like that—'I was wrong.' Sure. Check with me again when I'm a fucking—"

He twined his fingers in her dreadlocks and kissed her. She hesitated, and then he felt her arms go around his waist and hang on tight.

"You think we can synthesize something together?" he asked after a while.

"I'll pop your chocks again if we don't. I'll take your whole fucking head off."

The Gina Aiesi School of Sweet Talk. He was going to have to get used to it.

Someone behind him made a throat-clearing noise. He turned and found Keely standing there looking embarrassed and amused. "I wouldn't interrupt if it weren't kind of important," he said, "but I think you'd better come over and listen to this."

Her first reaction was an unqualified No-Fucking-Chance. It sounded like a stupid way to get their heads blown up and toss the AI to the sharks at the same time. She could tell little old Sam hated it, and as far as sense went, her money was on Gabe's kid. All the rest of them reminded her of some kind of retrograde experiment in techno-Walden-Pondism on the communal level, including the white-headed eminence who seemed to have all the answers. The old guy, Fez, he could sound pretty good, but Gabe's kid had been bolted together right on the first try.

She kept looking at the little box resting on the kid's leg, as if there were something to see there, and they all kept talking, including Ludovic. She had a feeling he was leaning toward it but would stand wherever she stood.

Abruptly the music clicked on in her head while they talked on, and the screen flashed messages from the Incredible Shrunken Entities. Shrunken heads.

I want you. . . .

Ninety percent of life was being there, and the rest was being there on time.

Be there for me one last time. Last stroke, you should pardon the expression, in a twenty-ump-year pattern. Sure, be there. And if she was, would she be anywhere when it was over?

"If we don't do it," Ludovic was saying, "someone else'll think of it, if they haven't already. It makes sense. If it's intelligent, you need something intelligent to fight it, and no one else knows it as well as we do. It might eat whole *expeditions* before anyone figures out how to put a stop to it. And by then it might be too strong—"

"They won't even do that," the woman named Jasm was saying. "They'll just string a new net and use that until it happens again. And it *will* happen again, because they won't know how to prevent it. Or stop it."

Keely was pounding away on the keyboard, more subdued this time as he transmitted the conversation to Mark and Art, who were identifying themselves as Markt now. Figured. That was a good one. She could have told them who was *really* fucking *marked*.

"If it's going to happen, it has to happen soon," Fez said apologetically. She knew without looking at him that he was talking to her. "While we're still running some clean lines. Otherwise we'll be socked in."

"Do you *know* we've still got some clean lines?" she heard herself asking.

"I've had the system running split-second checks at regular intervals. It hasn't come out of Phoenix or San Diego in this direction yet."

"Probably because we're mostly off-line, so it hasn't sensed the activity," said the good-looking one with the unlikely name of Gator. "And maybe it won't. Maybe as long as we're off-line, it'll stay away."

"What good is that?" said the little kid. Adrian, the one who couldn't read or write. "We'll have clean lines we can't use. That's as bad as being infected."

Her gaze returned to the little tiny box where Mark had been distilled into his new existence. *See past all the old trash to the core of what you thought you were loving all these years. A hot shot of truth. If it isn't the way you thought it was, can you take it? You really want to know anybody that* well*?*

She just didn't want her head getting blown up, she didn't want to stroke out in a fucking computer network.

I want you. . . .

What if it is what you thought it was, and more besides— *and it's in there* now, *and it'll never be out here again. Think you can take it?*

There was too much to face. Too much. After twenty-ump years she needed a rest. She was fucking *entitled*.

"We can use the sample to see what we're dealing with," Ludovic said. He picked up the cape.

"No," she said.

He looked at her, defeated.

"We can hook the cape up to the big system and use it as bait," she went on. "It's got the first edition, so to speak, and it wasn't on-line when Mark stroked out for good. The Big One'll run right at it. That sound fucked enough to work, right up there in the stupidsphere?"

Keely's fingers danced on the keyboard.

The screen blinked. >*What the fuck.*<

"Okay," said Fez. "What the fuck."

33

Fez was spooning fortified banana mash into her mouth as if she were an invalid, and though it made her want to squirm with annoyance, Sam held still for it. If Gabe could do what he was about to do, she could make peace with Fez, at least in her own mind. For the first time he had expressed admiration for her vision in constructing the pump unit rather than only revulsion for the power source. Having his open respect made up for a lot.

"I really did see the usefulness of it all along," Fez was saying, "as outré as I found it. A computer running on a power source that can't be compromised—"

"Unless you die."

"Then you can keep an extra set of connections in a potato and always carry it in your pocket. 'Is that a potato in your pocket, or are you just glad to see me?' "

Sam blinked at him. "Huh?"

"I should have known you wouldn't get it." Fez sighed. "The one time I make a dirty joke with you, and you don't get it." She started to say something else, and he stuck the spoon in her mouth. "Eat up. We want you to stay comfortable."

She swallowed and pushed the spoon aside. "No more. I'm fortified and banana-mashed to the gills. If you want to see to anyone's comfort, take care of my dad and Gina. I don't have to be anything more than a potato."

Fez regarded her solemnly. "You're still against it."

"Yah, I am. I don't think they can bring it off. It sounds like a computer game I once wrote. Or a bad B-feature that did well in the wannabees. Ever hear of something called *House of the Headhunters*?"

"No. But the title could belong to a good many of all the computer games ever written. The rest being variations on Parcheesi."

"Really?"

"No." Fez sighed again. "Truthfully, I don't really like it, either. I think there's a good chance we could lose them all. And if it were just Art alone in there with them, I'd never allow it. Art's always been viral at heart. Figurative heart. If he were a flesh-person, I'd watch him for sociopathic tendencies."

Sam raised her eyebrows. "Why? I never found him particularly antisocial."

"Not lately you haven't. But what's more antisocial than a virus? Besides, he never had to be antisocial by the time you came along. By then we were all at his beck and call. But didn't you find him just a little bit stuck on himself?"

"Yah. When I thought he was a person. Flesh-person, I mean."

"The addition of Mark makes me more optimistic," Fez said. "Not very much more, but some. Humans have always been smarter than viruses. Humans drive, viruses are driven. Even the intelligent ones. Three-plus humans ought to have a fighting chance against one intelligent virus."

"But it's not a virus," Sam said.

"An intelligent spike, then." Fez let out a long breath. "No matter what it is, it's still *driven*. No initiative—the big human advantage. I hope."

Gina and Gabe came over then with Keely, who was carrying the cape and the connections. "All clear," Keely said. "The diagnostic says the connections are free of all infection. But I still don't know if four each are enough."

"Mark says it will work with four apiece," Gabe said. "My left hemisphere and Gina's right."

Fez started to say something, but Gina turned to Gabe.

"You sure you want to run at this thing?"

Sam met her father's gaze evenly. They'd hardly spoken since he and Gina had decided to do it. She wanted to tell him not to, that the risks were too great, that he didn't know what he was getting into, but something in his expression stopped her. He was looking for her support, she realized suddenly. Not her help, or even her approval, but just for her *not* to discourage him. He'd had enough of that with Catherine. She looked down at the pump unit resting on her lap and cradled it protectively in both hands before she looked up at her father again.

"Yah," he said to Gina. "Yah, I do."

Gina shook her head. "You're a stone-home crazy fucker."

In spite of everything Sam smiled. It was the nicest thing she'd ever heard anyone say to her father.

They were lying side by side on a couple of narrow mattresses donated by Jasm and Graziella. Keely checked and rechecked the boot program before he divided the connections from the cape between them.

"When you connect," he told them, "the transmission and stealth programs will boot with you, and they'll stick by you till you disconnect. You can't accidentally disable them, but you might not always recognize them, and I'm afraid you won't be able to get a status reading whenever you need one. But whatever kind of controls you need, you ask—"

"Are you gonna fucking let us do this?" Gina demanded. "Or are you gonna fuck around till the fucking lights go out?"

Sam felt Rosa squeeze her hand, and she squeezed back. Keely looked up at her from where he was kneeling next to Gina.

"Sam, if you have to go to the bathroom, go now."

"If I have to go to the bathroom," she said with a nervous laugh, "you can bring me a saucepan, and everyone can look the other way."

"Let's just fucking *go*," Gina said, staring up at the ceiling. She reached over and took Gabe's hand.

"Okay," he said. Sam winced as he twisted his neck to take a last look at her. Suddenly she wished she'd thought to give him a hug or a kiss. Then his eyes were closed, and the program was running.

He was looking at a strange, half-finished room with black and white tiles and roofless walls against a backdrop of swiftly moving clouds. Or rather, he was trying to look at it. There was something very bright in the center of the room, undulating like a reflection of the sun on a ripply lake surface. It blinded him, blotting out most of the scene so that he would have to look away and readjust. He could sense Gina nearby. Her energy simmered like continuous, contained explosions. After a bit he turned toward her, and her visual was Gina as he knew her, but coming through strangely, the textures and colors shifting like a painting in flux.

She said something, but he couldn't understand it.

"Everything will be in phase shortly," said a voice from the bright light. "We're a little ways from full synthesis." And then: "Some trip, hey, Gina?"

The brightness became less blinding, not because it was fading, but because he was becoming adjusted to it. Gradually he came to distinguish a figure within the light, one figure but with two images superimposed on it, each image waxing and waning, sometimes in fragments so that it was a shifting composite rather than two separate images trading full dominance.

"Loads of room in here," the voice went on, and Gabe realized that it, too, was a composite. He turned to Gina again, and her image was smoothing out, the painting transmuting from impressionistic to photographic realism. And then it was like seeing her come through some transparent barrier, glass or water, before something gave, and he was perceiving her with total clarity.

The figure in the light moved aside to show them a four-paned window floating in midair against the backdrop of clouds. It put its hand on the windowsill; everything contained within the frame vanished, leaving a rectangle of darkness.

"Ipseorama," the composite voice said. " 'See distantly.' It's the word *television* would have been if the Latin and Greek roots had been reversed."

"Thanks," Gina said sarcastically. "I really needed to know that."

The figure was amused. "Just testing out the synthesis." It put one leg over the sill and paused, sitting half in and half out of the room. "You can see as distantly as you want to see. We're opening the line to the Phoenix node now." It climbed the rest of the way through the window.

Before he could think about it, Gabe's pov zoomed forward, through the frame and into the black.

A status line winked into being and marched across the bottom of the screen. "They're on-line to Phoenix," Sam said, and then felt foolish. The only person present who couldn't read a status line was Adrian. But nobody made any smart remarks. Maybe it was only natural to have someone call the action, so to speak.

Fez was hunched forward in the chair next to her, hands gripping his knees, staring at the screen intently. Rosa was still holding her hand, and Percy was camped next to Keely with his entire inventory of tools, hardware, and fragments of hardware. Gator had parked a supply of fresh batteries next to the screen, along with a couple of laptops. Everyone else —Jasm, Graziella, Kazin, Rodriguez, a few of Percy's merry little brigands, that drummer Flavia Something, and the Beater, looking old, tired, and anxious—hovered nervously. Another monitor nearby displayed the continuous diagnostic running on the big system while the patterns on the cape gyrated and squirmed like something live.

"I wish we could have tapped a full visual for this instead of just a status line," Sam said.

"We couldn't tax their capacity that much," Keely told her. "They'd have to cooperate in the transmission, even if I bugged their povs. Too much of a drain on their concentration."

"Could you crack in while this was in progress?" Fez asked.

Keely shrugged. "Maybe. Why?"

"If we lose contact with them, we could see what happened."

"If we lose contact with them, we wouldn't see much for long."

A new message appeared on the screen, just above the status line. >*Loading Headhunter programs.*<

"Headhunter programs?" Sam said. "A B-feature?"

"One hell of a surprise for your father," Keely said, smiling at the screen.

On the mattress Gabe looked jarringly peaceful, as if he were asleep and having the best dream of his life.

For Gabe it was like crouching at the base of an enormous generator, the vibrations shuddering all the way through to his bones. He could feel Gina's presence as well, an energetic mix of anger, fear, and ready aggression that spoke to his own apprehension and uncertainty. On the outside he had believed a little more in the idea of joining forces with Mark and Art —Markt, now—than he did on the inside in this ragged landscape of what seemed to be enormous shadows of almost-things.

"You think we can synthesize something?" The words came from Gina, but he recognized them as his own. "*Really* synthesize something," she added. "Something of us, to use against it."

He started to reach out to her and then hesitated. Actually touch anyone this closely? Suddenly the idea of that kind of contact was a hard, wordless fright.

"Part my brain and part yours," Gina said. "Doesn't get much more fucking intimate than that. If I can stand it, you can. What've you got?"

He tried to think. What *did* he have?

The house looked quiet enough, but then the whole street was quiet, and Gabe knew that was all wrong. *All* wrong—they were gone, a pile of dead chips on a cellar floor in Fairfax.

"Not quite." Marly grinned down at him and then threw a muscular arm around his shoulders. On his other side Caritha slipped an arm around his waist and nudged him with the handcam. "Hope you don't mind about all the modifications. Been a shitload since you last saw us. You thought it was a glitch in the program, but it was him all along. Art. Only I guess he's calling himself Markt now. More to him."

"More to everything," Marly added.

Gabe was too stunned to speak. There was no doubt they were real, or as real as they ever had been, not just phantoms pulled from his memory but the programs themselves, saved or restored, he wasn't sure which.

Programs?

"Try again, hotwire," said Marly.

The kid sitting at the laptop: *Stone the fucking crows at home! This stuff's infected!*

You thought it was a glitch in the program, but it was him all along.

Even after? Gabe wondered. *Even after the sockets?* He turned his attention inward, and there, deep in his mind, he found it, a little bit of a glow, the same glow that he saw in Marly's eyes, in Caritha's. It was like looking into an enormous dark box and discovering a very tiny, very perfect diamond. Incurably informed?

There was a pull outward like the one he'd felt when Gina had yanked him out out of a chair one night a lifetime ago. Her touch was unmistakable.

"Hate to interrupt you when you're contemplating the fucking jewel in the lotus," she said, "but it's here. The fucking program director's back."

"Good," Caritha said, hefting the cam. "I want that spike. I don't like programs that go around blowing up people's brains."

"Then let's go do a little damage," Marly said, and made a move toward the house, pulling Caritha and Gabe with her.

* * *

From within the new configuration of Markt, Art reconvened
and watched with real fondness. He'd always liked the first
part of the *Headhunters* scenario, where Gabe went barging
in with the women, a reluctant hero fast losing his reluctance
for the sake of people he loved, and then developing a taste
for heroics as he went along. That was the way he'd always
read it in Marly and Caritha, anyway.

Besides, it would help Ludovic if he just went to it as though
it were the enemy he had always faced in *House of the Headhunters*. Perhaps there really wasn't any other enemy for him
anyway.

Gina's enemy would be more difficult to articulate. He would
have to leave that to the Mark part of his new self.

Who do you love?
The only thing nastier than forty-seven miles of barbed wire
was forty-eight, and she hadn't had to go that far yet. Just
through this crowd of bangers on the tiny little dance floor to
a likely-looking head nodding up and down, and déjà vu shuddering through her like inner thunder, more than déjà vu.
Déjà-voodoo: had happened because she was reliving it now.
Who do you love?
Say again, doll, I didn't hear you that time.
She went through the door, stopped, looked at someone
pounding it out with two sticks on the hood of an abandoned
limo.
*Who abandons limos this time of night on this street at the
outer edge of Hollywood, land of the lost?*
She went over and peered into the back window, cupping
her hands around her eyes. The dark glass de-opaqued, and
she saw herself and Ludovic lying side by side with connections
trailing from their heads.
Disturbed, she stepped back, and Quilmar threw an arm
around her shoulders, drawing her into Valjean's long, narrow
kitchen. "Fucking *right* there's nothing fucking wrong with
porn," he said. "Porn is the fucking secret of life, sister-mine.
If you can't fuck it, and it doesn't dance, eat it or throw it
away. That's the fucking order of the universe, and I'm at the
fucking *top* of the food-fuck-and-dance chain. And I don't know
what *that* is"—he gestured at the limo, which was now on one
of the screens in Valjean's living room—"but it makes me
horny, and that's all that matters."

Easy one; she left Quilmar in the kitchen again, turned away from the grotesque sight of him attempting the forcible seduction of a major appliance, and found herself back outside.

!! U B THE ASS TO RISK!!
Many Main-Run Features Starring U!
COMPLETE ROCK VIDEO CATALOG, TOO!

Gina nodded. It wasn't going to waste its energy trying to fool her with little things. Which didn't mean she wouldn't have to be any less careful.

Know you once, know you always.

Who do you love?

Doll, why do you keep on askin' me that? You must be seeing something I didn't say.

Right; stone-fucking-home exactly. She could always see what he didn't say. With a fever in her chest. Nasty bridge, running from the top all the way down, hammering every step of the way, and she went, chased by her own growling need, but déjà-voodoo told her it was his, too. Her need and his, but hers had gone east, and his had gone west, hers had gone out, and his had gone in, and wasn't that always the fucking way of it?

Who do you love?

Oh, doll, wouldn't you like to know?

Sticks beating it out on golden garbage cans, a roadmark to tell her she was going in the right direction. *Move.*

The Mimosa was empty. She turned around and around, looking, but they weren't there now. They weren't hiding under the piers, they weren't watching from the shadows, they weren't anywhere. And then the ball of fire came anyway, and she started to walk through it.

More than a lot were left with when the smoking lamp started to burn low—.

Who—

. . . *Gina* . . . (So faint she didn't think she'd really heard it.)

There was a man with a different world in his eyes, still real, made of noise and light. More than a lot were left with—

Who do—

. . . *Gina* . . . (Yah, heard it this time.)

There was a man, real, taking the long way home, walking a strip that had once been by the ocean where she had run across the nasty bridge, but that was all in the fire now, too, along with all those things that might have been.

Who do you—

There was a man in a room, changed for the machines, not real now, and a stranger, real, on a stony shore under a gray sky, turning slowly to her.

Do you still want to?

Running down the long road. Sparks to lightning, white and otherwise.

Who do you love?

You tell me, doll.

He was there on the sand, waiting, and she made a move toward him.

Gina!

Something bumped her, and the memory came up like light.

You win the game as soon as you get them to say it. Then you do whatever you want. And she'd never said it, not once.

"Too fucking easy," she said, backing way, way off, until the Mimosa and the ball of fire she hadn't walked through was as small as something she might see from the wrong end of a telescope. "Where is it, really?"

Old habits, they do die hard, don't they. That's yours, ain't it—looking for Mark. And finding him.

She reached for Markt, but the sense of him was shockingly absent. Nor could she get a sense of Ludovic. She was suddenly and most definitely alone. Ridiculous, *someone* had just been calling her name—

And now you can find him wherever you look. What you've always wanted. Whether you know it or not. And I want you. I want you.

What the fuck was she supposed to do now?

Whatever's right, Gina.

Whatever's—

Markt looked sympathetic—both of him. He was there so suddenly, she didn't have time to be surprised, or even to demand where the fuck he'd been. "What's your weak spot, Gina? Better get to it before he does."

Weariness was a sudden ache all the way through her. "My weak spot. You got something we can make a list with?"

Markt glowed at her. "Who do you still want to love?"

* * *

"—*right*," she growled. She hadn't taken it through the wire, but she had imagined how it would be; how it was. Like floating through a tangible fog bank, and as each shadow pulsed, there would be a corresponding pressure deep in the head, an invisible finger pressing here, and here, and here, searching for some particularly sensitive spot. Like being molested in some weird, witchy way.

"I want you. . . ."

She was in a place from years before, and Dylan's strangely engaging nasal voice was speaking the truth for both of them. Mark was sitting on the floor, waiting for her reaction.

Laugh that old laugh, break it up and break it down. Hey, jellyroll—

But it wasn't anything to laugh about, was it? Missed chances, they don't have a lot of humor value, do they? So now there's a second chance. You gonna take it this time, or shine it on?

The desire in the room had been electric, was electric now. Not just the sex, but the full, rounded desire for completion. She'd felt that, too, the same way he had. Completion.

"But is there really such a thing as a second chance?"

Ludovic was standing over by the door. Mark turned up the music, and Ludovic melted away. Right, he hadn't figured into it then.

But he did now. He wasn't a missed chance. He was the one she was going to have to do something about.

Mark was still waiting. But this was an easy one, too. She opened her mouth to laugh that old laugh.

"Are you sure you want to do that?" he said seriously. "Looking for me all those years, and now you found me again. Wouldn't you rather save me this time? You could."

In the moment of hesitation, the pictures came to her. Two decades and some-odd of the show that had no end, her life, his life, their life, hit-and-run, kiss-and-tell, a little walk that had turned into a long run. *Who do you still want to love?*

Oh, lover, I been afraid you'd ask me that.

"Save me," Mark said, the plea in his voice carefully small. "I don't want to be this way. If I did, do you think I'd have made it so fucking easy on you?"

Oh, lover, I been afraid you'd ask me that, too.

* * *

They were flattened against the wall in the dark hallway, Marly's strong arm thrown across his chest. Gabe waited for the voice, wondering who it would sound like.

"It's gonna be different this time, hotwire," Marly whispered. "You ready?"

"What?" he said, confused.

"You're gonna have to be. Here it comes." Before he could protest, she grabbed him and swung him around to stand in the doorway all alone.

He was looking across the twentieth-floor terrace at Gina standing on the railing. She had the harness on, but he saw that the cords weren't connected to the railing this time. When she went over, she would be falling for real.

For . . . 'real'? Could it be 'real' *this* way, in here?

Oh, yah; it would be different, maybe, but no less *real*, a virtual fall and a virtual impact, but when she hit bottom, the effect would amount to something real.

Did she know?

He couldn't tell for certain. She seemed to know and not know at the same time, and something suggested she would accept it either way.

Schrödinger's Gina.

Gabe frowned; where had *that* come from? He took a step toward her.

"Floor's mined," Caritha said offhandedly.

Gina looked over her shoulder at him, her gaze both meeting him and going through him in an odd way. What was *she* seeing, he wondered. Did she even realize she was on the railing? What was *her* context?

You got to know your context, because you're only gonna get one shot at getting into it.

Yes, but if she thought it was one thing, and he thought it was another, then what was the *real* context? He burned with impatience and frustration. How was he supposed to know what to do?

"Whatever's right," Gina said. "How'd you like to get even?"

Even? He could almost have laughed. There was nothing even about Gina.

The loose harness connections on the rail swayed slightly in the breeze.

"Make up your mind," she said. "I gotta go one way or the other, I jump or you push me."

No, that was wrong, he thought wildly, but he had no way to tell her. It wasn't in her context.

"Gettin' late, hotwire," Marly said. Her voice sounded just a bit strange to him now. "Already know you can't argue. What's next?"

He turned in what he thought was her direction, and the images rushed over him.

Go somewhere. Go somewhere.

Floor's mined.

Change for the machines.

MORE DRUGS.

Run Personnel run.

Take a little walk with me.

Why the fuck didn't you watch where you were going?

The desire on the terrace was electric. Gina started to turn away from him. The scene blurred in front of him, briefly became an arc of stony shore around a lake. He was back on the terrace before he could even be startled, and he saw Gina's knees bend as she prepared to jump.

Somewhere, someone was laughing. *If you can't fuck it and it doesn't dance—*

He shoved the thought away. *If you can't argue, and you can't stop it . . .*

Last thing they'd expect.

Hey, hotwire—you're an asshole.

Yah, but I'm trying to quit.

Just as her feet left the rail, he hurled himself forward and caught her in midair, at the moment before she dropped.

Port in a storm, nowhere else to go. That bother you?

She already knew the answer to that, but he told her anyway. They toppled onto the sagging mattress in a frantic, urgent tangle.

That's what I've got: a port in a storm, he thought.

That's more than most people are left with when the smoking lamp starts to burn low.

The feel of her was even more tangible in this state, if that was possible. The sense-memory of her T-shirt against his hands was wildly vivid, the warmth of her skin a shocking contrast, and then the taste and smell of her flooded him, carrying him to her like a hurricane tide.

Her physical strength had caught him unawares, in spite of

that punch she'd given him. The power in her muscles had been astonishing. Or maybe it had been the force of her passion that had taken him by surprise, so different from long-ago, bloodless couplings with Catherine, no paler for being dim in the recollection.

Or maybe it had been the force of his own passion that had been the real stunner that night (was the real stunner *now*); until then he had all but forgotten that there was even the potential for passion inside him, let alone at this intensity. But he *could*, could then, could now—

We do what we do. We do it because we can. The words came to him now clearly, what he had only been able to understand in a primitive, gut-level way from the sound of her breathing in the dark. *I'm lucky I can dance, and so are you, and we're lucky we can dance together now. Take a little walk with me. A little traveling music, please. Here it comes. Be there for you. What does this remind you of, an open window or an open wound . . .*

The response poured from him without his willing it.

Well, the fact is, Gina, sometimes it looks like one and sometimes like the other, and it's really a combination of both. But what really matters, Gina, what really matters is, I climbed on in, because ninety percent of life is being there, and the other ten percent is being there on time, and it was time. And it still is, Gina. It still is time. But do I really have to tell you that?

No, he hadn't. But it had been good for her to hear it. She'd wanted to hear it.

Don't tell me who my enemy is; tell me who it isn't.

Okay, Gina; whatever works, whatever's right.

"How the fuck *did* you find me?"

"It wasn't that hard," Gabe said. "Not once I had the right associations."

There was a pause on the brink of one moment before the next.

"Jesus, yes, we've both got that, Ludovic. Run with it from there."

From there to anywhere, he thought. He could do that. What else did he have?

Take a little walk with me.

Right; that, too—a walk he'd taken, a way. Go *somewhere*. And what else?

Change for the machines.

MORE DRUGS.

Watch out, it can make you a little stupid.

Definitely got that, Gabe thought, bemused; definitely got a little stupid.

So? The kid said anything *could be useful.*

How about the C-word? Commitment.

Lover, sometimes that's all you got. Remember?

Sometimes, Gina. But not this time.

"All right," Mark said lightly, "I gave you that one. Now you can say I should have known better. That's okay, Gina. I got a million of them—"

—and they ain't all for you.

Gabe caught the rest of it, even if Gina hadn't. Apprehension hummed within him like a spinning sawblade. *Can't get her on a direct approach,* he thought, urgency rising in him and trying to become panic. *Got to go at her through the weak link, and that would be me.*

"Knock that shit off, hotwire," Marly said seriously, "unless you just want to paint a bull's-eye on your forehead and hold still for whatever's coming up next."

They were in the dark hallway again, flattened against the wall. But the hallway was different somehow, not quite right, and yet not totally unfamiliar.

"You're good. There's really no question about that, never has been."

"That's your cue, hotwire," Caritha said, and gave him a shove.

He was sitting at the table in Manny's office, and the smell of fried food was sickeningly strong.

"This was how I got you last time," Manny said. "Playing with your friends."

Gabe tried to look at Marly and Caritha, but his head refused to turn.

"See, you all tend to do the same things, gravitate to the familiar." Manny leaned forward, the bogus concern creasing his face as nauseating as the fried-meat stink. "You're so utterly predictable, it isn't worth the bother of plotting a decision tree for you. But our kind isn't. No trap doors, no twenty-story drops this time. Sticky field."

Gabe could feel it, sucking at him in the chair like quicksand. The ever-popular sticky field, mainstay of numerous B-features. Like the holo-to-laser trick, something else that was impossible only in the real world.

Something tugged at the edge of his thoughts, the bare, dim shadow of some idea, or—

Manny got up and came around the table to him. "And though you didn't ask, yes, it *is* me. Manny Rivera. After a fashion."

After a fashion. In spite of everything Gabe wanted to laugh. Poor old affected Manny Rivera, posturing even in this state. Although after the initial shock, Manny had probably taken to this like home. Anyone who could survive in the belly of the corporate beast would probably find this existence all but natural.

"*Me*," Manny said, "not that pitiful meat that walked and talked and played the villain in the set-piece of your life. Just as this is *you*, isn't it, Gabe, not the meat that breathes so slowly in some other reality. You left that behind to be where you are now, and it does breathe so slowly, doesn't it? Slowly, but it still breathes. Or can't you feel it anymore?"

The sticky field increased its pull on him and scrambled inside, trying to free himself, to get some sense of his body and his connection to it, because if he couldn't, there'd be nowhere to go if this failed, nowhere to go when it was over.

I can't remember what it feels like to have a body. No? Even after everything else? He wanted to scream in frustration, but he had nothing to scream with.

"Your life's all in your mind, isn't it? Good at dreaming, not so good at waking up—pretty bad, in fact. Stone-home bad, as they say in the world, the one you don't live in right now. You were right—you *are* the weak link. It's not hard to get to you. You just have to hold still long enough, and even *I* can work on you, even *I* can become so important that I can feed you a line of shit that will tie you in knots."

I can't remember what it feels like to have a body. All right, then, where was Marly, where was Caritha?

"Not something we can help you with, hotwire," Caritha said apologetically.

"Of course not," Manny agreed. "No body, no hotsuit to put on it."

He strained to look down at himself. No body and no hotsuit, but the familiar baroque pattern of snaky lines and geometric sensor shapes *was* there. At last the permanent tattoo.

I can't remember what it feels like to have a body.

Great people leave their marks. Everyone else is left with *marks—*

. . . with visual *marks . . .*

Manny was leaning forward to take it when Gina's face burst on him like a thunderstorm.

"Can't *remember*? Well, lover, it's a lot like *this*."

His face exploded with pain. The secondary hit of his body on the carpet was negligible, but he felt it clearly this time, his lower back hitting first, then shoulders and head, his heels bouncing a few times. From behind closed eyes he felt his mouth stretching in a smile.

"Jesus," said Keely. He knelt down to touch the left side of Gabe's face.

"What happened?" Sam clutched the unit on her thigh, her other hand resting on the wire leading to the needles in her stomach. "What's doing that, why is that happening? Keely, I can't read the fucking screen the way you can, goddammit!" One little yank; if that was what it would take to save her father's life, she would do it and hope it wasn't already too late, if that weird swelling in his face didn't mean he'd stroked out—

Keely was at the monitor again, scrolling the output backwards, forwards, and backwards again. Then he looked over the top of the monitor at Jasm, who was squatting next to Gina. "Jazz, look at her hands. Are her knuckles bruised?"

Jasm checked and then held up Gina's limp right arm. "You got it. Bruised and skinned a little." She glanced at Gabe and then did a double take. "Keely, something else." She leaned over Gina and pulled Gabe's shirt up. "You want to guess at what that is?"

Keely stared in silence at the sinuous lines and shapes pressed into Gabe's flesh. Then he blew out a long breath and shook his head.

"Keely, I'm gonna tear your fucking head off," Sam said tearfully. Fez put his arms around her, and she twisted away, keeping one hand on the wire leading to the needles.

"It's all right," Keely told her, laughing a little. "It's just the best case of stigmata I've ever seen. Actually, it's the *only* one I've ever seen with my own eyes, so let's say it's the best one I know about."

"Shit," said Gator, "they must be seriously hysterical in there."

"Wouldn't you be?" Keely said. He smiled at Sam. "Gina just belted your father a good one."

"Whack to that," said Percy, standing over Gabe and rubbing his own face. "Whack on sight when you been to the same party."

"What about those marks on him, what are those?" she demanded.

"From his hotsuit, of course," Keely said matter-of-factly. "You've worn hotsuits a time or two, you ought to recognize the marks they leave. Your father just discovered his whole body's a hotsuit, at least as far as his mind's concerned."

Sam stared at her father, not quite believing. The marks on his skin were fresh and deep, his swelling cheek looked painful, and the expression on his face said the best dream of his life had just gotten even better.

I feel pain.
That's sober as I remember it.

"Anybody can take shelter," Marly said. "Can you take on someone else's pain?"

"You're gonna have to try, at least," Caritha said, before Gabe could answer.

He was in somebody's living room, somebody's enormous, endless living room, currently filled with a glittery array of people eating, drinking, wandering in and out, watching the multiple screens on the walls, giving the thing in the center of the room a wide, courteous berth.

Gabe blinked at it. He remembered a creature eight feet tall, part ersatz samurai and part machine-fantasy, but this thing was so much more overdone that he was having trouble keeping it in focus. He thought he could catch glimpses of Marly at certain angles, Caritha at others; sometimes when it turned a particular way, he was sure it was Gina he saw within it, other times Mark, or Markt, and occasionally even himself.

Then it was a pillar of fire, and he remembered how he had ducked, expecting it to become a laser beam in the next moment. He got up and went over to the wall of screens.

Instead of the tech-fantasy porn clip, he was watching Gina. She was lying on a cot with wires in her head; behind her closed lids her eyes moved back and forth.

Gina-porn?

"That's a good way to put it," said a familiar voice. "If you can't fuck it, and it doesn't dance, eat it, *be* it, or throw it away. Lucky her. Not only can she dance, but she can be it, too. And so can you."

Abruptly the scene switched to Mark's bedroom, and he saw himself and Gina together. He looked away quickly only to find he was turning to the wall of screens again, all of them showing the scene in Mark's bedroom now. He put his back to them and there they were in front of him, above him, below him, on all sides, at every angle.

"It's no more of a prison than you were ever in," Mark's easy voice said soothingly. "After all, that's entertainment. Isn't it? One person's pain being another's entertainment. One person's grand love affair being another person's porn. That's all it ever meant to anyone. 'Don't know what it is, but it makes me horny, and that's all that matters'—other than that, nobody cares. It doesn't make a difference to anyone. A drop in the consumer bucket, to be drunk up, digested, excreted, and fed back into the food-fuck-and-dance chain. Food-fuck-dance-and-*be* chain, excuse me, whether it's you and Gina, or you and your virtual playmates, you and your wife, you and Sam, or just you and your carefully cultivated, fully formed pain."

The screens were splitting, multiplying, now displaying a myriad of pictures from both himself and Gina, each one different. His vision rebelled, unable to see them all at once, and they melted into a blur that ran and faded to a bleak grey color.

Ow.

She turned in a rush, looking for Markt. For all she could sense of him, or them, or whatever the fuck, Markt might have vacated as soon as she and Ludovic had gone through the window. "Enjoying the show?" she called angrily. "You get off on fucking with me like this?"

Laughter in the dark, flowing like music. Then Mark was pulling her onto the narrow bed in the room in Mexico. She hadn't been sure at first what he'd been doing, or even if he'd been sure, she remembered that, just as she remembered clutching his jumpsuit in both hands and tearing it away from him, driven by an urgency she hadn't wanted to identify at the time. Reveling in that intense familiarity and letting it cover over thought of anything and everything else, especially the feeling hat this would be the last she could have from him in this way, that he was going down the rabbit hole in his brain finally and for good.

Feeling? Shit, he'd *told* her, right out. . . . *you're gonna see this funny-looking thing, a piece of flesh clutching into naked console . . .*

So what was she doing here, with the feel of cloth and flesh so vivid?

"Because you can have anything you want, just by thinking of it. Make it over into what you wanted it to be, instead of the disappointment it turned out to be," Mark whispered. She felt his breath on her neck and strained toward him in reaction, pulling an arm out of her own jumpsuit. "Because the brain feels no pain."

The sensation running down her side with his hand definitely wasn't pain, she thought, letting herself open to it as it intensified; not pain, nothing like it.

"Pain is curable," Mark whispered to her. "It's the most curable thing of all, really, and it's the thing we all walk around feeling all the time when we don't have to. There doesn't have to be pain. Just us. No pain. Just us . . . us . . ."

Is there really such a thing as a second chance?

"It's not a *second* chance, Gina. It's a *new* one. And in spite of all that's happened—maybe even because of it—you want that. Do it any way you want to. Pain, your pain, my pain, it was all noise, and I've cleared it away for us."

What's wrong with this picture?

Echoes of phantom sounds bounced off the low clouds above the stony shore. Gabe stared up at the sky, wincing at the feel of the stones pressing into his back. In a moment the shadowed areas of the clouds would begin to shift and throb, and he didn't want to see that. Stones scraped the back of his head as he turned to look across the water.

The surface of the lake rippled as something began to fade in on the part of the shore directly in his line of sight. He could feel the pressure of its gathering, an unpleasant tightening sensation behind his eyes. With an effort he rolled over and sat up, keeping his back to the lake. The stones dug into him harder. When your whole body was a hotsuit, he thought, there were definite disadvantages. He pushed himself to his feet.

Something pulled at him from behind, trying to make him turn around. Caught off balance, he did a little staggering dance on the stones and managed to stay upright and still keep his back to the lake. "Gina?" he asked.

Her absence was a hole in the air.

* * *

The patterns on the cape weren't just unusual, Sam thought, watching them. There was something different about them. Sometimes she thought she could almost see pictures in them, not just shadowy shapes but real pictures, as if her mind were being teased into projecting images, or filling in color and detail. The longer she watched, the more tangible the pull on her mind felt, as if the patterns were somehow touching her in a very personal way. She wasn't sure that she liked it, but she wasn't prepared to say that she didn't like it, either. She wasn't prepared to say anything at all or, for that matter, listen to anyone else say anything, either. Good thing it had grown so quiet in the big room; no distractions. She could continue to meditate on the patterns shifting and reforming on the material.

But, God, she had to concentrate so *hard*. It was worse than when she'd been doping out the sympathetic vibration technique. Her thoughts kept nipping away, slipping out from under her almost before she could even make sense of them. It was like trying to catch sight of a number of very quick and elusive creatures that would dive into hiding places the moment she turned to them, so that all she ever saw was the very tail-end bits of them as they vanished. And that was the part she wasn't sure she liked at all, because it was like her mind was being emptied out, cleaned, sterilized in preparation for something else to come fill it up.

Something stirred on the fringes of her outer vision, disturbing her meditative state. She felt a surge of wordless, reflexive irritation that quickened to a flash/roar of blind rage.

Then she was blinking her watering eyes at the sight of Adrian standing in front of the cape, hands on his hips, looking bewildered.

"Are you all completely fucked?" he said.

"Not anymore," Keely said wearily. Wiping her eyes, Sam turned to look at him. He was rubbing his face with both hands as if he'd just woken up from a long, deep sleep. Which wasn't too far from the way she felt at the moment. "Thanks, Adrian. How'd you do it?"

"How'd I do what?" Adrian took a step forward.

"No, *don't*!" Keely said. "First, find some way to cover that goddamn thing up, or turn it inside out, or something."

Obediently Adrian turned the cape so that the plain, unpatterning side faced out and then rejoined the group. "That's the weirdest thing I ever saw," he said conversationally. "I kept trying to talk to you all, and you all just kept staring at those patterns—" He shrugged.

"I know," Keely said, watching the screen again. "Something similar happened to me the first time I saw it, but I pulled out of it on my own. It must be a lot stronger now. What makes you immune, I wonder?"

"He can't read," Sam said slowly. "Brain lesion in the visual center." Amazed, she looked at Adrian, who shrugged again.

"Then maybe he ought to be in there instead of Gabe and Gina," Keely said grimly. "A whole lot's happened since we all went under for a while, and none of it's good."

"What is it?" Sam said, craning to look at the screen. The figures on it still told her little.

Keely shook his head. "We're gonna lose them."

"All of them?" Fez said. He sounded as dazed as he looked.

"Oh, no. Just Gabe and Gina," Keely told him sourly. "Markt's just fine. At worst he'll stand the thing off, but it looks like he'll end up neutralizing the thing. But not before he sacrifices Gabe and Gina to it. Shit."

"I should have known," Fez said bleakly. "Art's always been viral at heart. Make that core. He's never had a heart."

"But Mark's part of him now," Sam said. "He wouldn't do that. Would he?" Her gaze fell on the Beater, standing silently on Keely's other side.

The Beater's face was expressionless. "I don't know anymore. 'Talent drives out sense.' Gina always said that about him. He's pure information, now. What does that drive out?"

"We've got to help them," Sam said, grabbing Keely's arm. "We've got to reach them."

"Sure," Keely said. "We might even be able to do it, we've got another person here with sockets. But we're fresh out of connections, and if we try to pull any from either Gina or Gabe, we'll finish them off. Sending in another fooler loop isn't going to do it, we need something conscious. A human. Any ideas?"

Sam was staring past him, at the pile of hardware he'd brought from Diversifications. "Yah," she said. "What kind of power do we have left, and how long will it last?"

Keely followed her gaze and then looked back at her with astonishment. "Sam, you am a genius."

"Yah, but will it work?" she said.

" 'Will it work,' the genius wants to know." He beckoned to Adrian. "C'mere, kid—"

"No." Sam stood up, holding the pump unit.

"But he's the only one who's immune—"

"They don't know him." She looked around. "Could someone else be a potato for a while?"

34

"Gina?" Gabe turned under the grey sky. "Marly? Caritha? Markt? *Anybody?*" Echoes of his voice danced all over, counterpointing each other. He took a few stumbling steps, fighting to keep his footing.

Why don't you look over here.

It was less a voice than a strong articulated urge. He refused to give in to it. "Somebody *answer!*"

Over here. Look over here.

At his feet the stones stretched away in a long, wide curve of shore, millions, billions, an infinity of stones, too many, and they were in there somewhere, he just had to find the right one. Except he wasn't going to live long enough to search them all, not even a fraction of them.

. . . died not of starvation but of old age looking for a way out . . . So why don't you just just look over here?

His pov began to move toward the source of the compulsion. He could feel it quite clearly, pulling at him. Not Gina's pull. With an effort he jerked his pov back to the stones as he stumbled along, but it slid away again, down to the water line, to the lake and the dark trees on the other side, past the trees to the stranger waiting on the other part of the stony shore.

"Gina?" he said without much hope as he turned all the way around.

There was a sudden bright light, and he was suddenly facing in a different direction entirely. "Guess again, Dad."

He could have believed it was another of Mark's apparitions (another of those visual marks, his mind whispered) except she was so obviously patched in, like a rough cut from the old days of hotsuits and head-mounted monitors. Old days . . . as if it had really been so very long ago.

"Yah, it's me," she said, walking smoothly over the stones as if they were an even surface like a floor. "It's Sam. I'm wearing your hotsuit."

He looked down at the permanent tattoo that was his virtual body. "What are you doing here?"

"Jamming." Her face rippled and flickered with mild line-noise. "Trying to give you a breather. It's been all over you and Gina. Where *is* Gina?" She reached out, and he took her hands. As patched in as she looked, the feel of her was star-tlingly realistic, and he could tell by the look on her face that she found the sensation equally real.

"It's not what you're used to," he said. "Things can change awfully quickly now. Maybe too quickly for you to keep up in that thing."

"Appropriate technology, Dad. Appropriate for me, anyway, since I don't have sockets." Her eyes shut tightly for a moment.

"What is it?" he asked.

"Keely's got a program disrupting the frequency so I don't trance out," she said. "Sometimes it makes my eyes feel funny. Like they're bouncing. I don't have long. Where's Gina?"

" 'Where' is not exactly the word. She's here, I just"—he looked around at the stones—"I just can't find the right con-text." He felt the pull at his vision reassert itself, and he started to turn toward the stranger without wanting to.

Abruptly Sam was in front of him again. "Jamming," she said. "Buying you some time. What's this about a context?"

What does this look like to you, an open window or an open wound?

. . . the Beater? Jim Morrison, or Visual Mark? Mozart or Canadaytime? The Living Sickle Orchestra . . . or that strange red-headed doctor. Her mind turned fitfully like a sleeping creature in the grip of a dream about to become real. Real dreams.

Come along with me.

When was I ever not there for you?

Come along with me now.

"It wasn't really that I didn't want your pain, Gina, it was that I could never take it away. Now I can."

What's your weak spot, Gina? Better get to it before he does.

Oh, you son of a bitch, you stupid fuck-up, my weak spot has always been you, and you know that, you've always known it. You do what you do, you do it because you can, and if that meant using my weakness against me, I just had to live with it.

She stood in the shadows on the courthouse steps, watching him pinned under Joslin's dead-white hand, she stood over him on the Mimosa, she knelt beside him in a thousand different places, waiting to see if he was going to turn blue or worse.

Can you top it, lover?

"Can you, Dad?" Sam asked.

I don't know," he said, holding the stone she'd found for him. Sympathetic vibrations, she called it. He was getting a sense of the program without really understanding it, but the way things were for him, he didn't really have to understand it. Which was a good thing; he couldn't fragment his attention to that extent.

"Then maybe that's the wrong context," Sam said. Her image rippled with noise again. "Is there something you know for sure?"

He groaned. "God, Sam, how does anyone know *anything* for sure?"

She looked at another stone and then smiled at him a little sheepishly. "Well, what've you got?"

Back to that again, he thought. He'd been through this, he thought, picking his way farther along the shore, using Sam's sympathetic vibrations on the stones.

"No, Dad," she said urgently, "what've *you* got?"

"It wasn't really that I didn't want your pain," Mark said. "It was that I could never take it away. And now I can. The brain feels no pain."

Maybe it was because she had never known what that would be like, maybe because she had missed the only other chance to find out all those years ago when Dylan had spoken the truth for both of them that night. Maybe that was why she was slipping now even though he hadn't even bothered to try to trick her. Take a little walk with me, yah, right into the jaws of the beast, with both eyes wide open and clear as rainwater, but God, to undo the years of getting toxed and renting furnished rooms with everything she needed and none of it hers and was *that* what it had all been about all along, was that *really* what it had all been for, all along?

"The brain feels no pain," he whispered.

"I feel pain," said Ludovic in a cool, clear voice. She looked up and saw him lying on his back in the graveyard. There was blood on his face. "Pain the day I met you, and it hasn't quit yet."

"So curable," Mark whispered to her. "There doesn't have to be pain. Just us . . ."

"Oh, come *on*, Gina." Ludovic sat up. The blood ran down his face in streams. "What would become of you if you couldn't cause someone some pain, raise a few welts now and then, draw a little blood, bring up the swelling?"

"That's not all there is to me," she said, feeling Mark try to tighten his hold on her (warm and so familiar, as if they had never led separate lives at all).

"I know that," Ludovic said. "The difference is, I'll take it. I *have* taken it. He never did." He leaned forward, stretching his hand out to her.

An open window or an open wound, whatever it comes up, Gina, I'll take it. The big bad c-word. Sure is big and bad. Never knew anything of value that wasn't.

His fingers brushed her face, and there was a roar like a hurricane wind that drowned out everything.

Had she gone to him this time, or had he come to her? And did it even matter?

"It's good," said Ludovic. He sounded a little surprised. She remembered that she had thought of him down in Mexico, and it was something he needed to know.

They didn't have to bother going down the hall to the room this time, they were just there, and he let her pull him down onto the bed.

"I know," he said, "this was never the easy part. You weren't smooch-faces." He laughed. "God, I love that. It's perfect."

She didn't understand how he could be there and also be on the stony shore at the same moment. But then, you could stand in the center of the burning flame untouched, too; the only problem was getting to the center without getting singed on the way in. And that was only impossible in the real world.

"I'm proud of you, Dad," she said impulsively.

He was still glowing, and yet he averted his gaze as if he were some lovestruck innocent.

"There's nothing to be embarrassed about," she added. "I know a little about this stuff. Maybe more than a little."

"Yah, but you're not supposed to see your father naked. Or your father's mind, anyway."

She started to say something, and suddenly Beauregard as she had last seen him popped into her mind, wearing a holo crown and hustling free preview tickets. "God, maybe it really *is* only impossible in the real world," she said.

"What is?"

She thought of Fez and laughed, feeling both hopeless and hopeful all at once. "Everything, Dad. Everything that matters. I hope not, I wish it weren't, but—"

The screen flickered several times; down in the lower right corner, the small icon warning of imminent power interruption appeared, blinking on and off.

"Oh, shit!"

"What is it, Sam?" He came closer, looking alarmed. "You're starting to break up—"

She threw her arms around him in a quick hug before something tore her away.

The Arabian-Nights-type tent was still ornately overdone, but it also looked disheveled now, messy, things out of place.

"This is certainly an unexpected and historic pleasure," Markt said too casually. "If the media is ever restored, we can state positively that interaction between the old technology and the new technology is indeed feasible."

"Where the fuck were *you*?" Sam shouted. "What are you doing? They're all alone—my father's all alone on those rocks, and Gina's out somewhere all by *her*self, and what the fuck is that? You said you wanted their *help* neutralizing that thing, you never said you were going to make them do it all by themselves!"

"They have to," Markt said quietly. "To a certain extent, anyway. One of us is too viral, and the other is too . . . *marked*."

"I'm not in any fucking mood for bad wordplay," Sam said. The icon in the lower right corner was blinking more rapidly, and she looked for the power-boost symbol. "You should have told them that before you let them go charging in to save the world. *Your* world."

"Yours, too," Markt said evenly. "Apparently you have some things you wish weren't impossible only in the real world. But then, doesn't everybody?" He looked away. "Sorry. We're on to something else now, and I can't keep it from biting off your power any longer. But thanks, Sam, you did the right thing.

That sympathetic vibration program really is a banger. And thank Keely for the jamming program, too."

The screen went blank.

Keely helped her work the headmount off. The rest of them were still gathered around her work island, and they were all looking at her, including the Beater, who made one hell of a nervous potato. She felt a sudden wave of excruciating embarrassment.

"How was it?" Keely asked her.

"Weird," she said, letting out a long breath. "You can see everything at once sometimes, and sometimes you can't see but what's directly in front of you. And we'll need at least four times the resolution we've got now, I don't think I got a fraction of the detail. There's all sorts of things—I don't know, symbols and elements and—"

You're not supposed to see your father naked. Or your father's mind, anyway.

"—or maybe not," she said after a moment. "Maybe we should leave well enough alone. Damn. I really wished I'd had sockets. Sort of. Or maybe not. Seeing someone's mind like that—"

Some residue of power surged through the hotsuit then, and she had the sensation of someone squeezing her hand. She stripped off the gloves in a hurry. " 'Scuse me, I'm going to slip into something a lot more comfortable." She headed for her squat space.

"Good work, Sam," Keely called after her. "You did it, you know."

"Yah, I did it," she called back over her shoulder. "For a while, anyway."

"Sam?" Gabe called. The jamming program was still running, but he could feel how it was beginning to stumble. It kept correcting, but that wouldn't last. Eventually Mark was going to overwhelm it, and he would be back at the mercy of that pull to turn around and see the stranger. Mercy? Bad choice of word.

And then they were just there, in front of him. He jumped, startled, unsure if it was just some wishful visualization.

Then he was rushing forward to embrace them, but they stepped back from his reaching arms.

"Can't, hotwire." Marly's expression was only half-apologetic. "You promised."

"You did," Caritha added. "I was there. And so were you."

He looked at each of them, but there was no appeal. He *had* promised, to Gina, all the things that were supposed to be impossible only in the real world, and without waiting for an answering promise. Because that was how it was, whether you heard an answer or not, whether it was the answer you wanted or not, whether you had to crawl over shards of broken glass or cold, naked stones. Even with a sympathetic vibration program.

Someday—if they ever got out of this—Ludovic might understand. It had been somewhat of a dirty trick, the promise and the choosing. Perhaps the choosing most of all, because Ludovic hadn't realized he'd been choosing. Markt knew by his graph that he'd have made the same choice regardless, but Ludovic would have obstinately insisted on going through it the way he thought he had to crawl over every single stone. Even with a sympathetic vibration program. He'd have wanted to do it, actively and consciously, claiming it as a right. A *right*—when the Art configuration had invested Marly and Caritha with himself long ago, and Ludovic hadn't even known it at the time. He still didn't realize it all the way through, and it was hard to see how he couldn't. Took it for granted, perhaps, that a simulation could grow *that* responsive by virtue of growing so many decision trees. Wander through the enchanted forest, yes, it's magic, must be magic.

The magic is, there is no magic.

Sound and vision, yes, but no magic. Pain and pleasure, yes, but no magic. Catastrophe and chaos, yes, but no magic.

Synthesis. But no magic.

Synners . . . but no magic.

None whatsoever.

Ludovic, this isn't bad news.

"How is that supposed to help me?" Gabe said, exasperated.

"Come on, hotwire," said Marly, or Caritha. It was hard to tell, now. They were both looking more like composites. "If you can face this, you can face anything."

He shook his head.

"If there was magic," Caritha, or Marly, said, "what would you need faith for?"

Gabe considered it. Then he turned around. Gina's fist was the size of a Hollywood Boulevard tourist bus as it came at him, and he was there for it.

She swung her legs over the side of the bed and stood up.

Night court. From high on the bench, the judge regarded her with a satisfied smirk. "You took the wrong turn getting up from that bed. Story of your life, eh, Gina?"

I can't be all fucking alone—

"Can't get you, but you can't get me, either." The judge tapped the gavel lightly and then pointed at the wall with it. "We can just stand each other off in here until I get *him*."

On the monitor she saw Ludovic frowning down at the stones.

Dammit all to fucking hell, Gabe, it doesn't make any difference which *fucking stone—*

"Not that it matters," said the judge, looking satisfied, "but how do you plead?"

"I don't plead," Gina said, feeling shakier than she sounded. "I never fucking pleaded in my life."

"No?" The judge was amused.

Get your claw off him, bitch, that meat is mine.

How'd you like to get even?

She turned away from the judge and got back into bed.

"Can *I* help *you*?"

Gabe hesitated. The common room was completely silent. Over at the cold-drink machine, Marly and Caritha were waiting patiently, Caritha tapping the cam resting on one raised thigh. She nodded at him. "Go ahead."

He looked down at the stones and then up at her again. "Oh, Christ. I *know* how this comes out."

"So hurry up," said Marly.

It's only impossible in the real world.

He sighed. "I thought you looked like you needed change for the machines."

"The more change, the less you know what's going on." Markt smiled dreamily, turned him around, and pushed him into the path of Gina's fist.

She swung her legs over the side of the bed and stood up.

"Open up in the name of the law!" The judge's voice, or maybe Manny Rivera's, doing Mark. "You are all alone in there. You took the wrong turn *again* getting up from the bed, and *you* are all *alone*."

She was getting closer to the center now. Mark's bedroom. *How's that for fucking symbolism*, she thought sourly. Maybe she wasn't getting singed on the way in, but things were definitely starting to get warm.

"Open up in the name of the law!"

She paused in the act of getting back into bed. "What did you say?"

The name of the law . . . the name of the law . . . The echoes danced in the gray air above the lake. Gabe could imagine them bouncing off the low clouds like maddened rubber balls. Now, what was that name, the name of the law? He could almost feel it, but it wouldn't come clear, wouldn't straighten itself out from the noise in his mind.

He looked at the stone in his hand and let it go. That was the bad news about the sympathetic vibration program. There was a sympathetic vibration in all of them, something that rang a response in him one way or another, but no way to tell which was the right one.

Who says it has to be the right *one? Will you just look over here?*

The name of the law . . . He searched, grabbing as many stones as he could, but the name wasn't in any of them. There might as well have been nothing at all. He felt like a fool.

Fool.

Fooler loop.

He raised his head to the grey sky and laughed aloud.

She swung her legs over the side of the bed and stood up. *U B the Ass to Risk.*

Yah, we're already clear on that, thank you one fuck of a lot.

Who you wannabee?

Gina laughed. *Have* you *got the wrong number, fucker.*

Really, Gina? Really? A very old room; surprising, this close to the center, but nothing should have surprised her anymore.

. . . because the larger pattern is contained in the smaller . . . She brushed the thought away, not even wondering who it belonged to.

Dylan's nasal, tuneful whine. *I want you.*

Who you wannabee?

But she had her own music with her, her own sound and her own vision. Nasty bridge, hammering all the way, the growl of her own need. Colors pouring down the bowl of the sky.

U B the Ass to Risk.

Lover, I always was. I'm lucky I can dance. Can you top this?

It was the *real* head of the food-fuck-dance-and-be chain, and it was going to try. She didn't run from it.

I hit him, but what can he do for me?

"I can find you," Gabe said.

—and the other ten percent is being there on time. It was time then, and it's time now.

"*Bravo*, hotwire," they all said. "All right, this won't hurt a bit. —Well, not much," Caritha's voice added.

It was like being tumbled in an enormous barrel rolling along a bumpy road, but somehow it wasn't unpleasant.

Got all the associations now, Gabe. One voice.

Was that what this was all about—associations? Just to find her? he asked.

Only in part. You were the fooler loop, she's the mirror. There she is. Better help her. She's strong enough to let you do that now.

There was a sensation of being shoved through some kind of thin but tough barrier, like a sheet of plastic. He landed on two feet in the pit. Gina was already straddling Mark with her hands on the connections.

The common eye-shaped area that was their life.

"But what do you think will happen?" asked the Mark-thing under her. "What do you think this is?"

A hard wave of dizziness hit her between the eyes, and she was staring up at herself holding the wires, ready to jerk them out.

Should've known it wouldn't be so fucking simple. U B the ass to risk, that's me. What did I wannabee, yah, how can you wannabee something and not know?

"There was a little bit of him left, then, do you remember? He opened his eyes and begged you to do it. Because the little of him that stayed with the body then, that was from the last time, in Mexico. Do you remember?"

The surprise of her own urgency, and his, and the over-

whelming familiarity, as if they'd never had any secrets from
each other. Because he'd already taken her there, to the lake
with the stony shore. The doctors had fed the image into her
brain to find out if she could see it as he'd meant it, but what
he'd meant was not what they'd thought. He'd taken her there,
and she'd been there for him.

"If you do it now, that goes, too.

"Can you do that, really? Can you end it, not just him but
that bit of yourself he kept with the part that stayed with the
body, that is here now? Can you die a little and live through
it?"

She tried to force her pov back home, but it was jammed
there, gazing up at her own face. Who *had* been there, looking
out of his eyes and begging her to yank the wires? Mark? Or
herself?

"If you don't believe you can be in two places at once, you've
forgotten everything you've learned. You, Ludovic, his simulated playmates, Mark—*me*. Do it, and everyone dies a little,
and can you do that, *really*?"

She could see herself waver at whatever she was seeing in
those eyes, her/Mark's eyes; the surge of brute hope she felt
from the thing at the sight was not as far removed from herself
as she would have wished.

That'll teach you to glory in your separateness, *your precious*
aloneness.

Ludovic reached around from behind and put his hands over
hers on the wires.

"Oh, it'll be even harder for you, Mr. Noble Gesture. Do
it, and you'll kill your taste for it, and you'll kill your last link
to *them*, your simulated playmates, and that's something you
might not be able to get back, ever. Can you do that, really?"

Ludovic's expression changed, and she knew that he was
seeing them.

"You gave up what you had of them, but see, here is what
I took from the volatile memory of your system when I ran
through, and it's every bit of them. Can you end it for them?
Wouldn't you rather do just about anything else but lose them
again, wouldn't you rather come and live with them and go
back to the way it was, not having to do anything, least of all
make Noble Gestures?"

"Last thing they'd expect, hotwire."

* * *

It should have been easy, but the desire for them was still there. The desire for them and the way things had been, for no good reason, just because—

"Because you can," Gina said. "But it's not the only thing you can do."

But it's different when you think you have no choice, and then suddenly you do after all.

"I simply do not fucking believe we have to do this *again*," Gina said, and her fist was coming at him. "There ain't *nothing* to them you didn't have in the first place, *hotwire*. And you *know* what you got."

"But how do you know whatever's right?" he asked, confused.

"You don't," she said. Realization came simultaneously with the words. "It's a damned Schrödinger world."

The name of the law.

On the stony shore he turned not because it was pulling at him but all on his own power. And she was there, just having turned around herself to look at him.

Her fist pushed through the air. This time he ducked, and it sailed past him to strike Mark.

Their hands came up together, and the wires pulled free.

The chain reaction went at the speed of light, unfeeling and unstoppable. It unraveled the pit around them, moved on to the lake with the stony shore, the common room, Mexico, Manny's office, Hollywood Boulevard, everything dissolving, running to nothing, and they were pulled along with it.

"I didn't even know for sure sometimes you were there," Gina told him.

"Likewise," Gabe said, feeling tired and exhilarated all at once. "You never know until you turn and look."

Abruptly he found himself back in the strange half room. Right; no need to go any further with it now, it was all happening by itself. He could sense it retracing every step the Big One had taken, undoing itself as it spread out in every direction, a starburst whose points touched Phoenix, Sacramento, Seattle, Japan, Mexico, London, Bangkok—

He turned to say something to Gina. She wasn't there.

* * *

"Hey," said Jasm. She had one ear to Gina's chest. "I hate to tell anybody, but I don't hear anything."

Sam looked down at her father. His face was still swollen, but the impressions from his hotsuit were fading rapidly. "When do we pull them out? Or do we just pull Gabe out?"

Keely motioned for her to be quiet. Sam looked at the Beater. He had refused to relinquish his new role as official potato, and she hadn't felt she could insist. Somehow, going in with them, even by old hardware, however briefly, whether to any purpose or not, had changed her status.

But the way the Beater was sitting, she could lunge quick and yank the wires out of his stomach. One hard jerk. If she had to do it to save Gabe's life—

"Whack to this," said Percy. He was holding the cape connected to the big system. The patterning side was blank white.

Easy now, Gabe told himself. He'd only looked at one spot. She could be anywhere in the room. Schrödinger's Gina—

The window still framed an area of black against the moving clouds. He took a step toward it and then stopped. The door swung only one way now, and it had already swung for him. He could wait, or he could go.

They floated in near-perfect rapport, balancing. With the virus gone, Markt was wide open, and she could see everything now, Markt's life and Mark's life and her life and their overlapping life together, right where it had always been.

"Let's dance," Mark said, surfacing in the composite. "Let's jump all night, let's burn it all down and burn it back up again. Let's die before we get old. Let's never die, ever."

She hesitated.

"It'll be better now than ever it was," Markt said. "And we're inoculated now. Even if it could come back, it couldn't touch us."

"I want you," said Mark. "Always did. Just couldn't find my way through the noise. But the noise is gone, and the wanting is still there."

Through the still-open window, she could see a very small and distant Gabe Ludovic, waiting.

"It's what I was born to do. And doing that, I can do anything now. I can be there for you. It was only impossible in the real world."

Her face pressed against his bony chest, hanging onto what

was left. Not just remnants now, but everything. *Better now than ever it was.*

"All the equipment we need is in our room," he said, leading her up the long hall. He opened the door, stepped inside, and turned, holding out his hand. Markt leaned close.

"The brain feels no pain."

It was a more persuasive argument this time.

He knew. He could sense it all through the dark window, and he knew it dwarfed his own offering.

Was that why they'd gone into this so easily? Did Gina want to be with him so badly? If she did, why had he come along? To be there to convince her to come out again after it was all over? Christ, he'd only known her a few months. After fifteen years of marriage, he'd been unable to persuade his wife to come out of a sealed office. How was he supposed to fight over twenty years of someone else, to compete with a, a whatever-it-was, a video, a synthesis, a sympathetic vibration?

Hey, Gina—come on out here and pop my chocks. Really, it'll make you feel better.

Sure. When the brain felt no pain?

What the fuck, as Gina would say if she were here. You got a punch in the jaw and, for a little while, a life. Keep asking, maybe someday someone'll put an egg in your beer. But not today.

He yielded to the pull toward the outside and faded away.

"I'd say about ten beats a minute, now," said Jasm, holding Gina's wrist. Sam tightened her grip on the wires in her stomach. There was a rustle as Gabe stirred on the mattress. Keely knelt down beside him and then looked up at Sam. "He's coming out of it."

"She isn't," said Jasm.

It was several hours before the feeling of disorientation and woolly-headedness even began to drop away from him. Gina stayed down. Ignoring his still-swollen jaw, he told them in as few words as possible what was happening to her, or what could be happening. Sam pointed out gently that he didn't know for sure, and he didn't contradict her by telling her he had looked and she hadn't been there. Not out loud.

Local portions of the dataline came back by the next morning, anchors recapping the big story every few minutes. The final count of socket casualties had yet to be determined. L.A. was still burning, and martial law was the order of the day.

The young guy called Percy offered him some 'killers. "They make me a little stupid," he said, pushing them back at the kid. "Thanks all the same."

He distracted Sam with a shower of attention, telling her everything that had happened before he'd seen her at the graveyard, even though she'd heard a lot of that. He didn't have to tell her anything about after, and he didn't try.

The following night Gina was still down, and he made a big deal out of tucking Sam in like a child in her little privacy area, her squat space, she called it. The ex-pump had been put aside, the contents transferred back into the big system, so it wouldn't be long before contact would be reestablished on the showy multimonitor arrangement they had. They were all waiting for that, he could tell.

Sam went to sleep, and Gina had still not come out of it. There were so many kinds of doors that swung only one way, and he could wait, or he could go.

Maybe there really is no magic, but for a few moments here and there, Gina, I think maybe there was. Just a few moments, but they were more than enough. And is that high enough up in the stupidsphere for you?

Go somewhere. Go somewhere.

He touched his swollen cheek. This was where he had come in; good place to make an exit.

There was no pull toward the outside this time, but he went anyway.

Epilog

The light on the voice-only phone meant he had email. He called the local exchange, and the grandfatherly man read it to him. Just a thank-you note from the school on the latest simulations for the geometry students. Gabe felt pleased. It was an isolated area and not a moneyed one, either. Custom-programs off the dataline would have broken their budget, whereas the little bit he charged for producing them let him live well enough, combined with the other little bit he made on the holos he managed to sell from time to time. He was glad of the income but disgusted by the dataline. Still run by a bunch of greedy bastards who wanted to charge by the bit, who had learned nothing. He was glad every day that he'd refused to put it in his house.

It was a pretty nice house, smaller than the condo in Reseda, but far more pleasant. It looked like someone lived there. Not in the best of style, perhaps—the furniture was a little of this and a little of that, and the last occupants had apparently gotten a deal on yellow-duck wallpaper. Cartoony yellow ducks sailed the walls in the kitchen, in the living room, and, mysteriously, on only one wall of the bedroom. Yellow ducks he could live with, though; they didn't bother him, and he didn't bother them.

The electrical system was less easy to get along with—he had to unplug the refrigerator to run the holo cam. But nothing, neither food nor holos, had spoiled yet.

The only thing he felt mildly bad about was his lack of gardening ability. The backyard seemed destined to remain scrub no matter what he did.

But the front yard was just fine. It stopped short about fifty feet from the front door, where the land dropped sharply down a rocky incline. From there he had an unobstructed view of the ocean. Someone was operating an underwater farm a few hundred yards out; with binoculars he could watch the dolphins popping up and down, hard at work at whatever dolphins did on underwater farms. On some days he did almost nothing else but watch them.

He'd thought at first that the solitude might make him strange, and then he'd asked himself just how much stranger did he think he could get, and after that he never gave it another thought. Being alone wasn't bad. If he really wanted to be among other people, he could walk the mile and a half to the village and do his shopping.

There was one media parlor/bar on the village's meager main drag, and only once had he ever been tempted to go inside. That had been not long after he'd moved into the house. He'd been walking by, and the front door had been open, and he'd heard his own name from inside. He'd stopped then and listened. The anchor had been reading a list of known socketed people who were still missing, fates unknown. Gina was also on the list, along with a lot of other people he'd never heard of. He didn't notify anyone, and he didn't worry, because he wasn't using that name anymore anyway.

Nor was he concerned that any available pictures of himself would give anything away. These days his hair was more grey than not, and long, down to his shoulders. He fit right in with most everyone else in the village. Appearancewise.

But a few days after that incident—or non-incident—he'd dreamed about everything, for the first time in a long time. It hadn't been much, a quick flip through some of the high and low points leading up to his departure from the broken-down inn on the Mimosa. After that the dream had been very detailed: the long, long walk, part of it under the not-so-hidden eyes of the survivalists and then the ride with the old guy to Santa Ysabel in the panel truck. He'd told the beautiful one, Gator, that he'd just had to get out and walk to clear out the cobwebs, blow the stink off. At the time he'd been sure she'd believed him, but in the dream she obviously didn't. It made him wonder if she hadn't known all along that he'd been leaving. Or maybe she'd wasted a day or two driving around in Flavia's car while the urchins picked through the cases under the piers, thinking he'd been jumped. Now he couldn't decide.

The next ride he'd gotten from Santa Ysabel had taken him due north several hundred miles. The dream got sketchy again about the time in Reno, which had been a mistake anyway.

Detail returned again when he got to the coast, well north of the L.A. area but far from San Francisco. The dream marched him through the Recovery and the way he'd established himself in the village as a refugee from the L.A. collapse. Much sympathy all around; everyone assumed he wasn't socketed, and he didn't tell them otherwise.

The dream might have taken him right up to the moment he'd gone to bed that night, except he'd forced himself to wake up and stayed awake for what remained of the wee hours and all of the following day, keeping busy and instructing his brain that it would not visit any more nostalgia on him.

It worked for a while. After a time he discovered he could weather the occasional dream about Gina. You could get used to just about anything if you endured it long enough.

Eventually he lost track of time. He'd been waiting for that to happen, but when it came, when he realized he didn't know exactly how many seasons had come and gone since he'd left the Mimosa, he was neither happy nor unhappy. It fit the context, it caused him no discomfort not to know how much time had passed between one thing and another. Working for the school kept him on a reasonable schedule.

He enjoyed the work more than he'd thought he would, even on the used, jerry-rigged equipment from the supply house north of the village. It wasn't exactly state of the art, but for his purposes he didn't need all the bells and whistles and dancing bears. *Appropriate technology*, he told himself, *and nothing more*. Words to live by. Better than *killed your taste for it*.

When he saw her standing in the front yard, he thought he was having another dream, the dream he had been dreading, where she appeared in his new context, grinning that smart-ass grin and announcing, *Hi, I'm not dead after all. I'm only impossible in the real world.*

Then Sam came around the side of the house, and he was sure he was hallucinating.

He closed the front door and went into the yellow-duck kitchen to splash water on his face.

"There," he told himself. "Just me and the ducks."

The knock at the door was very polite.

"Open up, Ludovic. This is real."

* * *

"A what?" he said.

"Eclone. That's why I was down for so long." She was stretched out on his second-hand couch while he perched on the footrest. Sam was wandering through the rest of the house; she seemed to like the ducks.

"They made a complete copy. As complete as they could," Gina went on. "It was the error-checking that took so fucking long."

"Thank God," he said suddenly.

"What?"

"You said 'fucking.' I thought you never would, I thought I'd die waiting for it."

She gave him a look. "You left before I could tell you what was happening." Almost an accusation. But he could tell she wasn't mad. "I came up starving after most of a week, and there was nothing but those fucking seal-packs from the survivalists, fucking banana mash, fucking *navy bean soup*. And *food porn* on the dataline. Would you believe the fucking *porn* channels were some of the first shit back on the air?"

He shrugged. "Sure. Why not?"

"I notice you don't have the dataline."

"No," he agreed, "I sure don't."

They'd stayed at the Diz—everyone was calling it the St. Dismas Infirmary for the Incurably Informed by then—for most of the initial recovery period, she told him. Getting around hadn't been terribly easy unless you had a private car. But the day the rental lots had reopened, she and Sam had left. Sam had had enough of communal living, and she'd had enough of everything else.

"What about the Beater?" he asked.

She shrugged. "What about him?"

"But you're not really in two places at once," he said over the messy casserole dinner. Odds and ends in a dish, but not survivalist fare, at least. "Since they made an electronic copy, and you're *here*, it means the clone is just a sophisticated, intelligent program. But not conscious."

"If she wasn't conscious before," Sam said, "she is now. She's been merged with Markt. And Marly and Caritha."

He nodded once, shortly. Of course, he thought.

"Which reminds me," Gina said, watching his face. She reached into her shirt pocket and put some chips on the table.

He stared at them. The yellow ducks swam around him crazily for a few moments.

"Unaffected," Gina said. "Markt copied the programs, left the originals for you. They're yours again." The chips gleamed in the lamplight. She pushed them into the middle of the table and left them for him to pick up.

"And you're wrong," she added. "From Mark's point of view, I'm there for him. That's good enough for me. You want the stone-fucking-home truth, I couldn't have stayed. Mark was born to do that. I was just born." She grinned. "Only the embodied can *really* boogie all night in a hit-and-run, or jump off a roof attached to bungi cords."

Sam excused herself and went into the living room.

"I guess," he said. "Doing all that for the sake of pouring it into simulated reality. After being here for—I don't know, however long I've been here"—her face told him that she knew exactly how long it had been, to the day—"that doesn't make too much sense anymore. Doing all that just to simulate doing all that."

Gina burst out laughing. "Simulate my ass! I did video just so I could do all that shit!"

Sam dabbed at the corner of her eye with her little finger. "It got a little hard to watch. No. It got a *lot* hard to watch." She let out a breath. "Everything that was going on and the thing I thought about most was—oh, shit, it sounds so stupid-ass when you say your heart was breaking."

Sitting on the couch next to her, Gabe patted her shoulder, trying to think of something full of fatherly wisdom and comfort to say to her. "We do what we do," he said after a bit, "and we love because we can. Can't argue with it and can't stop it—" He gave a short laugh. "About all you can do sometimes is stand it."

"I've got a hack for anything," Sam said. "Any program anywhere. Even that fucking spike, I hacked that. But I got no hack for this."

Gabe nodded. "Welcome to the world."

Sam gave him a sideways look.

"I'm sorry," he said, shrugging, "But that's about it."

"I was afraid of that." She dabbed at the corner of her eye again.

"Oh, go ahead and cry," he said. "I won't tell anyone you're not cool."

"Thanks."

He put both arms around her. "No problem. What's a father for, anyway?"

Sam had found him. As it turned out, he hadn't really been so hard to find, provided someone had been actively looking. There wasn't another independent simulation producer in a few hundred miles.

"Everyone else has pretty much gravitated to the center of the action," Gina told him as they strolled around the house together. It was night, the moon was up, and they hadn't stopped talking long enough to do anything else but start talking again. Talking and moving. It felt important to keep moving. "Even a lot of the St. Diz people. That old guy, Fez, he's consulting with some doctors and technologists they can trust. Mark's new existence is still pretty much a secret, but it opens up all new possibilities for healing brain damage, disorders, all that stuff."

"But you'd still need sockets," he said.

"Yah. You'd still need sockets." She paused. "There aren't that many socketed people around now certified safe. Not many people to help out with the new research." She almost went on, but something made her leave it at that, for the moment. He was relieved.

Some hours later she picked it up. The sun had come up, was already high in the sky. He didn't feel tired or sleepy; it was as if somewhere inside of him, some generator had come to life to turn out an endless supply of energy for him to run on as long as he liked. Not magic, of course.

"I couldn't keep doing it all by myself," Gina said. "Accessing them day in, day out, day-fucking-back-in again. I had to tell them to leave me the fuck alone for a while."

They had come to rest on the grass a little ways from the edge of the cliff.

"When they got insistent, I left. They want to revamp the new, inoculated net. I say that's good, that's a fucking good thing to do, but I ain't doing all the work."

"Inoculated," he said glumly. "I thought for sure they'd just ban sockets, and that would put paid to it. The end."

"No one's doing the procedure now," she said. "But that's temporary. Once they get the safeguards done right, they'll be back in business."

He frowned. "*Who* will be back in business?"

"Socket people. Socket doctors. The doctors are almost back in business as it is, certifying survivors. There aren't many, but there are more than anyone thought." Casually she pulled up a blade of grass and examined it. "I've been certified. Guess you haven't."

"No. And I don't want to be. The sockets should be banned."

"Forget Schrödinger. Yo, Pandora, how's your headache?" She grinned, and he couldn't help grinning back. "Mark knew. The door only swings one way. Once it's out of the box, it's always too big to get back in. Can't bury that technology. All we can do is get on top of it and stay the fuck on top."

He shook his head. "Appropriate technology. That's how I live."

"Yah?" She shifted position, leaning closer to him. "Think on this one. All *appropriate technology* hurt somebody. A whole lot of somebodies. Nuclear fission, fusion, the fucking Ford assembly line, the fucking airplane. *Fire*, for Christ's sake. Every technology has its original sin." She laughed. "Makes us original synners. And we still got to live with what we made."

Far out on the water, he could just barely discern a blip that must have been a dolphin breaking the surface.

"Think on it," she said.

"I will." He turned to her. "But it's going to take an awful lot of thought for me. I'm still—" He paused, and then shrugged. "Maybe there isn't even a term yet for what I'm still. But whatever it is—" He spread his hands. "This is it."

"That's all right. Take all the time you want."

He frowned a little. "From the way you were talking, it sounded like you were in a hurry."

"I was in a hurry to be here," she said.

There was a long moment when he couldn't say anything. "Is this like any port in a storm?"

"You have to fucking *ask* me that? What are you, stupid?"

He threw back his head and laughed. "I just wanted to hear it. Is that too high up in the stupidsphere for you?"

"Nah," she said, grinning. "That's just stupid enough."

"Excellent stuff, perceptive, imaginative, subtle and penetrating. A pleasure to read, and a writer to admire."
-- *Analog*

MINDPLAYERS
by Pat Cadigan

It is an era of mind-wipe and franchised personalities.... A bad time to be caught fooling around with technologically induced psychosis. So for Alexandra Victoria Haas, the choice between prison or psychological service is no choice at all, as she opts for the grueling months of pathos-finder training. Plugging into so many disturbed psyches could have powerful and dangerous after-effects for Allie. For in the volatile world of Mindplay, the rules change when they change, and everything is true...unless it isn't....

"Cadigan's novel is an energetic, intriguing, darkly humorous head-trip extravaganza." -- *Fantasy Review*

A Bantam Spectra Signature Special Edition.

AN201 -- 2/91

Bantam Spectra Special Editions

A program dedicated to masterful works of fantastic fiction by many of today's most visionary writers.

FULL SPECTRUM 2 edited by Lou Aronica, Shawna McCarthy, Amy Stout and Patrick LoBrutto

NO ENEMY BUT TIME by Michael Bishop

SYNNERS and MINDPLAYERS by Pat Cadigan

LITTLE, BIG by John Crowley

STARS IN MY POCKET LIKE GRAINS OF SAND by Samuel R. Delany

RUMORS OF SPRING and VIEWS FROM THE OLDEST HOUSE by Richard Grant

WINTERLONG by Elizabeth Hand

OUT ON BLUE SIX by Ian McDonald

THE CITY, NOT LONG AFTER and POINTS OF DEPARTURE by Pat Murphy

EMERGENCE by David R. Palmer

THE SILICON MAN by Charles Platt

PHASES OF GRAVITY by Dan Simmons

GYPSIES, A HIDDEN PLACE, and MEMORY WIRE by Robert Charles Wilson

On sale now wherever Bantam Spectra Books are sold.

AN158 -- 2/91

The first book in a stunning new series from
STEPHEN R. DONALDSON
Bestselling author of *The Chronicles of Thomas Covenant*

The Gap Into Conflict:
THE REAL STORY

The Real Story is set in a detailed, dynamic future where people cross the Gap at faster-than-light speeds, where technology has blossomed with extraordinary possibilities, and where a shadowy presence lurks just beyond our view. But that's not the real story....

The rivalry between Angus Thermopyle and Nick Succorso -- two ore pirates with legendary reputations -- begins with a meeting in Mallory's Bar. With the beautiful Morn Hyland between them, the conflict was bound to escalate -- but *that's* not the real story....

With **The Real Story**, Stephen R. Donaldson takes his readers into *The Gap Into Conflict*, a five-volume cycle of novels that explore the very nature of good and evil within each of us. It is certainly the most profound story he has ever told.

What's the *real* story?
Find out for yourself.

The Real Story
is on sale now in hardcover
wherever Bantam Spectra Books are sold.

AN 193 -- 1/91